CHRONICLES
of the
HOST

Exile of Lucifer

D. BRIAN SHAFER

Destiny Image Fiction

An Imprint of

Destiny Image® Publishers, Inc.
P.O. Box 310
Shippensburg, PA 17257-0310

ISBN 0-7684-2099-7
Library of Congress Catalog Card Number 2002-141110

For Worldwide Distribution
Printed in the U.S.A.

6 7 8 9 10 11 12 / 10 09 08 07

This book and all other Destiny Image, Revival Press, MercyPlace, Fresh
Bread, Destiny Image Fiction, and Treasure House books are available at
Christian bookstores and distributors worldwide.

To place a book order, call toll-free: **1-800-722-6774.**
For more information on foreign distributors, call **717-532-3040.**
Or reach us on the Internet:
www.destinyimage.com

Dedication

There are so many people who have been a part of this work in terms of encouragement and prayer and friendship. My eternal thanks to Pastor Ken Squires, for encouraging me in my dream; Pastor Ray Noah, for helping me launch this dream; Tom Westerfield, for being the first to believe in it all; Jonny Martinez, Benney Perez, John Rossnagle, Roy Burtt, Bryan Barnes, Jon Meister, Jacob Kobernik, Rob Belles and Jim Dallman, Nik Baumgart, and so many others, for all their time, prayers and friendship; Don Milam and Elizabeth Allen at Destiny Image for making it happen; Jeff Milam and Don Nori Jr. at Destiny Image for their hard work and great e-mails; all my friends and family and pastoral staff brothers and sisters at Marysville First and Valley Christian Center for their warmth and loving support.

And to Lori, Kiersten, and Breelin, for putting up with endless evenings at the computer: I love you very much.

Finally, to the Lord Jesus Christ, through whom all of us have a hope and a future. To God be the Glory!

"Some Thoughts About the Book from the Author"

Chronicles of the Host is a novel about the events in Heaven beginning before Lucifer's rebellion and following through to the disobedience of Adam and Eve in Eden. My intention in writing this book is *not* to reveal what truly happened in Heaven (because nobody knows except those who actually witnessed the events); rather, it is to take the truth given to us in the Bible and build a story around it.

My hope in writing *Chronicles* is to create a compelling and thought-provoking look at what happens when creature rises up against Creator in the supreme folly of pride. Such rebellion is at the core of all disobedience—it flies in the face of true power, which is rooted in God's established authority—and seeks to be empowered through cunning and sheer self-will. This was the problem then, and it is the same conflict being waged today.

In creating angel characters who oftentimes seem very human-like, I was attempting to demonstrate that they, like us, are moral creatures with the same freedom to choose that we have. Such freedom can be abused by men or angels. Many angels chose to rebel and will ultimately pay a terrible price.

Likewise, a scan backwards in the history of humans clearly exposes the bloody choices that we have often made. Do angels do and say the things depicted in this book? Is Heaven anything like it is described in this book? I hope that as you read, you will see that the point is not in the description, but in the principle.

Finally, in dealing with the Lord, I purposely hold any interaction between Him and the other characters until the end of the book. At whatever point the Lord is introduced, the story must shift dramatically. In other words, to introduce Him too early would be like calling the game in the fourth inning. But, I believe you will see God speaking loudly in His seeming silence throughout the book.

What is He saying? He is speaking of His long-suffering and graceful nature; of His hope that repentance might come—that his creatures will somehow return to Him. Often one misinterprets God's lack of intervention for disinterest or inability to intervene on His part. He deals with us in a manner similar to how He deals with angels: hoping that we will get it right, but finally and forcefully stepping in when we delay or ignore His subtle voice.

That said, I hope you will enjoy this book as much as I have enjoyed writing it. I hope it will be a blessing to you and will make you think differently about your approach to the Most High God—just as writing the book has done for me. If you would like to contact me about the book; or if you are interested in my speaking—at your church or even at a seminar—please email me at: **dshafer@dublinvcc.org.** God Bless!

Contents

List of angelic characters, in order of appearance:

Policas	—librarian in Hall of Record
Lucifer	
Serus	—servant to Lucifer
Michael	
Gabriel	
Rugio	—a warring angel, the Captain of the Fiery Host, who aids Lucifer
Pellecus	—a wisdom angel, former teacher at the Academy, who aids Lucifer
Octrion	—a worship angel, who feeds information to Lucifer, albeit unknowingly
Vel	—a warring angel, Commander of the Legion of Son, who aids Lucifer
Nathan	—a warring angel, Captain of Legion of the Lord's Holiness, who aids Lucifer
Prian	—a warring angel, Chief Angel of the Watch, who aids Lucifer
Sangius	—a worship angel, Minister of the Holy Flame, whom Lucifer tries to get on his side but does not succeed
Fineo	—a worship angel, Minister of the Incense, who aids Lucifer
Drachon	—a worship angel, Keeper of the Door, who aids Lucifer
Sar	—a worship angel, Singer of Praise, who aids Lucifer
Tinius	—a wisdom angel, Recorder of the Holy Annals, who aids Lucifer
Lenaes	—a wisdom angel, an Angel of Light, who aids Lucifer
Belor	—a wisdom angel, an Angel of Light, who aids Lucifer
Crispin	—angel of wisdom, a teacher of the Academy
Lucallus	—a teacher at the Academy
Berenius	—a student, angel of worship, who turns to Lucifer
Kara	—a wisdom angel, one of the 24 elders
Grel	—a teacher
Costas	—a friend of Octrion
Pratia	—one of the 24 elders
Belron	—one of the 24 elders
Rega	—assistant to the Chief Elder
Sep	—angel
Deter	—angel
Greka	—angel
Lamon	—one of the 24 elders
Sharma	—one of the 24 elders
Dracus	—one of the 24 elders
Dabran	—one of the 24 elders
Plinius	—an elder
Razon	—angel
Kreelor	—temple steward
Corin	—a teacher at the Academy
Zoa	—the four creatures that each have four faces and eyes all over their bodies; they are constantly standing before the throne

"Gracious and Eternal Sovereign,"

I beg You to take into consideration the following account of those events which have taken place from before the dark times until the fullness of the Son, which You, in Your infinite wisdom, commanded be recorded as a perpetual testament and chronicle of the Host. It is an honor to serve Your Holy Self in this capacity, and having been chosen for the task, I determined that nothing should be left to speculation—that all of Heaven should know of Your grace and justice.

I have spared no effort in my research, which has taken me to the four corners of creation, in an attempt to uncover the minutest detail. I have spoken at length with all of the actual participants, as well as reported those things to which I was a witness.

As a scribe, whose work involves gathering of facts, I would have enjoyed the opportunity to speak with some of the former subjects who now await their destiny at the end of the age, but as their whereabouts are difficult to ascertain at a given time; and since they are reluctant to speak to me for fear of retribution; and because they are by nature liars, I have had to content myself with the testimony of those who knew them before the rebellion and who witnessed their gradual plunge into the abyss.

To all who have aided me in this endeavor I am eternally grateful. I also wish to express my deepest gratitude to Polias, the librarian in the Hall of Record who helped detail the early times of the Kingdom. And so it is with deepest regard for Your Most Holy Person that I now dedicate these Chronicles of the Host and surrender them to Your keeping. May they forever proclaim, as all creation will one day proclaim, that You alone are worthy; that all power in Heaven and on earth rests with You.

An angel restored

Chapter 1

"Truly the Lord had marked him for great things."

Lucifer peered over his balcony, brooding about the recent developments in Heaven. He looked at the angels walking about the city beneath him. Their forms shone different-colored auras, reflecting the holiness within, the mark of their Creator. His eyes fell directly below and he saw his own image on the golden street. He studied the form staring back at him from the mirror-like pathway.

It was little wonder that Lucifer's name came to mean "light bearer," the Star of the Morning, as he was without question one of the most glorious creatures in Heaven. Lucifer's hair was his crown, pouring over the back of his white cloak in a golden cascade. His eyes were steely blue-gray, and could be both hard and soft at the same time, a reflection of the keen intellect and self-assurance he possessed. Lucifer cut quite a majestic figure, and his majesty was never more apparent than when he was enrobed with his special garments for most holy occasions.

He turned and walked along the balcony, nodding now and then to an occasional angel who caught his eye passing on the street below. Looking over the balcony once more, he continued to ponder his image. It was only fitting that the Lord's chief angel of worship, he who created and led the praises of the Most High, should reflect so beautiful an image. Lucifer could not help but compare himself to the other angels who milled about below him. Truly the Lord had marked him for great things. And yet...

He turned his eyes toward the Great Mountain of the North, where the presence of the Living God reigned in eternal brilliance. All the paths of Heaven led to this glorious place and one could not go anywhere in the Kingdom without casting a shadow because of the radiance emanating forth. At times the light streamed down the mountain, cascading like a glowing river, spilling into the streets of the City itself as the angels basked in the glory of a Creator whose presence was so pervading. Lucifer could only look for a moment, a glance really, before he shielded his eyes from the spectacle. He turned away.

"My lord," came a voice from inside the house.

No response.

"My lord," repeated the voice. Lucifer turned to see his chief servant, Serus.

"Yes, Serus, what is it?" he asked.

"Michael is here to see you," replied Serus, who was a little uncomfortable at the announcement.

"Michael? Well now, that is something," said Lucifer as he made his way into the beautiful mansion. Michael had not come to call for some time. Lucifer glanced at his reflection in a small mirror.

"It wouldn't do to keep the archangel waiting," he said, satisfied with his appearance. "I will receive him immediately."

"Yes, my lord," said Serus.

Lucifer followed Serus through his vast house, which was richly endowed with beautifully crafted ornaments of gold, jewels and crystal. His taste for things of exquisite beauty was well known in the Kingdom. Colorful tapestries adorning the walls hailed the Lord in various motifs as "Glorious," "Victorious," "Righteous," "Holy," etc. Ornate mirrors of various shapes and sizes hung on the walls and the light from the North poured into the house, creating an ever-present illuminance.

The odor of flowers hung heavily in the house and beautiful flowers were also represented in various art forms. Serus made sure to fill the many vases with pungent blooms, and the extensive gardens in the rear teemed with delicate blossoms. Lilacs were a particular passion with Lucifer. He entered the audience chamber where Michael stood waiting.

"Brother Michael," Lucifer said as he glided into the room and grasped Michael's hands. "What a pleasant surprise!" They embraced each other. "Or is it *Lord* Michael, now?" He smiled.

"Just Michael, my dear brother," Michael said with good humor. "There is only one true Lord in Heaven."

"And a splendid arrangement at that," Lucifer agreed, looking at the powerful angel who had entered his house.

The archangel Michael commanded respect from the entire Host of Heaven. While Lucifer was a creature of unmatched beauty, Michael was a warrior of virtue, with tremendous strength. Powerfully built, he had long brown hair like a mane over his broad shoulders. His handsome features were accented by his eyes, which were deep green and piercing. Michael was the chief warrior angel and the captain of the Lord's Host. As such, he commanded a large and loyal contingent of angels dedicated to upholding the authority of God and carrying out His will.

Lucifer looked at the jewel-encrusted sword that hung from a golden sheath around Michael's waist. The sword was the insignia of his rank as an archangel; an honor recently conferred upon him by the Lord with great ceremony. Lucifer had arranged the service and this was the first occasion since that he and Michael had spoken.

"You've come so very far, my friend," said Lucifer, indicating the sword. "It must be a great honor to have so much authority vested in you."

"The Lord is gracious," agreed Michael. "His confidence in me is truly humbling. I only hope I can be half the servant that this represents." He patted the sword's handle at his side.

"Come now, Michael," said Lucifer, "of all the angels in Heaven who could possibly be better suited as archangel? Who? Maybe

Serus here?" he said, pointing at the smaller angel. "That will be all for now, Serus."

Serus nodded and excused himself from the room, bowing as he went. Michael watched the little steward quietly shut the heavy chamber door as he exited the room.

"Well, actually that's why I am here," said Michael, a little disturbed with the way Lucifer had dismissed Serus. His sense of mission overcame this distraction and he went on. "In an official capacity, that is. I'm here to coordinate with you a ceremony for the installation of another archangel."

"Really? Another archangel?" said Lucifer, trying to contain his curiosity. "And so soon after your own pronouncement! To whom go the honors this time?"

"A friend to both of us. The Most High has decided that Gabriel shall stand in His presence with the full authority of Archangel, and will retain his responsibilities as Chief Messenger to the Kingdom! Isn't this a great honor for our brother?"

"Quite," agreed Lucifer. He looked up and drummed his chin with his fingers as if in deep thought about the service he must now orchestrate. "I shall have to make this a most memorable occasion for Gabriel. After all, how often does one become an archangel?" He paused. "Though it does seem rather commonplace with Him these days, doesn't it?"

Michael ignored Lucifer's casual use of "Him" in reference to the Most High.

"Let's go over the details," he said, quelling the uneasiness he felt brewing.

"Of course," said Lucifer.

He motioned to the other side of the room where a beautifully engraved conference table with high-backed chairs was set up. It was here that Lucifer met with his Council of Worship for the Most High. Michael approached the chair that Lucifer pulled out for him. His sword noisily scraped the massive leg at the end of the table.

"Sorry about that," Michael said, a little embarrassed. "I guess this will take some getting used to."

"Yes," said Lucifer, looking at the sword. "It will take some getting used to."

Michael was relieved when the meeting with Lucifer was finished. He didn't enjoy the fellowship with his brother angel as he once did. Something had changed in Lucifer's manner...but what was it? Michael pondered these things on his way to visit his friend Gabriel. As he walked, he mentally cataloged the person and position of Lucifer, trying to determine why he seemed so difficult of late.

Lucifer enjoyed one of the most prominent and seemingly rewarding posts in Heaven. He was chief lord over worship, a creative genius who could compose everything from a vastly sophisticated work with an angelic choir of thousands to simple praises of devotion that were utterly inspiring.

Not only that, he was the most attractive creature alive, and not just in outward appearance, though that was staggering. No, he possessed an inner beauty, a sacred presence difficult to describe. God had so created Lucifer that holy praise manifested from his very being, and one could not spend a length of time with him and not feel compelled to worship the Almighty. It was legend among the angels that to be with Lucifer was intoxicating, even enchanting, as one drank in the very nearness of God.

Michael certainly did not feel like worshiping as a result of *today's* meeting with Lucifer. Today he felt...was it tension? Resentment? Surely Lucifer, of all angels, was not jealous of the recent promotions of his old friends. His ministry allowed him access to the Eternal Throne, something reserved for only the Twenty-four Elders and a few select creatures. Lucifer's was a privileged position. As he neared Gabriel's house, Michael decided that he wouldn't make any hasty judgments about Lucifer until he consulted with his friend, but he was going to stay on top of the situation.

Since becoming a ruling angel, Michael felt that it was his duty to represent the Most High in all circumstances. Whether leading in examples of holiness and reverence to the Lord, or encouraging other angels in their tasks; or being on the alert for attitudes that reflected indifference or resentment to the Most High, Michael was diligent in his duties. His closest friends thought that he was a bit *too* diligent in his protective role and put it down to the zeal of a new appointment that would eventually fade away. But what many angels regarded as misguided enthusiasm, Michael considered honorable and reasonable service.

Michael was also without a doubt the Lord's most ardent and supportive angel. While all the angels held an allegiance to God, Michael was passionately loyal to Him and always had been—long before he was made an archangel. If other angels misunderstood his actions at times, that was all the more indication to Michael that they were not excelling for their King as they should be and that his actions might serve as motivation.

A commander by design, Michael longed for the times when the Lord would give him special services to perform, not so he could impress Him with his ability, but serve Him in humility. It was this passion for order in the Kingdom that stirred up his concern for Lucifer all the more. Gabriel's house was now in view. Perhaps together they could figure out a way to help their friend.

+≒————————≒+

Lucifer walked around the room, dictating to Serus the details for the ceremony. He spoke at a fever pitch, concocting and creating so rapidly that Serus had trouble keeping up with him. Serus had learned rather unpleasantly about interrupting his master while he was composing and dared not ask him to slow down. Every so often Lucifer would pause and ask, "Are you getting that, Serus?" and then continue on as before.

When the moment arrived for the creation of the manuscript itself, Lucifer sat down at the end of the table and shut his eyes in deep meditation. After several moments of silence the faint sound of many instruments and voices poured forth from Lucifer, spilling out of him. The music seemed to come from the area just over his head but Serus was never sure, and too afraid to ask. The sound grew louder and louder until it reached a crescendo of joyous worship to the Lord, a holy presence filling the room.

When the music reached this dramatic moment, tiny crystals of light, like thousands of shimmering diamonds, appeared in front of Lucifer, dancing and swirling around like sparks from a roaring fire. Serus watched as these beads of light pulsed with the music, creating a dazzling whirlpool that joined to form a glowing, pulsing sphere, which lit up the entire room. The light was so intense and the music so deafening now that Serus could scarcely remain in the room.

Louder...LOUDER...

Suddenly, all was quiet.

Serus waited a moment or two, quietly surveying the scene, and then unwrapped a large golden scroll that he had secured earlier. He placed the scroll on the table directly beneath the sphere of light that was hovering in front of Lucifer. He then stepped back a few paces as a single white beam shot out of the ball (or praise sphere as Lucifer called it) and began writing on the scroll as one would write on a tablet. As the scroll became more and more marked upon with the strange musical notations, the ball of light grew smaller and smaller until it disappeared completely.

Lucifer remained seated for several moments, his eyes closed, his hands folded in front of him. An exhaustion always set in after one of these creative episodes and it took a little time for him to recover his strength. Serus, meanwhile, rolled the scroll up and placed it in a long golden container, along with some other notes for the ceremony. It felt warm.

Finally Lucifer looked up and said, "Take that over to the Council with my compliments. Tell them the details for the installation of Gabriel as archangel are complete. And tell them that, as usual, I am most honored to be of service to the Most High in any matter."

"Right away, excellency," replied Serus.

"And then come back immediately," said Lucifer. "I have another task for you."

"As you command," said Serus.

Chronicles of the Host

Before the Beginning

In the vastness of eternity past (something which no creature can really grasp but of which there is no doubt), nothing existed except the Father, the Son and the Spirit in eternal harmony and perfection.

Theirs was, and is, and always will be a glorious relationship of complete accord, anchored in perfect love and righteousness, each His own Person, yet bound in a mysterious union which is One. The relationship of the Three has always been a point of debate and speculation among the Heavenly Host, and angels of the greatest scholarship have looked into this perplexing issue, but of course no satisfactory explanation has ever been offered.

The Kingdom of Heaven

So boundless is God's love, and so infinite His ability, that a decision was made to create a kingdom inhabited by a vast multitude with whom love could be shared forever and by whom ministry would go forth to and from the Almighty. Thus was born in the heart and mind of the Most High a kingdom called Heaven, where God's love would be eternally manifested to all He created, and through whom He would minister His grace and goodness to subsequent creations.

How can a foolish angel possibly describe the wonders of the Kingdom of Heaven except to say that it is all that one can imagine as well as everything one cannot possibly imagine? Splendidly crafted for the complete enjoyment of its future citizens, Heaven was (and is) a place of utter beauty, with streets of gold, seas of crystal, ever-blooming gardens nestled among gently sloping hills, babbling brooks crisscrossed with delicate footbridges, all underneath a canopy of the deepest, purest blue imaginable.

The Great City

At the very center of the Kingdom was the City of God, some-times called the City of the North or the Holy City that was the seat of God's presence and authority. Within the city was the Great Temple of the Most High. A myriad of beings would fre-quent the City, pouring into the Great Temple to worship their Creator and serve Him. It was in the City, at the Great Acad-emy of the Host, that the angels learned about God and their service to Him and to one another.

Perched atop a magnificent mountain—the Most Holy Mountain—the City, with its magnificent spires, could be seen from anywhere in the Kingdom. The City was surround-ed on four sides by a massive wall made of dazzling precious stones with bejeweled gates at the center. Once inside, the golden streets were laid out in a series of converging squares, the center of which contained the Great Square framing the Temple complex.

The City was thus the crowning jewel in the Kingdom out of which flowed the will, purpose and grace of God. As He over-looked the finished work and found it to be good, the Lord was savoring the next phase of the creation: those who would actu-ally inhabit Heaven and would serve the Kingdom in various ways, as attendees and messengers—the angelic Host.

The Great Temple

The Holy Temple was designed to allow thousands and thou-sands of worshiping angels access to the Most High. The Tem-ple was the largest structure in Heaven, with three gigantic columns on each on the four sides, each column crowned with a different precious stone—twelve in all. During times of wor-ship the complex was completely filled with worshipers singing praise after praise to their King and Creator. Many times the Lord's presence would spill out into the square and overwhelm it with billowing clouds of His glorious Self, consuming all in precious smoke.

A Summary

Thus was Heaven created a place of glory, beauty and life. Much more could be written and has been recorded in other chronicles, particularly the Chronicles of the Kingdom. One could fill many volumes on the subject, but as this volume chronicles events from the angelic view, I need not go any further. I refer you to these other excellent works in the Great Library.

How wonderful it was to be born into the Kingdom of the Most High God; in service to one so worthy; in eternal praise of His glorious works; witnesses to His creation. These were the bright times in Heaven, the glory days of old—days of sweet fellowship and sweeter worship.

How could any of us have known that a shameful darkness would one day prevail within our own ranks and usher in an unrighteous kingdom with which we are contending even to this day? How might we have suspected that one day we would be fighting a war against our brother angels, which would call upon our utmost loyalty and would turn on the greatest sacrifice of love ever made?

Gabriel lived just a short distance from Lucifer. The residences were situated on the same street—but what a difference! Whereas Lucifer indulged himself with great splendor, living in the largest house in Heaven (apart from the heavenly Temple), Gabriel chose to live quite modestly. Lucifer felt it unbecoming of so highly regarded an angel as Gabriel to live in such a plain manner, but it was very much like Gabriel to live this way, as he was one of the most unassuming and humble angels in all of Heaven.

Gabriel was everyone's friend and confidant. He was well loved and respected, quick of mind, playful almost to the point of rowdiness. But the most endearing quality about him was that one could entrust himself to Gabriel. This is not to say that the other angels were not trustworthy, but only that Gabriel's very person invited one's trust without reservation, a special gift from the Lord. It was to nobody's surprise therefore, when the Lord announced that Gabriel was to become the Messenger of the Kingdom, for who better to serve as messenger than the one angel everyone called a friend, and in whom everyone trusted?

"Michael! Over here!" called a voice from the garden in front of the house. Michael turned to see Gabriel standing under a magnificent tree, motioning Michael over and eating a piece of fruit.

"Hello, Gabriel," answered Michael. "Or is it Lord Gabriel now?" he added, borrowing from Lucifer's greeting to him earlier.

"Lord Gabriel," said Gabriel, embracing Michael. "I've got to admit it sounds strange putting those two words together, doesn't it?"

"Yes, like lord and Lucifer," Michael answered. "Now there is a disturbing combination to say the least."

Gabriel immediately drew the conclusion. "I suppose you've been to see our friend?"

Michael nodded. "Here, let's sit down," Gabriel said, tossing Michael a large yellowish green piece of fruit and motioning for them to settle themselves under the lush branches of the tree.

As they sat down, their attention was suddenly drawn to a fast moving figure walking in front of the house. It was Serus, carrying the newly created music for Gabriel's service. He saw the two angels seated under the tree, gave a quick nod of acknowledgment to them and went on his way. They watched him disappear down the street.

"That poor angel," said Michael, remembering Serus' curt dismissal by Lucifer earlier. He shook his head.

"Who, Serus?" remarked Gabriel. "I should be so poor, living in the finest place in Heaven." He looked for a reaction from Michael and went on. "I know a few angels who would like to have his position. I mean, serving Lucifer is quite an honor." Michael remained impassive. Gabriel casually bit into the fruit and continued, "Of course, I suppose there is a price to pay for serving someone as temperamental as..."

"Temperamental!" Michael finally exploded to Gabriel's amusement. "Lucifer is more than temperamental. What I saw today was simply unreasonable."

Gabriel's interest was awakened as Michael recounted the events of the meeting with Lucifer, the mocking of Serus as a potential archangel followed by his curt dismissal, the uneasy atmosphere when they were discussing Gabriel's promotion, and the uncomfortable feeling that accompanied him as he left the house. Gabriel listened intently to Michael's story. Then an amused look came over his face, as if he were imagining a scene far away in his mind.

"Wouldn't it be something if Serus ever *was* made an archangel?" he said. "I would not want to be around Lucifer on that day!"

"Is that all you can say?" said an exasperated Michael. "You've missed the whole point." He stood up, facing the Mountain in the North, squinting at its brilliance.

"All right, Michael," said Gabriel, looking at his good friend. "What exactly are you trying to tell me? That Lucifer is bizarre and difficult to be around sometimes?" Michael turned around to look at Gabriel. "Everyone in Heaven knows that. If Serus ever wants to leave Lucifer's service he can do so anytime. He doesn't have to stay. He chooses to stay."

Michael's face softened. "I don't know, my brother," he said. "Except that he is so unlike the way he once was. We were all such good friends. Now I hardly ever see him unless it is in official service to the Most High." He looked at Gabriel, his eyes teary, and went on. "I miss the old Lucifer...our friend Lucifer...the Lucifer who roamed the Kingdom with us from one end to the other...the Lucifer who laughed harder than any of us...the Lucifer who brought us joy and set our hearts to dancing...our brother the Morning Star."

Gabriel put his hand on Michael's shoulder. "I miss him too, Michael." He looked into Michael's eyes, filled with compassion. "Perhaps you're right. Maybe we can talk to him together and find out if something is wrong."

As he finished saying this Gabriel spotted Serus on his way back to Lucifer's house. Once again the little angel nodded a quick greeting and scurried off. "But one thing is certain," said Gabriel as they both watched Serus move down the street. "There is definitely a price to pay for serving Lucifer!" They both laughed and headed into Gabriel's house.

<hr>

Serus continued down the street, having delivered Lucifer's program of music. He wondered about Michael and Gabriel as he walked in front of Gabriel's house and saw the two of them talking. As far as Serus was concerned, all of Heaven could think whatever they wanted about his serving in Lucifer's house. Naturally, being connected to such an immense personality had its challenging moments, but it certainly had its rewards. Serus was convinced that most angels would love to be in his position; some on occasion had even expressed as much. For all his quirks (which Serus figured went with the territory of creative genius) Lucifer was the most energetic and capable angel in Heaven. His star was rising and Serus intended to rise with it.

Serus turned down the street leading to the enormous house, nodding to some angels who were talking. He enjoyed a sense of satisfaction as he walked by them, feeling their gaze upon him as he passed. He alone really had Lucifer's ear, or so he felt, and secretly thought it wouldn't be long before Lucifer would be proclaimed an archangel himself. Then there truly would be no greater house to serve in all of Heaven...apart from the Most High's, of course.

<hr>

"Serus! Serus!" the voice boomed from within the house.

"Yes, I'm coming," Serus called back, scrambling to shut the massive door and trying to remember if there was anything else he was to have done while he was out.

"Come out to the garden at once," came the voice.

"Right away, my lord," answered Serus, relieved that all was well and that he had not forgotten anything after all.

Lucifer's gardens in the rear of the house were a magnificent display of beautiful flowers, lush fruit trees, small idyllic ponds and scenic paths—the best in Heaven. The trails throughout the estate provided a favorite recreation for Lucifer, who enjoyed walking in the garden for his meditations. Filling the air was the ever-present odor of lilacs, the featured flower of the garden. Also filling the air was music.

Wherever one went on the trails, the sounds of lovely praises to the Most High were heard. This was designed to allow Lucifer to rest, meditate or stroll in a worshipful attitude. It was Lucifer's contention that one should surround oneself with that which he hopes to attain—in his case, he intended to create the most compelling worship experiences possible. Lately, however, Lucifer hadn't been outside as much. In fact, it surprised Serus that Lucifer was in the garden now.

"Did you deliver the manuscript?" asked Lucifer, who was gazing vacantly into one of the ponds.

"Yes, my lord," answered Serus. "They thought it would be spectacular, as always."

"Excellent," Lucifer said. He looked up and plucked a large berry from one of the vines and tossed it in his mouth. "Now, regarding the other task. It concerns the Council of Worship. I want to see all of them here immediately after Gabriel's installation. I especially want Rugio and Pellecus here. Tell them this is of utmost priority. Kingdom business, you know."

"I'll convey exactly what you mean," Serus answered.

CHAPTER 2

"Let's make an archangel, shall we?"

The Great Hall of Ceremony was charged with excitement. Great numbers of angels poured into the entryway outside of the holy parameter to watch another of their own, Gabriel, become an archangel. A few were fortunate enough to be in close proximity to where the ceremony would actually take place. Many others crowded the halls and the outer courts, unable to enter the immense room that was filled to capacity.

From the choir loft, beautifully adorned with vines of gold and silver, Lucifer watched the activity occurring below. He was robed in an immaculate blue cloak with crimson belt, his customary attire for special occasions. Octrion, Lucifer's chief assistant in matters of worship, stood by his side, organizing last-minute details with the choir.

"Look at them down there," Lucifer sneered. "You would think they were all going to be made archangel today!"

He smiled and nodded to an angel who had caught his roving eye in the sea of angels below. An official whispered something to Lucifer indicating that it was time for the ceremony to begin. Lucifer took his place on the dais and the choir snapped to attention.

"Well," he said, looking over the magnificent collection of worship angels who made up the heavenly choir, "let's make an archangel, shall we?"

A hush swept over the room as the excitement of the moment gave way to the holiness of the occasion. Lucifer looked around the room to make sure everything was ready. He then turned to the choir, and with a motion of his hand, the music began.

The sound of thousands of angels in perfect harmony filled the room with majestic, holy praise. Hundreds of instruments added to the magnificence as choir and orchestra blended together in the handiwork that only Lucifer knew how to create. Lucifer was pleased with the music. He glanced here and there around the room to see the looks on the faces of the crowd, who were entranced by the fruit of his genius.

After a few moments, a large golden door to the side opened slowly, and the Twenty-four Elders entered the room solemnly, taking their places at the front of the room. The Elders were arrayed in white cloaks with golden belts. The Chief Elder's belt was embedded with 12 large stones, each a different color. He carried with him a golden belt and a sword identical to the sword Michael had been presented with at his installation.

A trumpet flourished a majestic fanfare, signaling the beginning of the processional. All eyes fell upon the rear of the room, where Michael the archangel appeared in full regalia, wearing the sword which was his badge of office, and cloaked in a brilliant white robe. Behind him came Gabriel, wearing the same robe, but without the golden belt and sword. Their magnificent wings, usually unseen, were folded behind them in splendid dignity.

They approached the Great Throne with both honor and humility, their heads bowed and their hands folded in front of them. After walking the length of the hall, Michael stood aside, his head still bowed, while Gabriel continued on, stopping directly in front of the Great Throne where he was to receive his office. Suddenly a thunderous declaration sounded through the room:

"Holy, Holy, Holy
is the Lord God Almighty,

who was,

and is,

and is to come!"

The choir shouted the words in one voice. The rest of the angels in the room joined together in praise to the Most High God, whose presence suddenly filled the room in glorious light and love. Lucifer tried to steal a glance of the Lord but found the sight too awesome to endure. He saw smoke pouring from the Throne and enveloping first Gabriel, then Michael and the Elders, and finally most of the angels in the front half of the room. Eventually the entire room was filled with this holy fog. A voice issued from the smoke as Gabriel was bowed low before the Lord:

"Beloved, from this time forth, the Lord your God confers upon Gabriel full authority among you and all My creation in the commission of archangel, with the privilege of attending this Throne. He shall henceforth be known as a ruling angel and will bear the golden belt of majesty and the Sword of Truth as his insignia of commendation. This is a most holy ordinance to the Lord."

The ranking elder brought forward a golden belt and put it around Gabriel. He then presented Gabriel with the Sword of Truth. Gabriel took the sword, kissed it, and placed it in his waistband. The elder placed his hands upon Gabriel and prayed: "From this time forward, you shall be anointed of the Lord to serve Him; to keep His holy truth; to walk in humility and holiness; to hold as sacred all things dear to Him. Yours is a station of service, not of greatness, for the greatest station is that of a servant. So be it unto the Lord." The crowd then repeated the words, "So be it unto the Lord."

The choir began singing again and led the Host of Heaven in chorus after chorus of spectacular music. Gabriel took his place next to Michael and the two worshiped God together. As the ceremony drew to a close, the Lord's voice thundered above everything:

"Let him who has been created to serve, serve with all his heart. This is the will of the Lord!"

The entire room responded, "So be it!"

Outside the Throne Room many angels pressed forward to congratulate Gabriel. Michael watched his friend humbly accept the polite affirmations. Angels of every rank and station gave hearty words of encouragement to their new archangel, who seemed a little dazed by it all.

In the haze of white cloaks and the noise of many conversations a figure in a dark blue coat discreetly made his way out of the Great Temple. Lucifer decided not to stay around for the customary fellowship. Instead, he walked to a door saying as little as possible to anyone. Just as he reached for the golden handle on the door, he looked back into the mob of angels pressing around Gabriel. His eyes met those of Michael, who was watching him from the midst of the crowd. Lucifer nodded courteously to Michael, who acknowledged Lucifer and nodded back as Lucifer exited.

Serus had informed the Council of Worship that Lucifer intended to meet with them immediately following the ceremony. The Council had been developed by Lucifer as a means of supporting the ministry throughout the Kingdom by authorizing these angels to enact certain provisions regarding ceremonies, special services and worship at large. They acted in an advisory capacity— although lately they had been taking much more advice than they had been dispensing.

Because the worship before the Lord was an ongoing ministry, one Council member was always present in the Temple to ensure that worship was being carried out with the proper attitude and decorum. Lucifer referred to this person as his "Temple ears" and often called upon him for the latest information from the Throne. The angels selected for the Council considered it a great honor to have been chosen and served with unbridled enthusiasm. They represented all the different functioning classes of the Host. Lucifer purposely designed the group to be a balanced team of warring, worshiping and wisdom angels. They were divided this way:

Warring Angels:
Rugio—Captain of the Fiery Host
Vel—Commander of the Legion of the Son
Nathan—Captain of the Legion of the Lord's Holiness
Prian—Chief Angel of the Watch

Worshiping Angels:
Sangius—Minister of the Holy Flame
Fineo—Minister of the Incense
Drachon—Keeper of the Door
Sar—Singer of Praises

Wisdom Angels:
Tinius—Recorder of the Holy Annals
Pellecus—Esteemed Teacher
Lenaes—Angel of Light
Belor—Angel of Light

Lucifer did not usually call a meeting without prior notice given. The members arrived in groups of twos and threes and took their seats at the conference table, talking reservedly about the service they had just attended. The hushed tone of the room gave away the intense curiosity that everyone was experiencing as they all held one question in their minds: Why is he calling this meeting?

When Serus saw that everyone had arrived he announced to Lucifer that the assembly was ready to receive him. All eyes turned to Lucifer as he entered the room, dressed now in a simple white cloak. The angels began to stand.

"Please, my friends! Be seated! After all we're not here to install an archangel," he said smiling at everyone. They laughed.

"Aren't we?" asked Tinius in mock seriousness. The room burst out in even greater laughter and Lucifer nodded to Tinius and sat down.

"Yes, yes," said Lucifer as he sat down at the head of the table. "It is no secret among my closest friends that I contemplated offering my services to the Most High as a ruling angel. But you all know I serve my Lord in whatever capacity He deems appropriate. I am quite content to be His humble leader of worship, with this marvelous Council to aid me." He extended his hand toward the Council. "We were made for other things, you and I; to serve and not be served."

The group looked around at each other for an awkward moment before someone broke in with a remark about the ceremony. Everyone immediately followed with general praise for the inspired music that had been featured in Gabriel's installation. Lucifer raised his hands to silence the praise.

"Enough, my friends," he said. "Of course it was magnificent. How could my music be anything but magnificent? I have no choice but to create magnificent worship. Forgive me, but your comment holds a very personal meaning to me of late..."

Lucifer stood up and gazed over the heads of the group in a manner that reflected deep and disturbed thought. "Please understand me," he continued. "I don't mean that as a boast. It is my destiny...my lot to create magnificent music. Just as all of you have a destiny from which you would never deviate." He smiled a wan smile.

The Council was perplexed by Lucifer's melancholy behavior. Finally Rugio, the ranking warrior-angel of the council, stood up and assailed the awkward moment. "What is disturbing you, my lord?" he said.

Lucifer looked at the group seated at the table with deeply troubled eyes. "I apologize, my friends. I should not burden you with my private concerns. Please forgive me." He sat back down and regained his composure. "Now, let me progress to the reason for our meeting today..."

"Lord Lucifer," said Nathan, another warrior, "I think I may speak for the group when I say that we would invite you to unburden yourself here in this room. We are your brothers and your friends." The group agreed vigorously.

Lucifer surveyed the group around the table, meeting and reading each face, and with a great sigh relented. "Very well. I know I may talk freely, but please realize that this is a deeply grave matter that I have been thinking about for some time now and of which I have drawn no conclusion as of yet."

The smell of honeysuckles filled the air in the beautiful garden near the Great Hall. The golden-domed roof that covered the Temple shimmered in the distance. Gabriel watched his friend curiously. He knew that something was on Michael's mind, and had been ever since they left the ceremony. There had been silence between the two angels for a long time, when suddenly they both spoke out at the same time, calling each other's name. They laughed.

"Quite a service, hmm?" said Gabriel. "I have always enjoyed installations. But I never figured that I would be the one being honored. It's quite a humbling event, isn't it?"

"I found my installation to be not only humbling but purposeful. I have never been so filled with a sense of mission and service to the Lord as I am now," answered Michael, who felt a sense of pride. "I love my office."

"We've certainly come a long way," said Gabriel. "I always wondered what would become of us. Though I always knew you would be a leader of some sort, but an archangel?"

"Yes, and I always figured you to be a part of the worship ministry. Your heart for worship has always been evident," said Michael. He threw down one of the fragrant flowers he was holding. "Just like Lucifer."

"Very true," responded Gabriel, who realized that Michael wanted to interject Lucifer into the dialog. "Lucifer always seemed closer to the Lord than the rest of us, or at least I always thought so. I used to watch him worshiping God, hoping to learn the secret of such devotion. 'It is no secret,' he would say. 'Just love the Most High more than anything else.' The Lord certainly placed him well."

"Do you remember when we would all worship the Lord together in the Temple?" Michael asked. "I mean long before any of us had our appointments. You and I would sing with all our hearts. But Lucifer...he seemed to have the voice of God when he sang. Remember how the other angels would stop and listen to the beautiful praise coming from his mouth?"

Gabriel nodded, remembering the glorious light that Lucifer's face gave off when he sang praises to the Most High.

Michael went on. "And then God appointed Lucifer to the position of worship minister for the entire Kingdom. Do you remember that?"

"Of course," answered Gabriel, a little suspicious by now of where Michael was taking this discussion. "He did a wonderful job today."

"I remember that Lucifer was ecstatic," Michael continued. "He was finally doing what he had been created to do. He loved to worship. He always said that all he wanted to do was worship God...forever. And God brought it all to pass. We were so happy for our friend. And this was long before I was made a ruling angel. Do you remember all that?" asked Michael.

"Yes, Michael," said Gabriel curtly. "And...?"

Michael looked at his friend and decided to speak his mind even if it offended Gabriel. "I'm not sure. I believe he was...I don't know...did you see him after the ceremony? He didn't even come over to congratulate you. That's not how an old friend should behave. He should have been one of the first angels to share in your joy! Instead he barely even acknowledged you. I think he is jealous."

"Then why don't you go over and talk with him?" said Gabriel. "Ask him, 'Lucifer, are you jealous of Gabriel?' Then he'll tell you 'No' and you can forget about all this nonsense."

Michael was beginning to feel a little foolish now but continued. "I know you think I am being ridiculous about all this but something is wrong when the minister of worship acts so cold to everyone on such an occasion—especially his old friends!"

"Perhaps if you weren't so suspicious you could see more clearly," responded Gabriel. "Try treating him as a friend rather than a minister of worship."

"Alright, alright," said Michael. "I won't say another word about Lucifer...for a while anyway."

"Thank you," said Gabriel. "Not another word, please."

As he finished these words a long, low trumpet sounded from the north.

"Well," said Gabriel, "looks like I have to meet with the Elders. And so soon! Guess they just can't govern without me!"

"Well, they'll find that out soon enough," Michael said smiling. "I'm sorry, my brother. And I promise. Not another word."

Gabriel smiled at Michael as two great, muscular, translucent wings instantly appeared from behind him. The wings did not move rapidly like the wings of the seraphim; rather, they simply unfolded and gracefully lifted Gabriel into the Heavenly sky, carrying him toward the golden roof of the House of Elders.

Michael thought about their conversation as he watched his friend disappear in the blueness of Heaven. He determined not to bother Gabriel anymore until he either had something definite that would give credence to his suspicions, or until Gabriel was himself convinced that something was indeed wrong with Lucifer. Maybe Gabriel was right and this was all a lot of nonsense. Perhaps this sort of behavior was the way with some angels, particularly those angels gifted in such demanding and creative ministry as Lucifer.

As he reflected on these things, Crispin, a renowned angel of wisdom walked by and nodded at Michael. He was on his way to the Academy, just a short distance from the park entrance where Michael and Gabriel had been talking. Crispin was a noted teacher among the angels, and a favorite among those who were called to special service in the Lord's house. It was widely held that Crispin was one of the wisest angels in Heaven. Michael had sat under his teaching, as had Gabriel, Lucifer and many of the other angels who were now higher ranked. He was also a prolific writer and had recorded much of the Chronicles of the Kingdom and was a fountain of knowledge about everything concerning Heaven.

"Good day, master," said Michael.

"Good day, Michael," said Crispin, who was reading a book bound in silver as he walked. "Beautiful service, beautiful service, hmm?" he muttered.

"More books, eh?" teased Michael. "You already know more than all the other angels in Heaven combined! What could you possibly be studying now?"

Crispin turned to Michael. "One can never have too much knowledge, Michael. I hope you learned at least that much from me." He then assumed a familiar teaching demeanor that was legend throughout Heaven. "Michael, it is by knowledge that we were made by the Most High, praised be His name. And it is by the increase of knowledge that we grow closer to Him. You should spend more time *inside* the library rather than standing around gawking at it. You'll find answers there, Michael. Good day to you," Crispin said, as he turned and continued on his way.

Michael smiled and bade him good-bye. *Same old Crispin*, he thought to himself. He watched him disappear into the ornate, multi-columned library building, which was a second home to wise angels such as he who taught at the Academy. A burst of inspiration suddenly hit Michael as he looked toward the Academy and thought of what Crispin had just said. *Perhaps you're right, my scholarly friend*, he thought to himself. *Perhaps there are answers there!* He hurried to catch up to his old teacher.

CHAPTER 3

"Would a perfect God allow His creatures to turn on Him?"

The angels assembled in the room watched Lucifer, who seemed to be struggling within himself over what he was about to divulge. Finally, he looked at them and began speaking. "My brothers, just a short moment ago we were discussing the music I created for Gabriel's celebration. We all agreed that this was remarkably beautiful music. For that I thank you. But when I said that I have no choice but to create beautiful praise I meant that quite literally. I am bound by the parameters that the Most High has set forth within me when I was created. What choice have I but to reflect the beauty that God has placed inside of me for His glory? It is my destiny, is it not?"

They looked at Lucifer, not knowing how to respond.

"Poor Lucifer! So perfect...so frustrated!" said Tinius.

Everyone laughed nervously.

"No, my dear Tinius, I have been thinking about this for a very long time. Our Lord has created this realm called Heaven. He and the Son and the Spirit rule from the Eternal Throne and as far as we know They always have. We have been taught that there was never a time when They did not exist and that at some point They created each of us. Though why They have need of some of us I don't understand," he added, looking at Tinius in good humor. The group joined in at Tinius' expense.

"These three have created a perfect world," Lucifer continued. "I mean, have you ever really explored this Kingdom? It is astonishingly beautiful. Nothing has been left to chance. Everything is in order and designed to perfection. Everything."

Lucifer walked over to the large window and made a dramatic gesture indicating the panorama of the Kingdom outside. "A perfect world," he said, gazing out the window, the Great Temple's golden dome brilliantly shining in the distance. He walked back to the table and sat down.

"Now it follows that if one creates a world, one would desire to populate it with subjects, does it not? I mean, the Three-in-One cannot rule each other, can They? Though it might be interesting to see them try," he added. Some of the angels laughed.

Sangius, a worship angel whose ministry at the Holy Flame kept him near the Lord spoke up nervously. "This conversation seems quite disrespectful!" A few of the angels looked at him coldly.

"Please, Sangius, hear me out. I mean no disrespect. Our gracious Sovereign takes no offense at such conversation. It is too far beneath Him to concern Himself with our little scholarly episodes. Besides, I hear He has a marvelous sense of humor."

Sangius assented and Lucifer went on.

"As I was saying, with the creation of such a perfect world, there would be a desire to create those who would inhabit such a world. We have always been taught that so great is the love of our Lord, that He wanted to share that love with others beside Himself. And thus was sparked in the mind of God the angelic Host, that is, you and I. And we were not to be just a mob of angels, but angels of different assignment and distinct inclination; some given to worship, others given to war, some given to wisdom. But all given to serve God and carry through with His vision and plans for this or any other kingdom He may establish.

"Now that raises an interesting problem. I mean, having created such a place of perfection, He must now populate this perfection with imperfect creatures such as you and I. To my thinking this spoils the whole work of perfection. Why must this be?"

"Because the Lord in His wisdom willed it so," said Sangius.

Lucifer arose and walked over to an ornate vase filled with lilacs, ignoring Sangius' comment. The angels watched him curiously. "Consider this lovely flower," he said, taking one in his fingers. "Stunningly beautiful and fragrant to the smell, and yet it has no other function than to be exactly that." He sniffed the flower and laid it on the table in front of Sangius. He then knocked loudly on the table, startling some of the angels. "And this table and these chairs will never serve any other function than what they were designed for and for what we are now using them."

Lucifer moved over to an ornate cabinet and opened one of the drawers, pulling out a scroll similar to the one Serus had carried earlier. "And this music of mine. What is it except that which I must write because it was for such things I was created?" He dramatically threw the scroll across the room, sending it rolling across the floor.

"You, Tinius!" Lucifer said, pointing at the perplexed angel. "Could you be anything other than a worshiping angel? Look at you, Rugio! You're a warrior and nothing else." He paused for a moment and continued. "Friends, we are what we are because God has decreed it so. It has been taught to us from the beginning. No other reason!"

"And so it should be," said Sangius. "The Lord is all-wise. His will be done!"

"Yes, His will be done! Of course!" said Lucifer. "I am not questioning the Lord's will in any matter, Sangius. I simply wonder if you or I or..." Lucifer stopped and looked poignantly over the group. "I am sorry, dear friends. I am afraid I have brought you into my rather confusing dilemma and I have no right to impose such...uncomfortable thoughts on any of you. Serus, bring in some refreshments for us. I think it's time we closed this discussion—for the time being."

Rugio stood up. "No! Tell us what is on your heart, Lucifer. We agreed that you may talk freely here," he said, looking pointedly at Sangius, who, sensing the cold stares in the room, swallowed uncomfortably. "Am I not right?" he asked the council, who joined in affirmation with him.

Lucifer continued. "Very well, dear ones, but keep in mind that these are only meditations and not necessarily the truth. It would take an angel far wiser than I to find meaning in all of this. Far wiser."

From the other end of the table as if on cue, an angel stood up to speak. Everyone turned heir heads to Pellecus, a highly respected angel of wisdom who was a former associate of Crispin's and deemed the wisest member of the Council. Pellecus was a gifted orator who held angels spellbound when he taught at the Academy.

"The Lord expects us to wrestle with these deep matters," said Pellecus. "It is a grievous insult to Him when we simply accept things with no debate...no reason. I myself have studied these things and am very interested in what you are saying. In truth, Lucifer, many angels have deliberated such points. Please continue. And remember that a healthy discourse is always preferable to no discourse."

"So be it," said Lucifer dramatically, "but please, wise Pellecus, guide me through these rather murky waters if you find me drifting."

"Of course," said Pellecus, whose scholarship validated in the minds of everyone the issues that were being discussed. If the learned Pellecus deemed something worth discussing it must truly have merit.

"We believe that we have been given a great freedom in this Kingdom to come and go as we please," Lucifer continued. "But are we really as free as we think? I return to music as an example. Again I put it before you that I must perform as I was created to perform. Therefore I am not free but a slave to my creaturehood. Are we not therefore all slaves? Slaves to serve, I grant you, and to serve a magnificent God. Understand I would not have it any other way. I truly love my station and am bound to my ministry. But am I bound to it because I love it...or must I love it because I am bound to it? Where is truth in all of this?"

Having recovered from the earlier rebuffs, Sangius summoned the courage to speak up once more. "I propose we stop talking about this immediately. It is an affront to the Most High."

"Dear Sangius," said Lucifer. "How like you to defend the Lord's honor as if it needed defending. But then as Minister of the Flame you were created to passionately uphold Him, were you not? I would not expect otherwise from you."

Sangius folded his arms and sighed.

Lucifer cast a pensive look over the heads of the group. "The truth is that as long as you and I accept our places as they are, rather than as they might be, we will never be anything more than what the Lord intends for us to be. Perhaps we are slaves to our instincts, nothing more, nothing less."

"But we are not slaves!" said Tinius. "We are free to choose our course at anytime. We have always understood that. The service I render to the Lord is out of love and desire to obey Him. He created me wise and so I serve Him as a scribe. But not as a slave...I have chosen to serve Him just as I could choose not to serve Him." Tinius suddenly looked very uncomfortable. "I mean I would never choose such a thing..." He looked down at the table, and stopped talking. His eyes scanned the faces looking at him. "What angel would dare to choose his own course?"

Everyone looked at Tinius, and then back to Lucifer to see what his response would be. Lucifer began to slowly circle the table, deep in thought. Staring directly at Tinius as he paced, Lucifer repeated the words under his breath over and over, as if digesting the thought for the very first time, "Free to choose...free to choose."

Tinius started to speak again but Lucifer held up his hand to stop him as if an interruption of this revelation would be devastating. He placed his hand on Tinius' shoulder in a gesture of comfort, and then sat back down in his chair. Suddenly he said, "Could this be? It's so very simple...yet so very profound! Tinius, you are incredibly wise!"

"Me? Wise?" asked Tinius, timidly pointing to himself and breaking the tension of the room as the group exploded in laughter.

"Yes, my humble brother. If I follow your thinking, and please help me out, I believe that what you are telling us is this: Either we are everything that we will ever be according to the Lord's will at the time of our creation and therefore we go on about our ministry, knowing that there can be no deviation. Or we are free to choose our course at anytime, as you so brilliantly put it, and actually depart from the Lord's intentions for us and thus create our own destinies. Now let's assume you are correct, Tinius, in your second assertion—that while all of us have the desire to serve the Most High, we actually might choose different courses. For example, perhaps Prian would like to be a singer..."

"The Lord forbid that one," said Rugio. Everyone laughed as Prian, a hulking warrior angel who served under Rugio, grinned.

"But that's just my point," continued Lucifer as the laughter subsided. "Why would the Lord forbid such a thing? Are we a threat to Him? Is everything so carefully managed that there can be no variation?"

"But the Most High has already built variation into all things," responded a frustrated Sangius. "That is precisely why there are angels who minister in different ways. Can you imagine if every angel decided that he would follow his own course? It would be chaos!"

"Exactly!" said Lucifer. "And what is it that keeps Heaven from becoming a place of chaos? The fact that angels choose to continue serving the Lord according to His dictates. Yes, we have been taught that we have freedom to choose to serve the Lord. But that teaching was always on the assumption that we would in fact choose to do so. It's really an ingenious way of keeping the Host under His control, isn't it? I mean all we've ever known is that it is glorious to serve the Most High. Who would ever think of not serving Him? Yet, how do we know that glory cannot be found down other paths as well? Who better knows us than ourselves?"

Tinius jumped in. "I don't think that's exactly what I was trying to..."

"Isn't that how you perceive it, Pellecus?" asked Lucifer.

Pellecus looked around the table at the angels, many of whom were former students. All eyes were upon the revered angel, who began speaking. "I have in the past debated some of these very issues with others at the Academy, particularly Crispin. They too were highly disturbed at the thought that any angel could or would choose to differ with the Lord in anything. Mind you, I never encouraged that such a thing should happen, only that such a thing could happen if an angel willed it so.

"Now why is such a notion so disturbing to us? So disturbing in fact that it has cost me my fellowship with most of the other wisdom angels and my seat at the Academy. I don't even remember when I last spoke with Crispin. I'll tell you why." He pointed his finger at the group. "Because knowledge is dangerous. Because realization paves the way for new thinking. That is why the Lord is Almighty—He possesses the greatest knowledge and whoever has the greatest knowledge will always be greatest. How has He created this marvelous Kingdom? By knowledge! How does He maintain it? By knowledge!

"Dear ones, the danger to the Lord's order is not in thinking about being contrary to His purposes, but in acting contrary to His purposes. That was the point I could never get across to Crispin and those other narrow-minded scholars at the Academy. They were so bent upon thinking properly that they forgot how to think at all."

"And what was your final conclusion on the matter?" asked Lucifer, who was now seated with the others, listening to Pellecus.

Pellecus thought about his answer for a moment or two, and then began. "Lucifer, I believe you are essentially correct when you say it is the angels who by their choice to serve the Lord are not allowing chaos. Everything we have ever known points to the truth that the Most High is the Creator of order and design and purpose. In other words, if by choosing not to serve would result in disorder, then by choosing to serve we angels are actually creating order, design and purpose."

"Which would indicate..." prompted Lucifer.

"Well, it would follow that if the Lord cannot sustain order without the choosing of His creation to act in such a way as to sustain that order, that the Most High is in reality not all-powerful as we have always thought. Very powerful, indeed. But all-powerful? All-knowing? Ever present? The fact that we have free wills just as He does, indicates that we are far closer to Him than we've ever realized."

He stood up dramatically, all eyes upon him. "Do you think a truly perfect God would allow His creatures to have the ability to turn on Him? Is that wisdom? Do you believe for one moment that if the Most High was all-knowing that He would tolerate our discussion here and now?"

The room fell completely silent as everyone reacted differently to the somber discussion: Some looked around, certain that they were being spied upon by Michael's angels and were about to be set upon; others tried to digest what was being said, not knowing how to react; others simply nodded in stupefied agreement.

"And," Lucifer went on, almost whispering from the other end of the table, "if God is not all-powerful, all-wise, all-knowing, all-everything, then how can He possibly be perfect? And if He is imperfect, by what authority does He rule over us who are also imperfect? Pellecus?"

Everyone turned back to Pellecus for some sense of security, or confirmation, or even a rebuttal to such a daring statement. Pellecus was a little uncomfortable now but went on, "Disturbing thoughts perhaps, but on the whole true."

The room teemed with the tension that comes with stumbling onto something which is better left undiscovered; a feeling of trespass...of crossing a line...of seeing what one should never see, and yet having seen, of wanting to see more...of profaning that which is sacred.

"There is always a feeling of disturbance when one confronts the edges of truth," said Lucifer, breaking the spell. He had decided to conclude the meeting. "Thank you, dear Pellecus, for that wonderful summation. Thank you all. My hope is that by exploring such concerns as these we will be all the more loyal to the Most

High, knowing that He truly depends upon our service to perpetuate His order. Serus, let's have those refreshments now! My apologies, brothers, that we never did cover the items I had originally planned to cover. Thank you all."

The meeting broke up and the angels enjoyed the food and drink brought in by Serus. Much of the after-meeting conversation was about the order vs. chaos controversy. Lucifer made sure to ease the mind of some of the angels who were disturbed by the discussion, particularly Sangius and Tinius. He then singled out Pellecus and Rugio, quietly asking them to stay on after everyone else had departed.

Suddenly a trumpet sounded, causing several of the angels to look around at each other. "Well, that is interesting," said Lucifer, looking out the window. "It seems as if there is to be an assembly of some sort at the Great Temple. I'm afraid I must attend. Thank you all for coming. Serus will let you know when we are to meet again."

The Council was ushered out of the room by Serus and toward the front door. As they left they thanked Lucifer for the meeting and interesting discussion. Sangius took Lucifer's hands as he left and said, "I know that you are only thinking aloud. There's no harm in that."

"There's never any harm in thinking," Lucifer replied. "Goodbye, dear Sangius."

Lucifer crossed to the side of the room where Pellecus and Rugio were waiting for him. He watched Sangius depart and said, "I would say that today's meeting was quite fruitful. We have broken the surface and the Council seems to be with me."

"Most of them," agreed Pellecus. "I'm not sure about Sangius. He may prove troublesome. We need absolute unity on this."

"Don't worry about Sangius," said Lucifer. "I'll take care of him. We'll have to meet later," he told them. "I must attend this Council. Pellecus, your clarification was splendid. Such wisdom will reward you one day."

"I trust that it will," agreed Pellecus, as he exited. Rugio bowed slightly and followed Pellecus out the door.

Chapter 4

"Weren't you listening? It's the Creation!"

The Great Library was the repository of the recorded knowledge of God—those things that He had chosen to reveal to the angels of wisdom and knowledge for the instruction of the other angels, as well as an eternal witness to His grace and mercy. All the important truths were stored there, including the Chronicles of the Kingdom, great books of wisdom, books of praise and hymns unto the Lord, and a recently installed book which was curiously blank, simply called the Lamb's Book of Life. The Library was housed in the Academy of the Host.

In order to prepare the angels for their posts of ministry, the Academy was established at the Library where the great teachers such as Crispin, Lucallus and others taught the great truths of the mysteries of God. Many of the former students at the Academy had risen to positions of prominent service in the Kingdom, including Lucifer, Michael, Gabriel, and others.

Crispin always made it a point to teach his sometimes over-eager students that the pursuit of knowledge was really a fruitless endeavor if those things being learned were not incorporated into the angelic life. "Knowledge is the key to all things," he would say.

"But if it doesn't produce excellence in your service to the Most High, and if it doesn't cause you to love Him more and yourself less, or if it doesn't inspire you to fervency in your ministry, you might just as well have never been created."

Michael always enjoyed Crispin's teaching. He hurried up the stairs where Crispin had entered under the massive archway housing the front doors of the Library. He looked around the great hall, where hundreds of angels were involved in scholarly discussions: Some were very animated in making their point, others reasoned quietly. Michael smiled as he saw a group of angels being ushered into the very room where he himself had been taught by Crispin.

He walked the halls, greeting some of his former teachers as he went. Michael peeked into a room and saw several hundred angels seated on the floor in front of a platform. The room itself was circular, with very high ceilings that let in light from the outside through large round windows near the top. It could hold some ten thousand angels, though today's class was relatively small.

"Who's teaching in here today?" Michael asked one of the angels.

"This is Crispin's class," answered the angel, a little perplexed at the archangel's presence.

"Thank you," said Michael. "I think I'll join you."

Michael took a place on the floor very near to where he had sat as a student. The angels around him looked at him, amazed that the noted angel should attend their class. Michael decided to end their speculation about him and said, "Crispin taught me that one can never learn too much of the Lord's truth. Today I'm here as a student, not as a ruler."

Crispin entered the room from the rear and walked up to the three-stepped dais that was in the center of the room. The students were seated casually on the floor, encircling the platform. Michael watched as the revered teacher sat his books down, gathered his notes and cleared his throat, a routine he had witnessed a hundred times before. Crispin looked over the class and noticed Michael, seated to his left.

"Well, it seems that even archangels can learn something," he said, the class laughing. "Welcome to my class again, Michael. I trust you find today's lesson interesting, hmm? As well as the rest of you," he added, scanning the room.

For the remainder of the session Michael was entranced as Crispin taught on the creation of the angels. Crispin was a marvelous teacher, who involved the students in lively discussion while he spoke. Michael enjoyed listening to the students ask questions, remembering some of these very issues being brought up when he attended classes at the Academy.

"In conclusion," said Crispin, "let me simply say that as angels we are privileged to serve with the greatest dignity and freedom any creature can have, because we are free to live under the wisdom and love of a Creator who takes an interest in our ministry and who preserves us for even greater things. There is not one angel in all of Heaven who can know the mind of God and what plans He has for His creation. How grateful we angels should be that we were made for such things."

Crispin sat down, assuming an uncharacteristically informal posture. "I love my role and I hope all of you love whatever ministries you are called to as well. One never knows where service to the Most High might lead. Just look at Michael: a prime example of God's grace and purpose working in the life of an angel. We certainly never expected such an honor, did we Michael?" asked Crispin.

All eyes were upon Michael, who jumped as if awoken from a dream and said, "No. Of course not. I never sought such an honor and I certainly never deserved it. But God has chosen me and He will choose some of you for great things as well." He looked up at his old teacher with a how-did-I-do? expression.

"Well done, Michael. I see that you were listening to some of my lectures anyway," Crispin said as the other students laughed. "Any other questions before we conclude?"

"I have one," came the familiar voice of Berenius, an angel of worship who loved to spar with Crispin and the other teachers on difficult issues. Berenius seldom asked a question without an ulterior motive in mind—usually he was just trying to bait a teacher into some intractable theological problem.

"Yes, Berenius," said Crispin. "What is it?"

"I have yet to hear a satisfactory answer concerning true freedom. I mean, master, you have spent a great deal of time discussing freedom and yet I am still confused as to its nature. How can we angels have such great freedom if we must obey everything we are told?" asked Berenius. Many of the students winced as they heard the question. Others echoed the question with "Yes" or "Answer that one!"

Crispin read the mood of the class and replied, "You certainly have a knack for picking subjects that are far too lengthy and involved to give a satisfactory answer to in this setting. Perhaps we can take up the subject of our freedom in the next session." Crispin began gathering his things and continued speaking. "You see, Berenius, I am in a sense not free to delve into this matter right now because my responsibilities take me elsewhere at this very moment. True freedom and responsibility are compatible. I would go so far as to say that one cannot be truly free unless one is given some sort of parameters, boundaries, to make that freedom meaningful. The Lord in His wisdom created boundaries for us and in doing so assured us of freedom. Sounds like a paradox, I know, but it is true."

"A paradox indeed," said Berenius, who gathered his things to leave. "It seems as if the Academy is rampant with paradox."

The students began leaving the room, some saying that Crispin didn't have the answer, or Berenius was far too clever for him, while others said that Berenius was just a troublemaker and wasn't really interested in the answer. Crispin watched them as they filed out.

Michael turned to Crispin and said, "I certainly don't remember the students being so brash when I was at the Academy. Even if we disagreed with the teacher we didn't make an issue of it like Berenius."

"Yes, Michael, things have changed at the Academy since you attended classes here," sighed Crispin. He closed his eyes as he remembered. "The students were once so diligent in the pursuit of knowledge about the Lord and the Kingdom. They were tremendously interested in learning about their roles and their service to the Lord." He looked at Michael. "Now it seems that so many of them have an agenda that is quite their own, as if they're not satisfied with the traditional truths which the Most High gave us and which we have always been taught. No, they're always questioning, always debating. Like Berenius. Of course Berenius comes by it as a result of his association with Pellecus."

"Pellecus?" asked Michael. "What does he have to do with this?"

"Pellecus has a number of angels who follow his rather confusing teachings," said Crispin.

"But he doesn't teach anymore," answered Michael, a little confused.

"Oh, he teaches," said Crispin. "Just not here at the Academy. Pellecus will always teach. The Lord created him to be a marvelous teacher, very gifted, very brilliant. He was a favorite at the Academy, you know. And he leaves quite a legacy. His influence over a number of the angels he instructed as well as many of the teachers is enormous."

"Really?" asked Michael with growing curiosity.

"Oh yes," said Crispin. He looked around the room making sure they were alone and said, "But I can't put the blame of this attitude which is setting in entirely on Pellecus. True, his teachings are a bit on the...independent side, but I feel there is something greater...something more going on here." Crispin looked around and leaned into Michael, speaking quietly. Michael leaned in to hear his words. "Michael, I believe there is a movement which is much more dangerous than some radical philosophy that has infected some of the teachers and students at the Academy. I believe there is something under way which is quite critical, even dangerous to the peace of this Kingdom. And I believe I know who is responsible."

<hr />

The Great Hall of Assembly was energized when Lucifer arrived following the trumpet blast that had summoned him. He passed groups of angels who were talking among themselves trying to figure out what was going on. Normally, assemblies such as this were only called with advance warning. This was beginning to look like a very important occasion—particularly since all he could see were highly placed angels.

Lucifer found his usual seat near the center, where a seven-stepped circular platform was situated. It was from this platform the Chief Elder spoke, and Lucifer was looking around to see if he was anywhere nearby so he could find out exactly what was happening. He noted that though many of the more important angels were in attendance, there were none of the warrior class present, not even the archangels.

"It seems that the Lord is only interested in singers and sages today," Lucifer said to Octrion, a chief worship angel who was seated just behind Lucifer. Octrion was only a few steps lower than Lucifer where the music ministry was concerned, serving as an assistant in many worship experiences. He was also one of the best sources for the latest news in the Kingdom, because Octrion loved to talk to everyone. If anyone would know what this was all about, it was he.

"So it seems," said Octrion, looking around at the growing number of angels. "But it only makes sense if what I have heard is true."

"Really?" said Lucifer. "And what have you heard?"

Octrion looked this way and that, then whispered to Lucifer, "I heard that the Lord is about to announce that one of us worship or wisdom angels is about to become involved in a spectacular new ministry!"

"Interesting," said Lucifer, speaking loudly enough for the angels seated around them to hear. "But who in this room deserves such an honor? All honor belongs only to the Most High. I bear my ministry with no expectation of reward. My pleasure is in serving the Lord—nothing more."

Some of the angels around him whispered to one another. "Well, that's what I heard," said Octrion, a little embarrassed for having brought the subject up. He sat down again.

Lucifer thought about what Octrion said. Could it be that this assembly was called to announce some great promotion? He looked around the room again to see if other noteworthy angels were in attendance, but could find none who could compare with his own station. Among the angels present there was only one obvious choice for some new position as far as Lucifer was concerned: himself. Perhaps Octrion was right...

Suddenly the murmur of the crowd began to dissipate as the Elders solemnly entered the room and made their way to a section near the center that was reserved for them. Gabriel, whose capacity as Messenger to the Kingdom necessitated his being at all important functions, solemnly followed the procession. Many whisperings of Gabriel's name could be heard throughout the room as the angels saw the archangel enter the room. Since he only attended very important assemblies, this could only mean something very significant was about to be revealed.

Lucifer watched as the Elders seated themselves one by one until only Gabriel was standing. He then climbed the platform steps, carrying a large, white scroll that the Chief Elder had handed to him previously. The recently confirmed golden sheath carrying his sword of office shimmered as he mounted the steps.

All eyes were upon Gabriel as he prepared to read from the golden scroll. Generally the Chief Elder read the proclamations at these gatherings, but since Gabriel was reading, this must be something truly grand! With great ceremony, he broke the seal on the scroll and began unrolling it. Lucifer cocked his head forward, keenly interested. Gabriel began reading...

⚜ ——————— ⚜

The labyrinthine passages of the Great Library that led to the private rooms of the ranking wisdom angels who taught at the Academy were something that Michael had always wanted to see. They were off-limits while he was attending, though he and Gabriel and some of the others had thought up some never-used schemes to gain entry. Now he was accompanying the greatest teacher at the Academy down these very halls to discuss something dark and brooding. He could not help but wonder if somehow Lucifer fit into all of this, and meant to bring his name up at first opportunity. They arrived at Crispin's chambers and entered.

"Here we are, Michael," said Crispin. "The sanctorum, as it were."

Michael was not surprised to find that everywhere he looked were stacks and stacks of books. From the top of the room to the floor were volumes on every subject in Heaven. Crispin noticed Michael gawking at the enormous number of books that lined every wall.

"Don't be too impressed, Michael," he said. "They belong to the Library. I'm just borrowing them. Better make a note to myself to return them sometime. Here, have a seat," he said, clearing a chair in front of his desk which was piled high with books. Michael sat down and Crispin began.

"Now, before we get into any of this let me say that though I may mention some important names, I have no real evidence to either vindicate or nullify my thoughts. By that I mean there is no clear picture of any of this. It's really bits and pieces—but they begin to add up as one takes them as a whole. And remember: In the history of this Kingdom since its creation there has never been an incident where an angel rebelled against the Lord. So, what I'm telling you is that I am accusing no angel of any crime against the Lord. You understand what I'm saying."

"Yes," said Michael. "Of course."

"Good. Then let me begin by giving you a little background as to what has been happening in recent times, since you and your group left the Academy. As you know, the Lord devised the Academy of the Host as an instructional ministry to all angels—particularly those angels who showed the greatest promise in their areas of gifting. Not all angels are going to become archangels, any more than all angels can become teachers. The Lord knew this when He created us, and so he developed this school as a place where the skills of all angels could be sharpened. As to those angels who don't excel as some others do, they are not looked down upon by the Lord at all. They are simply given other tasks to perform. But remember, the greatest task any angel can perform is to glorify God in his duties, however great or humble." Crispin said these last words with an impassioned resolve.

"After the Academy was set up a number of wisdom angels were selected to become the instructors, of which I was one. Ours was a very important ministry and one we did not take lightly. The Lord set us to studying the deep things of the Kingdom for a very long time, until we were ourselves ready to teach. It was during this time of preparation that I became acquainted with Pellecus. After much laborious study, the time came that we began teaching and training angels for their posts of ministry and have been doing so even up until now.

"The first groups of angels to enter the Academy proved to be those destined for the greatest appointments of ministry. This was the season when you were a student, Michael—as were Gabriel, Sangius, Tinius, Kara, Lucifer and many others. Look where these angels are now serving in the Kingdom! You and Gabriel of course went on to the Warfare Academy since that was where your inclinations seemed to take you. Lucifer of course took up his ministry in worship. I must admit rather selfishly that I would have liked to see one of you teaching here.

"Now, as the number of angels in Heaven is known only to the Lord, this Academy will serve until every angel has had a chance for instruction—except for the angels who minister around the Eternal Throne, of course. Those rather mysterious fellows were created for unique service which keeps them in the presence of the Lord continually."

"What will happen to the Academy when all of the angels have been through its doors of instruction?" asked Michael.

"I don't know really," answered Crispin. "I simply know that the Lord in His wisdom will place every angel into various avenues of service as they show promise and desire here. The Academy has done well in its role of chief educator to the angels. As I said, the teachers here hold enormous influence with some of the most highly placed angels in the Kingdom—which brings me around to my concerns.

"As you witnessed in class today, there are certain angels who are finding the teaching at the Academy to be rather confining to their way of thinking. I don't mind a good scholarly discussion, in fact I welcome it. But these angels are not merely debating. They are strongly questioning and in some cases outright denying the veracity of the teaching."

"But these are the teachings of the Lord to the Host of Heaven," said Michael. "How can they question the truth of Almighty God?"

"They never do, Michael," said Crispin. "Instead of denying the truth from God, they accuse us teachers as having fallen away from the truth and they have become the custodians of truth—the guardians of the sacred teachings. The problem with all of this, Michael, is that they are teaching doctrines which incite the kind of independent, disrespectful and proud behavior you saw earlier."

"And what does Pellecus have to do with all of this?" asked Michael.

"Pellecus," said Crispin with a sigh. "My former colleague. Finest teacher the Academy has ever had. Pellecus could teach a class on any subject and hold the students completely enraptured. His authority was unquestioned and his wisdom renowned—he was the perfect teacher. But he began delving into very disturbing matters, subjects which transgressed the lines of discretion; things which were better left a mystery. After a while he was trying to bring the other instructors into his world and began challenging us, always wanting to debate another point.

"Now I'm certainly not afraid of growing in knowledge. I enjoy learning. But the knowledge Pellecus was cultivating was increasingly at odds with the orthodox teaching of the Academy. And as I taught you quite well, Michael, any knowledge which opposes, denies or attempts to weaken the truth of God is at best foolish angelic philosophy—at its worst it is a dangerous doctrine which must be dealt with."

"What exactly was he teaching?" asked Michael.

"Understand Pellecus was far too clever to publicly teach anything which was completely radical. Instead he taught by innuendo and implication. You know, lots of what-if and could-it-be statements. What did he teach? A number of things, but the centerpiece for every discussion always came back to the fact that angels are moral creatures with a freedom to choose rightly or wrongly. I had no argument with him there. It is a standard teaching at the Academy. We all know that the Most High has created us with the capacity to choose right and wrong, praised be His name. And we choose to serve.

"But Pellecus taught freedom in such a way that some of the angels felt imposed upon by the Lord, as if He was presuming upon their right to serve Him any way they so desired. 'Why must we serve the Lord in such and such a way if we are truly free?' they asked. My head swarmed with that question regularly."

"I don't remember any of those things being discussed," said Michael. "At least not to any degree. Of course I was spending most of my time in warfare."

"Yes, well it was not the rage it is now," said Crispin.

"Was Lucifer under Pellecus during this time?" asked Michael.

"Lucifer was never actually under Pellecus," said Crispin. "But he did begin to spend more and more time with him as I recall. Pellecus was quite taken by Lucifer. It was soon after they became acquainted that Pellecus' attitude began to change. Try as I and many of the other teachers did to undo the damage we felt Pellecus was causing, it proved quite impossible. When events finally progressed to the point where he said that angels are actually the ones who maintain order in the Kingdom and that the Most High is actually dependent upon their obedience, we had to act officially. I petitioned to have Pellecus removed and so he was. We have spoken very little since." Crispin remembered these things with a feeling of sadness.

Michael was drinking all of this in, quelling the anger he felt rising against Pellecus. Then he said, "And where does Lucifer fit into all of this? Do you believe he was the one who started Pellecus on his...mission?"

Crispin swallowed hard and said, "I am not very good at this sort of thing. Ask me about the foundation of Heaven or the righteousness of the Most High and I am quite comfortable. But these matters...I know you and he were very close...I hope that..."

"Master," said Michael tenderly, "Lucifer was my friend. He still is as far as I am concerned. I hope that somehow this can all be made right. The reason I came today was in fact to discuss Lucifer. But my allegiance is to the Most High God and if there is something Lucifer or anyone is involved in which threatens the purpose of this Kingdom, then I will pursue that point." Michael placed his hand upon Crispin's shoulder. "Thank you, Crispin, for your concern." He then sat back down and continued, "Tell me about Lucifer."

"When Pellecus fell into disfavor and left the Academy he was quickly courted by Lucifer, who asked him to sit on his Council of Worship. I believe they are quite close, or at least as close as anyone can be close to Lucifer now. They suit each other's needs. Pellecus provides Lucifer with a scholarly credential on the Council, which is desperately needed in that rowdy crowd, and Lucifer provides Pellecus a position of some importance, though to what end I have no idea. Apparently he was taken in by Lucifer's flattery and muddled teaching; it's his own fault for straying from the truth. If one turns his back on the truth, Michael, one is liable to believe anything, no matter how untruthful."

"Have you ever thought about publicly exposing them?" asked Michael. "I don't mean like when you had Pellecus removed from the Academy. I mean exposing their teachings for what they are in a scholarly setting—like a debate of some sort. Then perhaps Lucifer would return to his post and minister as he was intended."

"I appreciate your confidence in me," said Crispin. "When the truth is on your side you will eventually be vindicated—provided you know the truth. I must admit I've had such notions. Privately I'm ready to take Pellecus and Lucifer on here and now. And this is the reason, Michael. Pellecus will say all kinds of things which angels might find both disturbing as well as enticing. Of course Lucifer would not speak publicly on these issues—he would allow Pellecus to speak for him; his prophetic voice, so to say. But when it all comes down to it, they have only their wits and their pet philosophies. I have the truth of God and the truth is everlasting, Michael."

Crispin looked at Michael. "But I don't want to debate anyone just to try and best them. If by debating Pellecus I could put an end to this idle speculation about freedom that has infected this school, then I would challenge him. I'm afraid it isn't that easy."

"What exactly is the nature of this...infection?" asked Michael.

"Well, it's been around since we were created, I suppose," said Crispin, "this idea of how far an angel can exercise his freedom before he opposes the Lord. Where does one draw the line—that sort of thing. I suppose Pellecus has vented the argument. You saw Berenius in class. He's just one of a number of angels who seem eager to...try their own way."

"Is that the dangerous movement you were talking about in the classroom?" asked Michael. "These angels who seem bent upon their independence? Berenius may be brash but he doesn't appear ready to take on Heaven just yet."

"Independence! We have independence already," fumed Crispin as he thought about the rather smug expression on Berenius' face. "Besides, Michael, he isn't alone. There are others who are part of something that goes beyond academic discourse. I am not afraid of radical ideas. It is radical action that is disturbing. As long as the angels keep it in the classroom I suppose they may think what they like—they will anyway. But there is more going on here than simply a radical philosophy. There is coordination and perhaps manipulation toward an actual outcome. But to what end?"

"And you believe Lucifer is the mover?" asked Michael.

"Mind you, I have no real evidence for any of this. But you yourself mentioned his behavior of late. I too have seen a change in him. I find him seething and potentially explosive. Not at all the angel I once knew. Then there's Pellecus, spewing this divisive doctrine all over the Kingdom, encouraged, if not coached, by Lucifer. Pellecus teaches only what Lucifer allows these days. Of that much I am sure. Finally, look who sits on the Council of Worship! Every angel handpicked by Lucifer—all of them former students of Pellecus and all of them now in places of great authority. Let's see...there's Tinius, Lenaes, Rugio, who is one of your own commanders, Sangius, and quite a few others. From what I understand they are devoted to Lucifer."

"Everyone in Heaven knows about his Worship Council," answered Michael. "They've been meeting together for matters of worship for a long time."

"Worship Council?!" said Crispin. "Maybe they once met to discuss worship. Lucifer hasn't involved them in worship since way before your archangelry. The Council should be done away with. It's nothing more than a group of troublesome angels with nothing better to do with their time than sit around Lucifer's enormous house and talk about such nonsense!"

"But why would Lucifer, who brings us into the Presence of the Most High, consort with this group of malcontents?" Michael asked.

Crispin thought about his answer for a moment, reflecting on the two Lucifers he knew: the angel with the voice of God who once shone brilliantly in the Academy, and this melancholy figure who was restless and driven. "Lucifer is Lucifer," Crispin finally said. "He has always been a deep one. I remember when he was in my classes here. He would simply sit back and drink in the lecture with his eyes closed. In the beginning I thought he was not paying attention, but whenever I tried to call him on it he always had the correct response."

"I remember," agreed Michael. "He always knew the answers!"

"Brilliant mind," said Crispin. "But his attitude began to change. Not that it stopped his ministry—no, no he was always excellent in what he does with music. And he seemed to truly enjoy his worship post. Maybe he still does! As I said, I always hoped he would teach, but I think he had greater things in mind for himself."

"Crispin," Michael asked, feeling a heaviness within him as he asked the question, "can an angel truly rebel against the Most High—I mean outright oppose Him?"

Crispin weighed his answer carefully. He then looked Michael over and said, "Michael, could you ever oppose the Lord?"

"No!" Michael said. "Never!"

"And why not?" Crispin asked.

"Because I love the Lord my God. I will always serve Him. I would never betray Him."

"But you have not answered my question," said Crispin. "Could you ever do anything to oppose the Lord?"

Michael wasn't sure where Crispin was taking him. "No, I could not...ever," he said.

"Could not, or would not?" asked Crispin.

Michael suddenly realized what Crispin was teaching him. The fact was that though he would never turn against God, he actually could if he wanted to by a simple matter of choice. This being the case, any angel could betray the Lord if he so desired. "I would not, though I could," said Michael solemnly, "if I chose to do so. But I would never so choose."

"And so it is with all angels," said Crispin. "These are the exact issues which Lucifer and Pellecus are escalating. Ultimately, the choice is ours to make, Michael. But what those who would oppose the Lord don't realize is that His Kingdom will continue regardless of their choosing. It is nonsense to believe that angels are responsible for the continued order of the Kingdom through their obedience. If an angel ever chooses to disobey the Lord, the Kingdom will continue as always. Any opposition to God cannot possibly win. The tragic part is I really think they believe they could win, or at least force a compromise on the part of the Most High. I doubt, however, it will ever come to an actual rebellion. Such is the deception of pride."

"So why doesn't the Lord do something about this?" asked Michael. "Surely He knows what is being discussed around the Kingdom by Lucifer and Pellecus and others. Why does He not do something about them?"

"I can only say that the Lord is all-wise. And He knows what must be done at the proper time. Remember, Michael, Lucifer has not actually committed any rebellious action. Maybe he will not.

Perhaps the Most High is giving Lucifer time to think things through. Either way, God will not oppose Lucifer's or any angel's choice to betray Him."

"But why?" said Michael, who was quite disturbed and had framed in his mind how he would deal with such dissenters.

"Because the Lord loves His creatures too much to violate their ability to choose freely. What is devotion to God if it is forced or created beforehand? It is worthless. True love must come from a choice to exercise that love. If God does not allow for the possibility of some of His angels to oppose Him, then He is actually demonstrating that He is not in control. He is not inviting their disobedience, but He must allow for the potential.

"Strange, hmm? God is only in control if He allows the possibility of His creatures getting out of the bounds He has constructed for them. And the reason is clear. If He must exercise power to keep His creatures from willfully disobeying Him, then He demonstrates an inability to deal with them justly. He must let them choose because there are consequences for their actions. That is the difference!"

"What kind of consequences?" asked Michael.

"Well, I don't really know," said Crispin. "The point is, Michael, that if Lucifer, or Pellecus or you or I ever decide to rebel against the Lord's authority, the fact that we can rebel is not a sign of His weakness. It is rather a sign of His strength and confidence that He can handle such possibilities."

"So what do we do?" asked Michael, whose head was buzzing from the discussion.

"Watch. Listen. Be cautious but not overly suspicious," said Crispin. "These are in fact our brothers and perhaps there is hope for their fellowship again one day."

The sound of someone running down the hall loudly knocking on doors, mixed with muffled voices, could be heard coming from outside Crispin's room. "What is going on now?" Crispin asked, heading to the door.

He opened the door just as Grel, a teacher at the Academy, was about to pound on it. Grel was trying to tell Crispin something, but Crispin could not make any sense of it. He could see other angels running about in the halls, all jabbering with similar excitement. A long trumpet blast sounded, signaling to all of Heaven that a major proclamation had just been made. Michael looked at the two angels and asked urgently, "What is it?"

"The Lord Most High," said Grel, "has just announced through the archangel Gabriel the establishment of a new realm, to be populated with an entirely different creature! A physical realm. A world unlike any other. And we angels will be witnesses to this! Think of it, Crispin! We always hoped for this possibility and now it's happening! Come on!" Grel hurried out the door and disappeared into the throng of angels.

"What is he talking about?" asked Michael to a teary-eyed Crispin. "What is it?"

"Weren't you listening? It's the Creation!" answered Crispin, who hurried out of the room to join the rest of the angels who were celebrating the news.

Chronicles of the Host

The Creation

The greatness of our Lord was never made more manifest to the angels than in His Creation of the Heavens and the earth. Long discussed in Heaven, the announcement of the Creation stunned the Host. God in His wisdom and love had determined to design a physical world—a dimension of material substance with which He might interact, having populated it with physical beings.

Thus did the Lord announce through the angel Gabriel this joyous news, which was received by the Host in great excitement and celebration. To all it seemed a time and place of tremendous future service to the Lord; to some it afforded more personal advantages...

Chapter 5

"What are they searching for that they must go to Lucifer to find?"

The streets of the City were filled with angels celebrating the wonderful news. There were buzzes of information everywhere as angels excitedly exchanged views on the event: "I hear that angels will be allowed to visit the new world." "It can't be as beautiful as the Kingdom." "I wonder who will govern the planet—an angel perhaps?" All sorts of information was flying about—all of it guesses, most of it completely wrong.

Lucifer was hurrying home through the crowd of noisy angels. Every few steps he stopped to agree with this or that angel on how wonderful this was. "Lucifer!" a voice shouted. "Lord Lucifer!" Lucifer turned to see Octrion running toward him.

"So the Lord was going to announce another great ministry?" asked Lucifer as Octrion came near. "Octrion, you couldn't have been more incorrect."

"Who would have thought this was to be the announcement?" said Octrion, a little embarrassed. "But doesn't it make sense that the Lord must at the very least name some more archangels to help administer the new world?" He smiled at an angel who bumped into him accidentally.

"Octrion, you overestimate our importance," answered Lucifer, who noted some angels gathered around them. "The Lord will choose whomever He deems worthy of such a task. Archangel or not, I intend to serve Him as always."

"I'm glad to hear you say that, Lucifer," came a voice from behind.

Lucifer turned around and greeted Gabriel. They embraced each other for a moment and then Lucifer spoke up. "Well! The messenger at last! Since when do my friends keep such marvelous news from me?" He smiled.

"I only learned about it a short while ago myself," said Gabriel, who nodded in greeting to Octrion. "I was summoned to the Temple and the next thing I knew I was handed a scroll and told to prepare for an assembly."

"There was really very little to go on from the proclamation you read," said Lucifer. "All I could gather is that the Creation which everyone has speculated about for some time is actually going to happen. Is there anything else you know?"

Gabriel looked at Lucifer and Octrion hesitantly. "Very little. I know about as much as everyone else. The angels will be witness to the event, that much I know."

"Octrion was suggesting that perhaps the angels would also be involved in governing the new world," said Lucifer. "Isn't that what you heard, Octrion?"

Octrion looked up at Gabriel and nervously responded, "Actually I...I mean I really can't be sure. There's so much talk..." He looked down, mumbling.

"What do you think, Gabriel?" asked Lucifer. "You are so much closer to the source than I or poor Octrion are these days. What is to be the administration of the new world?"

"Lucifer, I do not know any more than you," said Gabriel, a little tense at Lucifer's question. "But here's some good news for you! As part of the celebration of the event, you will have opportunity to create your most significant work—the Creation hymn! The Elders wanted me to convey to you that they desire an extraordinary effort to celebrate this announcement. Hymns, praises, choir—everything. Your music will be remembered with the event itself!"

Octrion offered his congratulations to Lucifer, who accepted them warmly. "The Elders? Please thank them for me," said Lucifer. "I am honored to serve them and the Lord in this capacity...as always."

"Excellent," said Gabriel. "I shall tell them immediately! Just look at it, Lucifer! It's as if every angel in Heaven is coming to the Grand Square to celebrate this announcement. Good-bye, my friend. Farewell, Octrion."

Gabriel disappeared into the sea of angels. Octrion looked at Lucifer and wondered why the worship minister looked so displeased. Finally he said, "My lord, this is a great honor! The Creation set to your music! I will serve you in any way I can in this effort. My deepest congratulations to you!"

"And my deepest regrets," snarled Lucifer. "The most important event to happen to this Kingdom since its own creation and my part in it is to write more music!? Is that all they believe I am capable of?" He looked at Octrion, who was astonished by Lucifer's words. "I'm terribly sorry, dear Octrion. Of course I am honored. I only hope my little contribution will be of some use. That is what I was trying to say."

"Of course it will be of use," said Octrion. "It will be inspiring to all of Heaven. And think about it: Apart from the Lord, you will be the only angel who is involved in the Creation itself. Not directly, of course, since we are not God, but...I mean..." He dropped his voice to a nervous mumble.

"Octrion, you have an annoying habit of never finishing a complete sentence, " Lucifer said. "I think Gabriel was right about all of Heaven turning out. Just look at all these angels. You'd think they were all going to be a part of this."

Octrion felt uneasy and saw an opportunity to escape Lucifer's company. "There's my good friend Costas! I will talk to you again, my lord. Please call upon me when you need anything! Costas! Costas!" He melted into the crowd.

Lucifer scanned the crowd, watching the angels come and go. A small ensemble of musicians began playing to add to the carnival atmosphere of this joyous time. Many angels were dancing with a joy Lucifer had not witnessed for a very long time. One angel tried to grab Lucifer by the cloak and pull him into the dance, but Lucifer politely refused. Finally he saw Kara, one of the Elders, approaching him through the throng.

Kara was a strong ally of Lucifer. He was a wisdom angel who was widely respected and who sat on the Eldership. He was therefore privy to the deliberations of the Elders and kept Lucifer abreast of what was discussed at the meetings. Lucifer enjoyed this information, which gave him a pulse on certain events in Heaven.

Lucifer never quite understood why Kara held him in such esteem, but ever since they attended the Academy together Kara was devoted to him. Like Lucifer, he dreamed of greater things for himself and felt that by acting in the worship minister's behalf from time to time he was advancing both their causes.

"What a joyous day, my brother," said Lucifer, embracing his friend.

"And a noisy one," replied Kara. "What do you think of the news?"

"What do *you* think of it?" asked Lucifer.

Kara understood and motioned Lucifer to follow him. "Let's get out of this mob where we can talk," he said. The two made their way through the crowd until they came to a place between two pillars which were a part of the Great Hall of Assembly. They could see the Grand Square from here, filled with the noisy, happy, dancing, singing celebrants who were thrilled that God was about to embark upon a new creative venture.

Kara made sure they were at a place where no angels might overhear their conversation. He looked at his old friend and smiled at him. "I know what you are thinking, Lucifer. And the answer is, I don't know."

"What are you talking about?" asked Lucifer.

"Lucifer, since we both got out of the Academy and have been serving in our places of ministry—what is the one thing you have always aspired to do?" asked Kara.

"Why, to serve the Most High with all my heart," answered Lucifer.

"Yes. But it wouldn't hurt your feelings if the Lord gave you a more, shall we say, authoritative role in the Kingdom, hmm?" Kara looked at him with a penetrating gaze. "I know you. And the first thought which crossed your mind after the pronouncement was, *Who will rule over this new creation?* Am I right?"

"And what were *your* first thoughts?" asked Lucifer. "Go on. I'm listening."

"From what I gathered at our meeting the person responsible for ruling will be called a steward," said Kara. Lucifer tried the word himself, saying "steward" several times under his breath to see how it sounded. Kara continued, "The Lord intends to turn the new world, which will be called *earth*, over to this 'steward' who will be responsible for all of its resources—wealth, creatures, everything! Who the steward shall be nobody knows."

"So you believe that the Lord will select an angel to steward ...what was it called, earth? Is that what you are telling me?" asked Lucifer.

"Yes, but I have no idea whom He will select. But He must choose an angel since there are no other creatures capable of such a task," said Kara. "And I presume He will allow the Elders to deliberate with Him as to which angel is most capable and deserving of the task. Perhaps He will even consider a recommendation from us." Kara watched with interest to see what effect his words had on Lucifer.

"Really?" said Lucifer. "Well, my interest in all of this is a simple curiosity and nothing more. What with all the rumors flying about on the street already I am only attempting to divide the real from the ridiculous."

"I'm afraid that is all I can tell you right now," said Kara. "And any future knowledge I come upon will put me at tremendous risk personally if I am too...casual with it. At least until the Chief Elder allows us to speak freely. You understand, don't you?"

"Of course," said Lucifer, patting his friend on the back. "I would never want you to violate your office simply to satisfy my idle curiosity. Think nothing of it."

"Now," said Kara, "it seems you are in for a great honor!"

"Yes," said, Lucifer, "the Chief Elder has asked me to compose the music for the Creation."

"Correct!" said Kara. "That's what I was coming over to tell you. I am the one who suggested the idea to him."

"As if I was not burdened enough," fumed Lucifer. "Why did you do that?"

"Because my friend, this will be a great opportunity for you to demonstrate your ability to...steward your talent. Understand?"

"Yes," said Lucifer. "I believe I do understand." He thought to himself for a moment and then said, "I would imagine that a great many angels will be displaying their ministries in innovative and enthusiastic ways while the Lord decides who will govern earth. And I would also think that if a certain angel were selected he would be free to appoint certain other angels to accompany him and help administer. Particularly if that angel was well placed and able to...shall I say...motivate interested parties in the decision. Is that what you had in mind?"

Kara was lost in thought, feeding upon Lucifer's words. "Yes," he said, as if in great relief, "of course." He looked around carefully to make certain they were alone. "You alone know that I desire a new work. Something that will take me away from the endless drudgery that comes with serving as an elder. Please understand I love my office. But the possibility of something completely new...something I have control over..." He looked at Lucifer for some hint. "So you would take me to earth with you! You can be Chief Steward and I can..."

"Quiet!" said Lucifer, looking around. "Kara, I admire your ability to sway an argument in the Council. But your ambition will get the better of you one day. You're dreaming much too far in advance. You have us on the earth and it has not even been created yet." He placed his hand on Kara's shoulder, sensing that the conversation had shifted in his favor. "I am sure that whoever the Lord and the Elders select will be a worthy angel. But if I were presented with such an honor I assure you that I would want to bring with me the most talented angels in Heaven." He looked intently into Kara's deep green eyes. "You Kara, are remarkably talented."

Kara felt an excitement building within him—a sense of warmness that one can feel brewing within their inner being when a destiny is being realized. He then said very seriously and in a hushed voice, "You asked me a moment ago what my first thoughts were when I heard the news about the Creation. These were my thoughts: *Lucifer must be made steward. I must do whatever I can to get him appointed.* That's when I spoke to the Chief Elder about the music. Lucifer, you must do well on this. You must exceed even your own abilities this time. The Elders must be as completely taken with it as I shall be!"

"And so they shall," said Lucifer. He looked up in thought, his eyes scanning the Heavenly skies. "This work will be my greatest triumph—one which I will invest with all my talents and abilities." He laughed. "Actually I have been holding back a bit lately. But not this time. The Hymn to the Creation must be my greatest achievement in all my service to the Lord. It will encompass everything I know about music. I want all of Heaven singing my songs about the Creation, humming my melodies about the Creation, hearing my music even while the Creation itself is unfolding." He looked at Kara boldly and said, "And throughout eternity whenever the angels think of the Creation, they will not be able to do so without Lucifer's music playing in their minds."

"Excellent work begets excellent reward, hmm?" said Kara. "I understand. And when the Lord decides to reward such excellence with the stewardship, and I lead a delegation of Elders to your house and beg you to serve..." said Kara, already framing the proceedings in his mind.

"I would never object to any decision of the Elders or the Most High," answered Lucifer. "I would reluctantly, but graciously take on the task. And both of our situations would change drastically."

"So be it," said Kara, as they clasped arms and parted.

The Grand Square of the City was one of the most beautiful and busy places in the Kingdom. The square itself was paved with lovely precious stones that were polished and perfectly fitted, forming a beautiful geometric mosaic. All of the impressive buildings which surrounded the square were the official buildings, housing the various ministries of the Kingdom. To the north was the Great Temple complex, where the presence of the Most High resided; facing the Temple, from the south, stood the Hall of Assembly where the Elders functioned in their service to the Lord and the Heavenly Host.

On the east side was the House of Wisdom, where all the archives of Heaven were stored, including a vast and mysterious vault of sealed scrolls and books which had yet to be opened and which were forbidden to all. On the west sat the enormous Great Hall of Ceremony, where important occasions such as Michael and Gabriel's installations occurred, or where special services unto the Lord were held. Normally the square was brimming with angels going about their daily business, but today the square was practically empty, except for a large figure sitting by himself and thinking deeply.

Michael's mind was absorbed with recent events. His talk with Crispin, while confirming some of the things he was thinking about Lucifer, had also opened a great door into a much larger, much darker problem. If Crispin was correct, and there was a concerted effort on the part of Lucifer and a small number of angels to introduce an independent attitude among the Host for their own purposes, he needed to do something right away.

But what could he do? Crispin advised caution. But Michael's nature was to attack problems headlong. He could speak with Gabriel about it again, but he had promised his friend that he would not bring up the subject until he had good evidence that something was amiss. There had to be a different way to get at

Lucifer without arousing too much suspicion, and without treating Lucifer unfairly.

As Michael sat in solitude where recently thousands of angels had converged to celebrate the announcement of the Creation, he saw Serus walking toward the Great Hall where the Elders met. Since the announcement, Lucifer had cloistered himself in his house, working feverishly on the music, receiving no visitors, and conducting no business except for his occasional Council meetings. Michael watched as Serus walked up the marble stairs holding Lucifer's latest work and disappeared into the gigantic hall. Michael wondered if there was a way to talk to Serus without arousing too much suspicion. Perhaps he could get through to him.

"Blessings on you, Michael."

Michael turned to see Sangius, the Minister of the Holy Flame walking toward him.

"Sangius!" said Michael. "Greetings in the name of the Most High! How are you, my brother?"

"Quite well," said Sangius. "Excellent, in fact."

Sangius sat down next to Michael. The two had been much closer friends at one time, but now the different directions in service they had chosen had kept them from any meaningful fellowship. Sangius sat back, closing his eyes in a very relaxed manner.

"You do look well," Michael remarked. "I have never seen you looking so refreshed."

"That's because I am fresh from worship, Michael. I almost forgot how to really worship our Lord, what with my official office and serving on the Council. You know, Michael, as Minister of the Flame, I am quite near the Lord's presence much of the time. I am very privileged to hold such a position that places me so close to His holiness. Yet even so I felt myself growing more and more distant." Sangius had a dreamy look in his eyes as if deep in thought.

"But today you are refreshed in His presence," said Michael. "What happened?"

"Two things really," said Sangius. "A discussion we had at the Council made me realize that I had to choose to worship the Lord regardless—out of my will to do so and love for Him. I am a creature with freedom and I choose to worship the Most High!" Even as he said these words a glow began to appear around Sangius' face. "I choose, Michael! The other thing which refreshed me was that I choose to no longer be a part of the Council of Worship." He laughed. "Or perhaps the choice was made for me. Either way I am free."

"Really?" said Michael, quite interested.

"Yes. I suppose it was a mutual parting of the ways," said Sangius. "One or two meetings after the Creation was announced Lucifer asked me to step down." He laughed. "How I must have disappointed him! I guess I was not the kind of angel he needs on the Council. So he chose another angel to take my place and I feel quite unburdened."

"Really? Do you know who he chose to replace you?" asked Michael.

"Yes. An angel by the name of Berenius," said Sangius. "Ever met him?"

"We met once," said Michael, remembering Berenius' conduct at the Academy. Even as he answered Michael felt ashamed and angry at the conduct of the angels in the classroom that day. "Tell me, Sangius. What goes on in those meetings?"

"That's as suspicious a question as I have ever heard," said Sangius. "I'll be glad to tell you. I have no more obligation to them." He sat back, relaxed. "In the beginning, Michael, we would discuss various aspects of the worship ministry in Heaven. You know...how to involve more angels, whether or not a piece of music suited the occasion. That sort of thing. It was truly a legitimate, deliberative body functioning in the manner which had been described to me when Lucifer asked me to serve on it."

"Excuse me for saying so...but you don't have any real musical gifts, do you?" asked Michael, as diplomatically as he could.

"Who, me?" said Sangius. "I have about as much musical ability as you, my friend. I have musical disability." They laughed. "But I know worship."

"So why did Lucifer want you on the Council?" asked Michael.

"I never really knew," Sangius said thoughtfully. "And I never asked. But I believe it had more to do with my position as Minister of the Flame than anything else. You see, only a few of the members, such as myself, have any real knowledge in matters of worship. Most of us...them...serve in other capacities. All highly placed, capable angels for sure—but musical? Not really."

"So what you are telling me is that Lucifer's Council of Worship is seated with angels who have little ability in the worship ministry. Doesn't that seem a bit strange?"

"Of course," said Sangius. "But Lucifer has his reasons. He wanted a variety of angels so that the ministry could affect every facet of the Kingdom—wisdom, warrior, and worship. At least that is how he explained it to me. It made sense at the time."

"So why did he ask you to resign?" asked Michael.

Sangius shook his head at Michael. "I guess it was because I was increasingly at odds with the rest of the group, or seemed to be. I just wasn't comfortable with some of the discussions—especially toward the end."

"What did they talk about, Sangius?" asked Michael pointedly.

"I am ashamed to tell you, Michael," said Sangius. "And I am embarrassed for having sat on that Council for so long."

"It's very important that you tell me," said Michael, "much as it causes you distress." He noticed Sangius' attention directed elsewhere. "What's the matter?"

Sangius was staring out toward the square, with just the slightest hint of anger in his beautiful brown eyes. His reddish aura was slightly manifesting. Michael looked out onto the square and saw Serus walking back across the square toward Lucifer's house. Serus looked over and saw Michael and Sangius together but continued walking as if he didn't see them. Sangius watched him until he turned out of the square down Lucifer's street. He turned toward Michael.

"He certainly gets around!" Michael said, as he watched Serus disappear.

"Now there's the angel you should talk with if you want to know about Lucifer," said Sangius. "Of course you wouldn't get anything from him. He's totally devoted to his master."

"I know very little about Serus," said Michael. "I know he didn't do well at the Academy. But he found a choice position for himself, that is if you don't mind working for...hmm...how do I say this?...a potentially difficult taskmaster."

"Well done, Michael!" said Sangius. "I was thinking along less cordial lines!" They both laughed, and Sangius excused himself for the indiscreet remark. "I am sorry, but after serving on the Council I feel I am owed some satisfaction! Truly, Michael, that Council bears watching."

Michael wanted to know more about the Council and decided to tell Sangius about his conversation with Crispin. He went over the details about the prevailing sense of change at the Academy and cited his witness of Berenius' behavior in Crispin's class. Sangius nodded from time to time as if he saw a puzzle coming together in his mind.

"What you tell me makes perfect sense," said Sangius. "Though I haven't been privileged of late to many of the discussions. 'Closed room,' Lucifer called them. I know that the Academy plays a significant role in their talks, mostly receiving negative criticism. Of course Pellecus has no love for the school anyway. I suppose with me off the team Lucifer has a completely free hand with the Council. I was the only one who ever questioned him on some of the discussions, and rather weakly, I must admit. From time to time Tinius will raise a question but a rather intimidating look from Rugio will usually set him down. I suppose any opposition, however weak, cannot be tolerated by Lucifer." Sangius then added with humor, "No need for closed-room conferences now!"

Michael looked at the angel with compassion. "Sangius, are all of the angels on that Council with him? I mean, are their loyalty and obedience unquestioned?"

Sangius continued, "Lucifer is definitely in charge, I can tell you that much. Even though the learned Pellecus and a number of other angels who command great authority in the Kingdom sit on the Council, they all pay homage to Lucifer. I personally found their loyalty to him solid and unswerving, while their disposition to the Most High was disturbingly close to disdain. I believe they would follow Lucifer anywhere." His eyes shifted to Michael ominously. "Perhaps they shall."

"But why?" asked Michael. "What hold does he have on them?"

"The same hold he had on me, I suppose," said Sangius. "Lucifer has a way about him that makes you feel...important, needed, and that you're going to miss a tremendous opportunity if you don't join him. He makes you feel like you're on a great journey—part of some great plan. He inspires confidence in an angel—particularly if that angel is searching, or hurting, or discontented."

"About what?" Michael retorted. "What are these angels searching for that they must go to Lucifer to find?" Michael's passion was rising within him. "What could they be hurting about...or discontent with? These are some of the most exalted angels in Heaven! Apart from Pellecus, who has brought disgrace upon himself for teaching questionable doctrine, I see no reason that any angel should have such an attitude. Why don't they speak with an Elder...or bring it to the Temple if they have a problem?"

"I can only speak for myself, Michael," said Sangius. "I joined the Council because I felt it would serve the worship ministry to the Kingdom. But the more time I spent with Lucifer, the more unsure I felt about...everything. The changes in my attitude were all very subtle...very quiet. But within a short time I didn't approach my places of service with the same passion I once did, and I felt my closeness to the Lord slowly slipping away.

"Meanwhile the Worship Council became more and more important to me even as it became more and more antagonistic towards the Kingdom. I also noticed the agenda becoming increasingly hostile. Rather than promote worship Lucifer began promoting himself. Again, Michael, it was all very subtle. And whereas in these new discussions centered on the Lord's *ability* to reign, now they centered on His *authority* to reign!"

Michael bristled at this statement.

Sangius looked at Michael with tears in his eyes. "I finally came to a point where I had to choose to believe Lucifer or to believe the holy teachings. I began searching. I immersed myself in the truth. I began to differ with the group in meetings. I voiced favorable opinions of the Lord. I took up His cause. In doing so I found myself increasingly isolated from the others. In my final two encounters they started the closed-door meetings in which I sat outside the conference room with Serus to 'see to my comfort.' " Sangius smirked and added, "It wasn't long after that I was asked to step down. By then I wanted to stay on if only to upset the agenda. But I'm glad I left. If I had given myself over completely to Lucifer as some of these others have, I might never have been able to worship the Most High again."

"What now, Sangius?" asked Michael. "Where are they taking this...recklessness?"

"I don't know for sure. The last meeting I attended they were very excited about the Creation. It seemed to hold great possibilities for them."

"So they discussed the Creation in Council?" Michael asked. "Interesting."

"By then I was not in the same room, you understand. But they have previously discussed what they would do if and when another world was ever made available. Lucifer would of course be archon—ruler. And this lovely Council would govern with him. It was all such a horrendous and prideful fantasy. I did happen to overhear a few things as I waited outside. Of course one can hear much when one is listening outside a door." (Michael smiled at this.) "It seems the coming Creation is very much on Lucifer's mind right now—and not just because he's writing music for it. Believe me, music for Lucifer has become merely a bridge to greater things. He actually believes that if he was made ruler of the new world, a great many of the angels would join him there! What disturbs me, Michael, is that I believe he is quite correct in that assertion."

"Sangius, would you be willing to say these things to some other angels?" asked Michael. "I don't mean reckless, talkative angels. I mean friends to both of us?"

"Of course," said Sangius. "If you think it will help end this nonsense." His eyes slowly shifted toward the direction of Lucifer's house; the direction Serus had walked. "But we must be careful. Lucifer has ears all over Heaven."

They stood up to leave and he and Michael began walking together. As they exited the massive gate on the south end of the square Michael stopped walking. Sangius turned to see what was happening. Michael, clearly troubled by the unfolding sinister story, looked deeply into Sangius' eyes, and asked, whispering, "Sangius...what do you believe they really want?"

"That's easy," said Sangius. "Whatever he really wants."

+≍————————≍+

On the opposite side of the very wall where Michael and Sangius had been talking, a figure stealthily peeked out of the flowery shrubs. He made sure that he was quite alone, then stepped onto the stone path. He was almost giddy, armed with the knowledge of a conversation that would prove profitable to his future. Serus intended to tell Lucifer exactly what he had heard—when the time was right. This should prove his worth to his master once and for all.

+≍————————≍+

Chronicles of the Host
Heaven's Anticipation

The time for the Creation was fast approaching. All of Heaven was in a state of joyous anticipation, and waited anxiously to see their God in creative action. The scribes were preparing their scrolls to ensure that every detail would be recorded for the archives. The Elders announced that the angels would have a gallery from which they could watch the entire proceedings. But the questions that loomed on every mind, whether spoken or held in reserve, were these: What will the Most High do with the new world? Who will serve there? Who will rule in the Lord's name?

CHAPTER 6

"All I need is a show of strength— something impressive!"

Lucifer fulfilled his promise to Kara. He began work immediately on his Creation music and the only angel who saw him was Serus—even the meetings were dispensed after a short time. Occasionally angels walking down the street would see glimpses of their worship minister at the window, or catch a brief glance at him on the balcony, but for the most part he stayed in his study and worked.

As time went on, Serus continued his errands to and from the Temple, conferring with the Elders on the progress of the music. Angels would stop him in the streets and inquire about Lucifer, who had seemingly disappeared. He gave reports on how brilliantly "their" music was coming together and hurried on his way. The only other visitors who were admitted to the house were Pellecus and Rugio, who always arrived together, and only after being summoned.

Soon, the Chief Elder felt that they needed a more direct communication with the minister of worship, so Kara suggested that a liaison be appointed to act on the Elders' behalf and volunteered to serve in that capacity. He was instructed to visit with Lucifer immediately. Serus, who happened to be with the Elders when the liaison was established, raced ahead of Kara to prepare his master for the visit. When he arrived and explained the situation, he was surprised to find that Lucifer was delighted to receive Kara, as if he was expecting him. Shortly thereafter Serus was ushering Kara into Lucifer's presence. He excused himself from the study and left Kara alone with Lucifer.

"Good Kara," said Lucifer, "I'm glad you have come." They embraced each other. "I've been needing to talk with you. I trust the Chief Elder thought well of the idea of an embassy to me." He smiled and added, "The music I have created is stunning!"

"I had hoped as much," said Kara. "The Elders are thrilled with what they have seen thus far." They sat down on two golden chairs with dark crimson cushions. Kara noticed a strong odor in the room. "Your idea to get myself made a liaison *was* brilliant. What is that fragrance?" he asked.

"Surely you've heard of my love for lilacs," said Lucifer. "They're my only weakness, you might say. I keep them around me always. I plan to speak to the Lord about these beautiful flowers and make sure that He fills the earth with them." Lucifer looked at Kara, folding his hands in front of him. "Which brings up what I wanted to discuss with you. How go the plans for the Creation? Any mention of when this will actually happen?"

"Nothing specific is known to any of us," said Kara. "Only the Lord knows the hour. But I understand that the Three-in-One will coordinate this effort together—Father, Son and Spirit are in complete accord on this."

"Of course They are," said Lucifer. "They wouldn't have it any other way. As to the other matter...the question of stewardship. Any indication from the Elders on that?"

"I have been discreetly but firmly urging your name to various members of the body. Some of them, Pratia and Belron for example, were talking about you before I ever even mentioned the possibility. I'd say you have fairly wide support among the group."

"I need overwhelming support," said Lucifer. "You know the Lord will not select anyone to an office without agreement within the body. They must all be won over if possible."

"Your music will take care of that," said Kara. "There is one rather awkward development. You know Rega, the assistant to the Chief Elder?"

"Oh yes," said Lucifer. "He and I have had some interesting talks from time to time."

"Well, he remembers some of those 'talks.' He told me that he will only support you if you pledge to appoint him to some office after you begin governing."

"Rega always has had an appetite," said Lucifer. "But I need his support. Tell him that I will do what I can, but that I can do nothing until the appointment becomes official."

"Very well. I will report back to the Elders that you are working devotedly on the music and that you will have it completed within...how long shall I say?"

"Actually I have been finished with the project for some time," said Lucifer.

Kara looked at him in shock.

"It's quite true," said Lucifer. "I have needed this time of isolation to garner support in other areas which may play an important part in the future of the Kingdom. You see, Kara, there are larger issues at risk than the appointment of earth's steward— much larger. I will tell you everything when the time is right. I wrote the music quite rapidly and have sent Serus out with bits and pieces to whet the Elders' appetite—you know, keep them interested. Your appointment as liaison was critical at this point, though poor Serus was enjoying himself as go-between."

"But what are these other issues?" asked Kara. "You can trust me."

"I do trust you," said Lucifer, placing his hand upon Kara's shoulder. "And you are doing a splendid job. Keep up the excellent work and I promise you that your efforts will be rewarded. I am simply not at liberty to disclose these things right now. It is enough for you to know that as always I have the Kingdom's best interest at heart."

Kara left Lucifer's house feeling encouraged. For the very first time he was beginning to believe that Lucifer would be appointed steward and that together they would lead the new world. As he walked down the street he saw two angels coming toward him: Pellecus and Rugio.

"Greetings, brothers," said Kara.

"Greetings, Kara," said Pellecus, who had seen Kara just depart from Lucifer's house. "What takes you away from the Elders?"

"Some rather urgent business with Lucifer," said Kara proudly. "We meet together occasionally. As do you."

"Really?" said Pellecus. "That's quite interesting."

"Yes," said Kara. "We're really quite close. I am the liaison between the Elders and Lucifer on the matter of the Creation music. Exciting times ahead, hmm?"

"I'd say revolutionary," said Rugio.

"I suppose they are," said Kara. "And where are you two honorable angels headed?"

Rugio began to answer, "We're meeting with..."

"Gabriel!" interrupted Pellecus. "And I believe we best be on our way. Never good to keep an archangel waiting. Farewell, brother."

"My regards to Gabriel," said Kara as they parted company. Kara watched as the two continued down the street and slowed in front of Lucifer's house. He stood behind a large tree and watched them enter Lucifer's house, wondering why they had lied to him. Or perhaps they thought of some urgent business that they needed to conduct with Lucifer. It didn't really matter to Kara. He was on a mission for the greatest angel in the Kingdom and was now more determined than ever to win the Council of Elders over in the matter of the recommendation of Lucifer as steward.

Pellecus and Rugio were ushered into the council room where Lucifer was waiting for them. "What were you and Kara talking about?" asked Lucifer.

"Nothing of substance, my lord," said Pellecus. (He had been addressing Lucifer as lord ever since Lucifer insisted that it was necessary for the unity of the group as well as the sake of decorum.)

"We merely came across him after meeting with you. I gather he is not yet intimate with the movement. Though Rugio very nearly brought him in—bantering such words as 'revolutionary' and informing him of our meeting with you."

Lucifer glared at Rugio. "We must be discreet, commander," he said, "and cannot take chances with casual chatter—and especially not to an elder whose final regards in this matter are still developing. There's no shame in it, Rugio. Pellecus has himself on occasion been given to carelessness." Pellecus looked grimly at Rugio.

Lucifer invited the two to the conference area. "No, Kara is not yet intimate with us," he said. "But he will be very soon. And it is true that his devotion to the Lord is quite well known." Lucifer went to a gold inlaid cabinet and pulled an ornate key out of his cloak. "In fact, I would say that apart from Michael and one or two others, Kara is regarded as the most loyal and devoted angel in the Kingdom."

Lucifer opened the cabinet and retrieved a brass tube that opened on one end. He then walked back to the table. "Kara has cultivated, with some prompting on my part, a very public image which inspires confidence and trust." Lucifer looked squarely at the two angels and went on in a hushed tone. "Privately, Kara is extremely loyal to me. I have not brought him in completely because I want to see which way the Elders are going to go with their recommendation to the Almighty on the stewardship selection. If the vote should go against me, I want him to be able to continue his association with the Elders without the appearance of being biased towards me. He is quite useful to me on the Eldership. How do you think I came by the information on the stewardship in the first place? But…Kara also happens to be extremely ambitious and cunning and must be handled cautiously."

"So what happens if they recommend another angel?" asked Rugio. "Or what if the Lord decides on His own steward apart from the Council?"

"That is highly unlikely in either case," said Lucifer, who motioned for everyone to take a seat. "The Most High will desire the Elders to be involved because it is His nature to share such authority. He must give the Elders *something* to do. And He will consider their counsel quite seriously. He knows that to place in such a significant position an angel who is either unknown or untested would be inviting critical feelings from the Host—feelings which are steadily increasing among the various ranks, are they not? I'm ready for your reports. But first..."

Lucifer opened the brass container and pulled out a scroll, which he unrolled all the way down the length of the conference table. On the scroll was inscribed various headings and categories, which were divided into three sections covering the three main ranks of angels: warrior/ministering angels, wisdom/proclaiming angels, and worship/praise angels.

Under each category appeared the names of the most influential angels in Heaven along with their positions, ranks, ministries. These were categorized under the following designations: Loyal, Likely, Probable, Possible, Unlikely, Impossible.

The angels in the "Loyal" section were those Lucifer knew he could rely on completely, such as the angels on the Council, Kara, and other ranking angels who were sympathetic to change.

The bottom portion of the scroll was headed with the designations "Unlikely" and "Impossible," and underneath these titles appeared a list of angels as well. The names found here represented those angels who were most loyal to the Lord, such as Michael and Gabriel, Crispin, and many others. A recently scrawled in "Sangius" appeared at the bottom of the list with a question mark next to it.

"This is how I view the situation thus far," said Lucifer, poring over the scroll. "As you can see we have some work to do. But I'm happy to say that there is a definite trend in our direction ever since the news of the Creation was made known. It would seem that Kara is not the only ambitious angel in Heaven. In fact, there are quite a few angels who see my...our movement as an opportunity for greater achievement in a less strident kingdom."

Rugio and Pellecus looked at the scroll, making an occasional comment about names that appeared on the list: "Oh, you may move Sep to the 'loyal' side. He is definitely with us," or "I'm not sure if Deter belongs in the 'likely' category or not," or "Greka has moved from the 'possible' to the 'loyal' category in such a short time!" They examined the entire scroll and were quite encouraged. Lucifer rolled up the scroll, and asked for a briefing on the latest developments...

"I am happy to tell you that almost my entire command is ready to follow me anywhere," said Rugio, beaming. "They are desirous of a change and feel that the new world promises a great adventure for them. I am also in contact with other commanders who are sympathetic and will join us when prudence allows. They have angels in their command whom we can count on."

Lucifer looked over at Pellecus, who began talking. "Many of the teachers are with us," said Pellecus, "and therefore many of the current students. They think that they will be able to teach with fewer constraints in the academy that I told them I plan to create in the new world. Those at the Academy who are still tradition-bound are of no consequence as they are starting to lose students to the more vocal angels like Berenius, who I must say is doing a splendid job."

"Excellent!" said Lucifer. "I knew I was right in reading Berenius' character. But if we're not careful all of Heaven will join us on the new world and there will be no angel left to serve the Lord!" They laughed. "Except Michael and Gabriel...oh yes, and possibly that simpering Sangius."

"Don't forget Crispin," said Pellecus. "He'll be needed to maintain the Academy!"

"Enough of this, my friends," said Lucifer. "We must not celebrate too early or too openly. If there is anything that must be stressed to all of our contacts it is the need for utmost secrecy. If our ultimate intentions are exposed prematurely everything we have worked for will be lost."

"Remember," said Pellecus, "that there are some who are already suspicious. I'm afraid that some of our bolder angels have become rather brash of tongue lately."

"Then you put a stop to it," snarled Lucifer. "The supreme challenge in liberating the angels is in not allowing them to become too liberated. I believe, Pellecus, that you need to advise caution among some of your disciples. Now as to suspicions already raised, there may be a *few* angels who suspect that something is stirring, but all they can ascertain is that there is movement...undercurrent. They can't possibly predict the outcome or its source."

He held up the scroll as a point of reference and said, "I am convinced that the Worship Council is ready for the complete presentation. Now that Berenius has replaced Sangius, I have wholehearted support and can speak quite openly. I'll have Serus announce a meeting as soon as possible. We must meet before the Creation begins and while our strength is growing. I will instruct each angel on the Council to press his influence with those angels who are under him or work with him.

Lucifer stared icily at the two angels, as if he was looking right through them and into the future he envisioned. "We must begin setting up the new authority now; to have it in place and ready to take control once the stewardship has been given to me. I'll report to the Council everything we have discussed: They'll be pleased and encouraged to know that the Elders Kara, Pratia and Belron are already with us. Rega will follow soon now that his appetite has been aroused. I will also report that the Academy and the warriors are beginning to turn."

"*Some* of them, my lord," said Rugio. "The majority of the legions are still loyal to the Most High. I would hate to do battle with them. Though if it ever comes to it I will." He patted his scabbard.

Pellecus and Lucifer looked up at Rugio, surprised at this aggressive declaration. "Thank you, Rugio," said Lucifer. "But I never said we would need *every* angel to be with us. All I need is a show of strength—something impressive that will underscore the need for my appointment should the Lord waver for any reason. If urgent support for me is widespread, it will take on the appearance of a general consensus among all the classes of angels: wisdom, warrior and worship. Then, following such a demonstration on my behalf, the Elders, at Kara's passionate and skilled pleading, will insist on my appointment and the Lord will comply out of desire to maintain peace and order in the Kingdom." He smirked. "You know how He hates division."

"Do you really believe you can shame the Most High into giving in to your plans?" asked Pellecus.

"I don't intend to contest the Lord publicly, merely persuade Him privately," said Lucifer. "You and I know that we could never defeat the Lord outright, He's much too powerful. I will never be greater than He, but I can be *as* great as He. He will see the need to share power or face a ruinous conflict. Of course it may never come to such a scenario if I am elected outright. Either way, I will be made governor."

"And what about Sangius?" asked Pellecus. "Now that he is no longer with us on the Council isn't it likely that he will...talk to someone?"

"Sangius serves us whether he is on the Council or not," said Lucifer. "Naturally I would prefer him to be in a place where we could...look after him a little more closely.

"However, since he is no longer on the Council we need not fear him. There is not an angel in Heaven who will take him seriously. He has compromised his reputation at the Temple and there will be talk among the Elders of asking for his removal from the Ministry of the Flame. Kara will see to that. All he will do is detract from his credibility with his ridiculous tales of what goes on in Lucifer's ministry."

"You are quite sure of this?" asked Pellecus.

"You let me worry about Sangius. I should have known he was too weak to commit to anything so important as what we are undertaking," Lucifer concluded.

Serus entered the room with a tray of drinks. "Ah thank you, Serus," said Lucifer. He and the others each took a small gold, jewel-encrusted glass in their hands and held them up. "Here's to golden days for us all," said Lucifer.

They drank the deep blue liquid that filled the cups.

"Serus, I want you to call the Council together as soon as possible," Lucifer ordered. "And tell Octrion that I have completed the

Creation music and wish to take him up on his offer to help me. I want him to begin preparing at once."

Serus nodded and backed out of the room. As he shut the door behind him a burst of laughter spilled out of the room. He looked around the luxurious surroundings which served as both his ministry to Lucifer and his home. He wondered what the golden days would mean for him? Surely Lucifer had something special in mind for his most devoted servant! When the time was right he was going to ask Lucifer about it. As he walked down the corridor he stopped abruptly. He had meant to tell Lucifer something else, but didn't know if he should go back in the room after he had been dismissed. He decided he could wait until later to tell Lucifer that he had seen Sangius and Michael speaking together.

＋══════════════════ ═══╬

Michael had mixed feelings as his friends began seating themselves around the table in his house. Crispin and Sangius had arrived already and knew what this was all about. Gabriel, however, presented quite a dilemma. It was not that Gabriel was thickheaded, but he was very cautious in his judgments concerning his brothers. He always thought the best of any angel, giving them the benefit of any doubt, and one had to be very diplomatic in discussing such delicate issues with him. He was already suspicious that Michael had a grudge against Lucifer, so it was essential that the information be delivered in a sensible, logical way, that it, as little of Michael as possible.

Michael, Crispin and Sangius were already seated at the table when Gabriel arrived. He couldn't believe his eyes when he saw his old teacher at the table, and rushed forward to greet him. "Master Crispin!" said Gabriel, picking up the scholar and hugging him. "It's been so long! How are things at the Academy?"

"Put me down and I'll tell you," said Crispin. Gabriel apologized and gently set his teacher back on the floor, giving him another hug in the process. Gabriel then saw Sangius, and though he was rather surprised to see him at this meeting he greeted him warmly. "Brother Sangius! Good to see you!"

"And you," said Sangius, clasping his arms. "You make a remarkable archangel!"

"What about me?" said Michael in a feigned slight. They all laughed and Michael invited everyone to be seated.

Michael's house was just off the Grand Square. He had built it so that the front door faced the Great Temple. He always enjoyed the Temple being the first thing he saw every time he left the house. His largest windows also were on that side of the house and the light from the Lord's presence often filled his home to such an extent that he could hardly see. But Michael loved it. He bathed in God's glorious light, worshiping Him with upraised hands and drinking deeply of His presence. Today's meeting, however, was vastly different from anything so joyous as worship. Everyone looked at Michael as he began speaking.

"Let me first say thank you to Crispin and Sangius for coming. You both know what will be discussed here today and will in fact be doing most of the talking." He then turned to Gabriel, who had a puzzled expression on his face. "Gabriel, this meeting is for your benefit as much as anything. Or rather it is for me to tell you some things which you might not find so believable without other witnesses. I only ask that you hold all your questions until you've heard everything we know up until now, and that you keep your mind open to the possibilities about to be unveiled. With that, I guess I'll turn this over to Crispin and Sangius."

Gabriel, perplexed as ever, turned first to one and then the other as they decided who should speak first. Crispin began by recounting the things that he and Michael had discussed in his chambers the day the Creation was announced. He described the tense situation at the Academy, and the dismissal of Pellecus because of his radical teaching. He used Berenius as an illustration of how some angels were beginning to question the truths of God; he mentioned Pellecus, and his association with Lucifer both in the Council of Worship and as a probable vehicle for Lucifer's own philosophical agenda. "My feeling," said Crispin in conclusion, "is that the angels who are showing up at the Academy with this tainted viewpoint are simply the leading edges of a much larger, much more sinister movement."

Sangius next spoke about his association with Lucifer, his work on the Council of Worship and his slow plunge into Lucifer's reckless world of criticism, suspicion and ambition. He told about meetings that were particularly offensive toward the Lord or the Kingdom, and how the Council members were passionately loyal to Lucifer. He concluded by recounting his recent dismissal from the Council and the recovery of his integrity through worshiping the Lord and loving Him as never before.

Throughout the testimonies Gabriel gave no response, showing very little emotion, except when Sangius spoke of his own hurt, at which point Gabriel felt tremendous compassion. When they were finished Gabriel sat quietly for a moment or two and then spoke up.

"I owe you an apology, Michael. Earlier I cut you off and told you to leave this Lucifer business alone. I can see now that your feelings are justified or at least have the appearance of something real." He looked at the group. "The day the Creation was announced Lucifer was trying to pry information out of me as to who would be governing the new world. Octrion was with him, jabbering away as usual. I could tell the two of them had been discussing it. I can see where you might have been suspicious."

"What do you think we should do, Gabriel?" asked Michael, relieved that Gabriel was at least considering his position in light of the new evidence.

"I believe that the last thing we should do is make too public an issue of this. Not yet anyway," Gabriel answered. "This calls for patience and deliberation."

"I agree completely," said Crispin. "We must not allow Lucifer or any of those angels friendly towards him to know that we are observing their movements with such interest."

Crispin leaned back in his chair and assumed a professorial attitude. "He'll give himself away at some point. He must if he is ever to...do whatever he intends to do. The Creation now seems to be the focus. Perhaps as it unfolds Lucifer will overreach himself and then we'll have him."

"I don't want to *have* him," said Michael. "I want him to come to his senses." He gave his old teacher a resigned look. "But you're right, Crispin. The Creation seems to be the prime consideration in all of this." He shook his head and made a baffled expression. "Except that the Creation was only recently announced and Lucifer has apparently been garnering hidden support for quite a while now."

"That's his way," said Sangius, who was considered the resident expert on Lucifer's secret world because of his recent post on the Council. "Lucifer has always envisioned an opportunity for which he needed to prepare. He told the Council once that his appointment to the worship ministry was a result of his own musical effort rather than the grace of God. How did he put it? Ah yes, he said that 'music is merely a tool like any other tool—a vehicle to something greater.' What makes Lucifer so dangerous is that he believes he has a destiny that he must fulfill. This drives him. And, naturally, in order to fulfill that destiny he must prepare.

"So he has been slowly building up support through the influence of the Council; through the teachings of Pellecus; through his own ability to charm and ingratiate himself with others, by promising future benefits for present loyalties. I believe that he views the Creation as the opportunity he has been looking for—though in what way he intends for it to be of use to him I am not sure."

"Just remember," said Gabriel, who was increasingly uncomfortable with the discussion. "This is Lucifer we're talking about. Our Chief Minister of Worship—the Anointed Cherub. In spite of everything, including my own conversations with him, I find it hard to believe that he would try anything so vain...so traitorous...so stupid. I admit that the things you have told me bear looking into. But Lucifer is our brother and until he actually does something wrong he is innocent. I really think we need more information before we move on this."

"Agreed," said Michael. "But as an archangel you must realize your responsibility to the Most High in keeping order in this Kingdom. And if there is a seditious group of angels who are planning something in connection with the Creation, then that is criminal enough. We must stand ready. You heard what Sangius said.

They actually believe that angels maintain order in Heaven through their obedience; and that if the day comes when angels disobey, the Lord will no longer be able to maintain the Kingdom! Gabriel, these are very damning statements!"

"And very damning charges," said Gabriel. "I am only saying that caution must be the byword in all of this."

"Perhaps it would help to bring an elder in on this," offered Sangius. "That way when the time does come when we need to involve the Lord, we will have gone through proper lines of authority."

The group looked at each other as if to read one another's thoughts on the idea.

"Sangius might have an excellent point," said Crispin. "It's always wise to have an authority covering you. It makes for a more credible argument as well as a more proper approach."

Michael thought for a moment, looking to Gabriel for his opinion. "Well?" he said.

"It could be the wise thing to do at this point," said Gabriel. "But we'd have to be very sensitive in our choosing. I think all of the Elders are competent and trustworthy. But if Lucifer's influence extends to the Academy as you say, then it might also extend to the Elders. The Lord forbid that he should corrupt *that* body!" Gabriel's bluish aura began manifesting even as his words sickened him. The thought of corruption to such degree and in such high circles of authority affected him greatly.

"We would need someone we could completely trust," Gabriel continued. "Someone who is acquainted enough with Lucifer to see that these concerns are a possibility, however remote. Most of all, we need someone who will hold this in the proper confidence it is due."

"I know just the elder!" said Sangius. "Lamon! He has always had difficulty with Lucifer."

"I don't want someone who will be looking to bring Lucifer down," said Gabriel.

"We need someone who will be completely objective; whose interest is the welfare of the Kingdom."

"Sharma comes to mind," said Crispin. "He is quite closed-mouthed and quite faithful. He often teaches at the Academy."

"How about Dracus?" asked Michael. "Talk about faithful! He's a terrific commander."

"He talks too much," said Sangius. Michael frowned.

"Look, we all have our favorites, I'm sure," said an amused Gabriel, who could see Michael's patience wearing thin. "I suggest we put it to a private vote. We'll write down names and whomever we can all agree upon, no matter how long it takes, will be our contact. Now, I suggest that none of the names that have been mentioned thus far should be candidates so we may be in complete accord."

Everyone agreed to Gabriel's suggestion, albeit somewhat reluctantly. Michael retrieved a scroll and a writing instrument and handed them to Gabriel.

"Now," said Gabriel, "first let's write down the character traits of the person we want involved with us. I suggest we narrow the list to seven traits." Everyone agreed and Gabriel continued, "All of the Elders are tremendous, but at this point we must select only one. What qualities do we want in the angel who will be working with us on this? Let me have your suggestions."

One by one Gabriel wrote down the desired character strengths that the group gave. As the list grew, a portrait of an angel was coming together. In Gabriel's mind the angel who would be privileged to such information must be completely above reproach, possess an impeccable reputation and most importantly, be an angel of utter integrity. He must be widely respected as well, because should this become a public issue there would be need for such credibility and authority. As he thought about these things he already knew for whom he would vote.

The group went over the list, deleting repetitions or other suggestions that were either vague or otherwise unsuitable for the task. When they were finished Gabriel spoke. "These are the characteristics that the elder must have in whom we will confide: Trustworthy, Confidential, Levelheaded, Patient, Faithful, Proven, and Objective. These are certainly qualities that we need in this angel. But to these I would like to add one other: He must demonstrate tremendous devotion to the Most High. He must love God passionately. All of the other things we want in whomever we bring in are meaningless if this angel does not love the Lord God with complete abandon—as I know all of you do. Brothers, it is for our King we are making this choice. Choose well."

Gabriel handed out the golden tablets for the angels to write down their selections. The mood of the room had changed dramatically since Gabriel spoke. They all took their time, deliberating mentally the names and faces of the Twenty-four Elders. Michael finished first and handed his tablet to Gabriel. Next Crispin finished and finally Sangius. Gabriel then added his own tablet to the stack. He looked at everyone and then began reading.

Everyone noticed a smile on Gabriel's face, at first barely perceptible, but then turning into a grin. The decision was unanimous. It seemed to everyone in the room that only one angel who sat on the Council of Elders fulfilled every character trait they were searching for—especially in unquestioned devotion to God. Gabriel read the name of Kara four times.

―――――――――

Chronicles of the Host

Creation!

The Host of Heaven watched on in joyous celebration, with Lucifer's wonderful music playing and the voices of thousands of angels singing in great harmony, as the Lord began unfolding the design of the ages. Father, Son and Spirit in perfect Oneness had devised a plan of utter brilliance yet pure simplicity; of violent action yet subtle change; of the invisible and eternal giving way to visible and material.

Thus it was that the Lord God Almighty, Creator of the Kingdom of Heaven in all its majesty, brought forth the Heavens and the earth in all their mystery.

And mystery it was. Not only was this to be a completely different world, but an altogether different sphere of existence, a dimension of material reality! No angel had conceived such a thing— even the wisest angels were astonished when the Lord made the Heavens and earth out of physical substance—something many angels considered to be so beneath His dignity. Who can know the mind of God?

CHAPTER 7

"We know that you are an angel who can be trusted."

All of Heaven turned out for this marvelous event. A rumor started that there were only certain places from which the spectacle could be seen, but the Elders assured everyone that the Creation would be visible from any point in Heaven. Just to make sure, however, some angels crowded rooftops, others were seated on the higher hills, and still others traveled to the very border of the Kingdom. Every angel in Heaven would remember this day!

Even Lucifer was dazzled by this historical occasion, though he was a bit dismayed that his music wasn't playing as central a role in the event as he had hoped. Still, it was glorious music for a glorious day! He attended the early proceedings, spoke to a few Elders, and then departed, disappointed that Kara was nowhere to be found. After making final adjustments to the program, he satisfied himself and departed, leaving Octrion in charge of the choir. Lucifer decided to watch the event from his balcony. When he arrived he met Serus, who was just coming out the front door.

"And where are you going?" asked Lucifer.

Serus winced when he heard the voice. "I was just...I mean...I wanted to see the Lord make the new world like the others."

"Like the others! I sometimes wonder, Serus, why it is that I keep you in my service," Lucifer said. "But if you want to be like the others..."

Serus thanked Lucifer and rushed out the door and down the street, never looking back. Lucifer went inside and walked up the grand staircase, humming some of his music, which he could hear from outside. *That should please the Elders,* Lucifer thought to himself. He walked over to the glass-paned doors that opened onto his balcony. As he opened them his music became much louder. *Octrion is taking that a little too fast,* he thought.

He walked over to the side of the balcony and looked down. Angels were rushing here and there, discussing the best vantage for watching the event. All of them were making their way toward the northern edge of the Kingdom. Looking over the roofs of Heaven, Lucifer saw angels all around the City, some seated, others standing, all waiting for the Lord to begin.

"Lucifer! Down here!"

Lucifer looked down into the crowded street.

"Here! By the gate!"

Next to the large gate that stood in front of Lucifer's house was a figure waving at him. It was Kara. Lucifer motioned for him to join him on the balcony. Kara glided up over the lawn and landed next to Lucifer, who looked disturbed.

"What is wrong, my friend?" asked Kara, whose embrace was not reciprocated.

"What are you doing here? You should be with the other Elders bearing our cause to them. Especially today!" Lucifer paced around the balcony, quite annoyed.

"I saw Serus and he told me you were here," Kara said sheepishly. "I wanted to give you the good news personally!"

Lucifer's demeanor changed. "Really?"

"The Council of Elders have all but decided that they shall make a formal request to the Most High that you be made the steward of the new world!" Kara had tears in his eyes. "It's surely yours!"

"It certainly sounds encouraging," said Lucifer, motioning that they should be seated at a beautiful table nearby. "But it's not mine, my friend. It's ours. Yours, and mine and others who have been loyal during these trying times." Lucifer thought a moment and added, "And the Lord's, of course. Though I doubt He shall take any real interest in it after He has turned it over to me." He smiled at Kara and poured him a drink from a purplish crystal and gold decanter on the table.

"So when do they make the request?" asked Lucifer.

"Well, it isn't official," said Kara, taking the drink. "But it will be soon. After the Creation is near completion. To do so beforehand would be imprudent. It will have to be taken up officially, of course. But with my guidance I think we should have no problems."

A thunderous sound rocked Heaven. The balcony trembled with the noise and a great cheer could be heard in the distance. Kara quickly finished his drink and prepared to leave. "Will you join me with the Elders?" he asked Lucifer. "It might serve you well to be seen with us."

"No, not yet. Perhaps later."

"Well then, blessings upon you, governor." Kara's wings unfurled and carried him upwards. "This is certainly a time of history making! The creation of a new kingdom...or should I say two new kingdoms? Farewell!" He disappeared into the blue Heavenly sky, filled with angels awaiting the spectacle.

"Yes, my friend, this is an unique occasion," Lucifer said to himself. He set his glass down and went inside the house, closing the balcony doors behind him. Walking over to his writing desk, he unlocked a cabinet drawer and took out a gold-bound book that was entitled *Prophecies of the Morning Star*. The book had a golden lock built onto it. He took a crystal key from the desk and turned the lock. Opening the book, he began to write.

The *Prophecies* was the book of Lucifer's own recorded wisdom, personal prophecies and significant revelations he believed held special meaning for him in the future. He had been encouraged by Pellecus to record all these important thoughts for the archives as well as to lay a foundation of future spiritual authority—just as the Lord had recorded His own wisdom and used His writings for purposes of authority in Heaven.

A second thunderous noise, this time of trumpets, shook the room as he set the book down. This was followed by the voice of the Lord:

**"Glory to the Lamb of God who was slain
before the foundation of the world!"**

Lucifer recalled these words, which had greeted all of the angels when they were first created, and wondered what they meant. "The Lamb of God?" he muttered to himself. "Again?" He stepped back out onto the balcony in time to see a dazzling light going forth from the north and penetrating deeply into the Heavenly sky. He watched as the single shaft shot forth, disappearing into the blackness of the deep. *I didn't expect it would begin so soon,* he thought.

He watched as a magnificent chandelier of crystal and light swayed gently back and forth, still moving from the tremors caused by the tumult. *Such immense power,* he thought to himself, feeling a surge of respect for the awesome nature of the Almighty. Still he wondered if such power is truly inherent or may be somehow acquired.

Another general cheer went up from outside. Lucifer decided that he had better join the Elders. He quickly put on one of his official cloaks and looked at himself in the long mirror. Behind him in the reflection lay the book he had written in, still open. He smiled as he read what he had just written:

*Two kingdoms are born today;
two thrones shall rise;
one to greater glory,
the other to despise;
The Old Throne births the New;
The Greater births the Least.
To One a day of famine,
To one a glorious feast
So it is, O Morning Star*

This prophecy foretold;
The Greater now gives way to thee,
Thy wonders to behold.

The Chronicles of the Host

Creation!

The Lord Almighty had designed a vast, inky canvas called the universe onto which he was going to paint the Heavens and the earth. The excited angels sat on the very edges of this new physical realm, engaging for the first time a dimension about which they previously had only been able to speculate. They touched this multidimensional world timidly, ran their hands through it, and some of the bolder angels actually penetrated it, moving in and out of it with ease.

All eyes, however, were cast to the north from which came the thunderous voice of the Lord. Suddenly, the shroud of darkness was pulled back by the Spirit, whose presence enveloped a black, watery lump, the shape of which was imperfect and changing. Above and around the formless mass, the Spirit of God seemed restless and brooding, waiting upon the word to be spoken by the Father, in accord with the Son. He need only give the word…

Then God said:
"Light!"

As quickly as the Lord spoke the word all of Heaven shook to its very core. The angels were buffeted violently by the mighty resonance of the spoken word. Light streamed forth from the very presence of the Most High, bursting into the darkness and scattering it. (This was the light that Lucifer had witnessed from his house.) Angels who had situated themselves within the newly formed physical universe were blinded by the brilliance and tossed about like so many leaves in the wind.

The newly formed light was a type and form of illuminance that they had never before witnessed. Some of the angels actually touched the light streaming forth from Heaven and found it warm, and consisting of tiny particles which they could sense moving through them, completely unlike the pure, immaterial glory that radiated from the Lord's Person.

They observed as the light coursed through the universe, creating what many angels described as a tunnel, until its beam collided with the earth, allowing the angels for the first time to fully see the new world in its unformed state. The Spirit remained vigilant, hovering over the ball of water which was now lit up for all of Heaven to see. The angels shouted for joy that day as the Lord decreed that henceforth the darkness in the universe shall be known as "night" and the light in the universe shall be called "day." And suddenly the first creative act was over...

And there was evening and morning,
the first day.

Most of the angels stood around in complete awe of the event, talking excitedly about what they had seen. Scribes sought to record every detail, interviewing witnesses and compiling notes that would later be entered into the Chronicles of the Kingdom. Scholarly angels such as Crispin explored the new dimension and found that they could move in and out of this physical universe with great ease, traveling from the Kingdom to the outer edges of the immense, dark expanse as quickly as they thought about doing so.

Other angels approached the earth itself, the obvious future focus of God's intentions, which was bathed in the light of Heaven. They wondered what the Lord would achieve with this misshapen piece of physical matter. What were the angels to do in such a world? The Host anxiously debated questions that would be answered in the Lord's timing as the Creation progressed.

―――――――――――――

One angel in particular wondered what all this meant for his own future. Serus slowly made his way back toward Lucifer's house. He watched as the other angels walked by in groups, laughing and talking, genuinely enjoying each other's fellowship. Serus had long ago resigned himself that to serve with Lucifer meant sacrificing some aspects of one's communal life. After all, it was Lucifer who took him in after his poor showing at the Academy and gave him a position of real prestige. So what if he didn't do well? Let others like Michael and Gabriel be adored. Serus shined in service to Lucifer—the greatest angel in Heaven.

This was the reasoning that Serus had been entertaining lately. And still sometimes he missed the company of others, particularly in joyous seasons such as this one. He now wondered what this new season would bring to him. He looked up at the imposing house in the distance—Lucifer's palace—and could see the magnificent gardens in front and his master standing on the balcony. No doubt he would be in a foul mood about something. This was the angel in whom Serus had placed his trust and his future. He had long given up the idea of serving in the House of the Lord, as the greatest positions had been assumed.

He decided that the greater angels would not welcome him as he wasn't gifted musically, wasn't wise enough to be a scribe, and didn't have the ability of a warrior. And so he served in the shadow of one greater, hoping some day to cast a shadow of his own.

―――――――――――――

Kara looked uncomfortable as he sat across from Michael and the others in the room. He had never been invited to Michael's home before, and now, in the presence of Gabriel, Crispin and Sangius, he could not help but be suspicious as to their intentions. As an elder who sat upon the Council it was not unusual to have an audience with other angels, but usually the circumstances were much more official, much more public. This invitation came quietly and begged discretion until the meeting was over.

"Quite a remarkable demonstration of our Lord's plans for Creation," said Crispin to nobody in particular, trying to break the awkward tension that hung in the room. Everyone agreed generally.

"Lucifer's music was outstanding," added Gabriel. "As always." Kara was dispassionate at the mention of Lucifer, only nodding in agreement with the statement.

"Yes," chimed in Sangius. "It was a brilliant stroke of the Council to recommend that the Creation be accompanied by his music. That was your idea, wasn't it, Kara?"

"Oh, I think several of us came to the conclusion than an angelic influence was in order," said Kara.

"After all, it is we who will serve the Lord in the new world, is it not?" asked Crispin.

"I have no idea what the Lord's ultimate intentions are for the new world," answered Kara. "Far wiser angels have been speculating that one ever since I can remember. But tell me, Michael, it was not to discuss the Lord's plans, which none of us know anything about, that you brought me here, was it?"

Michael looked around the group and started to speak, looking rather uncomfortable.

"Well, not exactly," he said.

Kara studied the faces of the angels in the room. All of them were respected and completely loyal, and represented the various angelic ministries in the Kingdom. Had they heard about his meetings with Lucifer?

"Kara," Gabriel began gently. "We know that you are an angel who can be trusted. We asked you here because of all the angels on the Council, you were the one whom we believe we can entrust with some very important and volatile information. This is regarding matters which call for utmost discretion and confidence, but which we felt proper to bring to a Council Elder before going further with it."

"I'm delighted and honored that you would select me for such a role," Kara answered, relieved that they only had some Kingdom matters to discuss. This was turning out to be much more ordinary than he thought. "If there is anything I can do to resolve an urgent matter, I am certainly at your service. Now what exactly can I do for you?"

Little by little the group began to divulge the story of their collective discoveries; of whispered conversations and petty jealousies; of the impure doctrines finding their way into the Academy; of the smugness of the Council of Worship and the nature of the recent meetings; of Lucifer's change in attitude toward his former friends; of whisperings of references to the Lord's inability to maintain the Kingdom; and of the possibility that hidden within this morass was a systematic plan of some sort which threatened the very peace of the Kingdom—all pointing to Lucifer as its source and strength.

Kara sat back in his chair in a long silence. He looked gravely at each angel who sat around him. He sat quietly for a few moments and then spoke. "It was very wise of you to bring this to my attention. There certainly seems to be something worthwhile here to investigate further. Tell me, have you mentioned any of this to any other angel?"

"Not one," said Michael. "We wanted to speak with you before we brought anyone else in on this."

"Excellent! Well did the Most High proclaim you archangel, Michael," said Kara. "You are certainly correct in not allowing this to go any further than this room. More damage can be done with information that is recklessly tossed about than when it is handled discreetly. And this certainly calls for discretion."

"So what do you intend to do?" asked Crispin pointedly. Everyone looked at Kara.

"To act," he responded. "But not in an obvious and public manner. You all have done your duty. It is now up to me to take this further. There are certain parties to whom I will give this information. In fact I'm sure one party will be extremely interested. And hopefully we can deal with all of this privately and perhaps even redeem the situation. Naturally, I will pose an investigation of my own as well."

"But what are we to do in the meantime?" asked Michael who wanted to begin some sort of proceedings right away.

"Nothing. I know it is much to ask of you, my friends. But as you know, there is an authority structure within the Kingdom in which we must operate. You have done your duty in bringing me this information. Now it is up to me to carry it on to the next step. I will of course keep you informed of my findings, as I am sure you will update me as you gather any other information. But at this point what I am asking you to do is to remain silent about this. These reports must not go beyond this group. The time may come when I will call upon you to act. But until then, you must refrain from reacting."

The group sat silently for a moment or so after Kara left. Finally Michael spoke up: "What does he mean, we must do nothing? There is too much at stake to do nothing!"

"That is precisely the reason that Kara is asking for discretion," said Crispin. "Excuse me for saying so, Michael, but your strong-headedness is liable to make this whole affair much more confusing and hurtful than it might have to be."

"Crispin's right, old friend," added Gabriel. "I'm afraid I must agree with Kara at least for now. We have done what we agreed to do. Now we must let it rest with him."

"I cannot believe any of this," fumed Michael. "We are just supposed to walk away from this as if nothing is happening?"

"Just until Kara calls upon us for assistance," said Crispin. "He probably will want us to testify someday. But like Kara we can continue discreetly to investigate the matter. I believe he would expect that much from us."

It was not Michael's nature to do nothing. He longed for a fight—a showdown that would end the matter once and for all. But he knew that he must honor the decision of the group. He looked at them and dramatically said, "For now I'll go along with this. But the day will come when we will have to fight Lucifer. And when that happens..."

"You'll be leading the way," interrupted Gabriel, "with all of Heaven behind you!"

Everyone began laughing at the image of Michael bearing the Lord's standard with thousands of angels behind charging a bemused Lucifer and a terrified Serus, holding Lucifer's cup in one hand and a scroll of music in the other. Even Michael had to laugh.

"Here's to Michael," said Gabriel in mock toast, "vanquisher of Lucifer!"

They all raised their arms in feigned toast to their future general.

The Chronicles of the Host
Days Two and Three

With the creation of light, the unfolding of the plan for which every angel had held possibilities came together. Long had there been speculation and discussion among the more learned angels that the Lord might create another realm in which He would vest His love.

Thus with earth had God laid out a place where He could truly demonstrate to all of creation His glory and righteousness. The angels watched in complete awe as their Lord commanded and the misshapen, chaotic mass slowly became an intricately designed world, more and more complex with each creative episode.

Then God said,
"Let there be an expanse in the midst of the waters,
And let it separate the waters from the waters..."
And God made the expanse and separated
The waters below the expanse from the waters above the expanse;
And God called the expanse Heaven
*And there was evening and morning, **a second day.***

And so it was that the Lord commanded the waters of this murky planet on the second day to separate themselves into two bodies, being forced apart by a vast firmament that God called Heaven. Many angels thought this curious as the Kingdom in which they lived was also called Heaven, but it was later explained to them by the sages that this was a Heaven unique to the earth, a physical Heaven and part of the material nature of all of the new creation. (In the interest of clarification I shall refer to the earthly Heaven thus, and the Kingdom of Heaven thus.)

Then God said,
"Let the waters below the Heavens gather into one place,
And let the dry land appear...."

The waters on the surface of the planet quickly eased in their violent movement while the waters above, separated by the firmament, continued in a churning and volatile state. At this time the attention of the Almighty was focused supremely upon the earth, as the waters upon the surface began to abate, exposing large masses of dry land (hence the name earth) while the water which surrounded the dry land, and which again became volatile and ever-moving, was now called seas.

Then God said,
"Let the earth sprout forth vegetation,
Plants yielding seed,
And fruit trees bearing fruit after their kind,
With seed in them on the earth,"
And it was so...
*And there was evening and morning, **the third day**.*

And then a truly spectacular event began to take place upon the planet...one which almost every angel in Heaven witnessed, as on the third day the earth began to produce from itself grass and herbs and all manner of plants, turning the once muddy brown land into a beautiful garden, second only to Heaven itself in variety of flora and fruit.

Surely this would be a marvelous home for the future residents, whoever they might be. Many an angel speculated on whom the Lord would choose to live on earth, and to whom would go the honor of being the governor of the new world, not knowing of course that God in His wisdom had already chosen...

By the time the earth had sprouted the many plants that the Lord God had made, most of the angels had already visited the new world. They had seen God's wonderful design take shape and shouted with joy as each step of the process came together in perfect harmony. They watched as the Son and Spirit worked together with the Father in a united effort of love, creating a world which would one day be enjoyed by...

Chapter 8

"I can tell that the news is overwhelming."

"Angels, of course," said Pellecus, in a rather annoyed tone. "Whom else would the Lord create such a realm for? Do you see any other creatures capable of appreciating such a world?"

The group Pellecus was lecturing nodded in agreement, whether or not they believed Pellecus knew what he was talking about. The angel who had asked the question felt a little foolish and determined not to ask any more.

"Look at these delicate flowers," said Pellecus, pointing to a mass of flowery shrubs. "God has so devised them that they are almost perfect, and yet they are made of simple material substance. Incredible that the Most High should make such a world! It will be interesting to see what creatures the Lord adorns the planet with."

Pellecus led the little group of angels through a meadow and sat them down by a gently lolling stream. He had begun to take such instructional tours with angels deemed by Lucifer as likely future cohabitants of the earth after the most recent Council meeting. Other angels were making trips to the new world as well, all of them amazed at the Lord's creative imagination.

Pellecus looked up and saw Lucifer approaching through the field. "All right. That's enough for now," he said, dismissing the angels. Many of the angels vanished toward Heaven while some disappeared into the woods to continue their exploration of the earth. Pellecus watched them go and then addressed Lucifer.

"I had forgotten how much I miss teaching," he said.

"One always enjoys teaching when allowed to do so without interference," said Lucifer, who sat down on a large rock next to Pellecus. "I promise you, Pellecus, that one day you will head up the greatest academy ever and without any constraints as to what you may teach. Provided, of course, that you teach those things on which we are in agreement."

Pellecus nodded silently as he dreamed of the day when he would preside over such an academy.

"I must insist however," continued Lucifer, "that until we have that luxury presented to us, you be careful in what you are teaching the angels regarding their authority over this planet. Until the Lord decrees my position as steward, we can only speculate publicly—like every other presumptuous angel in Heaven is doing."

"Of course," said Pellecus.

"And you must particularly refrain from using my name in connection with any of this. As far as all of Heaven is concerned I am only interested in upholding the Lord's will in the matter of the future governor. Do you understand?"

"Yes, my lord."

"Good. Now some news. Kara has come to me with quite an interesting development. It seems that Michael and Gabriel and some others have become suspicious of our activities."

"What!?" shouted Pellecus. "How could that be?"

"Fortunately," continued Lucifer, "Kara told them that he would assume responsibility for the situation and set them on the benign task of waiting for his signal...which of course will never come. A brilliant move on his part. I knew that his public character and reputation for integrity would serve us one day."

"What do we do?" asked Pellecus, looking around, a bit nervous at this latest turn of events.

"For now we continue on as before...but with extreme caution," advised Lucifer. "Kara will continue to brief them with useless information which will give us the time to build our support. I'm much more concerned with the Elders' recommendation to the Most High that I be made lord of this planet than by the carryings on of Michael and his curious angels. By the time they get anywhere near the real story I will have been vested in this planet as its legal ruler and the issue will be moot. You know how sentimental the Most High is about such things; forgive and so forth."

"You make it sound so easy...so sure," Pellecus answered. "But let me remind you that Michael is no fool. A bit of an alarmist to be sure, but not a fool. Kara must be terribly cautious."

"So I have reminded Kara," said Lucifer. "Remember, he has a stake in my being made governor as much as you or anyone else." He nodded at a group of angels who were strolling by. After they passed on he continued. "Some of these angels are so completely loyal to the Lord that they will not see an opportunity with me on this planet. I cannot imagine why they should continue to serve with heads bowed in Heaven when they could live with heads held high on earth. And in a material world! Look at the tremendous possibilities that exist here. We can actually manipulate creation itself!"

As he said this a large rock nearby began to quiver and then slowly rise above the ground. It stayed aloft, floating about three feet off the ground. "If nothing else earth will at least be a diversion from the monotony of Heaven. Think of the power we will hold over whatever creatures the Lord uses to populate this planet! I shall be glad to lay down my office of worship to govern a world over which we have such control."

"And if you're not named governor?" Pellecus asked gingerly.

The rock crashed to the earth, breaking into two similarly sized pieces. Lucifer picked up one of the pieces and looked at it. "In that case we'll have to take other measures in hand," he said, tossing the rock into the stream.

Serus paced Lucifer's balcony. Inside he could hear the low murmuring of a meeting. This was not just any meeting, Serus had been assured. This was, in Lucifer's words, a "pivotal assembly of the key players" who would be involved in whatever it was that Lucifer was planning. Serus peeked in the window and could see just a corner of the large table around which the representatives of the angelic factions aligned with Lucifer were seated. From time to time Lucifer's voice was heard above all—sometimes followed by laughter, usually followed by silence.

As he gazed at the newly created lights that God had made to sprinkle the heavens—stars they were called—Serus wondered what his position truly was. Would he always be Lucifer's servant? The one to whom Lucifer turned for wine rather than wisdom? Was he destined to ride with Lucifer on this great crusade that he was planning, or would he simply limp behind picking up the debris left in its wake? He looked at the stars and saw that some shone more brightly than others—most, however, looked similar to the next. Would he be like one of these stars—a small speck of light in a large universe—nothing more, nothing less? he wondered.

"Serus!" came a cry from the house.

Serus entered the room in which the conference was being held. Several of the angels looked at him as he entered. Most ignored him and continued in private discourses with the angels to their left or right. Serus made his way to Lucifer, who was seated at the head of the table. He saw that Lucifer had opened his "Prophecies of the Morning Star" and that it was on the table. Lucifer motioned to him.

"Refresh yourselves, my friends," said Lucifer to the assembly. "We shall break momentarily and gather our thoughts." He took Serus aside and handed him a sealed scroll. "Take this message to Michael. See that it finds itself in no other hands. Then find Kara at the Hall of Elders. Tell him that the invitation has been delivered. Do you understand?"

Serus sighed. "Yes, lord. Is there nothing else?"

"You're very ambitious today, Serus. Yes, that will be all for now."

Serus remained where he stood. Lucifer turned to see that the little angel had not moved. "Yes, Serus, is there something else?" he asked in an annoyed tone.

"Well, sir," said Serus nervously, "there is something..."

"Well? Get on with it! I am conducting a very important meeting here!"

"May I speak to you alone, lord?" Serus asked.

"What! Now? No, you may not. You may, however, see me after you have obeyed my instructions. In fact I insist on seeing you alone. Perhaps you need to be reminded of exactly where you stand in the scheme of things. Now go!"

Lucifer's final words were so loud that the room got quiet for a moment as every eye turned toward the little angel speaking to his master. "Sorry, friends, just a little misunderstanding on the part of my loyal servant. Go on now, dear Serus. I'll speak to you when you return."

Serus bowed and left. As he walked downstairs he could hear Lucifer explaining the need for more training for "poor Serus" followed by general laughter. Serus felt good about his confrontation with Lucifer. At last he was going to talk with him face-to-face—even though Lucifer's words still rang loudly in his ears—*Perhaps you need to be reminded of exactly where you stand in the scheme of things.*

Do all angels wonder about their role in the Kingdom? Serus thought about this as he walked outside. Why are some angels clearly more preferred, or talented, or...chosen by the Most High than others? He thought of Michael and Gabriel and others who excelled in their ministry and place in the Kingdom. Happy in their service to God. He then thought of Lucifer and Pellecus and the others who seemed bent on some sort of contest with the Lord in order to attain their own places and positions by contrivance.

Does one really make one's own way by forcing the issue? He looked at the starry Heavens and wondered how things might have been had he remained a strong subject of God. Lucifer seemingly promised the only real possibility of advancement in Heaven. Where would Lucifer take him? "What shall become of you, Lucifer?" Serus whispered aloud. As he spoke a light streaked across the Heavens in a brilliant line. He watched as the head broke up into little glimmering pieces which all disappeared. Then nothing. He whispered aloud once more, "Lucifer, what shall become of you?"

———————————

"A message from Lucifer?" asked an incredulous Michael.

"Yes," answered Serus. "With his compliments to the archangel, of course."

"Of course," said Michael, taking the scroll. "Is there anything else?"

"No," said Serus. "Those were my only instructions."

Michael watched as Serus left. He thought about Sangius' words that Serus was probably the most informed angel in Heaven regarding Lucifer's true intentions for the Kingdom. If only he could speak to Serus on another level. Surely there must be something of God's design lingering inside of him despite the apparent conversion to Lucifer's attitude of late. He unrolled the scroll and read the script written in Lucifer's own peculiar style:

Michael,

I greet you in the wonderful name of the Most High, Beloved Creator of All Things, King of Heaven and Lord Over All:

Such wonderful times in which we live that we should be allowed to watch our Lord design and set forth an entire universe! I was utterly thrilled as He created the greater and lesser lights to rule the earth by day and night. And now springs forth an abundance of herbs and flowering plants that are turning the entire planet into a marvelous garden rivaling my own. Soon we shall see what creatures He deems worthy to inhabit this wonderful place. There is no end to His ability or His ability to astound, is there? That is why I write with so heavy a heart in such joyful and wondrous times.

Word has come to me that perhaps you and some others harbor certain feelings of resentment towards me. As we have always been brothers I desire to express to you my undying love and my sincere wish to win back your confidence. True, I have been vacant of late, but not because of anything untoward or brooding.

My position as leader of the worship of the Most High has held me captive recently. I beg you to visit me after this next creative phase is concluded. I understand that the fifth day is upon us and I must attend that glorious spectacle. Afterwards we shall meet, you and I, as brothers and servants of God, and will dispel any and all rumors that have bewitched your heart.

Your brother angel, L.

Michael read through the message several times, trying to ascertain the true intent of its sender. Was it possible that everyone was misunderstanding Lucifer? Perhaps he should at least give some room for doubt. Everything Michael had uncovered indicated that a small group of angels under Lucifer's leadership were planning...something. But what? There was no real hard evidence that indicated anything truly seditious or rebellious pointing back to Lucifer—bits of this and strands of that. Crispin was certainly convinced that there was something perverse happening among the Host. But does poor judgment or moody dispositions indicate treasonous intent? Could it be that Lucifer simply needed a friendly voice of encouragement rather than the suspicions of an archangel?

Michael's attitude all along had always been that if there was a chance for reconciliation between the angels then such an event must occur. A show of unity among the Host would benefit the Kingdom immensely, particularly with the plans for the new Creation unfolding. Such a show of love would also be pleasing to the Most High, would it not? Michael decided to meet with the others and show them the overture he had received from Lucifer. Or perhaps he should meet privately with Kara first?

"Michael! What a splendid surprise," Kara said, greeting Michael warmly. Michael had not spoken with Kara since he met with the others and advised a prudent course of action. Kara saw the scroll in Michael's hands. "I gather this meeting is coincidental to our discussion about Lucifer."

"Yes it is, Kara," Michael replied, handing the scroll over. "I received this from Lucifer and thought you should be advised."

"Really?" Kara answered, unrolling the scroll and beginning to read. He looked up from time to time at Michael, gratified that the archangel had brought the letter to him. It meant that he had the complete trust of Michael and the others. As he finished the letter he looked at Michael and asked, "What do you intend to do?"

"I don't know, Kara," Michael said. "I want to reconcile if at all possible but I'm not sure whether to trust him at this point. I must have an Elder's position on this."

"Yes, that is an issue," Kara agreed. "And we certainly desire to reconcile all parties in this affair if at all possible. The Lord's expectation of the Host is that we be able to settle such matters without His involvement. After all, Michael, if angels cannot settle affairs in Heaven, how can we possibly hope to govern the earth effectively?"

"How can 'we' hope?" asked Michael. "So the Elders *do* believe that an angel will be named to govern the new world?"

Kara acted uncomfortable, as if he had blundered into some sensitive territory that he should have left alone. Michael sensed the tension and indicated that Kara need not go on. Kara held up his hand and said, "Well Michael, I officially am not at liberty to say right now but as the present crisis is extremely volatile, I shall divulge some Kingdom information with you, strictly confidential of course. As an archangel you will soon be privy to this anyway."

Kara motioned for Michael to sit with him on a golden couch. He hesitated for a moment or two as if collecting his thoughts, and

then began his story. "Michael, as you know, the Most High created the Twenty-four Elders to worship Him at His Throne and to
dispense His authority among the Host. It is a tremendous honor
and one that none of us takes lightly. We are merely His servants
and recognize our role as completely submitted to His holy will. It
has never been the role of an Elder or any angel to approach the
Lord with anything other than the expected prayers offered in His
most holy name.

"Now Michael, before the announcement of the Creation was
made, the Most High in an act of marvelous grace informed the
Elders through the Zoa that the Creation was imminent." Kara
reflected a bit on the event, drinking it all in once again. "The Zoa
are curious creatures, Michael, unlike any other in the Kingdom,
and they have the closest proximity to His Person of any being in
Heaven." Michael had often wondered about these strange creatures who were tied so closely to the Throne of God and whose
appearance was said to be both beautiful and bizarre. "The Zoa
also informed the Council of Elders that there would be a 'steward'
named to exercise authority on behalf of the Most High, and that
the Lord would proclaim such person in due course. Naturally we
were thrilled! Think of an angel governing the greatest creation
since Heaven in the name of the Most High God!"

Michael could read utter delight in Kara's eyes, as if he was
lost in the thought of it all. "So how did Lucifer come by this information?" asked Michael. "If this was all as secretive as you say,
Lucifer should not have known until Gabriel himself announced it.
That's when all the rest of us heard."

Kara looked surprised at Michael. "What are you suggesting?
That an Elder would discuss sacred Kingdom business with other
angels? That's absurd! Lucifer found out precisely when you did—
at Gabriel's announcement."

"I'm not suggesting any Elders spoke out of turn, Kara," said
Michael. "I'm merely pointing out that Lucifer's behavior had
begun changing even before the announcement. That's all."

"Quite, quite," said Kara. "I see. Yes, well Lucifer was operat-
ing under some difficult situations, Michael. He was involved in

matters for the Most High—urgent matters of which even many of the Elders are unaware. You see, Lucifer understood that the Lord had selected him for a great promotion. We all knew it. But none of us knew what the promotion entailed. So when first you, then Gabriel were named archangels, Lucifer was a bit discouraged."

Kara was relieved that Michael believed the story, which was not entirely untrue. Lucifer *had* been selected for a great promotion—of sorts. The Most High apparently intended on allowing Lucifer to teach the new creatures on earth how to worship Him so that they might begin their lives in adoring fellowship. Kara had only just happened on this information and found it quite amusing that the very creatures that were to have been taught by Lucifer how to worship the Most High would now be learning how to worship Lucifer. He would enjoy telling this amusing detail to Lucifer.

"Discouraged to the extreme, I should say," said Michael. "I really think that he exceeded discouragement, don't you?"

"Of course," agreed Kara. "Lucifer is far from perfect, though the Lord created him with a divine beauty that reflects a sort of per-fection. I'll admit he has strayed a bit—acted out of sorts—but what angel has not?"

Michael was surprised by Kara's attitude. Recognizing that Lucifer had "strayed" was one thing, but making excuses for him was inappropriate for an Elder. "Of course angels are far from per-fect," Michael retorted. "But an angel with such responsibility as Lucifer must behave in a decorum befitting his rank. Lucifer is high-ly exalted—the Anointed Cherub—and must behave responsibly!"

"Agreed, Michael. That is why the Council spoke with him. You didn't know that, hmm? You see Michael, I have not been idle since I met with you and Crispin and the others. The Chief Elder and I and a few select others ministered to Lucifer and allowed him to purge himself of these attitudes. So now the matter is in its final stages."

"Except for the fact that nothing has changed," Michael answered. "Lucifer's attitude hasn't improved. If anything it has gotten worse. And the horrible situation at the Academy must be addressed as well."

"I tell you, Michael, that both Lucifer and the Academy are well on their way to recovery. Things sometimes do change in Heaven." He smiled.

"Well I certainly see no change in Lucifer's attitude," Michael responded.

"Yes, as this letter you handed me reveals," Kara said with a touch of sarcasm. He held up the letter. "Is this not the writing of a contrite spirit, Michael?" He looked deeply into Michael's eyes. "Perhaps you have been pursuing Lucifer for so long you have forgotten that he might in fact have a change of heart. You must give him the benefit of any doubt. Just as some of the Council has in its move to recommend him to the Lord."

"Recommend Lucifer?" asked a weary Michael. "For what?"

"That should be obvious, Michael. We are recommending Lucifer to the Lord as steward of the earth to rule in the Lord's name and authority. Or at least we will be shortly as soon as the matter has been deliberated. Decorum, you know."

Kara enjoyed the effects of his words upon the archangel of whom he was becoming less and less fond. Michael was astonished! All this time he had been investigating an alleged plan by Lucifer to somehow work his way into an authority which, should the Elders have their way, would now be handed over to him. It didn't make sense. Even if Lucifer *was* told that he might be appointed to some great promotion, the fact that he was working with such venomous fervency to realize such a possibility was at best unwise—at worst, unholy. Either Michael was the worst judge of character in all of Heaven or the Elders were completely taken in!

"I can tell that the news is overwhelming," said Kara. He placed his hands on Michael's shoulders and faced him with great compassion. "Michael, you asked me to help you as an Elder. I did that. I spoke with Lucifer and brought him into the Council for discipline. I believe he was forthright with us. He indicated that he had been misjudged in some matters and judged rightly in others. But he assured us that he was in no way involved in any plan to have himself honored. Lucifer promotes only the Lord and not himself. You can be sure of that, Michael."

Michael looked at Kara, deeply troubled. Suddenly the issue of Lucifer and the Academy and the turmoil in the Host seemed insignificant compared with this arrogance being displayed by the Elders. He was almost trembling with revulsion at the thought of mere angels approaching the Most High with this or any other recommendation as to how something should proceed. Creatures appearing before the Creator without invitation in order to promote one of their own! Abominable!

"Kara. The Council cannot seriously consider such a move," Michael finally said. "The Elders have no more right to present a petition to the Lord than I do! On whose authority would they make this...this suggestion?"

"Why it would be on our own authority, Michael," answered Kara, who knew that he must step delicately in this matter. "You see, we believe the time is coming when angels will have a greater...involvement in the Kingdom. The Creation bears this out. A steward to be named bears this out. We are merely expediting the fact."

"On your *own* authority?" Michael asked. "You have no authority except that given to you by the Lord! This makes no sense to me at all, Kara. Is the Chief Elder in agreement with this?"

"Quite," answered Kara smugly. "Wholeheartedly, I believe. As are most of the others." He looked slyly at Michael and added, "At some point, Michael, you must decide too whether or not you support the authority and wisdom of the Most High as we do. I assume you are with Him?"

Michael reared back. "What are you talking about?" he asked. "I am most loyal to the Lord. I am the Chief Commander of the Host and completely dedicated to the wisdom and authority of God! This you know, Kara." Michael's sword began to shimmer as a bluish aura began emanating from it. Kara looked at the sword and back again at Michael.

"Well then," said Kara quietly, composed once more and feeling the advantage of Michael's anger, "you must know that the Lord in His wisdom provided for the Council of Elders and vested them with His authority to act in the best interests of the Kingdom.

If you disregard the wisdom and actions of this body, you demean the wisdom and authority of our Most Holy God by implying that He has selected angels who are unwise—a most unwise thing for so wise a God to do. Wouldn't you agree?"

"I suppose," said Michael, recalling his conversation with Crispin at the Academy. "But even the wisest angel can choose wrongly, even if his intentions are pure. I suspect they can also choose wrongly with the most impure of intentions."

"I would only say the Lord have mercy on *that* angel," said Kara, haughtily. "But I suspect, Michael, that were something foul in Heaven, the Lord would have dealt with it by now. Yet I see Lucifer still in his office. I see the Elders in order. In fact, I see no angel in any danger of the Lord's judgment!" He laughed.

"Nor do I, Kara," answered Michael. "But then you and I are merely angels."

CHAPTER 9

"One day it will be the Son casting the shadow, not us!"

As Michael made his way to the Academy he thought of his disappointing conversation with Kara. How could Kara be so enamoured with Lucifer? Or *was* he? Maybe Kara was right. Perhaps Lucifer had been the quarry for so long that perspective had been skewed. Still, as he reflected on the meeting he began to see a disturbing logic that Lucifer and his proponents all seemed to rally around: that the Lord's apparent inaction was a validation of their progress. Kara alluded to this notion; Berenius was stirring it up at the Academy; Sangius admitted that the Council of Worship found comfort in it. Several times Michael had had the question posed to him: *Why hasn't the Most High acted if there is something amiss—even wickedness occurring in Heaven? Why would He tolerate such behavior?*

Crispin's answer to the question was couched in rather vague terms that offered nothing but the fact that the Lord is sovereign and will act when He deems it appropriate. But by not intervening, could God be encouraging such behavior within the Host? Was He ignorant of the affairs of Heaven as Lucifer thought; or was He merely a longsuffering God who held out for final reconciliation as Crispin held?

Michael entered Crispin's study deep in the heart of the school. Gabriel was already there, as was Sangius. Crispin looked up and greeted Michael warmly. "Well Michael, welcome back! How did the meeting with Kara go?"

Michael recounted the conversation with Kara, telling them everything. When he had finished there was a moment of silence. Finally Gabriel spoke up. "Are you quite certain that the Elders have spoken with Lucifer?"

"I am only certain of what Kara told me," said Michael. "He said that Lucifer was disciplined and they were convinced that he was repentant."

"It is possible, I suppose," said Sangius, "that he is changed."

"Of course it is possible," said Crispin, who was seated at his book-filled desk. "But we are dealing with an extremely cunning individual here. You were with him, Sangius. You should know better than any of us."

"Yes, I know," said Sangius. "But it *is* possible for one to change. That's all I am saying. I had lost my passion once. Remember, Michael? Shortly after I left Lucifer's service we talked."

"Of course. In the Grand Square," answered Michael.

"Now the Lord has graciously restored that passion. I know that an angel can change—provided he has not crossed too deeply into darkness."

Michael admitted, "Kara did point out that perhaps I have been hunting Lucifer to such a degree that I have lost the ability to see him in another light. Maybe he has changed but I just don't know."

"You all talk as if Lucifer wants to change," Crispin argued. "Hear me now. One can only change if one is willing to change. I see no willingness to change on the part of Lucifer or any of his followers. Not unless it buys them something."

"Crispin, I love you as my teacher," said Gabriel. "But you have become hard toward Lucifer. Have you no hope at all that just perhaps he could have had a change of heart? Did you not teach that the Lord has given us the ability to choose freely and therefore one might change one's mind?"

"I taught you well, Gabriel," Crispin said warmly. He sat back. "Yes, perhaps I am a bit of a doubter where Lucifer is involved. And Pellecus to be sure."

"And Rugio," added Michael.

"And Serus," chimed in Sangius.

"And about one-third of the Host of Heaven by your latest count," Gabriel threw in. Everyone laughed.

"I see the point, dear students," Crispin said. "Very well. Speak with Lucifer, Michael. Feel him out. I truly hope it helps resolve this matter so I can get back to my studies."

Sangius spoke up timidly. "Why can't we simply take this directly to the Most High? If He truly knows all then perhaps He expects us to come to Him with this."

"Your intentions are good, Sangius," answered Crispin. "But to do so would be to invite the same disgrace that the Elders are inviting upon themselves by approaching His Person. As I have always told my students, we angels are blessed and holy creatures— but that is all. We are in relationship to the Lord on His terms and according to His desires. Perhaps one day He will create a being with whom He communicates on the more intimate level of which you speak."

Sangius spoke up again. "I hate terribly to agree with Lucifer, but if we cannot go to the Lord with this, and we assume that the Lord in His wisdom knows and understands all that occurs in Heaven, then why has He not dealt with this? Lucifer frequently boasted at the conferences I attended that the fact that the Most High does nothing indicates that He is limited in His ability to know or act. I am telling you this lack of response on the part of the Lord emboldens Lucifer to carry on."

"It all goes back to the critical aspect of our ability to choose freely," said Crispin. "As I told Michael recently, the Lord will not violate our ability to choose. To do so would be to admit that He cannot govern in His own authority." Crispin began talking now with a dreamy look in his eyes. "If only I had been allowed to debate these issues with Pellecus. Perhaps we could have avoided all of this!"

"Crispin against Pellecus in open debate. That would be astounding," said Michael.

"Yes, but it will never happen," Crispin remarked. "Not unless there is some benefit attached to it that Lucifer sees. He keeps Pellecus fairly close to him."

Michael paced the room as if searching for the answer. He looked at the others for some sort of reassurance but saw none. Finally he threw up his hands. "We need wisdom in this, good teacher," said an exasperated Michael. "We need wisdom from someone who we know is loyal to God."

Crispin looked up from his chair. He thought a moment or two about what he was going to say. "Perhaps then a visit to the wisest and holiest creatures in Heaven is in order. We cannot counsel with the Elders at this point because we can't be sure of their intentions—or at least of their wisdom—while such an appalling recommendation is going to be deliberated."

"The Zoa?" asked Gabriel.

"Yes," said Crispin, looking up at Gabriel as if surprised that Gabriel understood his reasoning. "Those mysterious beings who move in and out of the Lord's Presence and who are more keenly held there than any other creature. Recall that Kara said that the Zoa brought the news of the Creation to the Elders, right? I am sure that if anyone can shed light upon this dark subject the Zoa can. And they are the only creatures in Heaven I feel certain that even Lucifer could never influence."

"But who has access to them?" asked Michael. He was hoping he could finally see one of these legendary creatures.

"Not simply an archangel, I'm afraid, Michael," answered Crispin, anticipating Michael's desire to visit the Zoa. "Besides, you have that letter from Lucifer. You must visit him."

"So the question remains: Who can visit the Zoa?" he repeated.

"Me," said Gabriel. "Though I've yet to see them. And the Chief Elder at times."

"Quite right," agreed Crispin. "As the Lord's chief messenger, Gabriel has access to the Zoa."

Sangius was getting a little lost in the discussion. "But what are they?" he asked. "I have heard of them, of course, but..."

Crispin sat back in his chair and assumed the role of professor. "The Zoa are marvelous creatures—very strange, very wise, very holy. Mind you I have never seen one, but in the Chronicles I have read that they are like the cherubim in that they are connected in close proximity to the Throne of God. They are full of eyes, front and back—a symbol of their wisdom I suppose—all-seeing and so forth. I know that there are four Zoa who have four faces of four different creatures of some sort. The Zoa cry, "Holy, holy, holy" to the Lord day and night and are constantly at the Lord's side except on the rare occasion when they dispense some vital holy decree such as the Elders received."

"And you believe that a visit to these creatures by Gabriel is in order?" asked Michael. "Will protocol allow such a thing—I mean unannounced and without invitation?"

"They will not turn the Lord's Messenger away," said Crispin. "My suggestion is that Gabriel visit the Zoa and you, Michael, attend Lucifer."

"Then it's settled," Michael said. "Gabriel, you will see the beasts with the four faces..."

"And Michael, you shall visit the beast with two!" Crispin remarked slyly as they laughed.

―――――――――――

Lucifer took his usual place at the head of the table. The merriment of the past few moments melted into a somber air as the angels focused upon their leader. Pellecus sat opposite Lucifer, glancing occasionally at the faces of the angels who shared these exciting, if not dangerous, moments with him. He liked to read the sympathies in the room as Lucifer spoke, making mental notes of those who seemed either hesitant or noncommittal on various aspects of the conversation.

"And now we can discern the end of this present creative act," Lucifer continued. "It is obvious that in every phase, or 'day' as He calls it, the Most High is designing a more and more complex world. Having started with the simplest material, light, the Creation has progressed to the point where the earth itself is budding with new life." Lucifer's eyes gleamed with excitement. "Have you seen the wonderful array of flowering plants and herbs He has created? Marvelous! What an amazing design! Each unique, each capable of reproducing itself."

"Indeed," remarked Pellecus, assuming the role of instructor. "From a strictly academic point it is all quite interesting. Our Lord has devised a material world—a physical universe in which His will may be manifested in even the simplest structures. And as our dear brother Lucifer has pointed out, the Most High is issuing an ever-increasing complexity. Thus we are now poised for the next phase..."

"Which by logical inference must take what form, good teacher?" asked Lucifer, who had already anticipated Pellecus' answer.

"Why, animated life, of course," said Pellecus, sitting back.

The angels sat back, stunned into complete silence. Pellecus enjoyed the rapt attention of a captivated audience. "But never fear, it cannot be superior to angels. If the Lord keeps to the design—and we all know that if the Lord is *anything* He is consistent..."

"If not predictable," added Lucifer to general amusement.

Pellecus continued, "Quite, my lord. He'll stay with the pattern and create animated life of an inferior material substance. Imagine! Living creatures who will walk the breadth of this world—drink from its waters...eat of its fruit...live in its seas...fill its air...endless possibilities!"

"But where does it stop?" asked Tinius. "How complex of a creature will He design? Certainly He would never create along the order of angels to inhabit this world, would He?"

"You weren't listening, Tinius," Lucifer responded. "If the Lord is going to entrust the world to an angel to govern it, He will most certainly not create angels to inhabit it. We have enough disorder in Heaven without it spilling onto the earth!"

The room exploded in laughter.

"Angels governing angels!" said Sar. "What chaos!"

"Exactly my point," said Lucifer. "The Most High is fixed on order. No, my friends, He will continue the pattern, as Pellecus said—you may be assured of that! He will not create spiritual beings to inhabit a material universe."

Lucifer stood up, deep in thought, and began pacing around the table seemingly unaware of the angels who watched him. "They must somehow be a little lower than the angels, yet capable of understanding the mysteries of God...capable of responding to Him freely...capable of obeying and loving those things the Most High holds dear." He looked gravely at the faces staring back at him..."just as we are free to do so."

"And how do you know this?" asked Tinius.

Lucifer looked at Tinius and answered. "You are a wisdom angel, are you not, Tinius? I am surprised that you have not yet understood." He looked at the group. "The Lord desires to be worshiped above all else. We all know that. Therefore He will create an order of life that can worship Him from this material plane. But He must give this life the ability to choose freely, or else He has created nothing more than a beast of worship." Lucifer sat back down.

"And suppose," said Tinius timidly, "that these creatures, whatever they are, decide that they will not be governed from on high—that they would rather choose their own course such as we..." Tinius looked awkwardly at his fellow angels. His words disappeared uncomfortably into the silence of the room.

"You implicate us in something sordid with such words, Tinius," said Lucifer. "We are merely discussing the aspects of creation here. I suggest you remember that."

"Of course," responded a sheepish Tinius. He melted into his chair.

"However," Lucifer continued, "I suspect there would be some recourse on the part of the governing authority on earth to handle such impertinence." He grunted a noise of disgust. "That is the critical flaw of this present Kingdom. We have a choice to obey the Most High. And so we choose to obey Him in a more enlightened manner that in the end will serve to further increase His authority in the universe. But what choices do we leave the Most

High in dealing with the choices we make? He is left with no apparent recourse because He has never contemplated an angel behaving contrary to His wishes. But one day He will see that our way increased the virtue and power of this Kingdom."

"How so?" asked Fineo, who seldom spoke up at these meetings. As Keeper of the Most Holy Incense he felt his role was not as significant as some of the others at the table. Yet he understood in such times that to remain completely silent invited being passed over in future appointments. Lucifer favored angels of quick mind and speech. "How can our independence from the Lord serve to magnify Him?"

"By demonstrating that angels are capable of creating their own destinies, my dear Fineo," answered Lucifer. "Think of it! By perpetuating and broadening the Lord's influence over creation in ways that perhaps never even occurred to Him, we are taking His design to its ultimate conclusion. Just as your incense creeps slowly through the Temple and overtakes us before we are aware, Fineo, so will the Kingdom be spread abroad throughout creation through our own innovation."

Rugio had been still long enough. The fighter in him was yearning for a contest; diplomacy and verbal jockeying were good to a point, but action was ultimately called for. "My lord, you say that we are nearing the end of this Creation and that is good and well. But nothing has been said about our...that is, your role in all of this. Where do we stand?" he asked. "When will you ascend?"

"Ah, Rugio," purred Lucifer, who moved over to the large angel and put a hand on his shoulder. "Always the warrior."

Lucifer walked over to a cabinet that housed many golden scrolls of worship he had created in times past. Opening the cabinet he indicated its contents and pulled one scroll out at random. "This represents much work, Rugio. Creating praise worthy for so exalted a figure as the Most High is not simply done in haste. It requires inspiration, thought, analysis. One does not patch together something as magnificent as one of my choral works with little consideration. Neither does a Creation take place as a result of mere chance."

He was speaking to all of them now, pointing the scroll towards them. "One must have patience when achieving greatness and one must be willing to attempt that which has never before been attempted. That is why the Lord is great. He performs that which has never before occurred. He creates His greatness out of His ability to do that which is unknown and spectacular. I put it to you that any creature who successfully breaches the unknown will become great."

Lucifer's eyes glanced at the large oval window that faced the Great City. The light, ever present, poured into the room. Putting down the scroll he walked over to the window and gazed into the busy streets of Heaven. "Events are moving much more rapidly than you realize, brothers. Just because you see nothing happening does not mean that there is inactivity. I promise you that very soon all we have envisioned will be realized!" He stood in front of the emblazoned window so that only his dark silhouette could be seen. "One day it will be the Son casting the shadow, not us."

Walking back to his place at the table Lucifer continued. "At this very moment Kara is introducing to the Elders a formal proposal to have me named governor of the earth. Sentiment in that body is sympathetic and increasing in our favor." He thought smugly of the secret agreements he had made with certain angels in the Council in exchange for their affirmation. "It seems some Elders are just as anxious to be set free as are we. At any rate, I cannot foresee any scenario which we will be unable to handle."

"What about Michael?" asked Rugio.

"Michael! Always Michael!" said Lucifer, perturbed. "How long must I endure this Council's fear of Michael? He is only an angel after all!"

"Well, lord," said a subdued Rugio, "he still commands the greater number of angels loyal to the Most High. They stand ready to enforce the Lord's will in any case."

Even as Rugio was speaking Serus entered the room and whispered something to Lucifer, who nodded his head in understanding.

"Serus, your timing could not have been better," Lucifer said. "To answer you, Rugio, Michael and I shall be meeting very soon."

Many of the angels stood up, aghast at the prospect of a possible confrontation with this great angel. Lucifer held up his hands. "No, no, my friends. I have not lost my mind in this. True, he is getting uncomfortably close, and of course, Rugio, I respect his strength and authority.

"But that is why I must meet with him. The best way to deal with one's adversary is to befriend him. I will assure him of my loyalty. As will Kara. I know Michael too, Rugio. He is fierce in his service to the Most High, but he is also quite open to sincere suggestion. I have yet to see him turn away a friend—especially one who has been acting rather out of character of late." Lucifer smiled.

"And as for us?" asked Rugio, who still believed that a violent confrontation was inevitable but was content to continue the game for now.

"Continue as always," said Lucifer. "Be cautious but not suspect. Visit the earth and learn of it. Divine its nature and your ability to manipulate its contents. We will one day rule there so become acquainted with it. Above all, build sympathy among the angels who are more ambitious than others. And be prepared to move. Creation will not last forever and events will soon overtake us."

Lucifer walked to the table where his book of prophecies lay open. "A new entry in this august book, my brothers, which I share with you now to inspire our effort. Sacred will be these writings one day as we rule a new world." The room was completely silent as Lucifer began reading:

And once was the time to see;
And once was the time to understand;
And then was the time to build;
And then was the time to command;
And now is the time to act;
And now is the time to demand.

And so He gave way to the Host;
And allowed them their freedom at last;
Father, Son and Ghost;
Henceforth from the past.

Thus are these writings fulfilled,
For all of the Kingdom to see;
And so it is I am like Him,
And so it is He is like me."

He took the book and slammed it shut dramatically, startling many of the angels, and then spoke in a quiet, almost reverent tone: "We are henceforth bonded together in destinies, you and I. Whatever the outcome, we shall be brothers to the end—whether in glory or in despair. We have transgressed the line of discretion and prudence. We now rise as one to a new height that no angel has ever seen...or plunge into an unknown and disgraceful abyss."

As Lucifer spoke a reddish aura began glimmering around the outline of his person. He held his hand down in the center of the table and the other angels followed suit, placing their hands on top of his. "Let this be a sacred oath and pledge together to be either creators or devastators of the new order. May we be forever revered or forever damned in this effort; eternally free or eternally cursed." The angels stood back as Lucifer walked to his seat and stood behind his chair, the reddish glow still outlining him. He bored into each of the angels with his blue-gray eyes. "So be it," he whispered, picking up his glass and holding it up. The others held up their glasses and repeated in hushed tones, "So be it."

CHAPTER 10

"I fear you are making a grave mistake placing yourself in Lucifer's hands."

Kara's impassioned argument for naming Lucifer as earth's future steward was going well. He had presented a marvelous and scholarly argument as to the sensibility of such an action. An angel was the only choice for the Lord, he said. Who else could the Lord trust with so important a task? And with Lucifer's ability in worship the entire world would be a tribute to the glory of the Most High. It seemed only fitting after such a distinguished record of unselfish service in the presence of God that such service should be rewarded. It was along this line of reasoning that Kara skillfully made his argument that was now being deliberated in the Council of Elders.

As he sat in the proceedings Kara counted heads. The Council seemed divided into three distinct factions. The vocal oppositon was led by Dabran, who was suspicious of Lucifer's ambitions. He continually tried to sway the undecided that Lucifer was unfit to take on such a task because it was not an angel's role to promote himself. Another group was undecided, but leaning toward a decision for Lucifer simply to keep the peace in the Council. These angels were Kara's target as the decision could be rendered with a simple majority of Elders. Finally, there were the dedicated Lucife-rians who viewed his speech as a mere formality to a conclusion already attained. Kara nodded to this and that angel and thought about his role in this endeavor as he excused himself from the gallery to allow a freer debate.

In other circumstances Kara might question the use of one's position to maneuver so important an issue. In this case, however, he felt justified. As an Elder, he was furthering the cause of the Kingdom, was he not? By helping Lucifer become the earth's stew-ard he was removing a future threat to the peace of Heaven and placing a highly competent angel in a place of service to the Most High. Lucifer would make a magnificent governor. He was a bit overbearing, perhaps, but over time he felt he could handle him, especially since he would be working closely with Lucifer in administering the earth. He pondered a heady future…

"Kara! Kara!" came a voice. It was Plinus, an angel very sym-pathetic to Lucifer. "You made a wonderful presentation!"

"How do you view the outcome?" asked Kara, who accompa-nied Plinus down the long hallway to the gallery where the Elders convened.

"Splendid! There were a few who felt that angels have no prece-dent for making recommendations to the Most High on such a mat-ter. It is after all a bold move," he said with an air of self-satisfaction in having been a part of such an occasion. "Wisdom angels! Always asking questions."

"Yes, it's about time the Council made a bold move," added Kara, who was perturbed at Plinus' smug manner. Plinus was of such low character in Kara's estimation that to speak as if he had performed an honorable task of his own initiation was repugnant. "I'm sure you were quite in line with everyone as always, dear Pli-nus. Very bold indeed!"

Before Plinus could respond the two entered the gallery and began greeting the angels assembled. The Chief Elder sat in his chair with the seven ruling angels. The remaining Elders were tak-ing their places around the crescent-shaped table that faced the ranking Elders. Kara felt good about his handling of the Council.

He thought of the time to come when Gabriel, one of those suspicious nuisances, would himself have to officially announce Lucifer's promotion to the Kingdom. *Delicious irony*, he thought.

"Brothers," said the Chief Elder, "please be seated. Before we embark on so important an action, I wish to thank this body for its generous spirit of debate and cooperation. We have proven to the amazement of some and to the disappointment of others (he looked playfully at the Elders who had held out against assigning Lucifer the position) that even angels can come to a reasonable consensus!" Everyone laughed. "Brother Kara, you have submitted to us that of all the angels in Heaven there is one who stands out from all the others in regard to this matter, correct?"

Kara stood up and began speaking. "Brothers, I would never submit to this body or any citizen of this Kingdom that there are not a number of angels who could serve well in this matter. Why, in this Council alone are many who could serve as governor of the earth and perform admirably! But as there may be only one steward for the Most High, I must confess that the name which continually presents itself—and not only through me but from others in the Kingdom—is Lucifer."

Voices in agreement filled the chamber as angels validated the name of Lucifer as their choice to submit to the Lord. The Chief Elder waited for the demonstration on Lucifer's behalf to subside and then recognized Dabran, who stood to speak.

"Not again," groaned Plinus to Kara.

"Quiet," said Kara. "Better he speak now than later."

"I realize that I do not speak from popular sentiment on this issue in this chamber," began Dabran, whose words were met with jeers from some of the angels: "He's jealous," or "Quit delaying things," or other such words.

The Chief Elder pounded the dais and raised his voice: "There will be a decorum commiserate with these proceedings! I will have no voice shouted down in this body. Do I make myself understood?" The angels nodded assent to the presiding Elder and began to lower their voices and take their seats.

Kara was disturbed by the rashness that the Lucifer contingent had been demonstrating of late. In casual encounters on the street or at the Temple those who supported Lucifer were growing in confidence and becoming more and more bold in their demeanor. Such attitudes are healthy to a point, but must be kept in check. Kara decided to speak to Lucifer about holding his disciples a little more tightly. As a representative of the angels to the Most High and as a leader among the Host, Kara felt it was his duty to make sure that dignity was maintained throughout the proceedings. As he saw it, it might be he and not Lucifer who could broker the great peace to come. A wonderful legacy!

Dabran and Lucifer had been opposed to each other on many issues in the Kingdom and Dabran had come to the conclusion that Lucifer was not at all the angel he appeared to be. "You who would put Lucifer as governor would do well to remember that he seeks only his own gain," he said. Many angels began muttering again, cajoling or laughing at the scholarly angel who opposed them. "Yes, his own gain!" Dabran continued forcefully. "I know that some of you have been bought with promises of appointments to serve under Lucifer—to the utter shame of all angels..."

"Sit down, Dabran," someone shouted. "Quit making a fool of yourself."

Kara watched with keen interest as the angels began to drown out Dabran's words with their demonstrations of loyalty to Lucifer. How masterfully Lucifer had cultivated such loyalty and in such short order. He truly was the greatest angel in Heaven.

Dabran continued on as if he didn't notice the noisy angels shouting. "Serve him well. But the day will come that you will regret ever having heard the name Morning Star!" The chamber exploded in angry cries for Dabran's expulsion from the room. The tension was overwhelming. Angels stood and accused Dabran of playing games with a most holy decision. The Chief Elder tried to regain control but to no avail. Dabran simply stood, quietly waiting to continue speaking. The Council slowly came to order again, amidst a few spontaneous outbursts.

"May I speak, Dabran?" asked Kara.

"Of course, Kara," answered Dabran, who was shaken from the ordeal but not defeated. "If there is one voice which I respect here it is yours, though I fear you are making a grave mistake placing yourself in Lucifer's hands."

"Thank you, dear Dabran," Kara said. He walked over to Dabran's seat and embraced the shaken angel. Dabran sat down as Kara stood to his side and began speaking. "Brothers, we all know that some have opposed this idea from the beginning. We are, as someone said, setting a new precedent, stepping onto unknown ground. But I must admit that it saddens me to see such arrogance displayed by some of the Elders in here. I would rather withdraw the name of Lucifer than watch Dabran be treated with such contempt." Kara's voice was growing more and more loud. "This is a deliberating body—a fellowship—where one voice may speak freely and without risk of the sordid display we just witnessed. I suspect that Lucifer would feel this way and that he will build the same individual freedoms on the earth.

"The Most High expects that we will be fair and cooperative in this Council. As to the issues of delegating certain future offices, yes, Lucifer has speculated with some about possible positions of authority that will be created on earth. But is that so wrong? Does not the God Most High, the Three-In-One, deliberate the great and secret things of the Kingdom?"

"You would compare Lucifer's dark deliberations with the most holy dialogue between the Father, the Son and the Spirit?" asked an incredulous Dabran. He stood up again, his anger building. He looked straight at Kara. "You would turn over stewardship of the Lord's greatest design to an angel who shows contempt for His Holy Name?" He turned to the other angels who were watching him intently. "I think you overestimate your influence with the Lord, dear Council. Creatures do not dictate to their Creator—nor do they even make polite recommendations no matter how official they may be. I will not remain here and be party to such a gross and...yes, unholy proposition!"

The room exploded in boisterous tumult as Dabran exited the chamber, accompanied by the same jeers and maligning he had received earlier. Kara watched him leave and waited for calm to be restored. Though uncomfortable with the nature of the debate, Kara knew the time had come to make an end of it.

"Brother angels! We stand ready to influence our Kingdom as never before. The Fourth Day has come and gone—the earth now has its own sun and moon and even stars that shed their light apart from our Lord. This can only mean that His attention will now turn toward the inhabitants of that planet—inhabitants who will need a gentle hand to guide them. I know, brothers, that these are stressful times. But we must be brave and humble in this task as we place our trust and confidence in the one angel who can maintain unity among our struggling angelry. I, Kara, elder of the Host, call upon this body to make official our designation of Lucifer as governor of the new world called earth; and for that name to be humbly placed before the Most High for His wise and most holy consideration..."

Michael entered Lucifer's house in a guarded mood. Crispin had convinced him that this was a proper course of action as Lucifer had initiated the contact. He also felt he owed it to one of Heaven's greatest angels to meet with him alone, but could not help but be suspicious of this sudden desire on Lucifer's part to speak with him. Serus conducted Michael through the vast house and led him into the garden where Lucifer was seated. Michael noticed immediately the worshipful state of mind that the garden invited as Lucifer's music filled the air, greeting visitors as they progressed through the estate.

"Ah, Michael," said Lucifer, who stood to embrace him. "Thank you for coming!" He indicated for Michael to be seated next to where he had been sitting. "Serus, see that we are not disturbed," Lucifer said.

After Serus disappeared Lucifer continued. "I know how awkward my message must have made you feel, dear brother," said Lucifer. "But it is for that reason that I wanted to speak with you to clear your mind of any thoughts you might have regarding my loyalty to the Most High. It is terribly awkward for me as well, I assure you."

Michael was clearly uncomfortable. Lucifer was the most influential angel in Heaven and here he himself was, a recently appointed archangel, accusing Lucifer of nothing short of disloyalty to God. "I'm sure that we can straighten the matter out, Lucifer," said Michael, "provided that you can set my mind at ease regarding some activities of which I have become aware."

"Of course," said Lucifer. "Anything I can do to promote harmony in this Kingdom will have my full attention and support."

Thus did Michael begin to divulge to Lucifer the results of his investigations and discussions with other angels. All of the recent events seemed to swirl about the two as Michael chronologically detailed Lucifer's apparent jealousy of Gabriel; the Council of Worship's potentially hostile agenda; the prideful attitude of certain angels friendly to Lucifer; the teaching at the Academy and the brashness of many angels there; Sangius' report of Lucifer's interest in the Creation; Lucifer's alliance with Pellecus and other angels who seemed bent upon great changes....

When Michael was finished he waited for Lucifer's reaction with great interest. As he made the charges his discomfort had taken on a feeling of vindication. He felt that he would finally begin to clear up this matter by placing Lucifer in direct line of his questioning. Also, by taking the matter discreetly to Lucifer and allowing him to give his own account, he felt he was doing the honorable thing. Surely the Most High would approve should this matter take on greater importance.

"Well I certainly look guilty, don't I?" Lucifer finally responded. He picked a berry from one of the nearby bushes and tossed it casually into his mouth. "And I can certainly understand why you and Gabriel and the others would be concerned." He laughed. "If I were you I too would be suspicious of me!"

"Well?" asked Michael. "Can you explain these things to me so I can go back and tell the others that we have nothing to fear in Lucifer?"

"Fear me?" asked Lucifer, who burst into laughter. "I thought there was no fear in this Kingdom." He looked at Michael with great passion. "Dear Michael, I preside over the worship of the Most High God, Creator of all. I bring praises to the Throne Room of Him who is above all. My music fills Heaven as we rejoice and extol the virtue of the Father, Son and Spirit. Tell me, Michael, if I was truly involved in these sordid excursions do you really believe that the Most High would allow me to continue in my place of service—much less approach His Throne and lead others there as well?" Michael noticed that as Lucifer spoke a hazy light blue aura manifested around him, which usually only occurred whenever Lucifer was leading the praises of the Lord.

"Our Lord is all-powerful, is He not?" continued Lucifer. "Yes, He is. He is in the process now of creating a world merely by speaking it into existence as you and I would speak to another angel. If these seditious antics were truly occurring how long would I or Pellecus or any of the rest of those you named be a part of this Kingdom? Why would the Most High tolerate corruption under His very throne? He would not, I say—not if He is truly all-powerful!"

"I cannot answer that," said Michael. "I know that Crispin believes that the longsuffering nature of our Lord possibly allows Him to put up with such behavior—for a season."

"Ah, Crispin," said Lucifer. "A capable teacher there. Very wise. And very jealous of the school's reputation and integrity. Perhaps a little too jealous, Michael."

"What do you mean?"

"I'm simply pointing out that when one is buried in one's tasks one can lose perspective and become a little overprotective of his domain—small as it might be. I love Crispin with all my heart. But he seldom leaves the Academy and for that reason is mistrustful of most who enter there—including myself and others who might enjoy debating a different point of view. Crispin is to you what Pellecus is to me—an academic voice with whom I enjoy scholarly discourse. Nothing more."

"Crispin would welcome debate," Michael said. "But open debate that would involve the secretive teachings that Pellecus promotes."

"Secretive teachings?" asked an amused Lucifer. "I would hardly call what most of the Academy now seems to subscribe to a secret teaching! No, Michael, Crispin would call secretive anything that he deemed unworthy of or different from the sacred teachings. Perhaps if he would entertain different thoughts from time to time he wouldn't find himself a part of such fantasies and see danger in every new idea." Lucifer smiled. "He certainly has agitated a great number of angels with this nonsense."

"So what does Pellecus teach?" asked Michael, finding himself on the defensive at this point. "Crispin is no fool. If he believes that there is dangerous doctrine being promoted within the Academy there must be something to it."

"I quite agree," said Lucifer. "Crispin is no fool. But you and I will never settle this here. This is a matter to be settled between Pellecus and Crispin. It always centers around those two, doesn't it? Perhaps there would be no better way to demonstrate my devotion to the peace and goodwill of this Kingdom than by helping create a lasting peace between them."

"What are you proposing?" asked Michael, curiosity aroused.

"You said yourself that Crispin would welcome open debate on the subjects that are in question. I propose that Pellecus and Crispin have such a debate to be witnessed by the instructors and students of the Academy. This would be a scholarly exercise unparalleled since the inception of the school, and would, I believe, lay to rest the notion that Pellecus' teachings are dangerous. Perhaps, Michael, it might even be discovered that the real peril to the integrity of the Academy comes from the unwillingness within to grow in knowledge. Pellecus has borne brutal reaction from the Academy. But enlightenment comes at a price for those willing to birth it."

Michael thought about Lucifer's suggestion. He didn't necessarily agree that a debate would lay matters to rest. But he did feel that by opening up the issue in such a setting it would at least clarify the positions of the angels involved, both students and teachers. He liked the idea.

"I'll speak to Crispin about it," said Michael.

"And I Pellecus," said Lucifer. "What a discourse that will be!"

As they continued talking Lucifer batted down Michael's arguments one by one with great skill: Sangius? He was upset with Lucifer because he wanted to become more highly placed within the Kingdom and Lucifer felt that his request was untoward. He did propose that Sangius take less of a role in the Council of Worship until an appropriate response to Sangius' request could be engineered. But Lucifer was "shocked" that he would take his anger to such extremes and actually accuse him of some malevolent purpose.

The Council of Worship? Indeed there were a number of angels from the various ministries involved in regular meetings with Lucifer. What better way to infuse all of Heaven with the worship of the Most High than by selecting high officers from each order and instructing them in the praises to Him?

Pellecus' teaching? The debate should settle that issue.

"Now we must come to something which I must concede is true and for which I am ashamed: my attitude of late," Lucifer continued. "I must admit it's a bit of a mystery even to myself, Michael. I have felt withdrawn lately and quite alone. I am no longer satisfied with the performance of my duties...it's as if I have lost touch with the Lucifer I once was..." He looked lovingly at Michael, his bluish aura reflecting off Michael's face. "How very proud I am of your rank, my brother. Indeed I should have shared in your joy instead of retreating from it."

Michael felt a stirring of compassion for Lucifer—something that he had not felt sincerely for quite some time. "Lucifer, I am here to help you in any way I can. I wish to have you for my friend and brother. As an archangel I am obliged to seek out any potential disturbances to the Kingdom and this is what has brought me here. Will you give me your promise, Morning Star, my once and always brother, whose sacred office lifts praises on high, that your purposes in this realm are pure?"

"I swear that, Michael. I have no intention in mind except that which I believe to be best for this or any kingdom that our Lord has devised."

"Then I must believe you, Lucifer. And I must report to the others that I do so believe." Lucifer started to embrace Michael, who held up his hand to stop him. "But hear me now, brother. Should you or any other angel prove false to this Kingdom, I will avenge the honor of the Lord."

"May you have the better of me, Michael, should I prove false," Lucifer said, grasping Michael's strong hands. "May you cast me out of Heaven, never to return, should I prove a liar."

Michael looked at Lucifer and softened his features. He laughed aloud and added, "May it never be!"

"My lord!" came Serus' voice from somewhere in the garden. He appeared from the direction of Lucifer's dwelling. "My lord. A delegation from the Chief Elder has arrived on urgent business!"

Lucifer looked perplexed and turned to Michael. "Michael, certainly you did not report these suspicions to the Elders?"

"No," answered Michael, who thought to himself that Kara certainly made short work of it. "I came straight to you!"

"In any case I would like you to receive the delegation with me. If perchance this issue has come to light I would like you to allay their fears with the words we have just shared here in my garden."

"Of course," said Michael as they made their way toward the house. Lucifer certainly didn't appear to have prior knowledge to the news he was about to receive. If in fact this were the delegation naming him steward, would he truly have asked Michael to accompany him?

<hr />

The Elders had assembled in the massive entryway of Lucifer's house. Michael could see Kara talking with some of the others as Lucifer led the way into the room. Lucifer and Kara looked at each other for a brief moment and exchanged knowing glances. Serus also saw the exchange between the two and was a little repulsed by the fact that Lucifer's plans seemed to be working out so splendidly.

"There he is," Kara announced. "Greetings, brother Lucifer." Kara rushed to embrace Lucifer and then stopped quite suddenly upon seeing Michael enter the room behind the worship angel. Kara gave Lucifer a wondering look and then added, "And the archangel Michael! How marvelous that you are here as well!"

"Yes," Lucifer quickly responded, taking Kara's hand. "I am glad to report to you and the other Elders that all is well in Heaven, though I am sure that is not what brought you here!" They laughed. He looked intently at Kara and repeated in a lower tone of voice, "All is well." Kara glanced again at Michael and nodded in acknowledgment.

Assuming his role as chief delegate of the Council, Kara solemnly said, "We are here, my lord, in an official capacity to announce that the Elders would have your name placed before the Most High as the greatest angel in Heaven and the most worthy subject to become governor of the new world! Brother Lucifer, we desire to see you become the steward of earth!"

Lucifer looked completely surprised. He turned to Michael who himself was watching Lucifer's reaction. "My dear brothers," Lucifer responded, "thank you for such an honor. I am deeply moved." He motioned for everyone to move into the receiving room where they gathered in the center.

"Noble honor fitting for so noble an angel," added Plinus.

"Thank you again. It's quite embarrassing really. The archangel and I were just now discussing issues which found me rather compromised. I hope, Michael, that this coincidence does not change your conclusion about me. I was not expecting this!"

"Lucifer, I honor you as always," Michael said, still astonished by it all but willing to go along discreetly.

"But surely we all recognize that the plans of the Most High cannot be anticipated by us mere angels," Lucifer said. "Who are we to bring this before Him?"

The Elders looked at each other somewhat confused, as Kara implored Lucifer as to the reasons that he must accept their recommendation of him to the Lord.

Michael could not believe what he was hearing. Lucifer and a few "malcontents" as Crispin called them was one thing. They could be explained and handled. But the Elders? The ruling angels who presided over all the angels in the court of the Most High, who sat in proximity to His Holy Person...the custodians of all angelry in the Kingdom recommending Lucifer to become the steward of earth? He had hoped that somehow within that body a voice of reason would prevail and dismiss this proposition out of hand. Michael began feeling a sense of despair for the first time—either he had completely misunderstood Lucifer in this entire affair, or Lucifer's influence had somehow crept into the sacred chambers of the Elders and deceived or corrupted even these most holy angels! Could one angel hold such persuasive ability? Could one choice divide a kingdom?

"And what does the archangel think of this?" Kara's voice boomed. He knew that Michael was bound by honor not to publicly reveal his prior conversation with Kara.

"I'm sorry," said Michael, a little dazed. "What did you ask?"

"It is quite astonishing, isn't it?" said Kara. "To think that an angel should be so honored. It will truly be a great day for all angels when Lucifer is made governor!"

"I should think that we must be sensible in this," answered Michael finally. "Lucifer said it himself: Who can know the plans of the Most High? If the Lord agrees that Lucifer should be named governor then I will naturally support my brother with all my heart."

"You have your doubts then?" asked Plinus, whose own meager influence was tied to Lucifer's success in this issue. "You think the Lord will name another?"

"I have no thought on the matter at all, Plinus," said Michael. All the Elders were listening to him. Kara looked at Lucifer who remained impassive. "I only suggest that until Lucifer or any angel is named by the Most High..."

"How true," Lucifer interrupted. "I would never assume such a position. Perhaps the honor will go to Michael...or Kara...or some other angel. You're quite right, Michael, nothing is settled until the Lord declares it so."

"Nevertheless," interjected Kara, "the Council has determined to place your name before the Most High and begs you to accept this honor."

Various voices in the room began speaking to Lucifer, who looked deep in thought as if wrestling the matter over in agonizing fashion. "You must!" "It is your duty." "Service requires it!" Lucifer held up his hands to silence the room.

"Brothers," he began. "Honor is for gods and we are only creatures. I cannot think of any reason why I should be so named. But if the Council urges me on in this regard, then I must out of respect for the Council accept their nomination and allow my name to be set with all humility before the Lord!"

And with all speed, I'm sure, thought Serus, listening at the door.

The room erupted in cheery congratulations. Kara read the official petition that would be brought before the Lord so all could hear it. Lucifer could only shake his head in mock disbelief as Kara finished reading the scroll.

"Thank you, dear brother," Kara said, "for taking up duty once more. We shall retire now and leave you to your business."

"My business is to do the will of the Father," Lucifer said. "But presently I shall go to the garden and meditate upon the greatness of our Lord. Let us never forget, brothers, how blessed we are to serve in such a Kingdom with such a King!"

The angels began to leave, talking as they went about the greatness of the occasion. Kara lingered behind and waited until all had left except Michael. When he saw that Michael intended staying on Kara turned to leave himself. "Farewell then, brothers," he said. "I shall personally take this to the Most Holy Place and deposit it with the Fiery Ministers of the Holy Throne. They will see it into the Lord's hands."

Michael watched as Kara left. He wondered what reception would be awaiting Kara at the Throne. He turned to Lucifer, still befuddled by it all and said, "Well, brother. This is quite a season for you."

"I'm still in disbelief," said Lucifer. "Though honored of course."

"As I said I will report to the others that we have sorted out some of the misconceptions that have been aroused. I'll also talk with Crispin about the debate with Pellecus. I'm sure they will be interested in the report from the Elders."

"I sincerely hope that because this was an issue that originated within the Eldership and not from the ministry of worship that your friends will see that I am not involved in some nefarious plot. It's quite absurd really."

"I'll report all that we have discussed," Michael repeated. The two angels embraced one another as Lucifer escorted Michael out of the room. As he turned to leave he caught a glimpse of Serus in the hallway. Their eyes locked on to one another and for a brief moment Michael the archangel stared into the eyes of Serus, the servant of Lucifer. Serus began to motion as if to say something, but stopped quickly when Lucifer turned to place his hand on Michael's shoulder. "Good-bye, my friend," said Lucifer. "I'm so very glad that we have cleared up this confusion."

"Good-bye, Lucifer," said Michael, still looking at Serus over Lucifer's right shoulder. "Thank you for being so candid."

Michael was, as had been the case more and more, glad to leave that place. It seemed that every time he chatted with Lucifer in order to clarify things the picture became less clear. Now he had to report to the group that he truly didn't know what he should believe. Lucifer seemed sincere. And his story made sense on the whole. But Sangius never indicated any jealousy toward Lucifer. And to complicate matters further, what about the Elders recommending Lucifer to the Lord?

All of these things swirled in Michael's mind in a cloudy puzzle. He looked toward the earth, now green with lush plants and herbs and wondered as to its future ruler. One clear picture did emerge, however—that of Serus indicating that he wanted to talk secretly to Michael while Lucifer was shutting the door. That might prove interesting!

Chronicles of the Host

Day Five

As the Lord continued in His wonderful plans, the earth became more and more interesting to the angels. For now the mind of God turned from the form of the planets to its creatures—and all of Heaven waited in great anticipation as the earth brought forth from the command of God something that had not previously existed in material form before: life.

And the Lord said,

"Let the waters bring forth abundantly
The moving creatures that hath life
And fowl that may fly above the earth in the open firmament of Heaven."
And God created great whales,
And every living creature that moveth,
Which the waters brought forth abundantly,
After their kind,
And the winged fowl after his kind:
And God saw that it was good.
*And the evening and the morning were **the fifth day**.*

CHAPTER 11

"If there is a rebel spirit in Heaven it flows from the Throne, not toward it."

"Lucifer! Lucifer!"

The shrill, excited voice of Octrion could not be mistaken.

"Yes, Octrion," answered Lucifer, who was returning from the Temple. "Must you bellow my name all over Heaven?"

"I'm sorry, lord," said Octrion, looking at some of the other angels who were watching the exchange. "It's just that…have you had occasion to visit the earth since the Fifth Day? Marvelous!"

"And noisy," said Lucifer. "Far too noisy to suit me." He nodded in greeting to a passing angel. "I think I liked it better when it was a floral world—a peaceful garden in the blackness of the universe. The place is now teeming with creatures of all sorts who make it their home."

Octrion began drifting off as usual. "Well, I just thought that you might be interested…that is…well since you might have a voice in what will happen on that world."

Lucifer looked sharply at him and pulled him aside. "What are you talking about, Octrion? What have you heard?"

Octrion looked rather timid and said, "I heard that you were being considered as the Lord's steward for the earth. A wonderful honor should it prove true."

Lucifer's anger subsided. "Steward over what, Octrion? Birds and fish? Perhaps when the Lord creates a more challenging creature I will be interested. I have no desire to be the zookeeper of the Most High. Farewell, Octrion."

Octrion hurried off toward the Temple, chatting with whatever angel might listen to him about the earth's newest life. Lucifer walked along the walls of the outer court of the Temple, glancing now and again at the earth looming blue and distant in the heavens.

Five seasons of creation, he thought. *When will it end? When will He make a finish of it?* He thought about the progress of recent events and was pleased. Kara's actions in the Council were flawless. And now they waited the strategic moment to address the Most High as to their recommendation. Everything seemed to be moving according to plan. And yet…he entered his house and walked to the edge of the balcony overlooking the Great City.

Toward the north was the Great Mountain, atop which was the Most Holy Place, shimmering as always in the distance. Within that sacred site dwelt the greatest being alive: the Most High God, Creator, King, Lord, the Father, Son and Spirit. God of mystery, God of power, all-knowing, all-seeing…

What do You see when You look upon the Morning Star now, O Most High God? Lucifer wondered. *Do You see an angel who is using the intellect You gave Him to further himself for the advancement of the Kingdom? Do you see a creature that You fashioned as an instrument of worship becoming the object of worship? Do You see a wretched malcontent grasping at opportunity? Or do You see at all?*

How did the Lord look upon this? Lucifer encouraged the others that when the decisive moment came, the Most High would do nothing except react gracefully to a foregone conclusion. Still, the question badgered away unanswered and looming: *How long shall the Lord allow me to progress? If He is truly Lord why does He not have me exposed and be done with it?* he thought to himself.

Lucifer perceived the Lord's apparent laxness as the subtle flaw in His character. The Most High is the nearest being to perfection that exists. But perfect? How could One who is so awesome in power, so splendid in beauty, which commands the adoration of every living creature—how could such a God be so impotent at such a time? Certainly the Lord's blind eye to Lucifer's plans indicated at best an unwillingness to confront him—at worst an inability to. Was He willing to confront Lucifer, but unable? Or was He able to confront him but unwilling? Therein lay the gamble of it all.

Lucifer knew that for all his planning and all his subtlety, he was taking an enormous, horrific risk. He knew that to lose in this meant shame, disgrace, loss of his high office—or worse. But to win...to win meant everything. Should he win in this endeavor and be allowed to rule as steward of the earth, without interference from on high, then he could at last fashion a world in which true freedoms were allowed—freedoms orchestrated around Lucifer's own teachings and dispensed by Pellecus and other wisdom angels through a true academy. No more bowing low to a benign God who cannot even discern or disable a rebel plot in His own Throne Room.

Rebel plot? Did he just think that? Certainly *rebel* is not the correct word. Lucifer assured himself that he was not a rebel, but a liberator. He didn't foment open strife, but healthy debate. A rebel would seek to turn the Kingdom over—Lucifer merely intended in sharing in it. A rebel would create havoc and deceptions to throw the enemy off. Lucifer felt himself an honorable angel who was only fostering the self-deceptions that Crispin and the others had bred into the Host, and used those to his advantage. A rebel would actively enlist support from others by influencing them to his way of thinking. Lucifer was only encouraging the feelings already resident among many of the angels and was offering a place of hope and comfort. One cannot deny one's own discontent.

Shall I pretend all is well here? Lucifer mused. *The truth is that if there is a rebel presence in Heaven it moves* **from** *the Throne and not toward it. God, in His desire to be loved, has allowed Himself to become indecisive and posturing,* Lucifer concluded. **He** *is the rebel, having rebelled from His responsibility to reign effectively by becoming sentimental. No being* *could expect to hold onto power who is unwilling to exercise it. The old Kingdom must give way to the new, just as the prophecy spoke.*

Lucifer looked toward the glowing, holy Mountain. *I know that I will never be greater than You,* he thought, *but I can indeed be like You. I cannot speak into existence as You, but I can govern that which already exists. I cannot create a world out of nothing, but I can move what has been created. I cannot construct a universe, but I can conduct one as I would any arrangement.*

Lucifer gazed intently into the shimmering light and began to speak boldly toward it in a monologue that he had rehearsed in his mind a thousand times before. "It is said that You are all-knowing. How can that be? If it were true, would You not be hearing my thoughts even now and responding? Yet I continue forward in my efforts unimpeded. What good is all of Your knowledge if not acted upon?

"It is said that You are all-powerful. How can that be? If it were true...Ah!" Lucifer angrily turned from the light, unable to hold his eyes upon the brightness any longer. He continued more forcefully, still looking toward the hill but not directly into the light. "If You were truly all-powerful would You have allowed my activities to flourish to the point that upwards of one out of every three angels is following me? What sort of power sustains such indecision?

"It is said that You are ever-present. How can that be? Were You present at the Council meetings when Your name was held in contempt by every angel there? Were You present when Kara misled Michael and Gabriel and those who would interfere with that which will soon happen? Were You truly present when I made the decision in my heart that You are not fit to rule? If these few examples indicate the power of Your presence then we are very lonely angels indeed.

"I am humble enough to admit, O Most High, that I am not all-knowing," Lucifer continued, arms folded behind him now as he paced the balcony, assuming a lecturing posture. "I cannot know the thoughts of angels, yet I can observe the intentions of their heart and thus influence them. Therefore the knowledge I have is of far greater utility than Your own. Neither am I all-powerful, O

Lord. Yet I can decisively exercise such powers as I have, not perhaps with *Your* authority, but certainly with my own.

"You are great, O Most High God," said Lucifer, "and shall always be great. Your holiness, Your purity, Your goodness—none of these shall ever be denied You. On earth we shall commemorate Your greatness periodically as we look into the heavens and recognize Your presence from above.

"I will never surpass Your greatness, Most Holy One...but I will not be denied my own. I will never rule from on high...but I *shall* rule. I will never come to expect the worship of all my subjects...but I shall be worshiped. I will never command the heavenly Host as one...but angels will be commanded of me. My authority will never accede Your own...but authority I shall have. And when in ages hence, Your power and presence on earth becomes increasingly dim in the minds of Your creatures—a shadow rather than a substance, a speculation instead of a certainty, a star in the evening sky rather than a light in Heaven—then shall there be truly one god to reign on earth.

"The Host will come to recognize this. The earth will come to recognize this. And even You will come to recognize this...and thus will the authority of the Morning Star be forever established on earth, just as Your authority is established in Heaven."

Lucifer then recited the prophetic words he had himself recorded:

The Greater now gives way to thee,

Thy wonders to behold.

Even though his rank and title gave him privilege into the Throne area of the Temple, Gabriel felt like an intruder as he made his way deeper into the complex. The heart of the Temple was the Most Holy Throne, from where the Most High ruled with all power and authority. The place was shrouded in mystery, and was a subject of speculation among the Host, for only exceptional angels were allowed access into this chamber. Even Lucifer, the Anointed Cherub, seldom ventured near this most sacred spot. And now

Gabriel entered into this most holy place to inquire about something that was perhaps unholy.

The Throne Room was two rooms really. An outer chamber served as a place of worship for the Twenty-four Elders. Gabriel noticed 12 seats on either side of the center aisle where the Elders would gather to offer their praises—and now apparently their advice—to the Most High God. The room was adorned in beautifully colored precious stones and gold, and a purplish-crimson curtain separated this room from the Throne Room itself. As Gabriel walked the length of the room he could hear voices on the other side of the heavily curtained doorway crying out "Holy, Holy, Holy" over and over again.

He gathered the curtains to one side and a shaft of intense white light beamed from the room and lit up the room in which Gabriel stood. He quickly let go of the curtain and the room was dark once more. Gabriel fell to his knees, staggered by the realization that the Most Holy Presence was enthroned behind that veil. He felt strangely ashamed for being in such a sacred place with such a sordid purpose. Overcome, he began to worship. He sang along in his heart and mind the words, "Holy, Holy, Holy." He lost himself in the praises to the Lord and soon had a calm about his mission. The situation with Lucifer seemed completely petty in the presence of so great a God. Who were Michael and Gabriel to assist the Lord in anything? Were they not behaving as arrogantly as the Elders by thinking of themselves protectors of the Lord's interests— as if He needed their little interference? God would deal with this in His way and in His time. Gabriel decided that it was proper to leave this all in the Lord's hands and carry out his expected duties and service to God without presuming to aid Him in administering the Kingdom. He started to leave, ashamed that he had even come, when from behind him he heard his name called out.

"Gabriel!"

<hr />

"Do you really think that Pellecus will debate me openly?" asked an astonished Crispin. "I mean in a fair and public setting?"

"Lucifer told me to make the arrangements," Michael said.

"Interesting," mused Crispin. "Bit of bait in there somewhere to be sure."

"Possibly," agreed Michael. "But we cannot assume anything at this point. If there is a possibility of a reconciliation in Heaven and a clearing up of this situation, then we must take up the offer...with your consent, of course."

"Of course, of course," answered Crispin, already making mental preparations for the contest. "I try not to assume the worst, Michael," he said, rising from his desk and looking through some of the scrolls scattered here and there around him. "Ah, here it is," he said, picking up a scroll with a crimson ribbon tied around it. "However, if I know Pellecus, he won't enter into such an event without some consideration as to its outcome." He looked up at Michael intently. "He's not one to take a risk unless he is confident that it will turn to his advantage."

"On the contrary," said Michael, "I'd say he is quite a risk taker if in fact he is throwing in with Lucifer in some unimaginable plot."

Crispin thought for a moment. He looked up at Michael and said, "I can only repeat myself, Michael. Pellecus would never venture into a contest without confidence as to its outcome. And I can assure you he would never 'throw in with Lucifer' as you say unless he was certain of THAT outcome as well." He paused for a moment. "If in fact there is something amiss in Heaven in which Pellecus has a hand, you can rest assure, Michael, that those who would oppose our Lord are extremely confident in their opposition."

He sat back down and assumed the role of instructor once more. "Understand, Michael, there is nothing wrong with being confident. It is by confidence that our Lord has created this Kingdom, knowing that His abilities are part of who He is. It is with confidence that He can speak the word *light* and create light. Lucifer cannot do that. No creature can do that. Only God Most High can do such a thing."

"So Lucifer and Pellecus are merely fooling themselves," said Michael. "Trying to attempt that which they will never be able to do."

"Confidence can itself be misleading, Michael. And misplaced confidence is a disaster in the making. But supreme confidence in one's own abilities, which seems to be the strength of this group, is an abomination. Our Lord will neither share His glory nor His power with angels. It sickens me to think that any angel would attempt such nonsense in the face of such holiness." Crispin had a faraway look in his sharp eyes. He caught himself. "Yes, Michael, I would be glad to debate Pellecus. Pass that along. Perhaps if nothing else this might be a lesson in humility."

"For whom?" asked Michael, smiling.

Crispin looked up and smiled. "For whoever needs humbling, of course!"

Gabriel turned and instinctively prostrated himself before the voice, not knowing whether he was encountering creature or Creator. The holiness that pervaded the room in the presence of this being crept like thick smoke which engulfed Gabriel. Gabriel kept his face low to the floor, not daring to look up, unwilling to speak until first addressed. The voice came again: "Gabriel! Stand up!" Gabriel slowly stood, his eyes averting the direction of the voice, still shaken by the spectacle, feeling as if he were more of an intruder than a petitioner.

Slowly Gabriel moved his eyes upward, scanning the figure that stood before him, and saw the most incredible creature in the Lord's entire Kingdom. Here stood a figure whose virtue and holiness was so pronounced, that one might be standing in the very presence of the Most High, if one did not know otherwise. Well could it be said that this was a very sacred creature to the Most High.

It was also a bizarre being, and true to Crispin's description, did indeed have the face of a beast—recognizable now as having a newly created counterpart on earth. The lion-faced creature motioned Gabriel forward, benign but commanding respect. As Gabriel observed the creature more closely he noticed that it was covered both front and back with living eyes which seemed to bore into him deeply. "This way, Gabriel," he said. "We know why you have come."

Gabriel followed the Zoa through the veiled doorway and into the room from where the light had earlier shot forth. As he stepped in he could make out the silhouettes of three other figures, whose forms were darkened by the spectacular light which emblazoned from behind. He could not see their faces, although in the eerie light he could make out the eyes of the creatures—hundreds of them—staring at him through the darkness. He could no longer see the lion-faced Zoa who had ushered him in and had taken his place with the other three. Together with the four creatures he stood, waiting for permission to speak.

<hr />

Chronicles of the Host

First Contest

The stream of angels heading into the Academy seemed endless. Never before had a single event surrounding the school attracted so much attention. Not since the first day of the Creation had there been so much anticipation on the part of the Host regarding an occasion. All elements of the Host were represented, as wisdom, warrior and worship angels, alongside Elders and other high-ranking angels poured into the Great Hall of the Academy of Hosts to witness the debate between Pellecus and Crispin.

<hr />

The hall was filled with lively conversation as angels on different sides of the issue discussed the arguments in question. Some angels had no real opinion on the matter but sided with whichever teacher held the most credence with them. Many simply came to see Crispin bested at his own game, while others held this as an important occasion which might determine the future position of angels in Heaven.

The teachers at the Academy were thrilled with the possibility that the issue that was so dividing them might be finally brought to light. The debate was organized quickly and news spread so rapidly and so far that there was not an angel in the Kingdom who did not know about the scholarly confrontation.

Berenius and a group of angels loyal to Pellecus were quietly baiting some of the angels who were closely allied with Crispin and the more traditional doctrinaires of the Academy. They knew that they held a comfortable majority in the hall and were smug with confidence. Berenius had a special interest in seeing Crispin humbled once and for all. This would be a wonderful event.

"We shall see, dear Berenius, how well your opinions are represented by Pellecus," said Razon, a wisdom angel who was a disciple of Crispin. Some of the angels with him laughed. "I should not like to go up against Crispin!"

"My opinions mean nothing," answered Berenius. "Whatever Pellecus has to say represents a truth I have embraced. If you desire to continue in the old teachings of Crispin that is your course. I prefer to be enlightened."

"I prefer to be correct," answered Razon.

"Then in preferring Crispin you are neither enlightened nor correct, Razon," said Berenius, as he turned away to find his place in the gallery.

Pellecus entered from the rear of the platform and a tremendous cheer went up for him—Lucifer had made certain that those angels friendly to him were quite boisterous. Pellecus looked up at the howling angels and glanced over to the side where Lucifer stood chatting with Kara. Crispin had not yet entered. Lucifer walked over to Pellecus.

"This is your day, dear Pellecus," he said. "This is the time for you to shine as brightly as you ever have. I need not remind you that our cause is in your hands." He looked up at a group of angels who softly supported Crispin, and who were rather subdued. "There are many here who need convincing—just a little more and we shall have them. They don't realize that the world I offer is so much better. Do well, teacher." He put a hand on Pellecus' shoulder. "Do well and I promise you that I will make your name great on earth!"

Pellecus looked up at Lucifer and then indicated the noisy crowd. "Why must our angels be so...common?" he finally asked. "They are loud and brutish. Look at Berenius for example—leading that pack of unruly wisdom angels. Most of them are unfit to enter the Academy, much less sit in on an academic exercise such as this. They discredit the intellectual and philosophical impetus of our movement and of this debate. They are making it a spectacle rather than a discourse!"

Lucifer laughed a little as if in agreement. "Dear Pellecus, I am not interested in these angels being educated. I am interested in them being loyal. You are a teacher and as such want a stage, a platform from which to teach. That is well and good." He looked intently at him. "But the strength of this movement, as you call it, is not in doctrine or truth or myths. The strength of this liberation is me. It is I whom they follow—not a teaching. It is I who shall liberate them—not a doctrine. It is I who shall lead them to earth—not a philosophy. Those things are useful, in that they provide a reasoned justification—but they are merely a reference.

"Whoever follows a teaching may one day turn from it. Whoever finds freedom will never turn it loose. It is freedom that the angels seek—order and freedom is what I offer. And that, dear Pellecus, is why these brutish angels are cheering you on today. Be glad for Berenius—he is one of our most bright and shining stars. Therefore I say again, do well. These brutes will serve us one day."

Before Pellecus could answer another cheer went up, though not as noisy as the first, as Crispin entered and sat next to Pellecus on the platform. Crispin turned to embrace Pellecus, who nodded affably at him but refused the embrace. Crispin took his place next to him.

Lucifer walked to Kara, greeting angels as he went. Kara was talking to one of the Elders. Finally he turned to Lucifer, who gave him a familiar look.

"No, my lord," said Kara. "There has not been a word from the Zoa or any source as to the petition. However it has been introduced in the proper manner and now we must wait upon the Lord's timing."

"No matter," said Lucifer. "I must say though, it is one of the chief flaws of our Lord that He takes an interminable period of time in making up His mind. I promise you, Kara, I shall not rule like our Lord!"

"I hope that this was a good idea," Kara said, nervously looking around. "I don't trust Crispin. And where is Michael...and Gabriel? Surely they are attending such an important event."

"You worry far too much, Kara," purred Lucifer. "Michael will be here, I am sure...and wherever Michael is Gabriel won't be far behind. They'll be here, encouraging their dear Crispin. This is the chance for which so many have been waiting, Kara."

"Yes, I know," answered Kara. "I am ready to be done with it all. In my opinion this is not a good idea. Suppose Crispin is victorious? What happens should Pellecus falter in some way? We will be made to look ridiculous!"

"Then in humble attitude I will concede defeat," responded Lucifer, "while knowing that my destiny cannot be altered." Kara looked at him puzzled. "You see Kara, when one is confident of his destiny, one must not allow events to dissuade him from that eventuality. Whatever happens today will have no bearing on our designs. If Pellecus does well, then we will have convinced more angels to our side. If he does not do well, then we become a mere distraction in the eyes of those who are suspicious—a philosophical nuisance which will soon go away.

"So long as our plans proceed I have no care whether the angels take me seriously or not. It is in fact to our advantage to remain a hazy distraction rather than an obvious contender for the loyalty of others. Remember this, Kara—true power dictates events whether or not those being influenced are aware they are being manipulated. Win or lose this day, we continue on course. And our numbers continue to grow."

Kara began to say something but Lucifer held up his hand to stop him. "It is starting," he whispered.

+≡———————≡+

"You are certain Lucifer is at the Academy?" asked a very shaken Serus.

"Quite sure, Serus," answered Michael, who, knowing Lucifer's ability to show up unexpectedly, was himself looking about him. "Very well," said Serus. "But not here."

Serus led Michael away from Lucifer's house through the lush garden in the rear. They walked down a path past the many varieties of flowers and shrubs. Michael followed Serus a few paces to the rear. Serus stopped now and then to surmise the area, and then move on a bit further. Finally he found a place he deemed suitable and secure and motioned Michael to sit next to him in the soft grass. Michael obliged and waited an awkward moment or two for Serus to speak.

"I know what you and the others think of me," Serus began. "Please don't protest, Michael. I know. And it is for good reason that you think the way you do. I am not, after all, the most popular angel in the Host!" He laughed a slight laugh.

"Serus," Michael said. "Please don't..."

"Of course being in the service of the greatest angel in Heaven," he continued, then catching himself added, "apart from yourself of course, Michael..." Michael grinned. "...has its advantages. Advantages that help make up for the lack of fellowship with the other angels." He paused and added, "or so I thought."

Serus picked a flower and began plucking its petals off one by one. "You see Michael, I have always been somewhere to the rear of the ministries of the Host. It is quite true that I could have been a wisdom angel of great import—perhaps a teacher in the company of Crispin and Pellecus." He looked at the flower, now bare of all but a single petal. "But instead I wasted my time of preparation in petty grievances. I chose to be hurt and was passed over until I eventually was attached to the ministry of worship and soon found myself in Lucifer's service."

He motioned in the direction of the gigantic dwelling. "The finest angelic dwelling in Heaven and the most important angel of the Host. Who could not be satisfied to serve under such circumstances, hmm? It was a tempting offer, Michael. And one that made me feel that if I could not prove my merit on my own, then at least I should serve one whose merit I could benefit from. This was my thinking, Michael, when I entered the services of Lucifer. I found, however, that things are not often as satisfying as one might believe—even to the point of emptiness." He plucked the last petal off of the flower that he held and threw the bare stem away.

"Serus, you know that our Lord never abandoned you," Michael said tenderly. "Your place in the Host remains should you ever return to it. But you must return with complete confidence in our Lord's love and determination to obey Him. He is our Commander and we are His servants."

A look of stark fear came over Serus. "No. No, you must not say that," he said, looking around as if he was expecting someone to break into their private conversation at any moment. "I will never be able to leave Lucifer. Do you realize what he would do to me? Why, if he knew you and I were talking at this very minute..." He looked at Michael with renewed defiance. "I am bound to Lucifer as surely as you are bound to the service of the Most High." He looked to Michael for some sort of comfort...sense...reason...

"Serus. We serve different masters, you and I. I am bound to my Lord out of love. You are bound to yours out of fear. Yet I assure you that our Lord's love vastly outweighs whatever fear Lucifer might hold you with. Lucifer cannot really harm you except in your heart and mind. He holds no power over you except that which you allow him influence. Some of these angels who have taken to him have surrendered themselves to him...but it was their decision. Just as it is Lucifer's decision to..." He stopped himself and looked at Serus. "Why did you want to speak to me, Serus? It was not to reaffirm your service to Lucifer. Was it?"

"No," whispered Serus, who looked around the garden nervously. "It was to question it."

Chapter 12

"This nonsense has gone far enough, Lucifer!"

Gabriel could not make out the features of the four figures who stood before him. He only knew that they were extremely sacred to the Lord, giving off a purplish aura as he had never before seen on a creature in Heaven. He began to feel a little foolish as he stood there, wondering how to proceed. Suddenly the purple aura brightened and the faces of the four could be clearly seen. Gabriel recognized three of the faces as coming from creatures that God had recently created on the earth:

"Gabriel," said the beast with a face similar to other angels, "your task is not to question the ability of the Most High God to reign, but to serve Him in humility."

"Gabriel," sounded another beast, this one with the face of an eagle, "the Lord is well aware of the events unfolding in the Kingdom. It is not your place to prevent, but to believe."

"And," continued the man-faced creature, "allow the Most High in His wisdom to deal with all the affairs of this Kingdom forthrightly."

"For behold," added the creature with the face of a calf, "the time will come when all things will be made right; when all things will be exposed; there will be nothing hidden which shall not be made known. There is nothing unknown to the Most High."

Then in chorus the four creatures said, "So be it! Holy, Holy, Holy is the Lord God Almighty who was, and is, and is to come!"

Gabriel was overwhelmed by the presence of these beings whose ministry to the Lord brought them to His very presence. Still he needed to satisfy the questions that prompted the visit to the Zoa in the first place. Before he could ask, the calf-faced Zoa spoke:

"You may ask what you will, Gabriel," he said. "And without fear. For behold, the Lord Almighty is aware of who loves Him and who is obedient to His name."

"You have found favor in the sight of God," added the lion-face. "And He commends you for your passion and perseverance."

The silence that followed was awkward to Gabriel. He took it as his cue that now was the time to approach the Zoa with his questions. He began with a recount of all the recent events, from his initial conversation with Michael to the recommendation by the Elders of Lucifer to the Most High. As he concluded he added, "I know, lords, as you have spoken, that nothing escapes the Most High. I know that none of the events that have unfolded and as I have relayed to you are unknown to you. That He will indeed prevail, we know. What we don't understand and must know...forgive me...what we desire to understand is, where is the Lord throughout all of this? At what point does He prevail before too much damage is done?"

"You seek answers, Gabriel, and that is good," spoke the man-faced creature. "And you attribute to us knowledge which is beyond us. Indeed we sit at the very throne of the Most High God. But we, like you, are merely creatures whose task is to worship the Lord God and to serve Him."

"We do not understand the mysteries of God," said the eagle-faced Zoa. "No creature can ever attain the knowledge of its Creator."

"This then is the error of Lucifer," said the calf-faced Zoa. "He has indeed transgressed the boundaries of his creaturehood and is assuming truths that are his alone, while attributing them to a more enlightened interpretation of the sacred teachings."

"Knowledge apart from the Holy One is presumption, Gabriel," said the man-faced Zoa. "Those who would presume upon the Lord's knowledge must also be prepared for the consequences of such a presumption."

"But that is exactly our concern," said Gabriel. "It seems, lords, that the Most High is distant from this dark affair. Where are the consequences of such blatantly arrogant behavior? Law we know exists in Heaven—but where is order?"

"The law, Gabriel, is within your heart," said the lion-faced one. "The Most High has created the Host with the capacity to choose freely to obey Him, just as He will create man with freedom to choose him as well. (This was the first use of the word *man* that Gabriel had encountered.)

"Man?" asked Gabriel, his curiosity overcoming his discretion.

"Yes, Gabriel, man—who will inhabit the earth in the name and authority of the Most High God. To man the Lord will give stewardship and dominion. With man he will have fellowship and enjoy holy communion. Earth is to be a place where the Lord will inhabit the very praises of man, and man will in turn worship God in the beauty of a perfect world."

Gabriel could not help but think of all the efforts of Lucifer. "And what of the idea that an angel might rule over earth in the Lord's name?" he asked timidly.

"Earth is not for angels," said the eagle-faced Zoa emphatically. "The Host have a home and a ministry here in the Kingdom God has created for them. No, Gabriel, earth is for men. Not angels. Earth shall be ruled by men. Not angels."

"But Lucifer..." began Gabriel.

"Lucifer will not rule earth, nor shall any angel rule on earth. Earth shall be stewarded by men. Earth is not a completely spiritual world—it is also a material world. God in His wisdom shall create a being who is both physical and metaphysical—a material being with an immortal spirit. Angels, Gabriel, have no place in such a world—at least not in the capacity which Lucifer envisions."

"But what will Lucifer's response be when he discovers all of this?" asked Gabriel. "He shall be devastated."

"I am sure you will do well in telling him, Gabriel."

"What do you mean, lord?" asked a grim-faced Gabriel.

"Naturally, as Messenger to the Kingdom, when the time comes you shall carry the news. Lucifer will hear and understand on that day. How he reacts only the Most High would know. But that will be the choice and responsibility of Lucifer alone. Your duty however is not to Lucifer, but to the Most High."

"Then tell him I will, when the time comes," Gabriel responded. "But from a distance I hope, my lords, from a distance." He smiled.

And suddenly they were gone.

Gabriel was very much alone. He was also surprised to find himself in one of the outer courts again. He looked about himself dazed and drained from the experience. He thought about the encounter as he walked through the complex. The message was both clear and puzzling at the same time—but the indication was that come what may the Lord would prevail. It hit Gabriel swiftly.

Of course! Of course the Lord will prevail, he thought to himself. *How very weak was the faith of those who were attempting to protect the interests of the Lord! We must not question the Lord's wisdom in this but draw back and allow Him to work! And what an inspired work of creation man would be!*

Gabriel sensed a liberty he had not sensed in some time since dealing with the whole Lucifer question. No angel can hope to compare himself with the Lord's ability to handle any situation. The Zoa had prudently but decisively rebuked him in this regard. The task of the creature was to depend upon the Creator—to follow His instructions and not question the circumstances. From this point forward they must trust fully in the Lord's ability and wisdom! The weight of the burden suddenly shifted from angel to the Maker of angels as Gabriel, refreshed from the meeting, fell to his knees and began to worship the Most High with a freedom he had never known before.

+≍——————≍+

The discourse between Pellecus and Crispin was to be a scholarly presentation of viewpoints. There was to be some limited debate, but mainly the idea was to clarify the major issues of contention, chief of which were the ideas of freedom and responsibility in the Host. Polias, the librarian of the Hall of Record, was chosen to mediate the event. He now took center stage as the hall became very quiet.

"*Brothers! Greetings to you in the name of the Most High God, praise forever unto His name!*"

The crowd responded, "So be it forever unto the Lord!"

While Polias went on, Lucifer scanned the hall. He watched as Gabriel entered the rear. He was obviously looking for someone. *Michael, no doubt*, Lucifer thought to himself. Kara also was watching for Michael, who had not as yet appeared, and then glanced at Lucifer to see if he had noticed Gabriel enter. Lucifer indicated that he had seen him. Gabriel finally settled himself near the doorway and focused on Polias' opening statement.

"*...thus it behooves us, who are the custodians of the great and eternal knowledge of the Most High God, to responsibly dispense such knowledge...*"

Lucifer ambled over to Kara. "Polias always did like a platform—he should have been given more opportunity to speak in the past so his present ramblings might be more tolerable."

"Polias is a fool," Kara responded, still watching Gabriel. "But Gabriel is not."

"Ah, Gabriel," said Lucifer. "Our dear friend...archangel and chief Messenger to the Kingdom. Sometimes, Kara, one can be so close to the source of truth that one misses it. Gabriel has no idea of the events that will soon overtake him. Never fear." He stared long and hard at Gabriel, noticing something about his appearance—a look of vitality and freshness as he had never seen before. "Does he look somehow different to you?"

As they spoke, Pratia, another of the Elders friendly to Lucifer, came up to Kara and whispered. Kara's eyes shifted to Lucifer as Pratia spoke and then, after a brief, friendly exchange with Lucifer, slightly bowed his head and walked away. Kara looked carefully around to make certain that those around them were listening to the droning of Polias, and then spoke in hushed tones to Lucifer.

"Pratia tells me that Gabriel just returned from the Temple complex—not the Host Temple, mind you—the Temple on the Mount."

"And?" asked Lucifer. "What are we to infer from this visit?"

"Well, one might assume that an announcement of some importance is forthcoming," said Kara. "But the fact is that Gabriel entered the complex unannounced—he was not summoned—and that goes against all protocol and tradition."

"And how do we know this?" asked Lucifer, mildly concerned but collected.

"Because Pratia has been engaged by me to make certain of Gabriel's activities and movements," Kara answered, rather proudly. "*Your* angels are not the only ears in Heaven, my lord. Also the Temple warden is, as you know, favorably disposed to joining us one day on earth. He gave the information to Pratia."

"Oh yes, Kreelor, the Temple steward," remarked Lucifer. "One of the most prattling angels in Heaven—perfectly suited to his task—which as Temple warden does not entail very much at all!"

"Nevertheless if Gabriel did in fact have conversation with someone at the Temple we must know if at all possible the nature of the conversation," Kara said.

"*And therefore, brother angels, it is with great anticipation that we meet together—not as feuding brothers—but as truth seekers...not as angels in conflict but as fellow travelers on an academic excursion...*"

"That would be up to you to discover then, Kara," said Lucifer, "you being the sympathetic advisor for Gabriel and his group. But since all of the important angels are *here* I must believe that he sought an audience with the Zoa."

"That would not be good," said Kara, himself considering the possibility.

"All the more reason why you must find out with whom he spoke," said Lucifer.

"The Zoa are incredibly loyal to the Most High and will never turn from Him. I must however believe that their reputation for wisdom is exaggerated."

"How so?" asked Kara.

"Because, Kara," Lucifer continued, "if the Zoa were truly these curiously bizarre and completely wise creatures they would have been aware long before now and we ourselves would have been summoned. The fact that Gabriel went begging to them for information tells me that our movements are unknown in even the highest circles." Lucifer smiled and added, "Ignorance under the very Throne, Kara. I rather wonder sometimes how our Lord maintains that Throne with such colossal ignorance in support of it." Lucifer saw Gabriel walking in his line of vision over and behind Kara's left shoulder. "Nevertheless, caution is always the byword. Investigate this at once and find out what information was exchanged with the Zoa. We must know."

"Agreed," said Kara, as they both turned to listen to Polias' concluding remarks.

"And now we come to the event itself. May the Most High receive all of the glory and honor from these proceedings...may His truth prevail as always...and may we leave here as we came—brothers of the Host, servants of God, one in mind, one in action!"

Michael didn't know what to think about Serus. The angel seemed contrite enough, even pitiable. Yet there was something that Michael did not trust about him. Perhaps the long association with Lucifer had so damaged his credibility that Michael could not see clearly. He wanted to be fair with Serus if this was a true repentance. Yet Serus still displayed the old defiance from time to time, especially where Lucifer was personally mentioned.

"What exactly do you find yourself questioning, Serus?" asked Michael. "I mean about your service to Lucifer?"

Serus looked about him nervously, as if unseen assailants were closing in upon him. Michael looked around again, alert to any presence around him but sensing none. He looked quizzically at Serus, who began speaking in hushed tones.

"I believe in Lucifer, Michael," he began. "I believe that he is the greatest angel in Heaven. I believe that the Most High created him for great and holy service. I believe that he is called the Anointed Cherub because the Lord has lavished upon him a special grace in the Kingdom. I believe that the Lord Himself could only surpass his music. I believe that his destiny is assured and that the Lord created him perfect in all of his ways. And yet," he remarked as he looked at Michael intently, "the Lucifer I just described and the Lucifer whom I serve are two different creatures."

"How so, Serus?" Michael asked almost tenderly.

"You knew Lucifer when he was different, Michael. You knew him before his heart began to change. I began serving him after he began to withdraw from the fellowship of the angels. Even so Michael, I have seen his demeanor change even more drastically—especially in the recent past."

"Since the Creation?" asked Michael.

"No. The Creation merely fits nicely into his plans," said Serus. "I refer to the time you were named archangel. Since that appointment was made Lucifer has been determined to make a name for himself which is greater than any other name—save the Most High's of course."

"Lucifer jealous?" said Michael almost laughing. "The Anointed Cherub jealous of me? That's absurd!"

"Nevertheless true," said Serus. "And of Gabriel. Do you recall when you saw me walking to the Elders with the music for Gabriel's installation? You were with Gabriel at the time."

"Ah yes," said Michael. "I do remember that because I was upset with the meeting I had just had with Lucifer."

"Well, that was not the only meeting held at the time," Serus remarked.

"Oh really?" asked Michael.

Despite his personal fears, Serus was enjoying the interview. Here he was—an angel of no reputation holding the attention of the archangel Michael. Lucifer had often said that words were the most powerful weapon one could use when used with discretion. Now he was proving Lucifer right.

"Yes, Michael," he answered proudly. "I convened on behalf of Lucifer a meeting of the Council of Worship shortly after

Gabriel's ceremony. And there were some very interesting words exchanged at that meeting."

"Such as…?" Michael responded.

"Mainly they were talking about the Most High," Serus said. "Mind you although I am intimate with Lucifer I am seldom included in the meetings. I just know that a couple of the angels were offended by their manner toward the Lord."

"Was Sangius one of them?" asked Michael.

"Why yes," Serus remarked with a bemused look. "How did you know?"

"He came to me, Serus," said Michael. "And told me why he had been asked to leave the Council."

Serus smiled, remembering that he had secretly listened to the conversation in the Grand Square. "Oh yes! I recall that. Sangius never did see things the way Lucifer did. He's not at all like the others on that Council—brutal, proud and blindly loyal to Lucifer. I must say I honor him for standing up to Lucifer as he did—though as you say, it cost him his seat in the Council as well as, I understand, some trouble in the Temple services."

Serus shook his head in disbelief. "And now I am to understand he is to be named the steward of the earth? Well that is what he has been after. I pity the creatures on that world if he administers earth in the same manner in which he treats the Council!"

"He has not been named yet," said Michael. "The Elders have only sought to recommend him to the Lord."

"The Elders! Michael, do you realize the extent of Lucifer's influence?" said Serus, shaking again in fear. "I was so ashamed for Heaven the day they all arrived and Kara made his announcement—as if Lucifer was hearing it all for the very first time. He is the most cunning creature in Heaven."

"Serus," Michael said. "Lucifer assured me that he was hearing these things for the first time that day. Are you telling me that Kara is with Lucifer in all of this?"

"Of course," said Serus. "Kara has always loved Lucifer. But from a distance. He sees in Lucifer a possibility for advancement—nothing more. That is the extent of most of the love held for our dear worship minister!"

Michael began to replay in his mind the many confidences he and the others had shared with Kara. How stupid of them! They might as well have had Lucifer in on the meetings, too. He would deal with Kara when the time came!

"I know that you are wrestling with yourself as to which master you should serve, the one who holds you now, or the one who never really let you go. The Lord Most High has never abandoned you. He has never abandoned even Lucifer, although it sometimes seems that Lucifer has abandoned Him. But that is between Him and Lucifer. Serus, what about you? Will you allow Lucifer to take you with him into this foregone catastrophe? He cannot win against the Lord—you know this."

Serus looked at Michael and smiled a forced sort of smile—a consigned look upon his face. "Don't you see it is too late for me?" he said. "Me and the others who have fallen in with Lucifer. I know, Michael, that you would say it is not too late. There are some angels who have thrown in with Lucifer completely—particularly those whom he has appointed leaders. And there are some angels who have crossed over with Lucifer who really don't understand why."

He sighed. "And there is me...caught in the middle, Michael—too afraid to leave Lucifer and too ashamed to come back to the Most High. I don't deserve the mercy of the Lord, Michael. That is why I choose to remain with Lucifer and suffer whatever fate befalls him, which I know I deserve equally."

"Serus, you can still turn to the Most High. You don't have to fall with Lucifer."

"Michael," Serus responded. "I have fallen already."

The hush that fell over the crowded hall at the Academy after Polias' introductory remarks was in sharp contrast with the chatter of the previous moment. All eyes were upon the two presenters—Pellecus and Crispin. Though no one outwardly admitted it, the debate was a microcosm of the larger disturbances that had taken

Heaven's center stage. Doctrinal differences were not what was being contested here. This was a preview of the coming conflict—a referendum on the recent movements by Lucifer and his group of angels. Thus did Lucifer whisper to Pellecus, "There is more at stake here than academic pride—remember that and do well."

Both of the esteemed angels were allowed an opening statement that was to be followed by free debate between the two. Polias was to be the coordinator—a task not relished by many who knew the potential liveliness of the coming discourse. The gallery would then be allowed to ask questions as well. Crispin looked to the crowded room but saw fewer friendly faces than he had anticipated.

"Counting heads, brother?" asked a very calm looking Pellecus.

Crispin looked at Pellecus and said in good humor and loud enough for all to hear, "If these angels are an indication of the power of your teaching, dear Pellecus, I may indeed be in trouble!"

The room broke out in nervous laughter.

Pellecus was amused. "True teaching always makes an impact."

Some of the angels in the hall burst out in support of Pellecus— some even jeered Crispin, taunting him as he sat stone-faced. Gabriel read in Crispin's face a sure retort and waited for him to speak. Lucifer too waited for the response.

"True teaching does indeed make an impact. But teaching truth makes a difference," said Crispin in an offhanded way.

Crispin's supporters, though outnumbered, applauded loudly.

"I teach truth, Crispin. Something that the Academy has long forgotten how to do effectively." Pellecus smiled at Crispin, who returned the smile, albeit with difficulty.

"Brothers! Please!" interrupted Polias. "May we get to the issues at hand before we start debating more personal items!"

Crispin rose to speak. He nodded at Polias. He then turned toward Pellecus and indicated a curt acknowledgment. Finally he surveyed the host surrounding him—a mixture of friends and antagonists, and began speaking with the demeanor that made him a legend at the Academy.

"Dear colleagues, brothers, honored ones and of course, my worthy opponent. What a delight to appear before you in such a setting. Where else could you expect to learn from the two finest teachers in Heaven than in this very room at this very moment!?" The hall exploded with laughter.

"One fine teacher at least," interjected Pellecus to the delight of the crowd.

Crispin laughed and gave Pellecus a "well said" sort of look and then continued. "In all seriousness, these issues which Pellecus and I will touch on today are critical to the knowledge of all angels. Critical to the extent that there are some who might take issue with the sacred teachings and so redefine them that they are no longer sacred. When one takes the sacred and profanes it, however noble the intent, one places that which was sacred into the dangerous position of becoming irrelevant and the personal tool of individual angels."

Gabriel shot a glance at Lucifer, who remained fixed on Crispin. Kara too glanced casually at Lucifer and then returned his eyes to the dais.

"I submit rather, that these doctrines are for the community of Heaven—which I believe is what the Most High intended them to be. We teachers at the Academy have been given the honorable task of teaching the Host the mysteries of God!" He laughed a little. "Not of course that a mere angel could know anything about the Most High save what He has revealed to us, but that is beside the point. Such as He has revealed, so are we responsible to teach and adhere to." This last statement he made forcefully to the delight of Gabriel and the others attending him.

"Now all of us here know that the Academy is a place where angelic ministry and service to the Most High is taught and learned. The whole reason for the existence of the Academy of the Host is to instruct angels in service to the Most High. All of you at one time or another have been through the Academy, and one day every angel in Heaven will have entered its doors. Why? Because the Most High God is pleased to share with us a very small portion of His knowledge. And I say praised be His name for that!"

The room broke out in applause. Clapping himself, Lucifer looked around at the angels, and sensed the charged atmosphere. He whispered to Kara, "These posturing angels! This could go either way today but don't worry. Nothing can interfere with the course we are on."

"At this event we are here primarily to discuss the issue of freedom and choice among the Host," continued Crispin. "I know many of you will be delighted to finally have opportunity to bring me to book...eh, Berenius?"

Many angels laughed as they looked at Berenius. For his part Berenius merely smiled at Crispin and nodded in agreement. "Depends upon the book, dear master," Berenius replied, to the delight of the crowd. Crispin laughed heartily.

"Well said, well said." He cast a serious look over the crowd. "Now, there has been a school of thought which has surfaced from time to time since we were first created. You all know to what I refer. Nevertheless for the sake of the argument, I will outline briefly the position of the Academy in terms of its traditional teaching, and Pellecus will give you the...what version shall you give today, Pellecus?"

"The correct one," Pellecus replied and smiled at Crispin.

"Oh yes, the enlightened version," Crispin said. "I do hope we will be enlightened."

"It would be refreshing, dear Crispin," Pellecus answered.

The angels in the gallery were thoroughly enjoying this duel of wits. Excitement swept the room with angel speaking to angel in hushed delight. For his part, Gabriel was only here to observe and support his friend. He found it difficult to follow the proceeding, however, because he was still basking mentally in his visit to the Zoa.

He watched Lucifer, who stood on the other side of the room next to Kara. The Zoa were completely certain that Lucifer would not be allowed personal authority on earth. Was it because of the way he had gone about it all? Or was there perhaps a greater plan unknown to all—even to the Zoa—something the Most High was holding in reserve for Creation's last and most pronounced act? He wondered about Lucifer's ambitions—what was driving him to make such an effort? And what would his reaction be when he discovered that for all his maneuvers he would not govern earth? What about all those angels to whom Lucifer had reportedly promised positions of authority in his new realm? Gabriel was amused at the prospect that he might be defending Lucifer soon from avenging angels who felt deceived and manipulated.

Gabriel looked over the crowded hall. *How many of these angels are aware of the extent of this drama that is being played out in Heaven's most sacred chambers?* he wondered. Though the Elders had decided upon the nomination of Lucifer as steward, many did so with an attitude of "better to do so and keep peace in Heaven."

But at what price? There were only a few dissenting voices in that body and they had been reduced to mere distractions by the determined majority. He wondered what the Host would think if they knew that their leader of praises, the Anointed Cherub, was using his high office for personal satisfaction and that the Elders were, wittingly or unwittingly, carrying him forward. It was unheard of and vile.

Yet the Zoa had urged caution. They had insisted that the Lord Most High had all under control and would in His timing deal with everything. Gabriel could not help but reflect upon how he or Michael or even Crispin might have dealt with Lucifer—with haste and great recklessness no doubt. How truly magnificent the Most High must be to endure such events with such patience and longsuffering—always knowing that an unpleasant conclusion awaited those who opposed His will!

***

"Now if I understand correctly," Crispin continued, "the point of this discussion centers on the idea of freedom and responsibility to the Lord Most High. I have heard it argued countless ways in the classroom—especially of late. But all of the questions essentially are born out of one: Does an angel have the ability to choose freely? Now this carries with it two subsequent ideas. If the answer is yes, then at what point does an angel transgress the lines of loyalty and become opposed to the will of the Most High? And if the answer is no, then what are we doing here?"

The room exploded with laughter.

"I mean, if we have no choices in what we do and who we are then how did we arrive here at a point where we have chosen two courses of very opposing thoughts? No brothers, the obvious solution is that we have choices and rights of choice given to us by the Most High, and that bears with it much responsibility. It also represents an incredible risk on the part of the Creator—risk that those whom He has created might go their own way—even outright oppose Him. It is therefore a great act of love and faith on the part of our Lord that He allows us such freedom of action!"

Crispin began walking the platform as he spoke. "But there are far more disturbing issues involved in all of this. Freedom and choice are simple matters of reality. The darker side of this becomes what an angel might do with such freedom and so many choices. I submit that we serve the Lord as a decision of our wills—not out of compulsion—but out of intention. And I further submit that any angel might—if he so chooses—turn from the Lord Most High and not serve Him. It's really all a matter of your choice and my choice.

"Now I have anticipated some of your questions, chiefly the idea that if an angel can oppose the will of God, what does that say about God's ability to control His creation? There are some who believe that our Lord sleeps—that they can go about their dark excursions —if such excursions exist—and the Lord will only blink an eye. Others maintain that because the Lord Most High is a God of perfect order, the risk of a chaotic conflict in Heaven would force a compromise rather than risk disorder. Let me assure my brethren that our Lord neither sleeps nor compromises!"

The room erupted in enthusiastic applause. Lucifer was unsettled inwardly but maintained a casual interest in appearance. Kara whispered to him that Crispin was certainly performing well, to which Lucifer returned an angry glare.

"Nevertheless, freedom is not to be taken lightly, my brothers. The choice to love and serve the Lord is the most noble choice we can make. But…it is not the only choice. When we do choose to serve Him, we do so for our love for Him, not because we are forced by some inherent nature to do so. Nor because we are created in slavery…."

Lucifer could hear some of the very dialog from his Council discussions being attacked point by point. He felt that Crispin was directing this line of reasoning at him personally. "I blame myself for this, Kara," Lucifer whispered. "I should never have permitted Sangius in the Council. I thought his weakness would serve me, not betray me!" Kara nodded in agreement as they continued listening.

"Do angels then, by their submission to the Lord, cause the Kingdom to remain orderly? Such nonsense! I maintain that even should every angel in Heaven march to the very Throne and state their opposition to the Lord, and threaten violent overthrow of the Kingdom, the Lord would merely shake His head in wonder that creatures would ever presume upon their Creator. No brothers, Heaven is not maintained by the obedience of angels, but by the steadfastness of our Lord. And it is in giving us these freedoms that the Most High demonstrates His omnipotence—that is, brothers, He not only gives us the choice to serve Him, but can deal with those who would not!"

Crispin sat down to a roar of applause from his students. Many of his colleagues in the Academy also burst out in joyful uproar. Pellecus took his place at the dais and the room once more was quiet. He looked at Crispin and said in a humorous vein, "Well done, angel! You are a very credible proponent of your viewpoints. It is unfortunate that your viewpoints are not credible!" Some of the angels howled with delight as Pellecus then began in earnest to present his case. Crispin laughed as hard as anyone at Pellecus' remarks.

Pellecus looked sharp and ready. Lucifer felt better knowing that a friendly gallery often yields positive results. He hoped Pellecus was at his best. Crispin was a worthy adversary—particularly in these settings. Lucifer leaned into Kara and said, "Angels are so easily swayed—particularly if the argument is concise and sensible. Now we shall see a true master at work and I guarantee, Kara, we shall leave here more greatly supported than when we arrived. Michael will regret ever having suggested this debate!"

"Dear brothers—I may still call you that, may I not?—even though in its wisdom the Academy has sought to keep me out of these chambers! As you can see, and to prove Crispin's well made point concerning choice, I have chosen to come back!"

Laughter and howling among the angels erupted as Polias sought to regain control. "Please brothers! Order!"

"Thank you, dear Polias," Pellecus continued. "Such disorder in such a sacred place! It seems, Crispin, that because these angels choose to be noisy rather than remain bound by tradition, they create disorder in an ordered environment! How like the scenario you painted." He looked accusingly at Crispin. "You have me dangling chaos in the face of the Most High in order to achieve some wicked goal. I tell you that true freedom is not chaotic as long as it is not unrestrained. You accuse myself and others of being totally without discipline, as if we were wild, raving angels set loose on an unsuspecting Heaven in order to promote chaos! That is preposterous! Do you sincerely believe that we have no restraint? No ability to refrain from excess? That is an insult to every angel who loves freedom and wishes to advance the Kingdom!"

Lucifer was delighted with Pellecus. "He is making Crispin look like an absolute fool," he said to Kara. "How embarrassed I would be if I was a teacher at this Academy!"

"However, let me address those concerns later, " Pellecus went on. "For now I wish only to portray a true picture of what I am advocating. Dear brothers, I am not promoting any action that goes against the sacred teachings given to us from the very hand of God. We live in concert with those laws. In the entire span of the creation of the angels until now there has never been even a hint of a rebellious action taken by an angel. I do not advocate such action."

"So what are you advocating, dear Pellecus?" asked Crispin. "If the astonishingly poor attitude I have witnessed in my classroom of late does not smack of a rebellious spirit, then what have I witnessed?"

"Something you have not witnessed for some time at the Academy, Crispin," said Pellecus. "Thinking. True thought. And to one who fears thinking, new ideas might appear as rebellious. You are witness to freedom."

"Freedom? Freedom from what?" asked Crispin.

"From...forgive me, Crispin...tiresome presentations of the Lord's teachings to angels," replied Pellecus. "You seem to forget, Crispin, that our Lord's words are living, vital and therefore fluid. You make no provision for the possibility that the Most High expects us to think through what He has taught us and to make application as needed."

"As needed? By whom?!" asked Crispin loudly. "By you? Must we apply the honored tradition of God's holy law of Heaven to your academic whims? Or to the dubious ambitions of other angels?" (He suppressed the temptation to look at Lucifer as he spoke these words.) "Of course we are to reason...to think. But within the parameters of truth—not outside of its scope."

"Truth has no parameters, Crispin. What you call parameters I call chains! Are you so miniscule in your scholarship that you cannot realize the depth of our Lord and that His words have no parameters? So vast is His mind, that His truth is unending, ever evolving. I choose to progress, Crispin, and so teach along those lines of progression."

"And what do you teach, Pellecus?" said Crispin. "Please enlighten us. What is it that you, and other highly placed angels so strongly advocate?"

"Merely this. Our Lord is much greater than you give Him credit, Crispin. You and these other teachers act as if He must be protected—surrounded by a sacred shell that somehow preserves His integrity. How dare you!? How dare you intimate that our God—who is even now creating a vast and varied new universe—must be represented by your narrow view? I suggest, Crispin, that our Lord is bigger even than the Academy—and therefore can be represented in many ways!"

"But where is truth in all of this?!" demanded Crispin. "If you or I decide to teach some pet doctrine we will always find a way to justify its existence. So long as there is no permanent basis of truth—something binding and eternal—then all else drifts and obscures truth! I could teach that Lucifer is God and many might believe! I beg your pardon, Lucifer, for the illustration!" Crispin said, bowing slightly to Lucifer.

"Quite alright, dear teacher," said Lucifer, uncomfortable at being drawn into the discussion in such terms. "It is the greatest promotion I have ever had!" The room filled with laughter.

"But," continued Crispin, "eventually truth will reveal that great as he is, Lucifer is not God...nor you...nor I."

"What is your point?!" shouted someone from the gallery in the area where Berenius was seated. Several angels echoed the words.

"My point? That truth is not something to be played with and tossed about and changed with every idle thought—truth is rooted ultimately in the Most High!"

"I am not questioning the origin of truth," said Pellecus. "Only your stagnant claim upon it!"

"I claim nothing save loyalty to the teachings of the Most High God!" shouted Crispin. "It is you and your teaching that is bringing disgrace to the Host!"

The crowd was getting tense as Pellecus and Crispin began raising their voices and gesturing with great emotion. The tension spilled out into the gallery as angels took sides and began arguing back and forth.

"I bring disgrace?" retorted Pellecus. "It is your antiquated teachings which bring disgrace, Crispin. You have lost the ability to think clearly and therefore forfeit the right to interpret the sacred teachings!"

"And you have so interpreted the sacred teachings that you have forfeited the ability to think clearly—your eyes have been veiled, Pellecus, by something dark!"

With that the room exploded. Some angels stood as if ready to fight, while others watched in amazement. Everyone was shouting. Berenius was leading a section of angels across the room, verbally attacking those who opposed Pellecus. Lucifer was delighted with the scene. Kara tried to regain some order but was shouted down.

Even Gabriel, who flew above it all and shouted for the angels to calm down, seemed unable to stop the uproar.

"This has been a long time in coming," said Lucifer to Kara. "Our side is passionate and willing to fight if they must! This bodes well."

"Lucifer, we must put a stop to this!" said Kara. "This is the end!"

"No, it's the beginning," said Lucifer, intoxicated by what he saw. "Angels in disorder—this, Kara, is exactly what the Lord will do anything to prevent. And this is only on a small scale! Picture such chaos Kingdom-wide. The Lord will not abide such a display of His inability to maintain control in general. Should it come to this He will compromise." Kara had stopped listening to Lucifer and was trying to arrest two angels who were starting to grapple with one another.

On stage Pellecus and Crispin were seated, silently watching the disarray. Crispin was horrified at the scene. He finally shouted to Pellecus, "This is what your teaching begets, Pellecus! Angel against angel!"

"Wrong, Crispin! You are witnessing the unleashing of freedom!" yelled Pellecus.

"Freedom!" Crispin said. "If this is the freedom you advocate let me remain a slave!" He walked off the stage and exited out a rear doorway.

Everywhere angels were involved in conflict. Polias was completely panicked. Some angels were arguing passionately while others were actually sparring. Some were in the aisles while others had taken flight and were battling in the air above the crowd. Gabriel was holding two wisdom angels apart. Kara found himself in the middle of the room helpless. And Lucifer drank it all in with satisfaction. He approached Pellecus.

"You see, Pellecus, how base angels are," he said. "They are so easily agitated. This will prove to our advantage should it be necessary to display force! Well done!"

"Thank you, lord, but I am not sure I made my point today," said Pellecus.

"Perhaps not, dear Pellecus," answered Lucifer, surveying the chaotic room. "But you made mine!"

Suddenly the doors burst open and a great shaft of greenish-blue light filled the room, casting its color on every face. In the light a silhouette could be made out. Whispers of "Michael" could be heard as the room quickly quieted down. Lucifer watched as Michael entered the room, envious of the respect this one angel commanded. Angels cleared a path as the archangel walked to the center of the room. All knew that the only time Michael's aura shone was when he was extremely provoked. Lucifer was curious as to how he would handle this.

Lucifer walked over to Michael and began to speak. "I was just about to put an end to this, Michael," he said. "It seems the discussion was a little more heated than we anticipated."

Michael either ignored or didn't hear Lucifer. He simply stood and looked at the angels around him, his aura slowly ebbing. Gabriel joined him and did not say a word. Finally Michael spoke loudly:

"Such a display! What has happened to us? Never before have I seen such an ugly and brutal side of this Host! You should all be utterly ashamed...."

As he spoke a thunderous noise filled the room followed by a crimson aura. Many angels were knocked aside as the reddish light streaked into the room and surrounded Lucifer. From out of this shell of light (which quickly disappeared) stepped three angels. It was Rugio and his two closest warriors, swords drawn. The three warriors pushed the angels closest to Lucifer away from him and set up a parameter around him. Michael was disturbed by this intrusion and looked hard into Rugio's eyes. Rugio returned the stare defiantly, holding onto his sword.

"Ah, thank you, Rugio," Lucifer said calmly, "but as you can see all is well here. The archangel, as always, has things in hand."

"You have trained him well," said Michael, still staring into Rugio's proud eyes. "However, Rugio, in the future you will remember that you are under my authority and not Lucifer's. You should have been here to keep the peace when this nonsense started."

"I'm sorry, lord Michael, " said Rugio, urged on by Lucifer from behind. "I came to assist you if need be. And here I am."

"Hmmm. Very well." Michael turned to the room and shouted, "These proceedings are closed. Now go...and repent of this ugly episode. Go!"

The angels filed out of the hall and soon the room was empty except for Michael, Gabriel, Lucifer, Kara, Pellecus and Rugio and his two warriors. Polias was also in the room waiting his turn to speak with the archangel. Michael walked past Gabriel directly to Lucifer and began speaking.

"How did this happen, Lucifer?" he asked calmly.

"Well, Michael, it appears that angels are willing to fight for what they believe," answered a rather smug Lucifer. He looked into Michael's eyes and said, "I am not responsible for this."

"I'm afraid that I am the culprit," said Pellecus, "or rather Crispin and myself. "You see, Michael, the discussion got a little involved and, well, soon the whole room was participating in the...discussion."

"I see. And you, Kara—a respected Elder!" Michael recalled his prior conversation with Serus that had revealed Kara's definite sympathies for Lucifer. "Why didn't you attempt to stop this?"

"Don't accuse me, Archangel!" said Kara. "I jumped in the middle of the brawl. Why not quiz your fellow archangel—he was as ineffective as any of us."

Gabriel remained silent.

"Perhaps this illustrates in a small way how a group of determined angels can upset the balance of things," said Lucifer. "A disturbing thought really, Michael. Something we should take up officially one day—you being responsible for order in the Kingdom and all."

"Do you realize what has occurred?" said Michael, upset once more. "A division among the Host! This nonsense has gone far enough, Lucifer. It stops now!"

"I have no arguments in Heaven," said Lucifer. "As far as the division of the Host, however, I believe it runs far more deep and wide than you realize. And I believe it has existed for a very long time. The fault does not lie with me. I suggest you search in much loftier places in Heaven for your answers."

Michael ignored Lucifer's snide comment. "If a breech has occurred in the Host, then we in authority must do what we can to mend the breech," said Michael. "A divided Host cannot possibly serve the Most High or honor Him."

Michael looked at Rugio once more. "Rugio, never again draw your sword in my presence, for on that day I will see you cast down!" Michael turned and left, followed by Gabriel and a stammering, apologetic Polias.

"I will see him cast down one day," said Rugio, replacing his sword. The other warriors attending him did the same.

"One day you will have that opportunity, Rugio," said Lucifer. "One day we will all witness the collapse of Michael and his righteous troop! But it will not be on his terms—it will be on ours. Such arrogance these angels display! Kara, you must talk with them and discover whatever Gabriel was doing at the Temple complex. Go now!"

Kara hesitated. "That might not be wise," he said. "Michael is rather put out with me. I believe he suspects something that might prove an imposition to me."

"If we don't discover what he knows it will be an imposition for all of us," said Lucifer, whose tone had a terminal ring to it. "All of us."

Kara said nothing, but acknowledged Lucifer's serious assessment. He nodded in agreement and disappeared, taking flight after Michael and Gabriel.

"Michael is correct about one thing," said Pellecus. "The house is divided. Two distinct camps are emerging."

"As it should be," said Lucifer. "The prophecy foretold it. However, we will have to have a credible show of support to succeed— particularly if the Most High needs added convincing. The fact that holy angels were actually fighting means we have cut a deep swath in the Host. I find these independent rumblings encouraging."

"And the fact that so many exalted angels were unable to contain the fighting is also encouraging," added Pellecus. "Only Michael was able to stop the nonsense—and that by his mere presence."

"Yes," said Lucifer. "I saw that, of course. His presence swept the room like incense sweeping through the Temple." He turned to Rugio. "It would be to our advantage that when the day of true battle occurs, Michael is not present."

"I understand, " said Rugio, patting his sword. "I will see to it personally!"

CHAPTER 13

"Was it really from this position all of Heaven was to quake?"

Michael and Gabriel stood near a cascading brook under a large flowering tree not far from the Academy. They said little as the throng of angels leaving the disastrous debate continued walking by. When it was evident they were quite alone Michael looked at Gabriel and spoke.

"Quite an academic exercise, hmm?"

Gabriel looked at him and smiled. "You mean an academic battlefield," he said. "That was not a discourse but a deliberate testing of the Host by Lucifer—and we actually abetted him in this. Shameful!"

"Even more shameful that we were unable to do anything about it," came a voice from the pathway. It was Kara.

"Yes," said Michael, nodding in greeting to Kara. "That was disturbing. The Host should have responded to your or Gabriel's authority—perhaps they would have listened to Lucifer had he attempted to quell them." Michael decided to be cautious with Kara, but was curious as to where the conversation might lead. He decided to venture a provocative thought. "Something is quite wrong, Kara—it's as if darkness is taking over the sensibilities of the angels. I feel I am losing some of them."

"Nonsense, Archangel!" said Kara. "You will find that the Host stands with their Chief Commander as always!"

"Yes," said Gabriel, "but who is their chief commander?" He looked up at the two angels, amused at their startled looks. "I'm only saying that the lack of respect for established authority causes me to question whose authority they are under."

"Speaking as an Elder I must admit that recent events have become intolerable and I shall take them up with the Council to be sure," Kara responded. "Perhaps we should discuss this with an even higher authority…"

Michael and Gabriel exchanged discreet glances. Gabriel read in Michael a cautionary expression.

"After all," Kara continued, "the Most High did create certain chains of authority and resource for us to access. Perhaps we should make this a Temple matter now. But of course…" He looked at Gabriel as if recalling something. "Gabriel! You were recently at the Temple and without summons. Was it possibly in connection with any of this?"

"What are you suggesting, Kara?" asked Gabriel, wondering what Kara might or might not know about his recent visit to the Zoa.

"I simply am suggesting that you were seen at the Temple on your own authority," answered Kara, "and if it was in connection with our little dilemma then I must congratulate your wisdom and your discretion—even if you did supercede official decorum by skirting established authority."

Gabriel wasn't sure how to answer Kara. "As a matter of fact I did visit the Temple, Kara, but the business is of such an urgent nature that I am not at liberty to discuss it except with the appropriate parties."

"I see," said Kara, trying to contain the offense welling up inside of him. "Ah, Kingdom business. One never knows where it will take an angel, hmm? I suppose then that in visiting the Temple you spoke with the Zoa?"

"Yes, Kara," said Gabriel, "as you know it is one of my functions periodically as Messenger to have an audience with them."

"Quite," said Kara, perturbed at Gabriel's pointed discretion. "Nevertheless, as you went unannounced and uninvited my presumption is that this was our business rather than theirs. And if ours, then perhaps it would not break your trust to share what was discussed. I am after all an Elder of the Kingdom, second in rank in Council."

"I respect that of course," said Gabriel, "but..."

"Kara, we cannot expect Gabriel to violate this confidence," said Michael in a subdued manner. He did not want Gabriel to reveal any intelligence to Kara until they had determined Kara's allegiance. He also determined not to allow Kara to know that he was aware of Kara's alleged alliance with Lucifer. "I was wanting him to tell me as well but realized that this too was as inappropriate request."

"Hmm. I admire your integrity, Gabriel. It speaks well of you," Kara finally responded. "As long as you realize that sometimes it is in the best interest of the Kingdom to know where discretion ends and wisdom begins."

"Thank you, Kara," said Gabriel. "I will remember that."

Kara looked at the two angels, knowing he was finished here. "Well, I must be off to Council. Please make me aware of any developments. I'm sure we will take up the behavior of the Host at the debate. Should prove interesting. Farewell!"

Michael and Gabriel watched as Kara's wings suddenly burst forth and he took flight. They watched him disappear toward the center of the City.

"How did he know you were at the Temple?" Michael asked.

"There are no secrets in Heaven these days, it seems," Gabriel responded. "I'm not sure who to trust now. But why would Kara be keeping watch on us? Isn't he with us in this matter?" He looked at Michael. "Or is he?"

"Let's go to a more private place," said Michael, looking around. "As you said, there are many eyes around Heaven these days. And there is much to tell about my visit with Serus. He proved quite revealing."

"Yes," said Gabriel. "So did the Zoa."

"Well *that* disaster could only have been encouraging to Lucifer," Crispin said with disappointment as the group was discussing the debate. "Not that I did poorly. I believe I rendered a fair and accurate presentation of the viewpoint of the Academy—but the outcome was an embarrassment."

Michael, Gabriel and Sangius looked with sympathy at their teacher as he sat behind his large table in his office deep within the heart of the Academy of the Host. They had gathered to discuss the visits with Serus and the Zoa, as well as the outbreak of conflict at the Academy between the two emerging factions.

"You're right about it encouraging Lucifer," said Sangius. "But he must be equally disturbed by the fact that Michael so easily stopped the brawl."

"Perhaps," agreed Michael. "But that was a complete surprise. If it ever comes to a real contest he will be ready. Still, I was gratified."

"Yes, and I'm sure he is preparing for it even now," agreed Crispin. "But as to a future contest, I believe that we will know very soon the outcome of this entire episode—what with the Day Six upon us."

"Day Six. How many more days until the Most High concludes this Creation?" asked Sangius. "Surely He must be nearing the end!"

"Never underestimate our Lord's ability to create," said Crispin. "If He so desired I suppose He could create indefinitely. However, I believe you are essentially correct. The order of Creation has progressed to a point of complexity wherein the final and crowning achievement must soon occur." He leaned back dreamily. "Day Six is proving itself most interesting. The Lord has designed the most wonderful beasts and other animals to inhabit the land." Crispin looked at Gabriel. "Only one creature remains—the greatest of all. The Zoa referred to it as man?"

"Yes," agreed Gabriel, looking at the others. "According to the Zoa, the Most High has determined that man will have dominion over the entire world—and without the assistance of or need for angelic involvement."

"No angels involved in the stewardship?" said Sangius, unable to contain his amusement. "What a very different world Lucifer is envisioning! How disappointing."

"Really makes all of this a moot point, does it not?" posed Michael. "Perhaps once Lucifer sees there never was an angel to be named he will realize that he has behaved foolishly and bring Heaven back into order."

"A reasonable observation," admitted Crispin, "were we dealing with a reasonable creature. But Lucifer? I know that you will call my judgment prejudiced but I cannot foresee him and Pellecus and that swaggering Rugio coming to terms so easily."

"Nor I," agreed Gabriel, "and the Zoa intimated as much. However, the Lord will prevail whatever the development. On that they were quite deliberate."

"Should it come to that," said Michael, "I will of course fight. But my hope is that Lucifer will see the foolishness in this and end it before it is too late."

"Angel against angel in Heaven," mused Sangius. "May it never be!"

"I'm afraid that it already is," said Crispin.

The conversation shifted focus as Michael related his discussion with Serus, Lucifer's chief steward. From time to time throughout the report, Sangius shook his head in disbelief. When Michael was finished recounting the meeting Sangius spoke up.

"So Serus has had a change of heart?" he asked incredulously. "I must tell you, Michael, that as much credence as I hold for an angel being able to change, I am truly at a loss here. Serus seems the most unlikely angel in Heaven to turn from Lucifer—with the exception of Lucifer himself perhaps." He laughed.

"All I can tell you, brothers, is that Serus seemed sincere," repeated Michael. He looked at Sangius. "Perhaps you're right. He was never able to make the final break with Lucifer. I'm not sure he ever will. Lucifer has a hold over him that defies his ability to leave him—even should he so desire. Fantastic!"

"Not so fantastic," interjected Crispin. "Think of Lucifer's ministry here. His ability to lead us into rapturous praise in which we are completely intoxicated indicates his ability to capture an audience." He looked up from his desk at the others. "Such astonishing power for one angel to exert over another!"

"I can only imagine the influence he could exert over earth," said Sangius, almost muttering to himself. Crispin, Michael and Gabriel looked at each other grimly as they thought of so powerful a being ruling the new world.

"Don't give Lucifer too much credit," warned Crispin. "True, he exerts a certain appeal and influence over others—but it is only that—an influence! Angel or man—if one succumbs to Lucifer it is by one's own choice."

"Man?" wondered Sangius. "You propose that man will have such freedom?"

"If, according to the Zoa, man is to rule in the Lord's authority on earth," Crispin responded, "it follows that he will be an exceptional creature and completely unlike the beasts now being created. So I say again, angel or man—one who succumbs to Lucifer does so on his own volition."

"What is it then to which Lucifer has succumbed?" asked Sangius.

"Lucifer has succumbed to Lucifer," observed Crispin. "And that is the reason I see little hope for an easy end to this matter. Apparently the others have succumbed to him as well: Pellecus, Rugio, Berenius..."

"Kara was certainly bent upon learning what the Zoa had to say," remarked Gabriel, still disturbed by the awkward intrusion in the garden. "I know he and Lucifer have always had a strong friendship but..."

"A friendship of convenience I would say," said Sangius.

"Come now, Sangius," protested Gabriel. "Surely an Elder like Kara would not allow the ambitions of an angel to compromise his position? Would he?"

"You don't know these angels, Gabriel," replied Sangius. "They are driven. Something possesses them to push on and on—closer and closer to the edge of complete madness." Sangius looked sympathetically at Gabriel who always wanted to believe the best about any angel. "Dear Gabriel, I wouldn't talk carelessly about these matters. I want to believe otherwise but I cannot. I have seen him for who he really is. If anyone could corrupt an Elder—even an impeccable angel like Kara—it is Lucifer."

Gabriel did not like the direction the conversation was going. He wanted desperately to believe that Lucifer had not compromised the Elders. Could one angel hold such sway among the Host? The Lord forbid it!

For the next few moments Michael and Crispin began outlining the reasons they felt that Kara could not be trusted further—or at least must be approached with extreme caution. Gabriel listened to the arguments made by both. He could tell they were trying to soften the blow in deference to his own misgivings about it all, but nevertheless they made their cases.

"It was Kara who led the delegation from the Council to Lucifer's house when they told him of their decision to name him steward," Michael said.

"And it was he who spoke to me of Lucifer, making excuses for his erratic behavior," added Crispin.

"Naturally Lucifer acted completely surprised the day the Council came to his house, but Kara was in shock to see me there as well," Michael continued. "That was when Serus began signaling me that he wanted to speak." The archangel began detailing his conversation with Serus as to Kara's alliance of convenience with Lucifer. He then summed it up: "If Serus is correct, then Kara is at the very least motivated to further Lucifer's ambitions in order to strengthen himself."

"Yes," remarked Crispin. "And you say he came to you immediately after the debate to discover what was said to the Zoa—on Lucifer's orders perhaps?"

"We are now accusing an Elder of something very dark," said Gabriel, quite disturbed. "Lucifer is one thing—he has always seemed prone to such possibilities; always an independent spirit. I am willing to believe that he is capable of these things. Pellecus we know has been poisoned by this perverse doctrine and seems bent on wreaking havoc in the Academy. Rugio is a bitter warrior who never received the rank and promotion he sought and is now seeking it elsewhere. These I can accept. But Kara? One who sits with the other Elders in attendance to the Most High God? I realize the evidence points to the possibility. But if this is true then who in the Kingdom is above suspicion?" He looked the group over.

"I would say no angel is above suspicion," said Crispin, standing up. "If Lucifer, who is called the Anointed Cherub; who walks in the paths of holy fire; who has access to the holy places; who leads the Host in praises to the Most High...if such a one can turn away from the true Light, then I would say any angel might turn to darkness."

***

Lucifer enjoyed his excursions to earth. Now that Creation appeared to be nearing an end, he was anxious as ever to get on with the task of stewarding the new world. He glanced up and could see the Heavenly Kingdom looming in celestial splendor, wondering when at last his freedom would come. Two strange looking beasts wandered by Lucifer, casually looking up at him as they passed. Lucifer watched as they disappeared into the woods. He marveled at the Lord's creative ability.

"There you are, my lord," came a voice. It was Pellecus, who was accompanied by Tinius. "I thought we would find you here. This seems to be your favorite place on earth."

"Yes," said Lucifer, "I love this spot. I have decided that it is from here I will govern. It is quite lovely and gives vantage of the Heavens and this beautiful world all at once. A medium between two worlds, so to speak. This is where I shall place my throne." He looked at Pellecus. "What developments have occurred?"

"Well, dear prince," said Pellecus, "the rather noisy climax of the debate has created much stir in Heaven. You did well to retire here for a season."

"Discretion is part of the game too, dear Pellecus," said Lucifer. "I bade my ministers farewell and told them that I was off to meditate on the coming greatness of the Kingdom—which in fact I am!" He smiled. "And where is Kara? I specifically requested his presence."

"An official matter has come up," said Tinius. "He was called to Council." He looked hopefully at Lucifer. "Perhaps news of your appointment?"

"Perhaps," said Lucifer cautiously, thinking it over. "Yet that would be of such enormous importance that myself and the archangels would be summoned as well. No, I'm sure this has to do with the outrageous behavior of Crispin's supporters at the debate. They will deliberate and it will be soon forgotten. Kara is good at making them forget."

"Rather an extended day this time," said Pellecus, looking at the teeming wildlife. A loud bark of some animal sounded in the distance. "If not a noisy one."

"Extended, how so?" asked Tinius.

"Well it is evident that the Lord has finished creating the beasts—he must now create the lord of the beasts." He shot a glance at a perturbed Lucifer and quickly added, "By that I mean him whom you will steward, my prince. Surely the Lord will not send an angel down to earth to keep his animals. No, there is greater work to be done here. He will create one who will manage affairs—under your careful hand, of course."

"You do well to remember that I shall govern this planet and not some earth creature—be he beast, bird or fish," said Lucifer, glaring at Pellecus. "However, I do agree with you that Day Six grows burdensome. I wish He would get on with it and finish the work." He looked at the others and added, "When His work on earth ends, mine will begin. Glorious days ahead, brothers!"

Lucifer led the group through a path already worn by the newly created beasts of the field. They surveyed the animals, amazed by the variety. "Notice that they are paired off," said Lucifer. "Like every other living thing on this world, these creatures are blessed with the ability of reproducing after their own kind. Quite an imaginative way of filling the planet, hmm? The creatures themselves become procreators."

"The Most High was wise in that He didn't allow angels the ability to reproduce themselves," said Pellecus humorously. "It would be difficult to imagine two Michaels for example! Or two Lucifers…"

"There is only one Lucifer," said Lucifer, smiling. "That is quite sufficient!"

"And a good thing—else we would have two angels wishing to be named steward!" Tinius added.

Lucifer looked at him coldly. "I only serve those who would have me named steward Tinius—I do not serve myself in this matter!"

"Of course, lord," said Tinius sheepishly.

"At any rate," continued Pellecus, "the Lord has decreed that these animals shall fill the earth. What a mind our Lord has. Such an imaginative mind! Look at them!"

Pellecus pointed to a group of gazelles gracefully bounding through a meadow, while nearby a lioness was playing with a cub. The sound of an elephant trumpeting in the distance added to earth's music. "Such a wide array of creatures," Pellecus went on. "A marvelous mind to be sure!"

"Marvelous indeed," admitted Lucifer. "But what good is a mind which is stagnant and closed to change? True, the Creation demonstrates the capacity of our Lord to think great, imaginative thoughts." An eagle soared lazily overhead and Lucifer watched it for a moment or two. "But I do the same when I compose a worship service, do I not? Yet my mind is ever evolving. Our Lord's mind remains fixed. This is precisely the point that you were making with the wisdom angels at the Academy, dear Pellecus! Such a pity we must come up against such a mind!"

"If I may digress, dear prince," said Tinius, "I must congratulate you on your boldness in dealing with Michael. Your meetings with him seem to have soothed his curiosities."

"As I said, Tinius, the best way to deal with your opponent is to deal with your opponent!" He laughed. "However, I only met with him the one time. Just prior to Kara and the Council barging in and demanding I take the stewardship of earth." He looked at the two angels, smiling. "Michael's look was priceless!"

"I speak of the more recent occasion," said Tinius. "Just before the debate."

"I have no idea what you are talking about, Tinius," snapped Lucifer. "I haven't seen or spoken to Michael since the meeting to which I refer. Except of course when he interrupted that splendid scene Pellecus caused at the Academy!"

"That is odd," Tinius responded. "Michael was at your door prior to the debate. Serus allowed him in."

"Serus never mentioned to me that Michael came to call," said Lucifer, confused and a little angry. "How do you know this?"

"I saw him myself," said Tinius. "I was on my way to the debate and observed Michael at your door. Serus looked quite agitated and quickly ushered him in. I naturally thought you were inside."

"I was not," said Lucifer. "I was in the Academy talking with Kara at the time." Lucifer's aura began to manifest around him. "So Michael spoke with Serus..." Lucifer's eyes now gave off a bluish glow as he became more and more agitated. He looked at Pellecus and Tinius.

"Where is Serus?" he almost whispered.

Serus was thinking about the conversation he had had with Michael. As he wandered through Lucifer's great house he wondered if he had not made a critical mistake. Surely word would get back to Lucifer that he had spoken with the archangel. A fear gripped Serus as he contemplated the confrontation with Lucifer— most likely in front of the entire Council. He wished he had never contacted Michael. And still...

He entered the room where the Council of Worship met. The room seemed strangely quiet given the usual activity that transpired here. He looked at the large table that served as the focus of strategy. It was from here that Lucifer had launched his bid for becoming earth's ruler. Serus began to circle the table, placing his hand upon the chairs that seated the more prominent members of the group. As he did so he thought of those angels and how their destinies were bound to Lucifer's.

Here sits the wisdom angel Tinius: reserved, careful, often doubtful. But quite clever. He smiled as he thought of Tinius' ever-present misgivings which Lucifer always artfully dealt with. Tinius was always prepared to raise questions though backed off defending the issues he raised. However, his ambitious nature tied him closely to Lucifer.

Next to Tinius, opposite Lucifer at the head of the table sits the esteemed Pellecus. The brilliant and bitter Pellecus had helped Lucifer fashion a philosophical impetus for their movement. He was shrewd, ambitious and, where the Academy was concerned, vengeful. Serus moved behind the chair and looked down the table to Lucifer's chair. The chair seemed filled with Lucifer's commanding presence. These two were skilled at manipulating the discussion between them to a desired outcome.

The next seat was reserved for Lenaes, the Keeper of the Light, a symbolic office granted him by the Most High. Lenaes was shrewd, reserved and calculating. Lenaes rarely spoke up in Council, but was probably one of the more dedicated angels in the movement. It was Lenaes who would become Lucifer's liaison to the court of Heaven one day—the embassy from earth.

The final wisdom angel was Belor, whose title Angel of Light bore with it the responsibility to teach accurately the truths of the Most High. Belor had long since departed from teaching and, like Pellecus, dreamed of the time when he could put to rest the notions of Crispin and the other arrogant angels, whose preferred teaching had driven him and Pellecus out of the Academy.

The next four chairs were reserved for the worship angels Drachon, Fineo, Sar and the recently chaired Berenius, who took over Sangius' position. Of the four, Berenius was by far the most cunning. Alert, daring and articulate, Berenius was a rising star in Lucifer's world and his future in the new regime was assured. Drachon and Fineo were bound to Lucifer for their love of praise and saw themselves in exalted roles on earth as leaders in the worship there. Sar was something of an outsider whose desire for prominence in Heaven found refuge in Lucifer's world.

Serus moved to the final four chairs which hosted the warring branch of the Council: Rugio, Vel, Prian and Nathan. Led by Rugio, who commanded the Legion of the Fiery Host, these angels represented Lucifer's strength in terms of the ability to wage war. Rugio was brutal, strong and loyal, but also tended to be headstrong and impetuous. His warrior charges Vel, Prian and Nathan blindly took their orders from him and together they represented a large number of warrior angels who were drifting to this adventurous cause.

Finally Serus came to Lucifer's chair. Slightly larger than the others, it was from this seat that the lord of a few opposed the Lord of all. Serus suddenly found the entire idea amusing. Was it really from this position that all Heaven was to quake? He felt both proud and ashamed of his master: proud, because of the boldness and brashness which seemed to be carrying Lucifer to a sure stewardship of earth; ashamed because in his heart he knew Lucifer was wrong.

He thought of the many conversations which had taken place in this very room; of things seditious and secretive; of things perverse and presumptuous; of things arrogant and abasing. He could see Lucifer, self-assured as ever, discussing disturbing issues in such a manner that by the time he was finished any angel might hold with him.

He could envision Pellecus affirming Lucifer's dialog with philosophical jargon and nonsensical angelic logic which, by the conclusion of the meeting, seemed to make perfect sense.

He also thought of poor Sangius, who had opposed Lucifer, and was disgraced by being removed from the Council and having his name besmirched at the Temple by angels acting on Lucifer's orders.

As these thoughts flooded his mind, Serus also thought of the words which Michael had spoken to him: how the Lord was always ready to receive one who was truly prepared to turn to Him. Hadn't Sangius recently recovered his joy? If Sangius could recover his name and fellowship among the Host, could not Serus? Yet there was a hesitation, a doubt which gnawed at Serus, and which hammered away at him accusing him of his unworthiness to serve the Most High. He was in too deeply with Lucifer and must now see it through to the end—not because he wanted to, but because he felt he deserved the same fate as Lucifer.

Serus had already secretly taken the position that Lucifer could not possibly prevail. At best he would be completely overwhelmed by Michael; at worst he would be completely destroyed. He glanced again at the chairs and thought of how each of these prominent angels might one day become a byword for rebellion. He tossed his own name in the mix as well. Serus was certainly not prominent, but he was as guilty as the rest.

He walked over to the large window from which Lucifer often brooded. The Temple looked glorious as usual, sparkling in the distance. If there were only a way that led back to that place of fellowship with the Most High he would certainly take it. His eyes fell casually to a chart on a side table that was a map of the Kingdom. He picked it up and lost himself for a moment as he surveyed the layout of Heaven.

All the paths lead to the Temple eventually, should one desire to make the journey, came a thought. He lay the map down and started to walk away when suddenly something deep inside him repeated the phrase. This time he looked around certain that someone in the room had spoken the words, but realized that the voice he was hearing was from within. A sensation suddenly stirred with him— something ancient, something sacred, something that he had not felt in a very long time. He could barely recognize it, yet it was quite distinct. It hearkened back to a different time, a happier time, a joyful time. It was the unmistakable presence of the Holy One.

"Serus!" boomed Lucifer. "Serus!"

No answer.

Lucifer glared at Pellecus and Tinius who had followed him back to Heaven after their discussion on earth. They looked at each other and said nothing.

"I am astonished that he is not here!" Lucifer growled. His aura was so bright that the room was filled with bluish light, casting an icy pallor on everything. "I will see him serve in the remotest part of this universe!" he bellowed. "SERUS!"

"Perhaps he is simply at worship," offered Tinius.

"Serus? At worship?" Lucifer laughed. "He worships here. No, I believe he is with Michael. Serus is the one angel in Heaven who could damage me. And now he is with the one angel in Heaven who could disrupt all of my plans? I have been betrayed!"

"My lord, until you speak with Serus you cannot possibly make that assumption," said Pellecus. "If he did speak with Michael, better to court him than punish him."

Lucifer thought about Pellecus's words for a moment. The blue aura began to subside as Lucifer calmed down. "I quite agree," he finally said. "I'll deal with him in my own way." Lucifer paced the room thinking. "Serus is easily swayed. Better to hold him close and offer him something than put him out where he cannot be trusted."

As he spoke those words the door opened and Serus ambled in. Pellecus and Tinius stepped out of the room and met Serus coming in. He carried with him a large scroll. When he saw Pellecus and Tinius he knew immediately that Lucifer was in the house and his casual attitude deserted him. Pellecus motioned in the next rooms and said, "He's in there." Tinius simply smirked at him.

Lucifer had by now completely regained his composure, realizing that in dealing with Serus a soft answer would yield much greater benefit. He asked Serus to sit down—a first in their relationship. Serus began to sit in a side chair but Lucifer motioned him to the table.

"No, no, Serus," said Lucifer. "Here, at the table."

"The Council table?" asked Serus meekly.

"Of course," said Lucifer. "After all, you aspire to sit on this Council one day, do you not?"

"I have always thought about that," admitted Serus.

"Excellent," said Lucifer. "What have you there?"

Serus held out the scroll he was carrying. "I borrowed this from the Academy library. Polias recommended it as a good source on the creation of the angels."

"Well," said Lucifer in an impressed tone, "you are certainly ambitious, Serus."

"I simply wish to be informed," Serus said guardedly. He was not at all accustomed to being treated with such cordiality.

"Don't we all?" said Lucifer, concealing his contempt for Serus. "Pellecus! Tinius! Come in here, please!"

Pellecus immediately recognized the scroll as he came into the room and took his place at the table. "Ah, the Creation Chronicles," he said. "Quite an interesting summation of the creation of Heaven's citizens, Serus. Wouldn't you agree?"

"I haven't read them yet," Serus answered. "But, yes, the creation of the angels is quite fascinating to me." He watched Tinius take his usual position. They all looked at Lucifer, his hands folded in front of him.

"There is, as you are aware, another creation occurring," Lucifer began. "Perhaps you will read about it one day as well. We just returned from earth, Serus." He indicated the other two angels. "Pellecus, Tinius and myself have come to a vital conclusion: The Lord will soon finish His marvelous work there. Afterwards, things should become very interesting in Heaven *and* on earth."

"Yes indeed," Serus concurred. He looked at Pellecus and Tinius who remained impassive. Serus remained quite wary.

"Indeed," repeated Lucifer, looking with compassionate eyes at Serus. "I'm sure you are aware, Serus, that great events are about to take place in the Kingdom. Wonderful events which are much bigger than you or I. Some of the Host are prepared for them, and some are not. But in either case there are set in motion plans which cannot be altered—either by an angel or archangel." He looked into Serus deeply. "Plans which include you, dear Serus."

Serus looked at Lucifer. For the first time Lucifer was addressing him as something of an equal—not on his own level to be sure—but as an insider; as one who is close to the situation. It felt good. Serus looked at Pellecus, who nodded in agreement with Lucifer's statement.

"That is wonderful, lord," said Serus. "I would of course be honored."

"I will naturally have need of a capable angel who will help me in certain administrations on the earth," Lucifer continued. "But it cannot be simply any angel. No, this position requires a discreet and trustworthy angel who can assume a position of authority and honor and serve well." He clasped Serus' hand. "I mean for you to have this exalted place, Serus."

Serus' mind was reeling. All of his ministry to Lucifer had led to this point. Every desire to serve in a place of honor had been dashed previously. Now Lucifer, soon governor of the new world, was requesting his services in an official capacity. He suddenly felt needed...wanted...respected. It felt intoxicating.

"Of course I expect the utmost in loyalty from those whom I appoint to such high office," Lucifer went on. "Both now and in the future." He looked at Serus. "You understand, of course?"

"Of course," said Serus, still overwhelmed by Lucifer's offer.

Lucifer shot a glance at Pellecus.

"You must understand, Serus," Pellecus began, "that what some might discern as sordid or malevolent is in reality a very simple progression of angelic destiny. By assuming the stewardship Lucifer is merely following a course long laid out for him. Greatness finds a way, you see?"

"I'm not sure I follow you," Serus answered.

"I believe what Pellecus is saying is that destiny cannot be denied," Tinius interjected. "Is that correct, Pellecus?"

"Quite right," he agreed. "But of course some angels *do* deny their destinies and thus we have the potential for conflict and for misunderstanding among the Host."

"Which brings me back to my point," interrupted Lucifer. "Loyalty, Serus, is extremely important now. You yourself know that there is a group of angels who are bent on destroying my destiny. Because they themselves have chosen to stay within their own boundaries they feel all of us must. I disagree. The Lord has designed us so that we might walk in fullness and freedom. I find that to be liberating. There are those who find it disturbing. Of course you know all of this."

"Well intentioned angels to be sure," added Pellecus. "And some of our greatest…Gabriel, Crispin, Michael…"

Lucifer watched Serus closely. He noticed the uncomfortable look upon his face as the net was beginning to draw up around him.

"Now," said Lucifer, "we must clear up a matter regarding some of these angels. Serus, know first of all that my love for even those who oppose me out of their ignorance remains firm. But know also that in their ignorance these angels have stirred up a great confusion surrounding me. Fear does that, you know. I am the most misunderstood angel in this Kingdom. Yet I press on—my destiny holds me captive."

The bluish aura began manifesting around Lucifer as his eyes bore into Serus' very person. Serus had never before experienced this intense feeling…alluring and comforting and yet unnerving. The dots of Lucifer's steel-grey eyes became a glowing blue as Serus saw the reflection of his own face staring back at him. He wanted to look away and break the intense feeling, but found himself more and more compelled to listen to Lucifer's reassuring words.

"Serus, your destiny is bound with mine. Just as the others in this room have sworn an oath of allegiance to their destinies, so you, Serus, are part of my destiny. It is inescapable, dear friend. We are bound together to rise or fall as one." He stood up and continued, the room filling with bluish haze. "You, Serus, are intertwined with me, just as these are. We are one in this. We cannot escape our destinies…"

Serus was feeling completely drawn in by Lucifer's dreamy words. He glanced at Tinius and Pellecus, who simply nodded in affirmation to Lucifer's words. But there was something vastly appealing going on. Here was one so great, paying homage to one so small. Serus felt woozy as Lucifer spoke, as if his mind was elsewhere and yet able to take in every word. So the price of destiny assured was submission given. He had been submitting for a very long time. The price did not seem too high.

Still, at the same time, another voice spoke to Serus. It was more subtle, more gentle, but equally compelling. The newly rekindled Holy Presence within beckoned him. It gnawed at him, breaking into the reverie and distracting his mind, vying for his attention. Strangely, he found both voices compelling.

"And now," whispered Lucifer, "let us talk about Michael."

"Of course," said Serus, once more directing his mind fully toward Lucifer.

CHAPTER 14

"We rise or fall as one."

The Chief Elder was trying to regain control of the special Council meeting. He watched in helpless exasperation as the Elders bickered among themselves regarding what had happened at the Academy. One after another the angels either defended the debate or castigated it, depending upon their standing with Lucifer. He finally sat silently as order disintegrated into angelic frustration.

Many Elders who had decided to seek the stewardship for Lucifer were now finding themselves in the embarrassing position of trying to defend the riotous activity at the Academy—something most angels found to be indefensible. Arrogance was one thing; blatant and open strife was unthinkable. Others were more blunt and outwardly recanted their decision and admitted that they regretted having promoted Lucifer at all.

Kara watched the proceedings intently, trying to determine the best course of action. He knew he must recapture the heart of the Council if Lucifer was to succeed. As Lucifer's chief proponent in the Council and early advocate of his appointment to the steward-ship of earth, Kara must be the chief defender of Lucifer. Neither he nor Lucifer had anticipated this violent of a reaction to the brawl.

Suddenly a thought occurred to him and he meditated on his course of action. When at last he was given opportunity to speak he took his place at the dais. The room fell quiet as he approached the platform. Respect for Kara remained firm and every angel honored him with his attention.

"I have just observed in this sacred chamber something which I never thought possible," Kara began, "at least since the ignoble affair at the debate!" He looked over the Council. "Could it be that even the Elders have a propensity for brawling?" Many of the Elders sympathetic to Lucifer began to smugly look around at the others. "Now I certainly am not comparing that rancorous debate in the Academy with these genteel proceedings, but if it were any more genteel in here I believe we would have to call upon Michael once more to quell things!" The Council laughed.

"No one questions the tension in Heaven these days, Kara," said Dabran, who was Kara's chief foe in the earlier debate on Lucifer's stewardship. "It is the *source* of the tension which I believe is critical." Many Elders roared in agreement. Kara looked around, quietly assessing the situation.

"Dabran, it is well-known that your love for Lucifer has grown...how shall I say this?...questionable of late," said Kara. "It is therefore not surprising that you would bring charges against him in this body—the very body, I might add, which whole-heartedly determined that Lucifer should be made earth's governor."

"Wholeheartedly?" asked Dabran sarcastically. "It was not with a whole heart that Lucifer was so named—but with a divided and weakened heart. And my love for Lucifer remains forever true. It is his behavior I will not tolerate." Kara noticed the Elders nodding for the most part in agreement with Dabran.

"You have quite a following in here yourself, Dabran," said Kara. "Perhaps we should have named you steward!" Laughter broke out.

"You seem to forget, Kara, that we can name nobody," Dabran shot back. "That is the Lord's prerogative alone. I seek no office for myself, unlike others in here who will one day regret having backed Lucifer." He pointed dramatically at Kara. "Mark me, angel! The time will come when every angel who sides with Lucifer will finally see his true nature—but by then it will be too late. That includes you, Kara."

Kara responded with great indignation. "Nonsense! I seek only the welfare of this Kingdom. I promoted Lucifer because he is the only angel with the ability to take on such an important task. Dabran, I will however agree with you" (he was now pointing back at Dabran) "that the time will come when those who oppose Lucifer in this will not only see his true nature—and will be astonished by what they see!"

The Lucifer faction of angels loudly applauded Kara's words. "As to the affair in the Academy I maintain that the fault lies equally divided between the two sides. You were there, Dabran. Antagonism came from both groups! It was not simply Pellecus' adherents who were the culprits!"

Kara looked at the Council with great passion. "We angels are the Elders of the Host—respected and responsible. And yet just a moment ago there was a chaotic situation in here which made me feel as if I was back at the Academy trying in vain to maintain order! Even the Chief Elder sat in complete impotence as this body broke out in argumentative nonsense! I am telling you that charges leveled against Lucifer are only fair if the Council charges itself! For I see no difference."

The Chief Elder sat up at the mention of his name. He then spoke as Kara finished: "Kara, perhaps you are correct. The charged natures of the debate precipitated the events both at the Academy as well in here. I will give you that. But would you at least agree that there is a tension in Heaven that has never before existed—a rift in the Host that threatens to profane this Kingdom? Something is amiss here."

"Of course," said Kara, "and that concerns me more than this brawl. What occurred at the Academy was only an effect of the larger problem among the Host. I submit in fact that the solution to the Host's current dilemma is not in shunning Lucifer but in supporting him. He is the one angel in Heaven capable of unifying the Host!"

The expected shouts and arguments amused Kara. He watched as Dabran again rose to speak for the group who wanted to withdraw the stewardship petition. Dabran gave Kara a bemused look, sighed and then began speaking. "I'm quite sure, Kara," he began, "that when you say that Lucifer is the solution to the dilemma you mean by his withdrawal in this affair, correct?" The room exploded in laughter. "How can the most divisive angel in Heaven be the source of its unity?"

"Lucifer is not a divider," said Kara. "His appointment will be a uniting force for all of the Host." Kara saw the bewildered looks on most of the angels. "Hear me out. The Creation draws to a close. The tension itself will naturally subside as these events end." Kara walked the front of the platform as he spoke. He pointed in the general direction of the earth. "If in fact Lucifer becomes governor of earth, his departure will mean that the Host will enjoy everything it wants. Those who support Lucifer's stewardship will be over-joyed that he will lead from the earth, and that angels will forever have a stake in the greatness of our Lord. Those who don't support Lucifer will be gratified that he will vacate Heaven and they can once again resume their duties, however dull!" The angels laughed heartily at this statement. Even Dabran smiled in amusement. "Lucifer's ministry will forever flourish. He is the Chief of Worship and shall always be—whether from Heaven or from earth. He is dedicated to his duties completely.

"I submit, fellow Elders, that to move against Lucifer now is a critical error in judgment which will invite more tension. Too many powerful personalities are now involved which will only compli-cate the situation should Lucifer or Pellecus be charged. I urge this body to allow the Creation to dictate events. When the Creation ends, I assure you, so will this conflict!"

The room applauded Kara's words. It was evident now that the Council was coming down in agreement with him. Dabran wait-ed for the applause to die down before addressing the group. "If I could only believe that to be true, Kara," he said, "I would most certainly drop the matter." He looked at the Council resignedly. "However, it seems as if you have the body with you once more in a matter involving Lucifer. I can only say that for myself, I hope that you are right. But I am doubtful that events will be dictated by

Creation. My feeling is that when the present Creation has ended something far more significant and disastrous is waiting to unfold."

Dabran looked with compassion at Kara and walked over to where he stood. Grasping Kara's shoulders he continued. "We have had our differences in here, my friend. This body knows where I stand in all of this. I cannot persuade you differently. You have chosen your course of action—as must we all."

He lowered his head in deep thought and then continued. "I must confess to you that I have an overwhelming sense of sadness—as if everything is about to change." He looked deeply into Kara's eyes. "And somehow, Kara, I am most sad because I feel that very soon your choice will lead you to a place to which I can never go...and that we shall never see each other again."

Before Kara could respond the Chief Elder called the Council to order as Gabriel entered the chamber. Kara watched Gabriel whisper to the Chief Elder and then take his place at the platform. Gabriel saw Kara, but didn't acknowledge him or any other angel. He read from a scroll as the Elders listened in rapt attention:

"To the Twenty-Four Elders of the Host,

The Most High, Lord of Heaven and earth, King of the Universe and Most Holy God, has determined the creation of His crowning and most sacred jewel. The Most Holy One commands all angels of the Host to witness this, the creation of man, in Eden, on the new world called earth, and so forever to share in this most holy and joyous occasion. So be it done unto the Lord!"

Gabriel finished, acknowledged the Chief Elder, and departed before anyone could throng him with questions. Dabran quickly broke off to a group of angels as the room buzzed with excitement. All over the room the word man was being tossed about. Finally! Kara thought to himself. This was news that should make Lucifer very happy. The final creature—he who would inhabit the earth and be governed by Lucifer—was about to be made. This could only mean that pronouncement of Lucifer as steward must shortly follow! Kara was glowing with anticipation for final victory. His thoughts were interrupted by his remembrance of Dabran's statement before Gabriel's announcement.

Kara walked over to Dabran.

"Thank you for your words, Dabran," said Kara. "But I believe you have spoken out of turn, as had many of the Host. This creation of man does not mean an end to our fellowship, but a beginning of a greater fellowship. A fellowship spanning both Heaven and earth. Lucifer shall surely follow as governor and peace shall conquer the tension in the Kingdom. It is time!"

Dabran looked at Kara tenderly. "Peace shall indeed reign in Heaven once more, Kara," he said. "But it shall not be by you nor me nor Lucifer. Events don't dictate to the Creator. Neither do angels. I suspect there is coming a rather large lesson in humility for all of us—Elders, archangels, and the Host at large."

"How so, Dabran?" asked an incensed Kara. "We have remained supremely humble in all of this. If anything we have been overly restrained in not fulfilling our destinies earlier." Kara's purplish aura began to manifest as he now spoke. "We are called to fulfill the destinies for which the Most High has purposed us. To walk away from that which drives us is foolish." He was almost whispering now. "This is only the beginning, Dabran. This is the age of angels...join us before it is too late!" Kara immediately took flight in search of Lucifer.

Dabran watched as he disappeared into the Heavens. "I fear it is too late already," he said to himself.

<hr />

Chronicles of the Host

First Citizen

Unlike the first day of Creation, which was filled with excitement for the unknown, the final event of the Creation found the angels anticipating that which had been long awaited: the creation of man. No angel dared postulate as to what form man should take, though many proposed that man must be superior to the other beasts of the earth if he was to be the Most High's crowning and adored jewel. Thus the commandment went forth throughout the Kingdom that every angel should bear witness to this, the glorious task at hand...to take place in a sacred portion of the earth called Eden. All of Heaven was pointed toward Eden...and yet the larger unanswered question hung heavily over the Host—who would rule in Eden, angel or beast? The very peace of the Kingdom seemed to balance on the answer...

+≡══════════════════≡+

Serus seemed happily his old self again. This was very gratifying to Lucifer, who for a time had questioned the loyalty of his servant. Lucifer watched as Serus placed the scroll of the "Creation of Man" music that he had just composed in its golden container. *How easy it was for one as weak-minded as Serus to be taken in by Michael and his pleas for loyalty,* Lucifer mused. He would one day settle accounts with Michael...but patience. Earth first, then Michael.

Kara came into Lucifer's great room unannounced. He acknowledged Serus and then greeted Lucifer heartily. He paused a bit in his step when he observed Serus.

"What news?" asked Lucifer, offering drink to his guest.

Kara brushed aside the drink. "Movement I believe," he answered, hesitating a bit while Serus milled about.

"Thank you, dear Serus," said Lucifer. "That will be all for now."

Serus politely nodded and left the room carrying the golden scroll.

"I think he can be trusted but until I am absolutely certain caution must prevail," said Lucifer. "Besides, Serus shall never be entirely privy to this Council."

Kara walked over to the table and saw a large schematic of Lucifer's intended administration of earth. At the top of the chart was, of course, the name Lucifer, written in bold flourished lettering. Under his name were the various ministries and the name of an angel who would lead those areas. Kara looked for his name but saw it nowhere. He didn't say anything at first.

"I see Rugio shall head up your warfare," he finally said. "Naturally."

"Naturally," agreed Lucifer.

"And Pellecus will establish your area of teaching and philosophy," Kara said. "And create your own academy I suppose?"

"Who else?" asked Lucifer. "It is his dream and he teaches what I tell him."

"Berenius at worship? Is his heart pure in this?" asked Kara, surveying the list.

"He worships as I please and whom I please," said Lucifer.

"All very interesting, lord," said Kara. "Some of the most capable angels in Heaven seem to be helping your guidance of earth. The man shall be very fortunate to be stewarded by such competent leadership."

"I quite agree," said Lucifer, waiting for the obvious question.

"I cannot help but see that my name is nowhere to be found," said Kara finally. "I'm certain that you have not yet devised my situation, or perhaps it was an oversight?"

"No, Kara," said Lucifer in good humor, "not at all. Your name will appear on the list…" (Kara beamed with pride.) "…after I have been named steward officially. You see, Kara, until I have the position secured none of these names mean anything. Least of all yours. I am withholding your name as a means of motivation for you to make certain of the outcome. You see?"

"Yes, I see," said Kara resignedly.

"Now, Kara, hear me out," said Lucifer. "You are the most important element in this mission. You are one of the three pivotal players in this."

"I'm listening," said Kara.

"Pellecus represents all that must be taught or re-taught to the Host. His ability to bring about a desired philosophy will be critical to changing the habits and behaviors of these poor wretches who have been taken in all these years by the Academy. Change what one believes and you change what one does—and ultimately who one is.

"Rugio of course represents my ability to wage war—the force and enforcement of the new world. It is unfortunate to thinking angels such as you and I that we should still have to deal with brute force—however—as we have recently seen the Host is not above brawling. For the time being Rugio and his commanders will see to our warfare. That brings me of course to you, Kara."

"And why am I the most important of these three?" asked Kara skeptically.

"You represent my ability to communicate with the authorities, Kara. You are my voice in Heaven that legitimizes what I am doing. You see how neatly the three areas work together? Philosophy, warfare and relationships—together you three are the heart of this crusade. That is why I am holding naming your position to the last, Kara."

"Which brings me to my news," said Kara, still upset and not satisfied with Lucifer's attempt at flattery.

"Ah yes," said Lucifer. "The reason you came. Well?"

Kara assumed the demeanor of an Elder, settling into a familiar role once more. "As you know, minister," he began, "the Most High shall very soon end His Creation with the completion of man. Hence your commission to write an inspiring work for the occasion. Another one of my proposals to keep you tied in closely with the event."

"So I thought," said Lucifer. "I have already completed it. When man is born he shall be greeted by my music!"

"And he had better get used to it," came a voice from the doorway.

"Ah Pellecus," said Lucifer. "Where is Rugio?"

"He shall be here shortly, lord," answered Pellecus, who took his seat at the table. "He is shoring up support in the Legion of the Northern Portion."

"Excellent!" said Lucifer. "You were saying of my music..."

"That man shall best be accustomed to your music, lord, as it shall be with him on earth always!" said Pellecus. "In one fashion or another."

"Well put," agreed Lucifer. "How fortunate shall this beast called man be!"

"As I was saying," continued Kara, "the Most High shall very soon create man. It is shortly after this is accomplished that the steward shall be named. This is all I know."

Lucifer paced the room a bit, thinking. "We need more, Kara," he finally stammered. "I cannot possibly make an intelligent move with so little information." He looked pleadingly at Kara. "Is this all you have?"

"My lord, it makes sense that none of the Elders would have all of the information," said Pellecus casually. "After all, the Lord prides Himself on His knowledge. It keeps Him ahead of us and therefore in control."

"Nevertheless I need more," said an angry Lucifer. "I am tired of Heaven's plodding. I am tired of waiting. I am weary of indecisive posturing by a God who is not powerful enough to rein in his angels, and yet clever enough to create a world. I am ready for action!"

"And so am I," came a new voice. It was Rugio.

"Rugio! You are always my inspiring warrior," said Lucifer. "Yes, my friend, you will one day see action—this I pledge!"

"I have returned from a discreet survey of the commanders of the Hosts by legion," he said. "I must report that though many are with us, including some of the most powerful angels in Heaven, most are undecided or completely loyal to the Lord."

"We must win over as many as possible while there is still time," said Lucifer. "However, we have always known that we should never achieve a majority in Heaven. That is why we have planned accordingly. That is why I asked you here, Rugio."

Lucifer invited the angels to be seated at the table. He took his usual spot at the head and after a moment or two began lecturing. "As Kara has indicated, typical of our Lord, we shall not know until the last possible moment what His ultimate intentions for earth are. I believe that earth is to be mine. The prophecy bears witness to this as does sensibility. Our Lord is a God of mercy and good nature.

"I believe that given the overwhelming response in the Council of Elders to have me named, even in spite of some resistance there, the Most High will in fact name me lord of the new world. And may I remind you that your stake in the new world is no small thing either!" The group looked around at each other, satisfied. "However, until that occurs we are merely speculating. I therefore place the following to you, my most trusted friends." Lucifer settled into his chair and began the lecture.

"The way I view things there are three distinct ways in which this will play itself out. The first way, and the way that we must work towards and hope for, is that the Lord will name me steward outright. There will be no questions and the authority shall pass to me. Michael, Dabran, Crispin—all of those who opposed us—shall suddenly be in the uncomfortable position of having to accept the Most High's decision."

"I shall particularly want to visit Crispin on that day," said Pellecus.

"I believe we all shall have some visits to make," agreed Lucifer.

They laughed.

"But until that happens," said Lucifer, "we must continue to be vigilant and industrious—and above all, discreet. We must not give up on any angel who might possibly join us. And we must not give in to those who will not. That is the first scenario and, I hope, the eventual one."

The group all nodded in agreement.

"But given the erratic nature that our beloved Lord occasionally displays, we must also look at a second scenario. It is quite within the realm of possibility that the Lord will request that I administer the earth from on high—that is, from Heaven—so that my duties here will not be hindered in any way. In such a case I would have to appoint an embassy on earth and establish my authority through another until some opportune time, at which point, I would vacate Heaven and assume complete control."

He looked the group over carefully. "I would entrust this temporary earthly ministry to someone whose ambitions would not become a nuisance later on." He looked squarely at Kara. "I'm afraid, Kara, that leaves you out altogether—at least in this instance and until I was firmly established. Only then would I bring you down to govern with me."

"I don't understand at all," protested Kara.

"You are far too clever for your own good, Kara. You are ambitious by nature and given certain advantages will take them. I therefore have decided that so long as I remain in Heaven...so shall you!"

Pellecus and Rugio gave each other a smug look.

"I must say that my loyalty for this body is certainly being tested," said Kara.

"It isn't that I don't trust *you*, Kara. It's simply that I don't trust your ambition."

Kara remained silent as Pellecus and Rugio snickered.

"And this brings us to the third and most difficult possibility," continued Lucifer.

"Which would be?" asked Pellecus.

"Rebellion. Opposition. In short...war."

Pellecus and Kara both jumped from their chairs. Rugio alone remained passive and fixed. They began to protest and Lucifer waved them down.

"You have just demonstrated the wisdom of having warriors on one's side," said Lucifer. "You two, largely ignorant of warfare, completely panicked at the mere mention of the word. Rugio however, trained in the craft of war, remained vigilant. And this is why war, though a catastrophic risk, is still a possibility—and a winning one."

"Nonsense," said Pellecus, fully recovered from the devastation of Lucifer's suggestion of war. "How can we face the Most High and the Host of Heaven, most of whom are loyal to Michael?"

"Several ideas come to mind immediately, Pellecus," answered Lucifer casually. "Do you think I have not thought this through? You overestimate the Host's ability to wage war—especially on itself. You saw what happened at the Academy—complete chaos! The angels untrained in war were virtually ineffective as compared to those who were warriors. Not even Kara or Gabriel were effective. I tell you that should it come to open conflict, Heaven will be thrown into disarray and the Lord will do anything to prevent this from happening.

"He cannot abide disorder—and that is our advantage. I promise you He will compromise rather than risk a rift that will forever echo His impotence in His own Kingdom. Trust me, friends, there is pride in this—yes, pride in the Most High God—and He will not allow His name or His Kingdom to be associated with such disgrace. He will *beg* me to take the earth's stewardship! That is why if it comes to war, we can win."

"Still it is an enormous risk," said Kara, still reeling from the horrifying thought of war in the Heavenlies that might jeopardize his standing in the Council of Elders. Kara's assumption all along was that if Lucifer did fail in this enterprise, Kara would maintain his place on the Council and explain that he had been completely deceived with everyone else.

"Something else happened at the Academy, if you recall," Kara continued. "Michael merely entered the room and the order was restored."

"True, Lucifer," agreed Pellecus. "Michael's commanding presence might put an end to any outbreak of conflict—as well as put an end to your dreams."

"May I remind you that you share in the outcome of my dreams for good or for bad," said Lucifer. "We rise or fall as one. We fight not only for freedom but now for our very existence. We crossed that line long ago."

"Still, Michael presents an enormous problem," protested Pellecus.

"Agreed," said Lucifer. Looking at Rugio. "Rugio?"

Rugio understood the cue and stood up to speak. "I am prepared with one thousand specially selected warriors to personally see that Michael will not be involved in the conflict on that day. We will hold him until it is over. Don't let Michael concern you any further." He sat down. Pellecus and Kara were incredulous at the prospect of even one thousand angels paralyzing the most powerful angel in Heaven.

"You believe that these angels will oppose Michael?" asked Kara with a sneer.

"As I said, these are angels whom I have selected personally," Rugio answered. "All of them have certain grievances against Michael and bear him no friendship. They are quite motivated to carry out the task. Yes, they will do well."

"So you see how it plays out?" asked Lucifer. "We ask for the stewardship. If it is denied, we march on the Temple. There we humbly restate our position as well as our intention to take, if necessary by action, that which we are requesting. Michael is taken by Rugio's guard and held in a remote part of the Kingdom and is prevented from interfering, and the angels are paralyzed. Another portion of our warriors led by Prian will hold the Temple. Nathan will take still another small group of warriors to earth and along with Berenius will make claim to Eden. The Lord, I assure you, will relent in the face of strife at His sacred doorstep and a collapse among the Host will soon follow.

"I know Him well. You must trust me on this. This is why, Kara, you are so vital to me now. You must continue to advance our cause in the highest circles of Heaven while there is time."

Kara looked resignedly at Lucifer, still stinging from his earlier rebuke. "Yes lord, of course," he said. "But the Chief Elder has had misgivings in light of the tension. Dabran has succeeded in getting close to him. He might even call for a more thorough dialogue on the issue."

"Prevent this, Kara," said Lucifer. "As Chief Elder, indecisive as he is, he is important to us. You must regain his confidence. It will do your own destiny good." Kara looked quizzically at Lucifer.

Lucifer walked over to the schematic of the future earth administration. He took a golden writing instrument and scrawled upon the scroll. He tossed the pen down and invited the three angels to look at what he had written. On the top near Lucifer's own name was now written the name "Kara" and underneath it "Chief Elder, Council of Elders, Kingdom of earth."

Lucifer looked at Kara and said," Does that encourage you to persevere?"

Kara looked at the potential title on the scroll and then back at Lucifer. He thought for a moment and then said, "I will have him pleading to join us before he even realizes what he is saying!" he said. Kara left immediately.

"Ah, ambition," said Lucifer after Kara left. "Lesson here. A little knowledge of another's weakness is a great strength to possess. Remember this as you administer earth. If one simply knows where the armor falls short, one need not possess all of the power."

And the Lord God planted a garden
Eastward in Eden;
And there He put the man
Whom He had formed.

Chronicles of the Host

Eden's Glory

Eden was incredibly still. Nothing on earth seemed to stir as the Host gathered to watch the crowning culmination of the recent events: the creation of man. The time of debating and speculating among the Host was about to end, as their curiosity would soon be satisfied. It was a glorious time in the Kingdom—all of the angels turned out for the event. For the Host knew that this was a special creature wrought by God, unlike any other yet created.

Innumerable angels blanketed the Heavens surrounding Eden, creating a shimmering white canopy. The usual boisterous excitement of the previous five days of Creation had given way to a solemn reverence. The Host quietly descended upon Eden in anticipation of man, like so many white and pink blossoms falling delicately off the fruit trees in the garden.

The garden itself was something of a curiosity to the angels. They knew that the Lord had taken special care in designing this spot on the planet, and though the entire world was beautiful, Eden was somehow sacred—completely set off from the rest of the earth. It was the most beautiful and fragrant spot on the planet. The lush trees, shrubs and flowers gave generously of their fruit, blooms and sweet nectar. So green and rich, so wonderful and colorful, so special was Eden that even from high above the planet one could easily see where Eden's regal prominence.

In the midst of Eden, God had created a stream that watered the whole of the garden. The angels could not help but compare it to the stream that flowed through their own celestial city, and wondered if perhaps the Lord was making a smaller, material version of their Kingdom on earth—a kingdom in microcosm so to speak. Unlike the stream in Heaven, however, Eden's stream eventually divided into four separate and mighty rivers. The rivers came to be called by men Pison, Gihon, Hiddekel and Euphrates, and carried their life-giving resources to the lands outside of the great garden.

By far the greatest mystery of all were the two trees which the Most High had planted in the very center of the garden. They were recent additions, and one could hardly walk through the garden without coming upon them. The purpose of these trees was not apparent, though many speculated that they were a special food for the man that the Most High was soon to create. And though they did not look extraordinarily different from the other trees in Eden, they were nevertheless quite holy to the Lord. The Host stayed away from them—or at least most did...

Chapter 15

"The Most High knows well what He is doing in this."

"Whatever these men are, they are certainly receiving enormous attention from the Most High," observed Pellecus.

"And from the Host," added Kara, who was watching the angels drifting in. "Even Michael is smitten today!"

"Indeed?" said Lucifer, as if only now aware of the conversation. "Michael the archangel has a weakness?"

"For man, lord," said Pellecus humorously, "and for anything else which the Lord holds dear."

"Yes, Michael does know who and what to love, doesn't he?" added Lucifer. "A good lesson here, brothers. Always hold dear those things that are held dear by your authority. It will help you immensely. It might even make you an archangel!"

They laughed as Lucifer led them toward the center of the garden.

"I'm sure that He will approve of the way that I handle these men," said Lucifer. "If they are special to the Lord, as is apparent, I will take extra care to steward them in a way pleasing to both Michael and the Most High—at least until I am firmly in authority. If they are anything like the rest of the stupid creatures that inhabit this world, they will be simply led. How easy to manipulate a senseless beast!"

"Eden is certainly a wondrous place," commented Pellecus as he looked around the garden. "A fitting place in which to create a man."

"And from which to rule a man," added Lucifer. Lucifer had already decided that he would rule from Eden rather than from the previous place he had shown Pellecus. He was gratified that the Lord had taken it upon Himself to create so lovely a site and could not help but respect the Lord's creative genius.

Lucifer continued leading the two angels to the center of the garden. As they made their way through the foliage Lucifer commented now and then about his future plans for the earth. Pellecus and Kara particularly relished Lucifer's lecture when their own names were mentioned in connection with some future administration.

"I hope, dear lord, that when I am Chief Elder over the earth's council we won't have to wait the interminable amount of time we are spending waiting upon the Most High when matters come up," Kara said in humor.

"I don't intend for that to happen at all, Kara," said Lucifer. "I suspect that the council on earth will have enough instructions from me that there will be no need for petitions and requests. You will find me quite clear as your sovereign."

Kara began to reply to Lucifer when Lucifer held up his hand to stop him from speaking. Kara and Pellecus watched as Lucifer's bluish aura began to manifest. He finally whispered to them, "There," he said. "Right there—in the center of Eden."

Kara and Pellecus moved up to where Lucifer stood and peered through a meadow at two large trees, standing side by side. Pellecus and Kara looked at each other rather at a loss and finally Pellecus spoke up.

"Are you certain that these two trees are sacred to the Lord?" he asked.

"Am I certain?" asked an incredulous Lucifer. "Of course!"

"But they look like any other tree in the garden," remarked Kara. "Why are these of special interest to the Most High?"

Lucifer looked at Kara glaringly as the jungle around them took on a pale blue character caused by Lucifer's aura. "How am I ever to rule here successfully if my own leaders are so dull?" he asked. "I have, as you know, developed a keen sense for those things which are holy to the Lord. I believe it comes with the special gift I have for worship. The reason I am able to lead such effective praises to the Most High is because I know Him. I know what moves Him. And I know when He is moved." He looked at the trees. "There is something moving here—something most holy. This spot is particularly important and one day I shall know of its significance personally! For it is between these two trees where my throne shall be placed."

As they made their way back, they watched the angels continuing their descent into the garden. "Is there an angel left in Heaven?" asked Pellecus sarcastically. "Or are they all in Eden?"

"Serus remains," said Lucifer, smiling. " I have set him to another task today. I thought it better to keep him safely occupied rather than risking another encounter with Michael. Serus gets ideas too easily."

"Serus is benign," remarked Pellecus. "I have been teaching him along our lines and he seems to have taken to it quite well." He smiled. "His ignorance is an asset, you know."

"Ignorance is only an asset when it is predictable," said Lucifer. "Serus' ignorance collides with his ambition. And that is dangerous. And that is why he is not here today."

The other angels began laughing when suddenly a serious countenance overtook Lucifer and he held up his hand to make them be quiet. He looked up towards the Kingdom and then back at Kara and Pellecus, who were wondering what Lucifer was hearing and seeing.

"It begins," he whispered.

At that precise moment a hush fell over the entire universe as a wave of love, flowing out of Heaven, showered down into Eden. It overpowered the angels as it moved through them. The love, like a liquid light, gathered above the earth and began streaming into the garden.

Kara, and then Pellecus, lowered their faces and could not bear to watch as the Presence moved by. Lucifer, who had never felt so keenly God's holy love, was himself compelled to lower his head, albeit still observing the event. Most of the angels had either turned away, prostrated themselves, or were otherwise averting their eyes, worshiping the Lord in soft but harmonious praise.

The stream of love burst upon Eden and flowed into the beautiful meadow near the two trees that Lucifer had just visited. It was here that God intended to create His finest work. Lucifer watched as the river of light piled high upon itself, and then divided into two smaller streams, the ends of which became hands. *The hands of God*, Lucifer thought to himself, struck by the awesome scene. He watched as the hands began to scrape the top of the earth, gathering dirt and clay into a small mound.

They worked the mound of dirt while the garden filled with light of such intensity that one could scarcely see what was happening. Lucifer dared not move but was curious as to the purpose of digging into the earth. Slowly, with grace and tender care, the nurturing hands began fashioning the small mound of dirt into a figure—a man. The creature was to be very like the angels in form and appearance, yet was unmistakably a physical being. *A man of dirt?* thought a bemused Lucifer. *Clever.* He waited to see what the creature would do upon awakening, but as the hands were finishing their work, the man did not move. He lay on the ground, on his back.

Lucifer watched as the hands tenderly caressed the form, finishing their work and crafting the most beautiful creature he had ever seen. He was fully developed, as all the creatures on earth were created, and had a quality of vitality and strength and beauty which made him quite different from any other living being on the planet. This was indeed a work of love on the Lord's part.

Some of the angels took a closer look at the newest creature in the universe and were also struck by the beauty of it. The light in the garden was beginning to fade now, and the angels encouraged themselves to move in even closer. Kara and Pellecus looked up and saw that Lucifer had moved in exceedingly close, almost to the edge of the meadow itself. *What a marvelous creature*, Lucifer thought to himself proudly. *He is beautiful. No zookeeper me!* He called for Pellecus to join him.

"Just look at this, Pellecus," said Lucifer. "It is certainly not an ordinary creature the Lord has made today."

Pellecus' academic curiosity had by now overcome his fears and he looked upon the naked figure lying in the middle of the meadow. "He is strikingly beautiful," agreed Pellecus. "He will be a wonderful addition to this world." He looked at Lucifer and added, "And a most adequate subject to govern, I suspect."

"But it doesn't move," came Kara's voice from behind as he joined the others. "It simply lies there."

"There is something different going on here, Kara," said Pellecus. "Something more wonderful than the creation of a mere sea creature or beast of the field. Those animals were wrought by a simple command. But this creature has the complete and personal attention of the Most High. He actually formed this man out of the dirt of the field and lovingly fashioned it into this marvelous design. Incredible!"

"Out of the dirt," repeated Kara. "How ironic—in a pathetic sort of way I mean—to think that the last and most beautiful creature made should come from the substance of earth. Rather humbling."

"Nonsense," said Lucifer. "It's brilliant! By creating the man from the earth the Most High ties it forever to its place of origin. What better way to instill appreciation for one's world than to come from its substance! The Most High well knows what He is doing in this."

The cloud of glory continued its vigil above the man. The hands had withdrawn into the light and the angels watched for the next action. All was quiet in Eden. "Still he doesn't move," Kara once again observed.

"The Lord pauses," said Lucifer, knowing that something was about to happen. "Let us move back a bit."

———————————————

Michael had observed from another vantage the fashioning of the man. He sensed the special love that the Most High held for the creature and immediately knew in his heart that there was a special destiny…a great purpose awaiting him. He also watched as the hands, enveloped in the light of liquid love, gently caressed the

earth and shaped it into the man now lying in the meadow. He saw
the hands disappear back into the shapeless form of light and begin
to dissipate.

The creature was supremely beautiful. Michael felt that were
he not a man he should be an angel. He lay completely still—almost
vulnerable, and yet strangely at peace. Was this to be the subject of
this world to be governed by Lucifer? Michael shuddered at the
thought of releasing so beautiful a creation into Lucifer's authority.

Suddenly the angels began singing in spontaneous praise to
the Lord. Michael recognized Lucifer's wonderful Creation music
and soon every angel was praising the Most High in rapturous harmony. Michael himself was overcome with the same joy and began
to praise God, lifting his hands toward the Heavens.

Lucifer too heard the music that he had created and enjoyed
its effects on the angels. Even Kara was caught up in worship as the
angel voices filled the Heavens and the earth. The angelic choir
continued singing even as three glorious lights suddenly appeared
over the man. Lucifer thought he could make out figures within
these lights but the brilliance kept him from seeing clearly. He
could hear thunderous noises as the figures within the lights
dialoged with one another. The angels continued singing as this
apparent conversation went on. Suddenly above all else came the
words:

"Let Us make man in Our image..."

The words were spoken quietly, and yet with such authority
that every angel was thrown about in chaotic disarray. Lucifer himself was violently impacted as if he had collided with an invisible
force and was thrown backwards. The singing was interrupted
momentarily as the angels slowly regained their posture.

Lucifer looked for Pellecus but the wisdom angel was still
recovering from the impact of the Lord's words. Kara too was slow
to recover. Lucifer turned to look once more in the direction of the

Most High. He had just regained his composure when the voice spoke again:

"...and after Our likeness..."

Though slightly better prepared for the words, Lucifer was nevertheless thrown backwards into the Heavenlies once more. All of the angels were disoriented for a moment as the Voice, which spoke as they had never before heard, issued forth.

Lucifer, once more fully recovered, along with Pellecus and Kara, perched himself above the garden and watched as the Three moved in closer to the man. The angels watched in complete amazement as one of the figures bent down toward the man and tenderly breathed into the man's nostrils.

A sound of a mighty rushing wind could be heard throughout creation (although not a leaf stirred anywhere on earth) as the breath of life moved from Creator to creature and the man became a living being. And because the man was created from the dust of the earth, he was named A'dam. No angel dared speak as first the Son and then the Spirit departed, leaving the Father alone.

A'dam breathed the first breath of air ever taken by a man. As his lungs filled, he slowly opened his eyes. The angels watched with intense interest as the man, A'dam, blinked his eyes and then turned them away from the light of the Father who stood nearby. The Father reached His hand out and A'dam took it and stood up. The man looked about him with a dazed expression on his face, taking in the world around him. He then looked to the light of the Father and was at complete peace, smiling as if by instinct. He instantly knew he was where he belonged...this was his home... this was his Father. They walked off together in the cool of the garden.

Chronicles of the Host

Creation's End

And so it was that the Lord Most High created man and declared him to be in His very image—an honor never bestowed upon the Host. Man was truly marked for greatness, as was the commemoration of these great events. For it was the Lord's will that a seventh day be decreed, a blessed day, a sabbath day in which A'dam would meditate upon the holiness and grace of the Most High in creating him. Thus did God declare that though all of Creation was good in His sight, this, the sixth day was indeed very good in His sight.

And God blessed the seventh day,
And sanctified it:
Because that in it He had rested
From all of His work
Which God created and made.

As A'dam, the man, walked the breadth of his new world in fellowship with the Father, it was the angels' honor to realize that the special bond between God and man was even more sacred than previously thought. No mere angel enjoyed the communion with the Most High as did A'dam. And though the Host felt no less loved by the Lord, they knew in their hearts that the name "Father" was especially significant to A'dam.

Most angels found great assurance in this, knowing that the Lord in His wisdom and love, had finally created a being with whom He would share Himself in ways that angels would never know or understand. There were some angels, to the shame of the Host, who saw A'dam in a completely different light...

"A'dam! A'dam!" cried Lucifer aloud. "How much more of this A'dam must I hear about?" he shouted to the Council. Tinius, who had simply remarked about some minor detail on earth, dared not look up at Lucifer.

"Is A'dam the only creature in the universe?" he asked. Everyone at the Council sat quietly, waiting for someone else to speak up. Finally Pellecus began talking.

"It is only natural, my prince," said Pellecus, "given the completely new state of affairs, that the curiosity of the Host is touched." He stood up as if in one of his old classes giving a lecture. "A'dam is different. A'dam is new. A'dam is highly favored of the Lord—and therefore the Host is merely curious."

"Curiosity is for fools, Pellecus," retorted Lucifer, "of which most of the Host is comprised, I am convinced. Sit down!" Pellecus humbly retook his seat. The warrior angels snickered in delight. "The longer he remains in Eden without being governed, the more accustomed to independence he will become," Lucifer continued. "I am weary of waiting!" He pounded the table with such force that Serus came rushing in to see if his master wanted something. This broke the tension in the room as everyone laughed.

Lucifer began outlining his current thinking. He was now more than ever ready to take over as governor. The new man was the first, but certainly not the last human to be made. There would be more. It was time to make this official. He looked at Kara, who had been invited to this special meeting.

"I cannot abide this inaction any further, Kara," Lucifer snarled. "Every day that the man lives is another day that he dominates that world. Why, he has even begun to name the creatures there! That is not his prerogative!"

"Ah yes," said Kara, amused at Lucifer's predicament. "It seems that the Most High has given the man some responsibilities on earth."

"I am responsible for that world," said Lucifer. "Not he." Lucifer stood up and began pacing as he talked. "How like our Lord to allow this...this A'dam...to share in the responsibility of naming the beasts. A'dam is himself a beast! Such presumption." He looked at Kara pleadingly. "Kara, you must make a move now. Or there shan't be any reason for me to be named steward. I'll not have my authority usurped by this mud-man!"

"Patience, Lucifer," cautioned Kara. "The Chief Elder is even now presenting your name to the Most High. I urged him to circumvent the Zoa who seem to be moving slowly on this. But be advised: This mud-man is a delight in the eyes of the Lord. Be careful how you refer to him—beast or not."

"Kara, you take me for a fool," said Lucifer. "You know as well as I that this unforeseen passion the Most High has for A'dam is a threat to us all. Do you realize that if we are not careful we angels may be serving A'dams rather than the other way around? It is a pathetic but distinct possibility."

"But unlikely," said Pellecus, who had recovered from Lucifer's earlier rebuff.

"How so, learned one?" asked Lucifer with a sarcastic tone. "Since when do you anticipate the thinking of the Lord? You who said that whatever the pinnacle of the creation was to be, that he would be lower than angels!"

"And so he is," said Pellecus calmly. "A'dam is a product of the earth. He is created out of dust. He is material, sensual, and therefore inferior. I confidently assert that the Most High will never relinquish dominion of the earth to him. Some responsibilities? Of course! Let him name the creatures of the earth...so long as your name is over all creatures on earth what does it matter?"

Lucifer began thinking through Pellecus' statement. He looked out the window onto the streets of Heaven. "Perhaps you are right, Pellecus. If this A'dam is to have a share of responsibility in the world, then I should be courting him rather than opposing him. I should be promoting him to the Lord—building him up and supporting him. Demonstrating to God that I too cherish A'dam. What better way to display my ability to rule over man than by being in harmony with him?"

"Sounds very plausible," agreed Kara. "For if the Most High has in fact determined that A'dam is to have a measure of authority, then you best serve your purposes by..."

"Recognizing A'dam's authority?" offered Lucifer.

"Well, yes," said Kara sheepishly. "It does not mean you are surrendering your own authority to him. After all, yours will be the final authority on earth. It has been prophesied. It must be that an angel shall rule and perhaps be assisted by an A'dam."

"To think that I might have to share *any* amount of authority with a beast. I shall never understand the way our Lord thinks. However, seeing one of their own in a position of some importance might help to keep the other beasts in line."

"A'dam is not quite a beast," replied Pellecus. "Not like the others."

"Are you presuming to lecture me, Pellecus?" asked Lucifer.

"I think, lord, that Pellecus is merely pointing out that A'dam is vastly different from the other creatures on earth," Kara said, attempting to deflect Lucifer's anger.

"Just so," Pellecus responded. "No other creature is like A'dam. Mind you this includes the angels. Every other creature on earth is animal. Brutish. Instinctive. Created by decree. But A'dam. He is created in the image of the Most High. He was enlivened by the very breath of God—and this is why the Most High delights in him."

"I know, I know. I saw him created, Pellecus. And I heard the Most High declare him to be made in His own image. But are we not all created in His image? Are not the angels created with God's image in them?" asked Lucifer.

"Well, yes. To the degree that—like the Lord—we are reasoning, moral creatures, we share some attributes of God. But A'dam shares a unique place in that he alone has been declared to be in God's image. We angels were never accorded such honor." Lucifer frowned and folded his arms in disgust as Pellecus continued. "The real question is not what image angels are made in, but what the Lord's ultimate intentions for A'dam are."

Lucifer looked at the Council and smiled wanly. "Ah well. Perhaps until I am named steward we can use the fact of A'dam's unique position in creation to our advantage." He took his seat once more.

"So you say, Kara, that the Lord will now be personally aware of the Elders' recommendation?" asked Lucifer. "Then we can only await His decision. I only hope the Chief Elder is proficient in declaring our position."

"You mean the *Council's* position," Kara answered. The Council of Worship laughed nervously.

"Ah yes," said Lucifer. "Good and well. So you see, my friends, it is only a matter of time before we shall be free from these chains and ruling earth."

"Or at least assisting A'dam," Pellecus said humorously.

"I shall only assist A'dam in relinquishing whatever authority he has taken which rightfully belongs to the steward of earth," replied Lucifer. "Which is me."

"I would like to assist the dirt man myself," said Rugio. "To think that he believes himself God's special creature! He could be so easily..." Rugio stopped himself.

"Not so easily, Rugio," said Lucifer. "The reason he believes he is special in the Lord's sight is because the Lord has so led him to believe. Observe how frequently the Most High visits and consorts with A'dam. He actually accompanies A'dam for strolls in Eden—in a severely diminished capacity, of course, or He would kill the poor creature! Visiting A'dam won't be easy, Rugio. That's why the best course is to obtain legal authority and then deal with whatever impertinence might exist."

"Perhaps, lord, whenever the day comes that such impertinence is to be dealt with, I might represent you in the matter and deal with this A'dam personally."

"Of course, Rugio," answered Lucifer. "But gently, gently."

Everyone laughed.

"And now the wait," said Lucifer, as the room quieted down. "I know that our Lord prides Himself on His ability to be patient in all things, longsuffering and all that. But I hope that His decision in this matter will take precedence over whatever else might be on His mind—whatever that might be!"

Chapter 16

"You must never eat of this tree."

A'dam loved Eden. Every day he learned something new about his world, and that made him feel closer to God. By now he understood that God had created him as a free man to love and be loved of the Father; to worship his Creator; to walk the breadth of Eden and learn of it; to name its creatures; to eat of its fruit. A'dam looked up to the Heavens and was supremely thankful.

As he looked skyward he saw a majestic bird that he had not noticed before. It was soon joined by another bird of the same kind. The two birds flew together gracefully and began circling the forest above A'dam's head. They then flew down and lighted near him on a large cedar log.

A'dam looked at the birds for a moment or two and named them. Upon hearing their new name, the birds screeched and took flight, disappearing into the deep blue sky. It had been this way ever since the Lord had commissioned him to name the animals. An animal or two, or sometimes a large group of animals would wander over to A'dam, who would name them and off they would go. He was grateful that at least he didn't have to go looking for them!

A'dam had everything he could possibly need in his world. All of the food he could eat was always a few steps away. He had plenty of cool water for drinking. The animals were his friends and he enjoyed a wonderful relationship with God, who would often visit him in the garden. He was truly grateful for his life. And yet...there was an emptiness stirring within him. A longing.

As he watched the male and female eagles disappear he once more realized that every animal in creation seemed to be in twos. The birds, the beasts of the field...all of these were accompanied by another of its own kind. He sometimes wondered as to the reason for this and found himself thinking about it more and more. Perhaps he would ask the Father about it.

He watched as two large animals with a brood of pups strolled up a garden path toward him and sat down in front of him. Without even giving it much thought A'dam called out their new name. The mother wolf came to A'dam and licked his hand and then trotted off into the woods, the pups bouncing behind her. The father wolf looked back at A'dam with his deep gray eyes, and then hurried off with his family. A'dam smiled at the family of wolves as they disappeared into the forest. He truly was learning much about his new world. But the greatest thing he understood was that he was quite alone.

+⇥——————⇤+

Michael was seated on a hillside in Eden, watching A'dam playfully wrestling a large black bear. He enjoyed A'dam's wonderful relationship to the rest of creation, and marveled at God's ability to design such a world. Everything seemed to function in a sort of perfection. The mist from the earth kept the ground moist and the animals watered. It was quite a world!

The bear trotted off after a while and A'dam watched it disappear into the woods to join its family. He plucked a berry from a large bush and sat right next to Michael. A'dam looked Heavenward and sighed deeply, as if searching for something...waiting for someone. Michael, too, looked up and saw nothing but the great fountain of the deep—a vast canopy of water that stretched in a band around the earth. It amazed him that the man could not see him and yet was so close—and the Host was under strict instruction not to appear or speak to A'dam unless commanded by the Lord.

"Michael!" came a familiar voice. It was Sangius.

"Greetings, brother!" answered Michael.

"Observing our friend here I see," he said, gliding down and seating himself on the other side of A'dam opposite Michael.

"Yes, and thinking of what a dreadful shame it would be if Lucifer was made governor over this beautiful creature," answered Michael. "I certainly hope Gabriel was correct about what the Zoa told him."

"Gabriel is seldom wrong," said Sangius. "Lucifer, however, will be horribly disappointed once word reaches him!" He laughed. "I sometimes wish I was still on his Council simply to observe his reaction!"

"Sangius, if Lucifer is turned down and this man is named steward, as the Zoa have suggested, will Lucifer be satisfied to let things go?"

"I don't know really," said Sangius. "Lucifer is apt to do anything. I suspect he is clever enough to know when he is through and will drop the matter. But then again, we're discussing Lucifer."

A'dam stood up and stretched, yawning as the midday sun struck his face through the tall trees. He picked up a stick and wandered off into the garden. The angels watched as he reached down and stroked a young deer, giving it a handful of lush green clover. He then continued on into the deeper parts of the garden.

"He is such a beautiful creature," remarked Sangius. "He is regal—almost angelic. And yet so innocent. He seems so strong and yet so fragile at the same time."

"Yes, Sangius," agreed Michael. "I have been studying the beasts of this world. Some of them could easily overcome A'dam. Yet peace prevails in Eden."

"I would certainly not want to see an angel come against so weak a creature," said Sangius, who caught Michael's fierce glare. "Although I certainly don't anticipate such a conflict." Sangius indicated the spot where A'dam had disappeared into the woods a moment before. Sangius ventured further and added, "Do you anticipate that there will be conflict between angels and man?"

"Any angel in particular?" Michael said, finally smiling weakly.

"I can only speculate of course," said Sangius, "but when Lucifer discovers that the 'mud-man,' as he calls him, will be made steward, he certainly will have no great love for him."

"Lucifer will never touch A'dam," said Michael resolutely. "This I vow. Neither Lucifer, nor Rugio, nor any angel in Heaven will touch a man unless it is decreed by the Lord to happen. I am sworn to uphold the Lord's honor in this."

"Well, Eden certainly suits A'dam," said Sangius, happy to move on to another subject. "He has all that he could possibly ever desire."

"Does he?" asked Michael. As he spoke a pair of swans swam gracefully by. Michael pointed to the swans. "I have observed that every creature on this world has another just like it except for A'dam. The beasts of the field have companion beasts with which to share life and perpetuate it. The birds as well. Even the fish. But A'dam? What does A'dam have?"

"A'dam has the Father," came the familiar voice of Crispin. "And what more could he possibly need than that?"

"Good and well, dear teacher," said Michael, embracing his friend. "And I realize that the Most High has a special and wondrous relationship with A'dam. I don't question the wisdom or plans of God. I simply feel a sense of protection for A'dam is all. Where that comes from I don't know, because the Lord has forbidden contact with him—yet I believe that the Most High would have it this way."

"Those feelings are quite simple to explain," said Crispin, who settled down next to Sangius and Michael on the bank of the pond. "Such grace," he said pointing to the swans who were making their rounds once more near the angels. "Ah, the imagination of such a creative Lord!" He looked at his former student with compassion. "Michael, the reason you have feelings of protection for the man is because of your loyalty and love for the Lord. He holds A'dam quite dear and therefore so do you. It is nothing more.

Angels and men will never relate to one another as do God and man. But in the Most High we share with man a common bond of loyalty and love."

"So then what is our position in regard to A'dam?" asked Sangius.

"I believe that Michael is already realizing our position," said Crispin. "We continue to serve the Most High as always, but with the added honor of serving him on earth as He sees necessary."

"But the Zoa said earth is for man, not angels," said Michael.

"Earth is for man to dominate and to steward," Crispin answered, "as Lucifer will soon find out. That is what the Zoa said. But we angels will have a role on this planet in serving the Lord by seeing His will for man ultimately carried forward—whatever course that might take us on."

"We serve God by serving man?" said Sangius.

"No, Sangius," said Crispin. "We serve God by serving God. And if in serving God we find ourselves also involved with man— then so be it!"

"A'dam!"

"A'dam! Where are you?"

A'dam knew well the voice of his Father. Everytime he heard it his heart leapt in him like one of the gracefully leaping bucks in the forest. A'dam looked around him and answered aloud, "Here I am, Father!"

A'dam stood, awaiting the arrival of the Most High God, his Father. He felt a gentle breeze blowing against his face, and suddenly the garden became pale, as a glorious light appeared before him. The robed figure in the light was a head larger than A'dam and not completely unlike him in features—although His face could never be seen clearly. The figure walked out of the light and extended His hand. A'dam could barely see to take the hand because the light was so bright. He finally shut his eyes and reached out blindly, feeling the Father's loving hands taking his own—the blinded A'dam guided by the all-seeing Father.

When A'dam opened his eyes an instant later, he found himself standing in front of the two trees that were planted in the center of the garden. He was completely perplexed as to how he had moved from the extreme edge of Eden to its center so quickly! A little dazed by it all, A'dam looked to his Father with a bewildered expression. The Father merely indicated the two trees and A'dam looked at them as he had done many times before. He had never before ventured this close to the trees, however, as there was a sacred presence here which seemed to forbid him access until now.

"What is it, Father?" he finally asked.

"My dear son," came the voice of God. "I love you more than you can possibly know. This you understand?"

"Of course, Father," replied A'dam. "I have always known You loved me."

"Know this then," the Father continued. "All of Eden is yours to enjoy. I have provided for your every want. There will never be hunger known to you, nor thirst, nor toil, nor fear, nor even death. Do you understand this, A'dam?"

A'dam was still puzzled by it all but spoke up. "Yes, Father. I know all of this. You have been so good to me." A'dam was not entirely sure what death meant, but he knew that he need not fear it.

"Know then that you may eat of every tree of the garden; every fruit-bearing bush, every melon and berry—all of that which grows freely in the garden—of all of these you may eat..."

A'dam instinctively looked at the two trees which stood before him. "And what of these, Father?" he asked. "Did You bring me here that I may now eat of these as well?"

"Hear me, A'dam," said the Father, in a grave tone which A'dam had never before heard. "You may eat freely of all that I have said. But of these two trees you must never eat. They are forbidden to you."

A'dam looked at the trees and the fruit upon them. They didn't look much different from many of the other trees in Eden. "But why, Father?" he finally asked. "I have always felt this was a special place. Are these trees set apart for You alone?"

"No, A'dam," said God. "They are set apart for you—and they are set apart from you. You must never eat of these trees."

"I don't understand," said A'dam, looking at the trees. "If I am not to eat of them, then why are they here?"

"The reason is not as important as the command. You must never eat of these trees. For on the day that you do you will die."

A'dam looked at the trees and back at his Father. "You would kill me for eating of these trees, Father?" he asked.

The Father looked down at A'dam with love so overwhelming that A'dam could scarcely stand before Him. "No, A'dam," He said. "I would never kill you. But by your own choice you would bring death to yourself. Therefore I say to you again, you may not eat of these trees, for on that day you shall surely die."

A'dam started to answer but suddenly the Father was gone. A'dam blinked a few times and rubbed his eyes. The garden once more took on its usual beautiful colors as the glory of the Lord faded. He looked around and all seemed normal. Slowly his eyes looked in the direction of the trees, which were swaying gently in the breeze. As he watched a solitary piece of fruit fell from one of the limbs and rolled a few paces in front of his feet. A'dam looked at the fruit.

At first he smiled. But then a terror began to grip his heart as the words of the Lord played back in his mind. He began to step away from the area, walking backwards. A screeching hawk startled him, and he turned and bolted, vowing never again to set foot in that part of Eden!

Chronicles of the Host

Eve

It was never the will of the Most High that A'dam should be alone. God the Father, in complete agreement with the Son and the Spirit, had determined that a suitable helpmate must be provided for A'dam. One who would complement him; one

*with whom he would share his life and his love; one with whom
he would build a new world. So the Lord set A'dam upon the
task of naming the animals, and in doing so, allowed A'dam to
realize that he was incomplete by seeing that all of nature was
accompanied by one of its own kind. And as A'dam named the
beasts of earth there was not found for him a suitable mate.*

*Now for the Host this longing that A'dam was experiencing;
this sense of loneliness; this need for another was incompre-
hensible. The angels were responsible to the Lord of all, and
though they enjoyed a fellowship among the Host, they had no
sense of such intimate need. Therefore they watched A'dam
from afar, some feeling compassion for his despair, others feeling contempt for what was an apparent weakness among
man—the need for others...*

*So it was that the Most High, upon A'dam's recognition that
he needed another suitable to himself, He brought forth another human—one with whom A'dam would share the glorious
life God had given him...*

> *And the Lord caused a deep sleep to fall upon A'dam,*
> *And he slept; and He took one of his ribs,*
> *And closed up the flesh instead thereof;*
> *And the rib, which the Lord God had taken from man,*
> *Made He a woman...*

"A woman?" asked Tinius. "What is a woman?"

"Haven't you heard?" said Pellecus. "The Lord has given
A'dam a mate!"

"It's quite delicious really!" said Kara, who was standing in
front of the window in Lucifer's council room. "Ties A'dam even
more closely to the other beasts on earth."

"Does that suit you, Kara?" asked Lucifer, who appeared from
the other side of the room where he had been discussing some

details with Rugio in private. Kara could see the hulking Rugio standing just off Lucifer's right shoulder.

"Why yes," said Kara, surprised at the question. "It suits me quite well. This A'dam is beginning to think himself an angel—hmph! Prideful creature! This places him firmly back in his element—and reminds him that he is a beast, nothing more."

The angels laughed.

"Perhaps," said Pellecus, "in so doing the Lord ties him even closely to Himself."

"Ah, Pellecus," sneered Kara, "always an opposing viewpoint. Why is it that whenever you and I discuss something we are on opposing sides of the issue? Is it your academic need for argument?" He smiled as a few angels snickered.

"No, Kara," replied Pellecus calmly, "it is my need to be correct!"

"Enough!" interrupted Lucifer. "We have much to discuss."

"No, Lucifer!" said Kara. "I am weary of Pellecus and his arrogance! I am an Elder to the Most High God! I have position and authority in this present Kingdom! And I will not be spoken to in such condescending terms!" Kara's purple aura was beginning to manifest. "I will be respected here!"

"You speak of arrogance?" replied Pellecus calmly. "You who would wave your credentials as an Elder with one hand while manipulating that same Council for your own gain with the other?"

"Enough, I said!" Lucifer said loudly. "There is too much at stake for your colossal self-posturing to interfere! Kara, Pellecus, sit down." Lucifer glared at the two angels. Kara's purple aura immediately dissipated and he took his seat. Pellecus sat down as well, trying to maintain an outward dignity. Rugio smiled at the entire affair, amused by it all.

"It seems, lord, your brightest stars are tarnished," Rugio finally said.

"Excellent point, Rugio, my warrior," said Lucifer, who took his seat at the head of the table. He looked at the members of the Council, his chin resting on his left hand. "I want to tell you a story. I saw a star fall once. It was very soon after Day Four when I was meditating on the earth. I looked up and there was a very bright light streaking across the twilight evening sky, like lightning that occurs from time to time. I watched as it became more and more brilliant and then suddenly broke up and disappeared. At that moment a majestic looking eagle glided in the air above me. At the precise point in the sky where the star had disappeared in the Heavens the eagle shrieked loudly, circled once, and disappeared toward the mountains north of Eden."

He looked at the Council. "It occurred to me that we are about to witness a Kingdom in decline, even as another is rising. We are that young eagle—poised and prepared. Ready to ascend." He looked harshly at Pellecus and Kara. "However, if we fail to remain completely united in this effort we too will burn out and break up just as that piece of matter did. All of us will be forever compromised. I suggest therefore that there be no more personal offenses— at least not until I am firmly in authority on earth. Then you may destroy each other if you are that stupid...*but not here and not now.*"

Everyone in the room was silent.

"Now something for which all of us have been waiting." Lucifer stood up. "When we first began this journey I must admit I had my doubts. There were times when I felt it was pointless to pursue so noble a course amidst so many in Heaven who lacked vision or depth of character. Now I see I was correct in continuing the affair." He held up a scroll. "I have in my hand an official decree commanding all of the Host to attend the Lord in assembly at Gabriel's next summons, at which time the Lord is prepared to name the steward of earth! Brothers, this is what we have been waiting for, fighting for, trying each other's patience for!"

"When did you receive that communication, lord?" asked Tinius.

"Shortly before this meeting," said Lucifer. "Serus brought it to me by special conduct from none other than the Chief Elder himself. I suspect the more important angels are receiving notice and then the Host in general will be informed."

"I knew of no such communiqué," snorted Kara. "Are you certain that is from the Chief Elder?"

"It has his seal, Kara," said Lucifer, handing the scroll to Kara.

Kara looked the scroll over. "Well, it certainly looks official," admitted Kara. "I still am confused as to why none of the other Elders were notified that such a summons was forthcoming."

"Perhaps this is an issue deemed too important even for you, Kara," said Pellecus with a hint of delight in seeing Kara somewhat compromised in his position.

"Nonsense!" said Kara. "I am privy to everything that happens at Council."

"So I see," sneered Pellecus. Berenius snickered also.

"It doesn't matter," interrupted Lucifer, as he snatched the scroll out of Kara's hands. "I understand that the Chief Elder received it from the Zoa. None of the Elders knew except him. I am less concerned that you are offended in this, Kara, than I am that we are finally seeing movement on this." Kara averted his eyes to others in the room, feeling quite uncomfortable.

Lucifer continued, "What matters is that a steward shall shortly be named and we shall all benefit from it. A new age is dawning, brothers, wherein angels will take the primary role—set the tone as it were." He smiled, thinking of his previous illustration. "I would say our star is on the rise."

"I would say that the Morning Star is on the rise," said Rugio. He stood up and raised his goblet toward Lucifer. "Glory to the Morning Star!"

The others stood to their feet and raised their glasses as well:

"Glory to the Morning Star!" they all said.

Lucifer stood to acknowledge their salutes. As he did a long, low, trumpet blast rang out. Lucifer looked at the Council and said, "It is time. I will see you all at the assembly. Kara, you will be seated with the Elders of course. I want you as near to the Chief Elder as possible. Pellecus, I want you with the teaching angels—especially near Crispin. The rest of you I want interspersed among the more important angels to glean their reactions. Farewell all. Rugio, please stay for one moment."

The room was soon empty except for Lucifer and Rugio.

"Rugio, my valiant fighter," said Lucifer, putting his hand on Rugio's shoulder. "I don't anticipate any deviation from the scenario which we just outlined. However, should there be the need for more strident action, have your body of angels ready to act on my command. Just as we discussed, understand?"

"I will, lord," said Rugio. "The archangel will not cause you any difficulties."

+≡———————≡+

One angel remained behind in Lucifer's house. Serus watched out the window as uncountable numbers of angels came in all directions toward the place of summons. He wondered if Lucifer, the worship minister to the Most High, would return as steward of earth. It certainly seemed likely. What would that mean to him though? he wondered. His recent meetings with Michael and the others angels had reignited some of the old feelings of passion he once held so strongly for the Lord. Michael had insisted that it was not too late to abandon this nightmarish course Lucifer had embarked upon and return completely to the loyal side of the Host.

He looked over the skyline of the City, toward the ever-shimmering north. The dome seemed more brilliant today, as if beckoning Serus with an even greater urgency than normal. *Always you call me,* he thought to himself. *Not with voice, maybe, but still you call.* He smiled wanly. *I'm afraid I have answered a call already.*

+≡———————≡+

Chronicles of the Host

Stewardship

All of Heaven was summoned to the great assembly in which the Lord would announce His plans for the stewardship. The Host waited anxiously to see if one of their own, an angel, would be made the governor over earth and man. Most felt that Lucifer would be so named, and quietly spoke as much in the crowded fields and skies of the Kingdom.

And yet, how could any angel have known the mind of God? How could any angel have divined that he who came from the stuff of earth would also steward it? A great cheer went up upon the proclamation, that A'dam, the man, would be given full authority over earth, to keep it for the Lord Most High; to nurture it; to care for it; to steward it together with the newly created woman.

As the angels left the assembly, a new sense of mission and purpose was realized. They knew now that theirs was not merely to serve the Lord in Heaven, but also serve Him on earth. They knew that A'dam was forever bonded to the Lord in a special, mysterious plan, and there would now be opportunity to serve God by helping the man and woman. But among most, the greater question was not what the naming of A'dam as steward would mean for earth, but what the rejection of Lucifer would mean for Heaven...

CHAPTER 17

"I don't intend to start a war in Heaven—I intend to finish one."

"What a wonderful event!" said Crispin. "Glorious!"

Sangius nodded his head in agreement. He could barely hear Crispin over the joyous celebration that was occurring in Heaven. Among most angels the name *A'dam* could be heard in lively conversation. Some angels admitted complete surprise, while others indicated that they had thought it possible but never dared suggest such a notion. Most were simply joyful in the Lord's decision. Others were completely astonished.

"Have you seen Lucifer?" Sangius asked.

"Not since the dismissal," said Crispin. "I must say that he demonstrated great self-control when the words 'A'dam the man' were spoken in connection with the stewardship." He laughed. "Every angel who sits on his Council looked at him as one when *that* announcement was made!"

Gabriel came over to where Sangius and Crispin were talking.

"Greetings, brothers!" he said, embracing them.

"Ah Gabriel," said Crispin. "Remarkable time in Heaven, hmm? The Zoa were quite correct, weren't they? Gabriel? Gabriel!"

Gabriel was looking intently at something behind Crispin. Sangius and Crispin turned to see an angry looking Rugio staring harshly at Gabriel. When Rugio saw the other two looking at him, he scowled at them and immediately took flight. He disappeared in a reddish streak across the Heavenly sky, buffeting several angels as he went.

"Seems as if we have some work to do," said Gabriel sadly. "Now that the question of the stewardship is settled we must mend the breech in the Host."

"That should prove interesting," said Crispin, as a celebrating angel merrily bumped into him and begged pardon.

"Nevertheless, it must be done," said Gabriel. "Where is Michael?"

"Like Lucifer he disappeared as soon as the ceremony ended," said Sangius, looking around.

"I wonder what Lucifer's intentions will be now," said Gabriel. "He will be the key to restoring good relations within the Host. I hope he is prepared to do so."

"And so he shall," came the familiar voice of Michael. The archangel glided in and landed next to Gabriel. "I have just had words with the music minister!"

"Good words or ill?" asked Crispin.

"Good words," said Michael. "The best. Lucifer has accepted the Lord's decision and will support Him wholeheartedly. In fact, he has invited me to speak to his Council in a special meeting he is convening on earth."

"On earth?" asked Gabriel. "That seems odd given the change in his circumstances."

"I wonder if Lucifer will have to ask permission of A'dam to hold a meeting there?" Crispin asked humorously.

Gabriel ignored Crispin's comment and said, "Do you really believe there is a chance at reconciliation?"

"I can only try," said Michael. "I must!"

"Then I will go with you," said Gabriel.

"And I," said Sangius.

"No, dear friends," said Michael with great compassion. "I thank you. But Lucifer was quite clear in that he wanted only me to attend. I think it will help him save face and ease back into the relationship."

"Hmph! Save face indeed," said Crispin. "I think a little humility is well in order for Lucifer and the whole Council." He looked at the others. "But I believe that our Lord would have us accept their overtures of reconciliation. If they can be gracious in defeat, we can most certainly be gracious in our case as well."

"Then it is settled!" Michael said. "I will visit earth alone. I feel that all will soon be well in Heaven once more. We will soon be one as a Host again! This horrible spirit which has darkened Heaven for so long will soon be with us no more!"

<hr />

No one dared look Lucifer in the face.

The Council met following the announcement as prearranged. But instead of it being a victory celebration it was an awkward and quietly tense scene around the table. Noticeably absent were the warriors. Pellecus and the others looked at each other from time to time. Tinius on more than one occasion began to speak but stopped himself. Berenius simply looked down at the table. Lucifer sat stone-faced at the head of the table, collecting his thoughts. A loud cheer from the celebration which was still going on in the City echoed through the room and seemed to awaken Lucifer.

"I have been a complete fool," Lucifer finally said.

The angels at the table began protesting but Lucifer held up his hands to stop them. "Yes, I said a fool," he continued. "How could I have ever believed that the Most High would take advice from the Elders? I should have realized that He only takes council with the Son and Spirit. And now He has done what He always intended—He has named A'dam as the steward."

"Abominable!" said Pellecus.

"A disgrace to all angels," added Lenaes.

"And a fact with which we must now contend," said Lucifer. "It certainly complicates matters but it does not mean that earth will not yet be ours. It only means that we will have to move by another route—perhaps the only route that was ever really open to us. The Most High needs to understand that we will have this our way!"

The Council looked at each other uncomfortably.

"Surely you don't intend to start a war in Heaven?" said Pellecus, who was speaking for the Council in this matter.

"No, Pellecus," said Lucifer, "I don't intend to start a war in Heaven. I intend to finish one!"

+≡————————≡+

Michael glided down to earth at the place where Lucifer had instructed him to meet with him. It was a barren spot, half a world away from Eden, where snowy mountain peaks jutted out of fertile valleys. He wondered how he should approach the Council. He wanted to see them all restored, but he also knew he must point them to their collective responsibility in this business.

"Michael!"

Michael turned and saw Serus.

"Serus!" Michael said. "What are you doing here?"

"I'm here to guide you to the meeting, Archangel," said Serus.

Michael was disappointed in Serus' attitude of late. It seemed that for all their talks, Serus had stayed firmly aligned with Lucifer. Perhaps the reality that Lucifer would never be named steward would force Serus to draw some redemptive conclusions once and for all.

"Where is Lucifer?" asked Michael. "And the Council?"

"They have begun meeting between those two jagged peaks," Serus said, pointing to twin rocky promontories. "Heaven is feeling a bit uncomfortable for them right now, as you can imagine. I'll show you."

Michael took flight and followed Serus to the mountainous area that Serus indicated. As they landed Serus said, "Right over here."

Before Michael could respond he felt himself set upon by hundreds of warrior angels, who were pressing in, swords drawn, creating a belt of light around him which grew more and more intense. Michael was able to draw his sword, but only for an instant as a dozen strong hands pulled the sword out of his hands. A thousand of the strongest warriors in Heaven were holding Michael, and still their combined strength could just barely contain him.

Several times he almost broke out. At one point he managed to snatch back his sword and began hacking away at the force that was holding him back—but more and more angels continued pouring into the battle. Soon he began growing weary. Michael recognized most of the angels—some of whom were under his direct authority. He commanded them to step back but they merely sneered or laughed at him. And through all of the shouting and excitement, Michael could make out the voice of one particular angel who was barking orders: Rugio.

Rugio walked calmly to the scene of battle. His chief aids Nathan, Vel and Prian followed closely behind. Michael glared at Rugio and then at Serus. Rugio laughed at the sight of Michael, trapped by his own legions. Serus did not look up at Michael.

"Well, Archangel," said Rugio. "It seems to me that I recall your having told me that the next time I drew my sword in your presence you would see me cast down." Rugio took out his sword and came close to Michael. "Cast me down, Archangel!"

The warriors holding Michael began laughing and cajoling him.

"I will still see you cast down," said Michael, who continued feeling out weak spots in the angelic prison which held him. Nathan handed Rugio Michael's sword. Rugio held it next to him as if he was wearing it. "I make quite a dashing archangel, hmm?"

Nathan and the other angels burst out laughing. "Quite so, commander," said Nathan. "It suits you well."

"Good," said Rugio. "We'll just call it a trophy of war."

"What is the meaning of this, Rugio? Where is Lucifer?"

"I believe he is in Heaven," said Rugio. "In fact, we should soon have word from him that we may set you free—that is, once our business with the Lord is finished. So relax, Archangel, and it will soon be over!"

Michael looked at Serus. "Serus, how could you betray me?" he said. "How could you betray the Lord?"

"You can only betray one with whom you had trust," said Serus. "You never trusted me, Michael."

"But I did," said Michael. "How else would I have ended up here? I trusted you, Serus! Serus!"

Serus took flight and headed back toward Heaven. He turned to Rugio. "My instructions are to meet Lucifer at the Temple and report on your situation," he said. "I will send word from Lucifer when Michael is to be freed!"

"Very good," said Rugio.

Serus disappeared into the sky. Rugio turned his attention back to Michael. "Serus is a fool—but he's a useful fool. Don't struggle, Michael. It will be over soon, I told you."

"What is Lucifer attempting?" Michael asked, still fighting against the force of a thousand angels. "It can't possibly succeed, you know!"

"You arrogant angel," Rugio snapped back. "You and Gabriel and the rest who think that your example must be followed by the entire Host! Well clearly that is not the case! Even now, Michael, Lucifer marches on the Temple with upwards of one-third of the angels to become steward. Yes, Michael. One-third of the Host decided they had enough of you and the rest of your pandering crowd!"

Michael suddenly lunged forward, just missing Rugio, before a flood of angels who pulled him back buried him again. Vel and Prian drew their swords. Rugio continued talking, relishing the moment in having so important a captive.

"The remainder of the Host will give way," Rugio continued, "especially when they have been told that the reason you are not present is because you refuse to fight against a brother angel! Brilliant, hmm? So you see, in this instance your example-setting ways will finally become useful, Michael, as you set the example to the rest of the Host not to resist!"

"This cannot possibly succeed," Michael responded. "Stop this nonsense before it is too late! For all of you!"

"Ah, Michael," purred Rugio, who was now toying with Michael's own sword. "It is already much later than you realize!"

+⚎━━━━━━━━━━⚎+

"Morning Star! Morning Star!"

The crowd of angels was shouting the name in a chant which all of Heaven could hear. Lucifer spoke to them from above, perched on the Temple roof above the entry. He was so proud of the angels who were turning out for him—the operation could not have unfolded any better.

Next to him on the Temple were some of the most important angels in Heaven representing the Academy, the Elders, the legions and the Temple. Lucifer made quite sure that the Host saw a united and encompassing movement within their body. Those members of the Academy (like Crispin) or of the Elders (like Dabran and the Chief Elder) who were not in accord with Lucifer were being detained in other quarters of Heaven—just as Michael was held on earth.

"Brothers!" Lucifer shouted, as the noise subsided. "Hear me out!"

"No! Throw him out!" came a voice, which was quickly stifled by a group of warriors who were assigned to prevent such disturbances.

"Yes, throw me out!" he went on. "Throw me out of the Kingdom if what I have to say makes no sense. But first hear me out!"

"We'll hear you, Morning Star!" a voice shouted, which was followed by a general consensus among the noisy crowd. Lucifer waited for the noise to subside.

"I know most of you are wondering what has happened to your Morning Star," Lucifer continued. "For some time now you have all been hearing rumors, whispers in the great halls—stories of subtle plots and sordid schemes. You have heard that I am a rebel and an insurrectionist. But let me tell you who I am.

"I am one who seeks only what is best for the Host. I am one who stands for the freedom of angels to reach their greatest destiny. I have no argument with the Most High! He is wonderful and He is God. Neither do I have an argument with Michael. And as you can see by his absence, Michael has no argument with me. But I recognize, as he does, that from time to time new eras of realization come into being. The Creation brought in the age of man. Now let man bring in the age of angels!"

Lucifer's angels burst into uproarious cheers. The other angels continued to watch cautiously. Some wondered where Michael was. Others awaited the response of the Lord Himself to such pride.

"Yes, I say the age of angels!" Lucifer continued. "You see next to me some of the greatest angels in Heaven. We are not monsters— we are liberators. We seek not to rebel in Heaven but to exercise angelic destiny on earth! Can an angel be stewarded by a man of mud—a beast? I say no! I say that angels must be allowed to fulfill the destiny to which they are called!"

⊹══════════════⊹

In the Academy classroom where Crispin was being detained with some of the other teachers, the noise of the cheering mob could be heard. Berenius was in charge of keeping order at the Academy through what was becoming known among Lucifer's followers as "the liberation." He looked at Crispin and the other teachers.

"Quite a bit of noise," he said. "Sounds as if Lucifer is making one of his magnificent orations!"

"You are right about one thing," agreed Crispin. "He is making a great deal of noise. I suspect it will get quiet when Michael appears."

"I don't believe the archangel will make it to this meeting," replied Berenius slyly. "At any rate, once Lucifer begins to lead these angels in praises to the Most High to demonstrate his devotion there will be no need for Michael. Worship is so moving, hmm? Lucifer has said that angels are like the cattle of earth, easily moved, easily led."

"It is only a matter of time," said Crispin, "before the Most High responds to your master's nonsense. And then we will see who is cattle and who is King."

⊹══════════════⊹

Gabriel paced the hallway outside the Zoa's chamber restlessly. Like everyone else in Heaven, he could hear the great noise of

Lucifer's mass demonstration going on. Why had he been ordered to remain here during the most important and critical event to happen to the Kingdom? Should he not be with Michael and the others? Instead, the Zoa had ordered him to remain until they were ready to dispatch him. Perhaps it was pride, but Gabriel wanted to play a part in this drama. He wondered what was happening in Heaven. A voice called to him from the darkness.

"Gabriel," said the voice of one of the Zoa. "We must tell you what is to happen in Heaven."

Gabriel turned and once more entered the presence of those who stood before the Lord in service to Him. The Zoa stood as they had the first time they met with Gabriel. The lion-faced Zoa spoke to Gabriel first.

"So many questions are in your mind, Gabriel," he said. "But we have already told you that there is only one answer."

"And that is found only in the Lord Himself," continued the Zoa with the face of a man. Gabriel could make out the thousands of eyes that made up the bodies of these strange creatures, staring at him in the darkness.

"Yes, I know this," said Gabriel. "I was wondering why I was called here and not allowed to take part in the conflict itself."

"Yours is the greater part of the conflict, Gabriel," said the eagle-faced Zoa. "For to you it has been given to know the events which shortly must take place. After which you shall seal this knowledge until the fullness of time when it shall be released."

With that the Zoa began to speak of incredible and frightening things which would one day take place. Gabriel could hardly believe what he was hearing, yet, with each word, understood more and more the great depth of love of the Most High. It also made him feel a sense of sadness for Lucifer, whose pride stood no chance against the power of such love.

———

"And so it is with humble but resolved heart that I appear before you today," Lucifer continued. "I am prepared now to voice before the Most High Himself our urgent request that A'dam be guided back to his inferior position and that an angel be named steward of the new world!"

Tremendous cheering went up among the crowd. Kara next stood up to speak.

"Dear brothers," he began. "As you are well aware I am an Elder, second in rank to the esteemed Chief Elder. It has always been my heart and purpose to serve your best interests. This you know. When we as a Council determined that an angel be named to the stewardship we knew that we must be careful in our selection. We knew that the angel who would serve God on earth must also be a proven servant in Heaven. Among the Elders one name continually surfaced. We deliberated and prayed and sought wisdom. Even the Zoa themselves brought word to us that a steward would be named. And thus it happened that we arrived at the decision to commend Lucifer, the Morning Star and Anointed Cherub to become earth's steward!"

Wild cheering broke out in the assembly. Kara looked over at Lucifer who gave him a knowing exchange. Even Pellecus was acknowledging Kara's competence as a crowd-pleaser.

"Brothers!" he went on. "Join us in recommending to the Lord the name of Lucifer as earth's steward!"

Lucifer stood once more, thanking Kara amidst the cheering, noisy sea of angels. The commanders of legions loyal to Michael were paralyzed, as they had standing orders never to take the offensive against Lucifer unless Michael was directing them personally. The other angels, those of the wisdom and worship classes, simply observed the carnival atmosphere in bewilderment.

"I thank you deeply for your confidence," said Lucifer. "But confidence may not be enough." The crowd grew still, wondering what Lucifer meant. "There are those who would oppose us on this—even now. There are those who are so fixed upon the ancient teachings that they are unaware of the prophetic nature of those texts. So bent are these upon keeping the old ways preserved, they have stifled the potential for creative destinies.

"You all witnessed or heard about the tension at the debate. Angel against angel in shameful disarray! Yet such a conflict was not only inevitable but needful! It demonstrated that angels who are resolved will fight for truth. I am prepared, brothers, to resolve this situation without conflict. I am equally prepared, however, that should it come to it, I will go to war for your freedoms. Are you with me to the end?!"

The crowd suddenly burst forth in wild cheering as they responded in dramatic affirmation to Lucifer's challenge. All of Heaven seemed a tangled mass of angels flying here and there, some scuffling with other angels, others demonstrating in unrestrained merriment. Lucifer looked down at what he saw as "freedom unleashed" among the Host and encouraged it on—whipping the angels into a greater and greater frenzy.

Lucifer turned to his Council.

"Appearances are everything—I told you that. Now do you see why I said we don't need every angel—just an impressive show of strength? The other angels don't even realize they have us outnumbered by two-thirds."

"Quite impressive," agreed Kara. "But I suggest we end this quickly before someone tells them."

"Perhaps so," said Lucifer, looking around him. "The demonstration has made its point. I will speak to the Zoa at once and demand, that is, make known our petition."

"My lord!" came the voice of a clearly troubled Tinius.

Lucifer turned to acknowledge him.

"Some of the angels have broken into the sanctuary of the Temple."

"What?!" Lucifer screamed. "Have we no order here? Who was it?"

"Amman and most of his troop," continued Tinius. "They were so emboldened by your words that they boasted they would bring you the greatest trophy of all—one of the Most Holy Emblems."

"My words were meant to encourage resolve, not idiocy," said Lucifer. "They have sealed their fates. Let them pay for it!"

"Serus!" Lucifer called out. "I will shortly become steward. As soon as I have exited the Temple you may tell Rugio to set Michael free. It is finished!"

Serus looked at Lucifer, flush with the coming victory.

"I will do as you command," Serus said, knowing Lucifer had won after all.

Michael was weary of the struggle. From time to time in the Heavenlies he could hear the great noise coming from Heaven. Those angels around him who were holding him also cocked their heads, listening to the great cheers and noises. Something important was happening up there. Was Lucifer actually going to win this battle? Or was something else going on? Michael was frustrated by the angels who held him. He wanted desperately to get into the fight.

"Sounds like the noise of war," said Rugio calmly, still holding Michael's sword. "War in Heaven. How did it ever come to that?" He snickered.

"Because of the war in your own spirit, Rugio," said Michael. "And Pellecus. And Lucifer. All of you have fought a war and lost. You have lost to pride."

"Don't lecture me on pride, Archangel," said Rugio. "You and your kind are the prideful ones. Lucifer is simply changing the order of things. Your pride will not allow you to recognize this."

"I pity you, Rugio," said Michael.

"I don't want your pity, Archangel," said Rugio sarcastically. "It is I who pity you. I will thoroughly enjoy seeing you come to terms with the new order in the cosmos. You will simply have to live with it. And who knows? Lucifer might even appoint me archangel of earth!"

Nathan pointed toward the sky at a bluish streak moving rapidly toward them.

"I believe it is Serus, commander," he said.

"So soon he brings the news," Rugio responded, looking at the sky. "I would have thought that the Lord would have held out a little longer than that! Looks as if it's over, Michael. Your deliverance draws near!" He smiled.

The bluish streak of light crashed violently into Rugio, knocking him down. Michael's sword went flying and Serus grabbed it and drove into the angels immediately around Michael. The sight of the sword of the Archangel manifesting its powerful aura panicked enough of the warriors that Michael was able to break free.

Rugio quickly recovered and tried to stop the panic. He ordered Vel to bring his angels back into ranks. Nathan and Prian grabbed their swords and looked menacingly at Serus, rushing towards the smaller angel.

"Michael!" Serus screamed.

He tossed the sword to the Archangel. Michael caught his sword and broke free from the remaining angels who were holding him. He lunged toward Nathan and Prian who turned at the last moment from their pursuit of Serus. The powerful sword smashed into the two warriors, knocking them far into the Heavenlies. Serus grabbed a loose sword and continued the fight.

The other warriors were thrown into confusion as swords and red light flashed in a ferocious melee. Many of the confused angels fought among themselves, thinking they had been attacked by a large group of Michael's warriors. About half of the contingent had scattered at the sight of the avenging angel. Some returned to Heaven while others hid among the desolate mountains nearby.

Rugio gave up stemming the panic and took out after Serus, cursing him. Michael intercepted Rugio and the enemies stared coldly at one another.

"So your little friend rescues you," said Rugio. "But it won't do you any good, Michael. By now Lucifer has already won the concession he demanded."

"The Lord will never give in to the demands of angels or any other creature," said Michael, keeping an eye out for surprise attacks from the many angels watching them. "You are totally deceived, Rugio. You fight for a wicked kingdom with no authority."

"It is you who is deceived," answered Rugio. "Let my sword represent my kingdom *and* my authority!"

With that Rugio screamed a warrior cry and lunged at Michael, his sword giving off a reddish aura. Michael dodged the thrust and came back hard. He knocked Rugio's weapon out of his hands. Rugio cursed Michael and went scrambling for his weapon. The angels around the fight were cheering Rugio on. Rugio picked up his sword and lifted it over his head with both hands and came down hard against Michael's sword. There was a loud crashing sound and Rugio's sword broke in half. He looked at Michael, holding the broken sword.

"As you said, Rugio," said Michael, "your sword represents both your kingdom and your authority!"

Michael took off to Heaven, telling Serus to come along.

Lucifer made his way into the Temple complex. He haughtily dismissed the Temple warden who, though sympathetic, still maintained an official decorum. His attempt to keep Lucifer from entering the holier recesses of the Temple went ignored.

As he neared the place of the Zoa, the atmosphere took on a reverence that seemed so bizarre in contrast with the riotous celebration going on outside.

He could hear the praises to the Most High which echoed in these chambers day and night. As he entered the antechamber to the Zoas, he saw a figure standing before him. It was Gabriel.

"I was wondering when you might come into this sacred place," said Gabriel sadly. He was vacant and not at all antagonistic, more resigned than revengeful.

"Away from me, Archangel," said Lucifer. "I have business here."

"Your business is finished here, Lucifer," said Gabriel.

"Out of my way, Gabriel!" Lucifer shouted. Behind him appeared two large warriors, adjutants to Rugio who had orders to stay close to Lucifer. They walked up menacingly behind Lucifer and stared at Gabriel.

"Your power is finished here, Lucifer," said Gabriel. "The Lord won't even have to move against you. You never had a chance."

"Remove him," said Lucifer, who started into the room where the Zoa were. "I'll deal with him later."

The two warriors started forward and Gabriel prepared to fight them when suddenly Kara came rushing into the room from behind. Lucifer turned around annoyed.

"Lucifer! Lucifer!" Kara screamed.

"What is it, Kara?" he shouted back.

"The Archangel! Michael!" he said, almost hysterically.

"What about him?" Lucifer said, trying to calm Kara down.

"He's here!"

———————————————

With the appearance of Michael in the City, the celebration quickly turned into violent conflict. Rugio landed not long after and was giving commands to the warriors loyal to his warriors. Everywhere angels were unsure of who was loyal to Lucifer and who was fighting for Michael, but within a short time the two sides sorted themselves out. Michael called out to his commanders and instantly they attacked with their legions, swooping down on Lucifer's angels. Brilliant flashes of different colored lights…swords smashing into each other…auras manifesting in explosive violence…battle orders screamed above the fray…war in the Heavenlies had broken forth!

Michael watched as his warriors valiantly fought with Lucifer's angels. Though the battle was never in doubt in his mind, there were times when it seemed that certain of Lucifer's stronger warriors were getting the advantage in different parts of the City. He smiled as he saw Serus diving headlong into the battle, chasing a panicked Tinius with his captured sword. Sangius flew over to Michael. As word spread that Michael was in the City, Lucifer's angels began to lose heart, and a panic ensued.

"I wish it hadn't come to this," he said, "but it looks like it will be over very soon! Lucifer's angels are fighting poorly!"

"They are fighting extremely well," said Michael. "But they are overwhelmed by the number of the Host who still love the Lord."

"Where have you been?!" shouted Crispin, sword in hand.

Michael could not help but laugh at the sight of Crispin with a sword drawn in full warrior stance.

"Have you actually used that?" Michael asked, indicating the sword.

Crispin held up the sword proudly, pointing to a small nick in its blade.

"You see that?" he said. "That was made on Berenius' proud head! I cornered him over by the Academy when the panic started and reasoned with him a little!" He smiled.

"And where is Lucifer?" Michael asked, scanning the City. "I would like to reason a little with him myself!"

"Lucifer? He went to the Temple, of course!" said Crispin.

Upon those words Michael's sword began to manifest a golden aura—one that he had never before seen. Crispin and Sangius stood back from Michael. Even as the sword grew in its shadowy outline, Michael's heart became more and more indignant as he heard the words of the Most High speaking into his heart. His countenance became strangely unfamiliar as he knew what he must do. The direction from the Lord was not an easy one. He looked at Crispin.

"What is it?" Crispin asked Michael timidly.

"The Most High," said Michael gravely, "has ordered that Lucifer and all with him be turned out of Heaven—no longer to be a part of this Kingdom. And He has given me the command and the authority to do this!" As he said this, the sword grew in such brilliant intensity of gold light that all three of the angels were blind for a moment.

"It is finished!" Michael said, and took off into the Heavenly sky.

Lucifer and Kara scurried out of the Temple, the two warriors following. Lucifer reasoned that if he could only get to Michael he might still carry the day. Gabriel walked behind, awaiting the inevitable outcome. He could only shake his head in disbelief at Lucifer's suggestion that he could get Michael to compromise at this point.

"Lucifer, you will have cost me everything," said Kara. "My position, my standing. I will be ruined in Heaven!"

"Enough," said Lucifer. "I very seriously doubt you'll be in Heaven long enough to worry about it."

They walked out of the complex and surveyed the battle scene. All around them were weary and wounded angels, mostly his, surrounded by a canopy of Michael's angels, holding them in. Not one of Lucifer's angels had been able to escape the parameter set up by Michael. In various parts of the City were the members of Lucifer's Council, once proud, now captives of Michael's troops.

Lucifer looked at the vigilant angels that surrounded them—captains and warriors loyal to Michael—now captors. "The net closes in," said Lucifer. "I have underestimated Michael."

"And Serus," came the voice of Rugio, who explained Serus' actions in helping release Michael prematurely.

"Betrayed in the end," said Lucifer, smirking. "How like that weak angel to throw in with Michael at the last! Serus, you are a disgrace and a traitor!" an enraged Lucifer screamed. His words echoed through the Heavenlies.

Michael came gliding in and set down in front of Lucifer. Gabriel came walking up behind Lucifer from the Temple. All of Heaven awaited this last act of the drama. Rugio stared coldly at Michael.

"Not that it matters, Lucifer," said Michael, "but Serus did not betray you—he remained loyal to the Lord. And that made all the difference."

"Let him serve the Most High," said Lucifer. "For all the good that Serus was to me I am better off without him."

Kara rushed toward Michael. He looked at the others with whom he had worked to see Lucifer named steward and indicated them to Michael.

"I beg you to consider, Archangel, that I am an Elder. I am not one of these rebellious angels! I have sought only a peaceful resolution throughout this affair. I worked ceaselessly..."

"Not now, Kara," said Michael.

"You worked ceaselessly with the rest of us," said Pellecus, who made his way to the top of the steps where Lucifer stood in front of the Temple. "I am not ashamed to admit it. We tried and we failed. The question is, Archangel, what now?"

"That is entirely up to the Most High," said Michael.

A sudden thunderous blast from the Great Mountain of the North rocked Heaven, sending many angels to their feet. The Presence of the Most High began to slowly pour into the City from the Mountain, engulfing the angels with a holy shroud. Every angel bowed low before the Lord. Even Lucifer went down on his knees.

High above them in the Heavenly sky, a figure appeared who was the color of bronze and wearing a white, flowing robe. The angels in the sky pulled away from the robed figure, encircling Him, heads still bowed low. The figure rode a fierce looking beast and held a sword in his hand.

"Behold, the judgment of the Lord!" the Voice said.

Michael pointed his sword to the extreme end of the Kingdom, as the Lord had instructed him, and suddenly a great gate appeared, which grew and eventually encompassed a quarter of the horizon. The Host was astonished and frightened by this strange sight at the edge of Heaven.

The gate was made of large white stones. There were huge, barred doors which swung open. The bars looked like bronze. Somehow everyone knew that this was a gate to be used only once—and not as a point of entry, but as a place of final exit.

Michael instructed the angels on the ground and in the air to divide, clearing a pathway to the gate. The path made its way through the crowd and up the Temple stairs, ending in front of Lucifer and his leaders.

Lucifer looked down the pathway that led to the extreme end of Heaven. It looked as if it entered the gate itself. The angels around Lucifer began looking around nervously.

"Surely we are not intended to go down...there," said Kara, pointing toward the dark. "This is ridiculous!"

Pellecus merely looked at the situation and resigned himself to whatever fate may overtake him. His expression was grim. He turned to Kara. "Looks as if you're no longer an Elder, Kara," he said. "In Heaven or on earth!"

Rugio felt for his sword but remembered he had lost it in battle.

"I will one day face Michael again in battle," Rugio said. "This I swear!"

"Not unless Michael enjoys fighting outside of Heaven," Pellecus said.

Michael indicated for the defeated army of Lucifer to begin walking toward the gate. All of the angels who had sided with Lucifer began begging for mercy. But, as if compelled, they began moving. The Host turned their backs on the guilty angels, ashamed and saddened that some of their own had actually rebelled against the Lord. Now, their horrible choices had led them to this even more horrible end.

Some of the angels were still defiant, but most were terrified. Most of them regretted having sided with Lucifer in such a reckless affair. A few of the angels, like Amman's group, who had particularly profaned the Most High in their break with him by presuming upon the Most Holy Place, were divided further from the group. Chains shackled them together and they disappeared into an abyss from which their screams could be heard and out of which there was no escape. They could be heard cursing and screaming as they struggled in their dark prison awaiting further judgment at the end of the age.

Lucifer was the last to leave the Temple steps. He muttered something under his breath as he passed in front of Serus, whose back was turned toward him like the others. As he made his way closer and closer to the darkness he became more and more enraged. How could this be? Why were they simply accepting this without a struggle? He could no longer contain the vicious feelings inside him and looked up at Michael. He decided that he would not accept defeat so graciously.

Michael saw the purplish light coming right at him. He didn't have much time to think and quickly wielded his sword. The angels watched in horror as Lucifer went up against Michael for one last battle. Michael brought his sword down and crashed into Lucifer who screamed in agony and went spinning out into the

Heavenlies. Lucifer growled like a beast and came roaring back. Back and forth the two mighty angels thrusted and parried, moving ever closer to the dark opening in Heaven. Lucifer swung his sword hard and it crashed into Michael's sword, sending streams of light all over the City. Their swords were locked in struggle as Archangel and Anointed Cherub faced each other. Lucifer's eyes were like glowing purple coals. He smiled at Michael's apparent distraction caused by the grotesque sight.

Suddenly, Michael's sword manifested the strange golden aura. Lucifer backed away a bit. Michael raised the sword high over his head. Lucifer looked at the menacing weapon and then back at Michael. His hateful eyes met the Archangel's determined eyes, ablaze with the righteousness of the Lord. Michael hesitated for just a moment, giving Lucifer enough time to strike down hard with his purplish sword. The Host gasped as Michael winced in pain and reared back.

Michael looked to the Lord in the sky and suddenly his sword began to shine even more brilliantly—a white gold which bathed all of Heaven in its sheen. A strength he had never felt before surged within him as he raised his sword for what he knew would be the last time in this battle.

"In the name of the Lord," Michael said, as he brought the sword up over his head, holding it with both hands. Lucifer saw the blow coming, unstoppable, unavoidable.

"This is not over, Archangel!" Lucifer managed.

Michael's sword struck Lucifer with an explosive force that shook the City and sent Lucifer reeling out of Heaven. He fell like a meteor, bright at first and then disappearing in the inky blackness of space. Lucifer was vanquished and all of Heaven broke out in solemn praise to the Most High.

Chronicles of the Host

The Dark Times Begin

And so it was that Lucifer and all those who had sided with him in his prideful attempt were disgraced and removed from the Kingdom of God. No longer would they enjoy the sweet Presence of the Most High; no more could they worship with their fellow angels and enjoy the beauty of holiness. They were cut off from the fellowship of Heaven and took refuge in each other's disgraced company.

And so they became increasingly embittered, as their rage ran unchecked, and they abandoned themselves completely to the so-called freedoms espoused by their leader. They took on the very image of the vile and contemptible behaviors to which they were becoming increasingly held captive. Soon the beauty of their outward appearance could neither hide nor contain the corruption that lived inside of them. And so they took on the hideous characteristics of the lusts which drove them. Angel became demon; messenger became monster; and Lucifer, the Morning Star, became Satan, the Adversary.

In Heaven there was rejoicing that the Lord's name had once more been vindicated. Yet there was the feeling among many that the struggle had only been interrupted; that the greater struggle lay ahead. The words of Lucifer rang loudly in Heaven, "This is not over, Archangel!" And thus did the Host in Heaven gird itself for the inevitable conflict.

The fallen angels soon regrouped under Lucifer's capable and vengeful eye. Time was against Lucifer and he realized that a judgment awaited him and the others at the end of the age. They knew that the recently created Sheol was to be their final destiny. And so Lucifer reconvened his Council, now called the Council of Liberation, and together they reasoned that unless the war could be continued from afar, all was lost. And so it was that Lucifer's host drew the lines of battle, from where they could still strike a meaningful blow against the Lord, on earth...in Eden.

CHAPTER 18

"The battle will be played out in the minds of humans."

The morning sun peeking over the mountains to the east of Eden was always a beautiful and welcome sight. A'dam loved the morning. He sat up and considered the great blessings he enjoyed. He had a Heavenly Father who loved him and took care of him; he had the most wonderful place to live; and now, with Eve at his side, he was complete.

He looked at Eve, lying beside him under the great tree in the meadow where they always settled for the night. She was so beautiful. He recalled vividly that day when he first called her Eve, because she had been taken from a part of him. She was bone of his bone, and flesh of his flesh—united as man and wife as the Lord's caretakers. He loved her so. He caressed her hair and she stirred.

Eve opened her eyes and looked at her husband. She smiled at him.

"Why do I always find you staring at me when I wake up?" she said.

"I cannot help it," A'dam replied. "I love you so very much that I enjoy seeing you there…knowing you are at my side. I am so thankful that the Lord has been so good to me."

"And to me," Eve replied.

A'dam stood up and stretched, yawning and surveying the garden. He thought about what he must do today and looked at Eve.

"Where did that face come from?" she asked, smiling at him. "So serious all of a sudden!"

"Eve, there is something I must tell you...show you," A'dam said.

"What is it, my love?" Eve asked. She stood up and came to her husband's side.

"Follow me and I will tell you," said A'dam.

Eve took her husband's hand and they began walking through the garden. She loved walking with her husband in Eden. But she was a little disturbed by his behavior this particular morning. What was bothering him so? What could be this serious?

"I have never seen this part of Eden before," she finally said. "Where are you taking me?"

"To the center of the garden," A'dam replied.

"Such eventful times in Heaven," commented Crispin. "This will certainly be an interesting situation for the chroniclers of the Kingdom!"

Michael and the others laughed at Crispin's remark.

"Ah, Crispin," said Michael. "I might have known your first thought would tend toward the academic!"

"My interests are academic to be sure," agreed Crispin. "But I want to make sure that all of creation knows what happened here. Realize, Michael, that if darkness can exist in Heaven it can exist anywhere!"

Michael, Sangius and Serus were all enjoying the company of Crispin in his quarters at the Academy. Serus had recently been invited into this circle and was making great strides in becoming reacquainted with the fellowship of the Host.

"I certainly found that out," said Serus. "I shudder when I think of how close I came to staying with Lucifer."

Michael smiled at Serus and said, "Yes, my little friend. The Lord never gave you up. And now instead of being steward to Lucifer you are apprenticed to me! I am very proud of you, Serus."

Serus looked at Michael. How different it was to be in the company of those who treasure service to the Lord! "You're right, Michael," Serus responded. "It was the Lord who never gave up on me. I thought I had transgressed too far. But I suddenly realized that my heart was not in it after all. I also realized that Lucifer was never going to win against the Most High God. What presumption!

"So it was that while in their proud assembly of leaders that I realized once and for all time that my loyalty and heart belonged to God Most High." He looked to Michael rather sheepishly. "I hate to admit it was just before they had designed the plans to hold you on earth while Lucifer made his move in Heaven. For that I am truly sorry." He looked down, ashamed.

Michael smiled. "Don't let it trouble you, Serus. Better a change of heart late than too late!"

"Well put, Michael!" said Crispin, impressed with Michael's response. "I could not have said that better myself."

Everyone laughed.

Serus continued. "So I made up my mind that when the right opportunity came up, I would do something." He began looking around the room, now becoming more animated as he relived the experience. "When I knew I would be returning to earth with a message for Rugio, I decided that it was time and just...well... attacked the mob of angels holding you."

"And for that we are all grateful," said Crispin. "You have done well."

Serus smiled, completely grateful of his new life and company of friends.

"So Heaven is clean once more," said Sangius.

"Any word of Lucifer?" asked Crispin.

"Nothing in detail," said Michael. "The Elders are meeting with Gabriel right now. He will have instruction for us soon regarding the whole business. As well as our roles on earth."

"Earth," said Serus, "is where you will find Lucifer."

"Would he dare such a thing?" asked Sangius. "He has already been removed from Heaven for his profanities. Would he dare defile earth as well?"

"You must understand," said Serus. "Lucifer does not consider himself beaten. If I know him he will call this a setback. He will redouble his efforts and continue the war. And the most logical place from which to continue is earth."

"I quite agree with Serus," chimed in Crispin. "The heart of the conflict was earth. That is where he will draw the next line of battle."

"But how?" asked Michael. "What can he possibly do on earth that he was unable to accomplish in Heaven? He knows A'dam has the authority on that planet. Like it or not he must abide by that!"

"Oh, he doesn't like it," said Serus. "Neither will he abide by it."

Gabriel entered the room and greeted everyone.

"Ah, Gabriel," said Crispin. "Perhaps you can enlighten our thinking. What will be Lucifer's next course of action? Will he storm Heaven or simply foul up earth?"

"Neither, dear teacher, "said Gabriel. "The Lord has instructed us that so long as A'dam has his authority on earth, Lucifer can do nothing. In short, Lucifer is powerless against the name and authority of God which A'dam carries."

"Interesting," said Crispin.

"So there is nothing Lucifer can do to A'dam," remarked Michael. "That is quite encouraging. Especially when you consider the transformation that our former brothers have undergone."

"Yes, they are quite hideous, "said Crispin. "I have seen one or two of them myself. They sometimes come to the edges of the Kingdom—completely profane and given over to their most base instincts." Crispin shook his head. "Distorted, frightening, ugly, cunning beasts they have become."

"The thought of *that* kind having access to A'dam is quite disturbing," agreed Michael.

"They never shall," said Gabriel, "provided that A'dam maintains the authority God has placed in his hands."

He continued telling the group of the angels' role on earth. The Host would be serving man as they grew in numbers. Specific angels were to be assigned to individual men and women. Angels were never to interfere with the choices or situations humans found themselves in unless instructed by the Lord. They were not to talk or appear to humans. They were simply there to guide and watch—and in some cases protect.

"Protect from what?" asked Crispin. "Everything on that planet is at peace with everything else!"

"Just because Lucifer does not have the authority now does not mean that he will not do everything he can to take it away from A'dam," Gabriel said grimly. "In such a case earth would legally come under the authority of Lucifer—at least until the end of the age when the Lord promises to judge these fallen creatures."

"Unbelievable! You mean A'dam could have his authority taken away?" asked Crispin.

"No," replied Gabriel. "I mean that A'dam could give it away."

⊹⇌————————⇌⊹

A'dam led Eve to the clearing in the center of Eden. She looked at him with a bemused "okay, what now?" sort of look. A'dam looked tenderly at his wife whom he deeply loved. As they stood before the trees a young deer came up and nudged at A'dam's hands, looking for tender young shoots he often fed the animals. He indicated to the deer that he had nothing and the animal wandered off.

"Eve, first of all know that I love you with all of my being," A'dam began.

"You didn't have to bring me here to tell me that," said Eve. "I know your love for me is true, as mine for you is."

"But my love for the Lord Most High must always come before you or anything else. You understand that, don't you?" he asked hopefully.

"Of course I do, my love," said Eve. She pictured in her mind the many evenings when A'dam consorted with the Father in the garden, or stared into the Heavens in communion with God. "And I promise you I will never be jealous."

"That is not what I am trying to say," said A'dam. "Rather, it is the Lord who is jealous."

Eve looked at him quizzically.

"The Lord is jealous? Of you? Of me?" She laughed.

"He is jealous of our love for Him. Jealous of our obedience to Him. That is why I have brought you here, Eve."

A'dam pointed to the two trees in the midst of the meadow.

"You know that the Most High has given us everything in the garden. We may eat, drink and enjoy the plenty that the garden produces. The animals are blessed with the same situation. We all eat of the fruit of the garden..."

"Yes," said Eve. "Go on."

"But we must never eat of the fruit of these two trees. The Lord has forbidden them to us. If we eat of this fruit we will surely die. The Lord told me this Himself—right here where we are standing now."

Eve looked at the trees. She smiled at A'dam.

"As you wish, A'dam," she said. "I shall not eat of these trees. But may I ask you what is so special about these trees?"

"What makes these trees special from every other tree is that we may eat of every other tree and not these. That is all there is to say." A'dam shuddered a bit. "I don't even like being near them."

"Come on, my love," said Eve. "It's all very interesting. And I promise we shall never come into this part of Eden again! Now, come and follow!"

Eve bounded off into the garden the way they had arrived. A'dam raced after her, grateful that he need not be worried about the trees. As lawkeeper in Eden, it was his responsibility to see that this command of the Lord be kept. Particularly since there was such a devastating penalty attached to the breaking of it. He took off after Eve, calling her as he ran. Suddenly, he stopped and looked back.

"Hello?" he called. "Lord?"

No response. The only noise was the wind blowing through the trees. A'dam felt foolish at the notion that there might be someone else in the garden when the only other human had run on ahead. Still he thought he had sensed another person. He shook his head and took off after Eve.

He could not possibly have known that Lucifer stood in the meadow near him, and had been there during the whole conversation with Eve. He surveyed the trees and then turned his eyes in the direction the human couple had run.

"Forbidden fruit?" he said, addressing Heaven. "If I may borrow Kara's phrase, this is delicious! And with a death sentence attached? Isn't that a little risky, O Lord? Didn't You learn Your lesson in Heaven when You lost one-third of the Host to choices? Choices are dangerous, remember?" He walked over to the first tree and put his hand on one of the lower hanging fruits. "But if that is the way it is played on earth, I'm up to the game. I've become rather an expert on the subject of choices."

<hr/>

"Come to order!" Lucifer screamed.

The Council of Liberation was meeting to discuss the next course of action. Most of the members of Lucifer's former Worship Council sat on this Council. Kara was a new member, taking the place of the traitor Serus, and had only recently been asked to attend. The Council met in a deep fissure of the earth, far below the surface. Lucifer had decided that he no longer wanted to be in proximity of Eden or its beauty officially until it was his to steward alone. Only then would he make good his promise to set up his throne between the two great trees in the center of the garden.

The rowdy Council got quiet as Lucifer stood to speak. He was pained by the increasingly malevolent characteristics that all of his angels were taking on. The beauty of holiness had given way to the reality of iniquity—and the angelic exterior was rotting away. Some of the angels were actually difficult to look at, though most in the Council still managed enough of their former presence that they continued on as before.

"Grim looking lot here, hmm?" said Lucifer, whose own appearance had taken on an angry countenance devoid of the joy he once maintained as worship minister to the Most High. The joy of the Lord had become a rotting corpse.

The angels laughed uncomfortably. Those whose appearance was more distorted than the others laughed the hardest.

"Rugio, you're looking particularly...convincing today," Lucifer said.

More laughter.

"It comes and it goes, lord," said Rugio, "depending on the mood. As long as I don't think about Michael too much I can maintain some dignity."

"Well. Perhaps one day we will recover your godlikeness!"

Rugio laughed. "Or at least bring Michael down from his, lord!"

Lucifer smiled in agreement.

"Well. All of us realize the precarious position we are in," began Lucifer. "Because of the stubbornness of the Most High, the blind loyalty of the Host, and A'dam's position of authority, we now face a war that seems to have little chance of success."

He paced around the large flat boulder that served as the Council's makeshift table. The Council sat around it listening to their leader—their only hope. The faint sounds of the angels already in torment could be heard echoing slightly through the room. It was chilling to those who knew their fate was taking them to a similar end.

"Up until now I would have told you that our chances were none and that we all faced certain judgment in Sheol like our misfortunate friends we hear screaming in agony day and night!"

A few of the angels shivered at the sound of the word *Sheol*.

"To be fair I warned Amman and his angels in particular that to profane the Temple as they did on that day was incredibly presumptuous. The Lord may be longsuffering but He will only be presumed upon to a point—this we all know! However, I am here to report that the Lord has given us an incredible gift in the form of two trees in Eden."

Lucifer enjoyed the effect of his words as the angels looked intently at him.

"Trees, lord?" asked Pellecus skeptically.

"Fruit trees," responded Lucifer.

The Council snickered

"Interesting gift. What sort of fruit do these trees yield?" asked Pellecus.

"Death."

The Council sat up.

"These trees yield death to A'dam and to Eve."

They looked at Lucifer, baffled. Some wondered if perhaps he was losing his mind. Pellecus tried to ascertain where Lucifer was going with this. Kara, who was accustomed to the more dignified deliberations of the Council of Elders was astonished at the lack of decorum. Lucifer held up his hands.

"Let me explain," he said. "Several earth days ago I was meditating in the garden. Yes, I know I'm not in the habit of frequenting Eden since the rebels in Heaven expelled us. But I felt drawn that day as if inspired. I knew that a strategy—a plan of war—was formulating in my mind. Thus I found myself in the center of the garden near the trees where I had promised to build my throne.

"As I meditated on these things the two human creatures interrupted my thoughts. I would have destroyed them if I could but they are protected by their privileges in the Lord and so I contented myself to listening."

Lucifer smiled and clapped his hands together. "It seems that the Lord desires A'dam and Eve to choose well or die! For it was explained to A'dam by the Most High Himself that should they eat of the fruit of these trees, covenant will be broken and they will live no more."

The Council looked at Lucifer vacantly, trying to digest the meaning of this. Pellecus alone seemed to grasp the significance and nodded his head.

"Don't you see?" asked Lucifer. "If A'dam disobeys God he breaks the agreement with Him. He will have transgressed and lost his position of authority. He will lose legal right to this planet and we will be rid of him once and for all. Then I will have authority on this planet and can carry on the war with a much more convincing argument."

"The fruit is nonsense really," said Pellecus who understood. "It is merely a point of choice. I doubt seriously the Lord will kill A'dam."

"Whether A'dam dies or not is hardly the point," said Lucifer. "The critical aspect is in the choosing. Choice is what lost us our place in Heaven. It may well be that A'dam's choosing will help us win it back!"

Kara sat up interested now.

"You are saying that A'dam must eat from these trees knowing full well that if he eats he will die?" Kara asked.

"Yes, Kara," said Lucifer.

"What creature in his right mind would choose against the wishes of his Creator?" he asked.

Kara felt the cold stares of every angel upon making so stupid a comment to so many who had made such a choice. Kara stared back defiantly.

"Then the challenge is to steer A'dam in the direction of that choice, correct?" said Kara, trying to move on quickly.

"Yes."

"We cannot even appear to A'dam right now, much less speak to him," Kara continued. "How do you propose to convince A'dam to do this? Surely the Lord has told him about you...about us."

"It won't be me telling A'dam anything," said Lucifer. "My voice is useless in Eden until I have authority on earth. It will be an earth creature that will convince A'dam to eat of the tree."

"An earth creature?" said Kara.

"Yes," said Lucifer. "There is only one other person to whom A'dam confides, besides the Lord."

Several angels muttered the name *Eve* with contempt under their breaths.

"Yes, just so," said Lucifer. "It is through Eve that we shall convince A'dam. He will listen to her, I am sure."

"And what will convince the woman to do such a thing?" asked Kara doubtfully.

"Another earth creature," said Lucifer, smiling. He began pacing the room.

"Earth creatures have a definite weakness for one another. And Eden is full of weaknesses, Kara. There is in the garden one peculiar beast who is more cunning, more intelligent, more capable than all the rest. From what I know of Eden there is only one like him. As it turns out his favorite place to dwell is in the area near the two trees. Eve has frequently seen him near that meadow and has befriended him, as she has all of the beasts in Eden."

He leaned over the stone table looking directly at Kara.

"And though, as you remind us, Kara, I cannot appear to the humans or speak to them outright, at least until I come into authority, I can use a medium which is well-known to the human creatures! I would say the war is about to take an interesting turn for the Most High!"

"You mean to say," said Tinius, "that you can actually teach the serpent to talk to the woman?"

"No, Tinius, hear me out," said Lucifer. "Brothers! I have not been idle in my visits to earth. I have found that we have a great advantage over the material nature of this planet. Not only are its contents able to be manipulated, but so are its inhabitants—so long as they are unknowing or willing. The beasts of earth—at least the lower beasts—can be quite easily controlled."

"By what means?" asked Pellecus.

"Through the mind," answered Lucifer. "Those beasts which possess a mind of some sort and a bit of personality are entered in through the mind. Granted they are stupid and instinctive and therefore easily controlled. The serpent seems to be somehow different and affords greater opportunity for exploitation. The greater the reasoning ability, the greater the potential to serve us. This includes A'dam. As we gain more of A'dam's confidence, we gain a greater potential to aid us."

"Or harm us," said Pellecus. "Should A'dam become incensed by these things."

"Agreed," said Lucifer. "That is why it is of utmost priority to strip A'dam of his authority. So long as a human operates under the authority of the Most High we are paralyzed. But once he has no legal right over us I suspect we will be able to force certain conclusions that will be to our advantage. The battlefield is not in Heaven or in Eden—the battle will be played out in the mind of humans."

Pellecus stood up.

"In the interest of clarification," he said, "and for an accurate rendering in our earthly chronicles, let me summarize. Through the serpent we will encourage Eve to independence. A'dam breaks covenant with the Most High and surrenders legal authority of this present world to us. All well and good. But what does that do to aid us in the end? Is not the war already lost?"

Lucifer glared at Pellecus, his purple aura beginning to seize him. Pellecus eased back into his place.

"The war is never lost," Lucifer said. "Once we have obtained right over these mud-men and distort the image of God, just as many of us have been disfigured, we shall have drawn the game. No winners, no losers. The earth will remain ours, Heaven His. How could the Most High possibly recover A'dam after he chooses against Him? Will He judge humans along with angels? And is it fair to so just a God to judge angels and not humans who are guilty of the same act of disobedience? If He will not condemn His most beloved creature for His own blatant transgression, how can He possibly condemn us who are guilty of a lesser crime?"

"Lesser crime?" mused Pellecus.

"Yes, Pellecus," said Lucifer. "Our crime was merely crossing a line which was implied and never fully stated. There was no law in Heaven forbidding our adventure. We chanced and we failed. In the case of A'dam, however, there is a law in place which, if broken, is an outright rebellious and willful action that is hostile to God. Stated law is always more powerful than that which is merely implied. I believe in the end we will be exonerated because of A'dam's fall—because his sin will be truly outlaw! The Most High will act, rather than see his most beloved creation condemned."

Everyone agreed.

Lucifer looked at Rugio and then Pellecus. "I told you that love would be the deciding factor in all of this. The Most High so

loves these creatures that He will do anything to see them preserved. Yet He loves them enough not to violate their ability to
choose freely to love Him or turn from Him. Such a dilemma! The
Lord has repeated the same mistake on earth that He did in Heav-
en, by creating something that can turn against Him. This is the
blindness of love—and this is why we shall win the war in the end!"

Lucifer stood to conclude the Council.

"Brothers," he said, "be encouraged. I promise you that the
next time we meet it will be in Eden. I swear to you that earth shall
be ours. A word of caution, though, on the angels who vacated
Heaven with us. Rugio, you must make sure your commanders are
keeping the legions intact. Many of them are recklessly chasing all
over the universe—some have even ventured near Heaven itself.
They are acting berserk and chaotic. This battle, though winnable,
is far from over and we must have organization, authorities, principalities and powers in place for the struggle to come. See to it."

"I will so organize," said Rugio, who began conferring quietly
with the warriors who sat next to him. Lucifer dismissed the group.

"Where to now, lord?" asked Pellecus, walking over to
Lucifer.

"I have a visit to make," said Lucifer. "To the serpent."

Chapter 19

"In a few moments, Archangel, it will be you and your angels clearing out of Eden!"

Eve's mind kept going back to what A'dam had told her about the trees. What a horrible thing to plant in a garden! She wished that the trees were not there. But A'dam assured her that as long as they remained obedient to the Lord's wishes, they need not fear. She determined that like her beloved, she too would never again venture into that meadow.

A rustling noise startled Eve and she turned to see the serpent, gracefully wandering toward her through the brush. Of all the creatures in Eden, the serpent was the most social and seemed especially to favor Eve. He was a beautiful beast, with smooth reddish-brown hair and gorgeous green eyes. He had powerful legs that he used in snatching fruit from some of the lower limbs of the trees. Eve liked the serpent. He was friendly. He was beautiful. But mostly she felt a tinge of compassion for the serpent because of all the beasts in the garden, the serpent was the only one of its kind.

He sidled up to Eve. She began stroking his soft coat. The green eyes looked into her eyes.

"You are my favorite creature in Eden," she said, gently caressing the animal.

The serpent nuzzled Eve as if it understood her. She laughed.

"If only you could talk," she said. "Then whenever A'dam was in other parts of the garden I would have someone to talk with. And so would you," she laughed.

From a distance, unseen to Eve, Lucifer watched the scene. He snickered to himself in delight.

"Don't you worry, Eve, " he said to himself. "The serpent will be talking to you soon enough!"

<hr />

Kara and Pellecus were looking for Lucifer. They had scoured the Heavenlies searching for their illusive leader. Kara suggested that they search Eden once more and thus they landed in the northern border. They could see many of their fallen brothers, in the air and about Eden, but their Lucifer was nowhere in sight. Kara was amazed at the hideous transformation of these who had abandoned their place in Heaven. Some were totally maniacal—shrieking and streaking about as if completely insane. Others lolled about, looked up at Kara, and then went back to whatever they were doing. Pellecus shook his head in disgust.

"So this is the freedom Lucifer promised," Kara said. As he spoke, a horrible looking angel dove at him, screaming, "In the name of the Most High God!" and then disappeared into the sky. Pellecus jumped back, startled.

"And to think some of these were the greatest in Heaven," said Pellecus. "Is it any wonder we lost?"

They continued on in the garden to an angel whom Pellecus recognized, perched in a tree. The angel, named Corin, was a former teacher at the Academy and knew Pellecus quite well.

"Hello, archangel," said Corin, ignoring Kara.

"Greetings, Corin," Pellecus said, ignoring the archangel comment. "Where is Lucifer?"

"Ah, Lucifer," said Corin. "The greatest angel ever. You shall one day see that, Pellecus. Believe me!"

Corin's eyes were black and void. Pellecus knew that the brilliant mind he once possessed as an instructor at the Academy had been given over to complete darkness. He inwardly bristled at such a waste.

"Corin, where is Lucifer?" repeated Pellecus.

"Lucifer is wherever Lucifer will be!" Corin answered mockingly.

"Dear Corin, my colleague, look what you have done to yourself by your disgraceful behavior in Heaven," said Pellecus. "If only you had listened more to what you were teaching than to what you were taught."

Corin looked at Pellecus with his black eyes and laughed a bizarre laugh. He began to shake uncontrollably and make strange sounds. Pellecus and Kara watched as the former teaching angel's face contorted and twisted into a misshapen image. He growled a guttural, unearthly sound and his countenance took on the simian appearance of a hideous, ape-like beast.

"Find him yourself, teacher!" he said in the growling, gravel voice. He then leaped off the tree and with a shriek disappeared into the ground. The other angels in the area laughed hysterically at the incident.

"We'll get nothing from these," said Pellecus. "They are completely given over. They are mad!"

"On the contrary they are quite controllable," came the familiar voice of Lucifer.

"Provided one knows what motivates them. Welcome to Eden."

"Lucifer, we must speak to you regarding the present disorder among the angels," Kara said. "This visit only confirms what I am hearing about our situation. We shall never win with angels who are completely insane!"

Lucifer smiled at Kara.

"I have been with the serpent, " Lucifer said. "Or rather I should say I have been in the serpent. Eve is completely smitten with the poor creature! I have found, Pellecus, that even an advanced beast like the serpent is very easily manipulated. Once I was within his mind I was able to drive those things that motivate him—play him, as it were, as our beloved archangel plays his trumpet at an assembly. I had him all over Eden. I left him at the top of a tree—completely unaware of how he had gotten there! It was quite amusing."

"Yes, amusing. The situation with our angels is quite disturbing," Kara said. "Some of them don't even recognize us."

"Ah, Kara," said Lucifer. "Your point is well taken. Realize that in fact some of the angels are completely mad—barely controllable even by me. Others are completely given over to the idea of particular unholy words and deeds. But of course until we have the authority we can do nothing. Believe me, all of them will prove useful in exploiting the weaknesses of men."

He looked at the two leaders, thinking again about his manipulation of the serpent.

"Can you imagine what we will be able to do once the authority is established in our own right?" Lucifer asked. "The Most High will end the war simply to preserve something on this rotten planet besides condemned angels!"

"So what are we to do in the meantime?" asked Kara.

"Kara, you act as if all of our angels have gone berserk. The reality of the situation is that the vast majority of the angels are keenly intelligent and motivated. Rugio is even now ordering them into the principalities and powers that I outlined earlier. I suggest that you each take a leading role in commanding angels. Order must begin from the head—which is me. You allow me to lead and I will see us through."

While they were talking Gabriel landed in front of them. He was carrying a scroll and looked directly at Lucifer. Lucifer smirked at the Archangel.

"Lucifer," said Gabriel, "I am here on business from the Most High God concerning your presence in Eden."

"The Archangel Gabriel coming down in person to deliver a message to a fallen angel," said Kara. "How delightful."

"And what does the Most High wish to tell us now?" said Lucifer. "To vacate earth as well?"

"You are not welcome on sacred ground, Lucifer," said Gabriel resolutely.

"Must we be so formal, Gabriel?" asked Lucifer. "We are after all dear friends, and one day when this is all over we shall be again."

Gabriel ignored Lucifer's comment.

"Not welcome?" said Kara. "Come now, must the Most High be greedy as well as unmerciful? Eden is the only hospitable place on this planet. Surely there is room enough for the human beasts and a few angels?"

"Nevertheless, know this," Gabriel replied, as he read from a scroll. "A'dam, the man, will have full authority over Eden. He carries with that authority the power and privileges of the Most Holy name. Unless the Most High, or one under the authority of the Most High, allows entry into Eden, no creature is welcome in this sacred place. So let it be as to the reading of this commandment which is most holy to the Lord."

"Very well," said Lucifer. "We go. But we shall return one day."

Gabriel looked hard at Lucifer.

"Know that the Host of Heaven will enforce this commandment as required," Gabriel said.

"No doubt, no doubt," said Lucifer. "We shall comply."

Gabriel took off and disappeared into the earth sky. Kara and Pellecus watched him leave and then turned back to Lucifer with a "what now?" expression.

"Why is it that the Lord always leaves open a door?" asked Lucifer.

He called for Rugio and the other major commanders who appeared almost instantly. They stood in front of Lucifer awaiting instructions.

"Alert the Host that no angel shall come near Eden until the proper time. Try to gain some order with those angels who are increasingly difficult to manage." He indicated Kara and Pellecus and added, "Our friends here are getting nervous."

Lucifer took Rugio by the shoulder and looked squarely into his eyes.

"We're playing the game now, Rugio. We lost the first game, but we shall win the second. Go now!"

Rugio took off with his commanders. Lucifer turned to Kara and Pellecus.

"I shall make quick work of this, I believe," he said, "so that the next time Gabriel comes to earth it will be he who is no longer welcome!"

⊹══════════════════⊱

"So you delivered the message to Lucifer?" asked Michael.

"Yes," said Gabriel. "He responded that he would comply but I have my doubts."

Michael and Gabriel were seated in a garden outside of the City. They were discussing the recent events in Heaven, and how they could best reorient the Host to the new circumstances. Most of Heaven was back to normal. A few angels wanted a more complete judgment visited upon Lucifer. They felt sure that the powerful angel would not give up so easily.

"Well, if Lucifer does not vacate Eden on his own, I will vacate him personally," Michael said. He noticed the troubled look on Gabriel's face. "What is the matter?"

"Michael, I have seen what rebellion does to an angel," he said, remembering his recent visit to Eden. "I saw the horrendous result of sin—the transformation. I cannot help but think about what might happen should A'dam choose a rebellious path as well."

"I am concerned too, Gabriel," Michael said, looking in the direction of Heaven, from where Lucifer's angels had been expelled. "I know that in Lucifer we have a determined adversary." He looked back at Gabriel. "But my hope is that he will not try to engineer another rebellion. That will be the finish of him then and there."

"But A'dam can turn, Michael," said Gabriel. "And that is what concerns me."

"All the more reason for keeping those fallen creatures out of Eden," Michael said. "Unless or until they are invited in, they have no authority there. A'dam is clever enough to realize that. He hasn't ventured anywhere near the center of the garden since the Lord spoke to him about the trees."

"Yes," agreed Gabriel. "But Eve frequently goes there."

"Only to visit the serpent," Michael said. "Besides, A'dam has warned her about the trees as well. He is the law keeper in Eden, Gabriel. It is up to him to see that the law is kept."

"And what if the law is not kept?" Gabriel asked. "I can understand the forbidding of Lucifer's angels in Eden. But why are the holy angels not allowed to help A'dam; to guide him; to keep him from…"

"Rebellion?" came the voice of Crispin.

"Just so," said Michael. "Why can't we be in Eden guarding the trees in case A'dam should come near. Why does the Lord forbid our interference with A'dam?"

"You are asking many questions, Michael," answered Crispin. "But it all centers on the same reason that the Lord did not interfere with Lucifer's decision to rebel."

Crispin sat next to Michael.

"Freedom," said Michael.

"Freedom, exactly," said Crispin. "Michael, if the Lord permitted you or me or any other angel to interfere with A'dam's choices to either obey or disobey it would defeat the reason for creating A'dam in the first place. A'dam was created to love the Lord—but if that love is not freely given it is not truly love. True love is not compelled—it is offered."

"That is wonderful—for you and me and Gabriel—and the other Host who love the Lord," said Michael. "But Lucifer and his angels are certainly not going to respect that boundary. They will try to get to A'dam—I'm sure of this."

"Whether they 'get to A'dam' as you say, or not, the choice is still A'dam's to make. The man will choose his own path. What he doesn't realize is that his choice is a critical aspect of the war."

"And suppose he decides to rebel," said Michael. "What then?"

"In that case," said Crispin, "we have a very different war on our hands."

✦ ━━━━━━━━━━━ ✦

"Eve!" A'dam called out.

He could hear his voice echoing through Eden.

"EVE!" he shouted again.

No answer.

She probably wandered off again with some of the animals, he thought to himself. A'dam was amused with Eve's fascination with the beasts of the garden. The animals loved Eve and came up to her whenever they saw her. She felt part of her responsibility as co-steward on earth required that she care for the animals at times—grooming the beasts; pulling a thorn out of a lion's great paw; or playing with the cub of a bear while the mother foraged for honey. He smiled as he thought about the time when a little black bear cub was stuck in a tree and she climbed up to retrieve it.

He decided to look for her deeper in the garden.

✦ ━━━━━━━━━━━ ✦

The little lion cub was playing with a lily that Eve had picked. He playfully pawed at the flower as Eve made it dance back and forth in front of him. She laughed in delight. *A'dam will be looking for me,* she thought to herself and decided she had better leave.

As she was standing to leave, a low moan echoed through the garden. It was the sound of an animal in pain. Eve rushed toward the area where she heard the sound. It was coming from the center of the garden. In a clearing not far ahead she saw the serpent, heading into the great meadow.

He was limping terribly and making noises as if he were hurt. Eve's first thought was to help the serpent as she had helped countless other animals. But she was reluctant to follow him into that area of the garden. She watched from a distance. The serpent suddenly plopped himself down at the base of one of the two trees. He began to whimper loudly, licking his front paw.

Eve stopped at the edge of the meadow. She called to the serpent to come to her, but he simply looked at her pitifully and continued moaning. She looked at the trees and felt blow across her face a cool breeze that chilled her. She decided to find A'dam. As she turned to leave the animal moaned again, much more loudly.

"I'm coming right back," she said. "I promise!"

She started back into the garden when she heard her name called out.

"Eve," the voice cried out. Eve turned around, completely puzzled.

"Eve!" the voice came again.

"Serpent?" she managed, feeling more than a little silly.

"Eve, please don't leave me," said the serpent.

Eve slowly wandered over to the serpent. She looked, wondering if perhaps her husband was playing some sort of joke on her.

"A'dam, where are you?" she called out.

"A'dam is not here," the serpent said. "Nobody is here except you."

"You can talk?" she asked.

"Yes, Eve," said the serpent. "Because of your great love for the Most High's creation, He has granted me a special gift to talk to you. I suspect that most of the animals in Eden will be talking soon. Such a testimony of your love for God and His world!"

Eve could not believe what she was seeing and hearing.

"I must go and get my husband," she said.

The animal acted as if it were getting up and then cried out in pain and fell again.

"Please don't leave me," the serpent said. "Besides, your husband even now is making his way here."

She knelt down to nurse the hurting paw. She found the thorn and pulled it out.

"There," she said. "Now I will meet my husband."

"No, wait," said the serpent.

Many of the holy angels were converging on the garden. It was as if they knew that a great contest was about to happen and they sensed that God's plan for earth was in the balance. They drifted in, like snowflakes on the mountains, creating a white canopy over the meadow. Like a flock of crows at a field of corn, Lucifer's angels also gathered in the meadow. Whereas the holy angels gathered in the Heavenlies, the fallen angels settled in and around the great trees in the center of the garden. They mocked the angels of the Lord with vile comments.

Michael and Gabriel arrived, setting off a clamorous assault by Lucifer's angels, who screamed curses and oaths, particularly cursing Michael. He simply ignored them. Kara arrived and saw Michael. He went over to him.

"I see we will have to clear these rebels out of Eden after all, Kara," said Michael.

"In a few moments, Archangel, it will be you and your angels clearing out of Eden," said Kara smugly.

CHAPTER 20

"All that God holds in contempt we shall encourage in mankind."

The serpent placed his head on Eve's lap. He looked up at her with soulful eyes.

"I am so grateful to have a friend in Eden," the serpent said. "I am all alone except for you."

Eve was quite nervous. She didn't want her husband to discover her near the trees. She could sense many voices—some compelling her to stay, others demanding she leave.

"You are my friend," she said. "But I must go now."

"There is no need to leave," said the serpent. "Your husband will be here shortly."

She looked at the serpent suspiciously, still feeling a bit awkward speaking to an animal.

"How do you know A'dam is coming here?" she asked.

"Ah, Eve," said the serpent. "I told you that the Lord most High gave me a special gift, did I not?"

"Yes," said Eve. "Because of my love for you."

"Just so," he said. "And the gift of speech is not the only gift He gave to me. He gave me a gift far more significant than mere speech. And because of your love for me, I will share that gift with you."

⊹≒————————≒⊹

"Why can't we intervene!?" asked Michael.

Kara laughed at Michael's frustration. By now Pellecus and Rugio and most of Lucifer's Council had joined the gathering of angels watching Eve and the serpent talk.

"You know the rules, Michael," Pellecus said. "We respect them—so must you."

Rugio laughed heartily.

"She'll take the bait," said Rugio. "And so will he." He looked sharply at Michael. "And then all your efforts to serve the Most High in this will have failed. Yes, Michael—you will have failed the Most High in this!"

Michael resisted the impulse to strike out at Rugio.

"Whatever happens in Eden," said Gabriel, "will be the choice of the humans. If anyone should understand the consequences of poor choices I would think it would be you, Rugio."

Rugio began to manifest his reddish aura, but maintained control.

"Nevertheless," said Pellecus. "It will be a very different world by the time the next sun comes up. A'dam will be here soon and then it will be finished."

"And so shall you all be," added Kara.

⊹≒————————≒⊹

"You wish to share this gift with me?" asked Eve. "But why?"

"Because it is a very special gift," said the serpent. "One which will make you very wise indeed."

"Wise?" said Eve incredulously.

"Why, yes," purred the serpent, who stood up and moved in closer to the trees. He now sat under the branches of the tree on Eve's right.

"But what does that mean?" she asked.

"To be wise means to be able to see," began the serpent. "To be wise means helping your husband steward in ways he never thought possible. To be wise means you will be able to act and feel and think in a whole new light—in short, Eve, to be wise is to be like God. And being like God is the duty of His creation, isn't it?"

Eve thought about these words for a minute.

"I suppose so," she said. "But how does one become wise?"

"That is the rather delicate part," the serpent said. "You see, even though the Most High desires that we be like Him, it requires on our part a certain action—a choice, so to speak—to begin down that glorious pathway."

Eve indicated that she did not quite understand.

"Let me explain it this way. If there was a way for you to become wise so that you might be a better wife to A'dam and a greater caretaker of the Lord's earth, you would make such a choice, would you not?"

"Well, yes," said Eve.

"Of course you would," said the serpent. "And that is because you already have a measure of wisdom inside of you. Now, if I were to tell you of a way to increase that which is already inside of you, that which the Lord has already placed within, you would most certainly want to know of it, yes?"

"Yes," said Eve. "If it would increase that which the Lord has already placed inside of me I would honor Him by increasing it."

"Exactly!" said the serpent. "I could not have put it any better." The serpent's eyes glanced in the direction of Kara and Pellecus and then back toward Eve. "If the Lord had not imparted such wisdom to me—a mere beast—I would never be able to speak with you. Imagine what would happen to you—made in the image of God Himself—were you to have this increased measure of wisdom."

"But what about A'dam?" she asked. "Could he have this gift as well?"

"My dear," said the serpent. "I would insist upon it."

A'dam was nearing the meadow now. He sensed in his spirit that there was something wrong, but he couldn't quite determine the source or the reason. But he knew somehow that he must get to the center of the garden. He hurried along.

✦━━━━━━━━━✦

"Are you prepared to make the choice, Eve?" asked the serpent. "A choice which will open your eyes for the very first time. A difficult choice but the only choice, really, if you are to truly honor the Most High in your stewardship."

"I suppose..." she began.

"The Lord has charged you with keeping His earth," said the serpent. "Clever as you and A'dam are, you will need more wisdom to fulfill this commission. After all, do you think you will always be in Eden? I am sure that one day the Lord Most High has greater plans for you. How can you possibly handle the things He has in store for you without the wisdom to carry on?"

"Yes," she said. "I want more wisdom. For me and for A'dam!"

"Of course you do," said the serpent.

✦━━━━━━━━━✦

"Your lord certainly knows how to confuse an issue," said Gabriel.

"I think he is being quite clear," said Pellecus. "He is merely presenting the woman with a choice. He is neither forcing her nor compelling her."

"He is tempting her," said Michael. "And that amounts to the same thing!"

"Poor Michael," said Pellecus. "You really should have listened more at the Academy. The woman has a free will. As you so ably pointed out a moment ago, Eve is like us angels who made our own choices. The consequences befell us. We were not forced into our decision. Neither shall she be. Lucifer is not allowed to touch the humans. This is all her game now."

"And I might add," said Kara arrogantly, "that she isn't playing very well."

✦━━━━━━━━━✦

"As you know, Eve," the serpent continued, "the Most High has graciously given you and A'dam the privilege of taking care of

His world. He has withheld nothing from you, correct? And yet it puzzles me a bit. Did He not tell A'dam that you must not eat from every tree in the garden?"

Eve looked up at the two trees, the light of the sun glimmering between the branches and shining on her face.

"All is ours except for these two trees," she said, a feeling of hesitancy coming over her. "A'dam received instruction from the Lord which was very clear."

"Isn't that odd?" said the serpent, glancing up at the large boughs. "I wonder why the Lord would withhold these two trees from you?"

"A'dam said that to eat of these trees means death," she said, moving a bit away from the tree.

"Death?" asked the serpent. "In Eden?"

"This is what the Lord told my husband," she said, looking once more at the trees.

"Now that is interesting," said the serpent. "For I am only a serpent and yet I am wise enough to know that you will not die."

The serpent looked up at Eve.

"Do you really think that the Lord would destroy His most precious creation?" he continued. "Do you think for a moment that He would allow a creature who bears His very image; with whom He walks casually for fellowship; in whom He has poured His great love and has authorized to steward the world—do you really believe He would allow you to die?"

Eve wasn't sure how to answer.

"You shall not die," said the serpent. "That is a ridiculous notion. I'm sure that A'dam has innocently misrepresented what the Lord meant. In fact, quite the opposite is true. The Lord Most High knows that if you eat of this fruit that your eyes will be opened and you will become the gods of this world—a god very much like He is. You will know good and evil. What better way to serve Him than by knowing the difference so you may avoid the one and do the other?"

A cold chill ran down Eve's spine. She shuddered a bit.

"Are you cold, my dear?" asked the serpent.

"Then why would God forbid it?" she asked. "If it is such a good thing, why would He tell A'dam not to eat?"

"Why indeed?" replied the serpent. "Makes little sense, hmm? That is why I propose that A'dam has misheard the Lord's instruction. If God would withhold from you the greatest gift of all, He would not be a very loving God, now would He? Yet we know that the Most High is a God of great love. Love withholds nothing, Eve. True love anyway."

Eve looked at the lowest limb of the tree. Several large, round pieces of fruit hung on the branch. She stood and stopped for a moment, staring at the fruit.

"Wise as God," said the serpent. "Can you imagine such a thing?"

Eve walked over to the branch and touched the fruit. It seemed ordinary enough—much like other fruit in the garden. She sniffed it. There was really little fragrance. Perhaps she could at least hold it and examine it a little more closely. As she held it in her hands it broke off and she made a startled noise and dropped it.

"It won't hurt you, Eve," said the serpent. "Do you really think the Lord would place something deadly in Eden?"

"No," she admitted, "there is nothing deadly in Eden."

<hr/>

"Gabriel, we must do something!" Michael said.

The area around the garden was by now filled with angels watching the exchange between the woman and the serpent. Lucifer's angels had crowded in around Eve and the trees in an unholy circle. The holy angels watched in horror as Eve came closer and closer to the trap. Gabriel looked at Michael and shook his head.

"If only we could intervene," he said. "But we are forbidden. She must make her own choice."

"I'd say she has already made it," said Kara with delight.

"Not yet, Kara," said Michael. "Remember Serus? He repented at the last moment and never fell into sin."

"Serus is weak," said Kara. "But Eve is strong. She won't turn back."

"Her strength may deceive you, Kara," said Michael.

"I'm counting on it to deceive her simpleminded husband," said Kara, "and here he comes!"

"Eve!"

A'dam ran to the tree and pulled Eve by her arm. The serpent slowly moved to the other side of the tree.

"Let's get away from this place—what are you doing?" he demanded.

"My love," she answered. "I am doing this for us both."

She picked up the piece of fruit and showed it to her husband.

"Together we will become wise as God and rule for Him to His glory," she said.

"Join me in this—if you truly love me."

Eve took a bite of the fruit. The juice ran down both sides of her mouth as she bit deeply into its meat. She then offered it to her husband. A'dam was completely shocked by this.

"What have you done?" he demanded. "You know that the Lord has forbidden this! You know what He has said!"

"Yes," she said. "I know. And yet I live."

A'dam turned from her. She grabbed his arm.

"Dearest, rule with me in wisdom!" she said.

"Wisdom? Where do you hear such nonsense?" he asked.

"From the serpent. He speaks and is wise," she said, looking for him. "He told me so. A'dam, you must listen to me. We can be like God Himself! A'dam, I ate and did not die. If you truly love me you will join me and together we shall become like God! We will know good and evil. We will be able to rule this world in a way fitting to the glory of our Most High Lord!"

"Eve," said A'dam, "I cannot."

"It is because you don't love me then," she said. "I am merely another beast in Eden to you."

"No, my love," A'dam insisted. "It is simply that..."

He looked tenderly at Eve, the fruit turning brownish already where she had bitten into it. He stared at the tree and thought about the Lord's words to him. Yet Eve lived!

He would prove his love to her. And if perchance she was correct, become wiser in the process! He took the fruit out of her hands and bit into it.

Lucifer's angels shrieked in delight as A'dam took the fruit. The holy angels groaned and wept bitterly at the sight of God's precious man turning rebel. Michael was stupefied. Gabriel looked on sadly. Kara was completely overjoyed. He moved away from Michael, not knowing what his reaction might be. Pellecus looked on studiously, watching the reactions of the Host. It was a chaotic mixture of rapt ecstasy and horrified sadness as A'dam transferred his authority to Lucifer.

The serpent began to snicker aloud. He called to Eve.

"Eve," he said. "How do you like it? Your eyes being opened, I mean. Gives one a new sense of life, hmm?" He laughed.

"What have you done?" Eve asked the serpent.

"I have done nothing, my dear," said the serpent. "But I fear you have undone everything!"

A'dam looked at the fruit and threw it down to the ground. He suddenly was aware of a feeling of horrible shame and nakedness. He could sense the unholy angels around him, laughing at him. Eve, too felt naked and alone. She looked to the serpent for some sense of comfort.

"What do we do?" she asked, fear in her voice.

"It's already done," he said, laughing.

A'dam quickly picked some large leaves off a tree and used them to cover himself and Eve. They felt vulnerable. Ashamed. Embarrassed. He decided that they must get away from the trees immediately. He took Eve's hand and started to run out of the meadow. They could hear the sound of laughter all over the garden.

"A'dam!" came a Voice.

"It is the Lord," A'dam whispered to Eve. "We must hide from Him!"

Lucifer realized that the Lord was present and quickly fell to the ground, prostrating the serpent. He tried to make the serpent scurry away but found he could no longer control the animal. He sat still, quietly terrified. The unholy angels, upon hearing the Lord's voice, quickly scattered. Michael and the other angels pulled back, turning their eyes from Eden. Many bowed low to the Lord, waiting the judgment which must surely follow.

"A'dam," said the Lord again. "Where are you?"

A'dam remained hidden behind a large bush. Eve sat next to him, quietly sobbing.

"A'DAM!" said the Lord. "Where are you?"

A'dam stood up. His poorly made covering of leaves was already falling apart. He held up a portion of it to cover his nakedness.

"I am here, Lord," he said. "I heard Your voice in the garden and it frightened me. I didn't want You to see the shame of my nakedness."

A'dam looked to the ground. Eve came up behind her husband and stood.

"Nakedness?" He said. "Who told you that you were naked? Who told you that you should be ashamed of anything?"

A'dam and Eve remained silent.

<hr/>

Michael and Gabriel were feeling the shame of watching God's creatures turn on Him for a second time. They could only look on in agonizing silence. The rest of the Host had quietly departed or were prostrate in the Lord's Presence. Serus joined Michael and looked upon the fruit of his former master's labor.

"This is freedom," Serus said in disgust. Michael looked at the little angel who had recently returned to the Lord. "Lucifer's freedom always seems to lead to rebellion and shame. If only I had seen the truth earlier, perhaps…"

"There is nothing any of us could have done," said Michael. "Even had we exposed Lucifer, his course seemed set—one way or the other he would have found a way to rebel against the Lord. It was his choice, Serus, not ours."

"Yes," agreed Serus. "But now his choice has become man's choice."

<hr />

"Did you eat of the trees which I forbade you?" the Lord asked.

A'dam could not look up at all. The Father he once knew seemed distant now. It was as if they were strangers. He felt ashamed, and embarrassed. He also felt anger building up inside of him. He recalled his conversation with Eve at that very spot and looked at his wife with intense hatred. The leaves he was grasping dropped to the ground and he pointed at Eve.

"This woman you made for me to be my helpmate—she tricked me. She is no helper to me! She gave me some of the fruit and I ate it!" He looked at her with contempt and added with great sarcasm, "Bone of my bone, flesh of my flesh indeed!"

Eve looked at her husband pitifully, sobbing.

"Eve," said the Lord. "What is it you have done?"

Eve looked up at the Light. She still could not see the serpent but sensed he was nearby.

"It isn't my fault," she said, fighting back the tears. "I was here to help the serpent. He began talking to me and deceived me. He laughed at me after we ate of the fruit. He drove me to eat!"

Eve stepped back. The Lord turned His direction toward the serpent. Lucifer trembled violently, unable to control the beast that was once his to command.

"Serpent!" said the Lord.

Upon the word *serpent*, Lucifer was shaken violently. The serpent came slinking out from behind the tree and stood in front of A'dam. Lucifer tried to leave the beast but it was as if he was imprisoned there for this critical moment. The serpent stared at the light where the Lord's presence was. He was terrified.

"You have done a grievous thing," the Lord said. "For this you are now cursed. You shall be cursed above all beasts of creation. You shall be humbled to the point that you shall eat dust! It will be as if you shall crawl on your belly—no longer dignified, no longer a prince among your peers. And hear this: I shall place between you and the woman an enmity that shall span the ages. Hear me, serpent! There shall be enmity between your vile seed and hers. And one day her Seed shall thoroughly break your crown, though you bruise His heel!"

At that moment the serpent gave Lucifer up with a loud wailing noise. The animal dropped to the ground, dead. Panicked and terrified, Lucifer flew into the Heavenlies to get away from that place of cursing. Michael and the others watched as Lucifer streaked past them out of Eden, screaming as if in great pain.

Lucifer could feel something happening to him, overwhelming him. He looked down upon Eden and seethed with a hatred for the Lord and all that He held dear, with an intensity never before experienced. His heart and mind were given over to complete corruption, as all that was once holy inside of him died. Lucifer had become the complete Adversary—the Satan. He glanced at Michael.

"As I said to you once before, Archangel, this is not finished!" he screamed.

He quickly disappeared into the earth.

Eve looked at the lifeless body of the serpent, then awaited her own punishment.

"Because you have done this thing, I will cause great pain to come upon you when you bear children. You and your husband will indeed fill the earth, but it shall be through much pain and sorrow in childbirth. Not only that: Because you rebelled against the authority of your God, your desire shall be toward your husband and he shall rule over you in earthly, carnal authority."

Eve stepped back, ashamed and weeping.

"A'dam," said the Lord.

A'dam shielded his eyes from the great light that he could no longer look upon.

"Yes, Lord," he answered.

"Because you listened to the counsel of your wife and did not keep the law in Eden, the ground will now be cursed. That which once yielded fruit will now yield thorns. That which gave to you freely will now have to be worked rigorously. By the sweat of your brow you will labor all your life simply to exist. And one day you shall return to the ground from which you came. For you have forgotten something, A'dam. You are dust—and to dust you shall return!"

A'dam turned away from the Lord and looked at Eve. He realized in his heart that he had shamed both of them. He had been given the responsibility to keep the law and failed. He took her by the hand, managing a weak smile. Together they left the area, weeping bitterly for what they had done.

Chronicles of the Host

Exile

Following the rebellion in Eden, the Lord determined that rather than risk further impertinence from the humans, He would set a guard around the trees. Thus did Michael command that two cherubim be placed around the trees with swords of fire which would keep any tempter to eat of these trees away. For the Most High knew that should the fallen humans eat of the Tree of Life, they should live forever.

Thus began the struggle for which we angels continue to fight this very day. The Great War that began in Heaven was now raging on earth as darkness sought to wage war against light through the lives and minds of humans. The Host never dreamed the critical role they would play in this conflict; that they would be intervening and encouraging, fighting and ministering, supporting and strengthening men and women on behalf of the Lord. They never dreamed that one day a human would be born of the Seed of the woman in whom God would invest His Very Self; that through a man would come the redemption of mankind...

Lucifer was brooding. Not even Rugio's report that the Lord had driven the humans out of Eden seemed to encourage him. He sat lost in thought, sizing up the situation and trying to discover what would be the next move. The Council gathered nearby awaiting his direction.

Tinius walked over to Pellecus, who was seated on a large rock in the great cavern where they were meeting. The other angels waited in awkward silence, exchanging awkward glances.

"How long must we stay in these gloomy quarters?" he whispered to Pellecus. "Surely we may inhabit Eden now that the humans have been forced out!"

"Not that it matters, but the last report I heard of Eden is that it is being overrun by thorns," said Pellecus dryly. "It is hardly the paradise it once was. It's quite desolate."

"How like the Most High to be so cruel in His judgment," said Tinius, "to remove the one completely beautiful spot from the earth."

"I hear that the Most High actually made clothes for the humans out of the skins of animals," said Kara, coming over to the conversation. "How bizarre!"

"Yes," said Tinius. "It seems that nakedness is suddenly offensive to the Lord! It never bothered him before."

He laughed, breaking the silence of the chamber. Everyone turned his way and then went back to what they were doing.

"The nakedness is not what bothers Him," said Pellecus. "It is the shame of the disobedience. The Most High now realizes He has made a grave error in judgment and is attempting to cover the indiscretion as it were with the skin of beasts. Pitiful symbol really of A'dam's fallen state."

"The blood of beasts to cover the shame of beasts," said Kara. "I sometimes wonder if the Most High knows what He is doing at all."

Pellecus smiled at the stupidity of Kara.

"I am weary of waiting," said an exasperated Tinius. He addressed Lucifer directly: "My prince, when do we move?"

All of the angels looked at Tinius, startled at the exclamation which broke into Lucifer's reverie. Some scowled at him; others nodded in silent affirmation; all eventually looked to Lucifer. He remained impassive.

Finally he looked up at Tinius.

"I have been thinking," Lucifer began. "I have been thinking about those things which the Lord said to me in Eden. He cursed me, you understand. And not only me, but realize you too are cursed. As I once said, we are in this together."

A chill swept through the room. Every angel knew that he had tied his destiny to Lucifer. Now they understood that they tied their grim fates to him as well.

"I know you sense this," said Lucifer. "There is, however, one consolation to A'dam's disgrace. His rebellion prolongs the war. Gives us time to prepare. Hear me!"

The Council gathered around the makeshift conference area, deep within the heart of a mountain. Lucifer found solace in darkness and preferred it to the light of earth. He rarely ventured on the surface anymore, although he anticipated that one day he would return in complete triumph. He could see the dark eyes peering at him.

"These are the facts—grim or great—however you wish to interpret them," Lucifer began. "First of all, the earth is ours," he said. "We have obtained legally what we could not take by force. A'dam's decision has wrested the kingship and the authority from him and it now belongs to me. That is the rule of law. We are the principle authority on earth. We also find ourselves in a grave battle with Heaven which centers on the fallen humans. It is through humanity that we shall wage our warfare."

"But how so?" asked Tinius. "The humans shall never trust you again."

Lucifer stood up, and thought a moment.

"I once remarked that the Lord has a propensity for leaving doors open," he said, ignoring Tinius' question. "Every time we are finally set back, He leaves room for us to react. Whenever we are cast down there is an opportunity to rise again. He has done so once more. The Lord is a great God but a poor strategist for the long term."

The angels perked up, hopeful that somehow Lucifer had a definite plan of action which could stop or delay the inevitable judgment that awaited them.

"What is your thinking on this?" asked Pellecus.

"Dear Pellecus," said Lucifer. "Always a question. My thinking is in terms of the prophecy that the Lord spoke to me. Do you recall the words?"

"You mean the Seed of the woman?" asked Kara.

"Yes," said Lucifer. "The Seed of the woman. Everything on this planet that yields life involves some sort of seed—a deposit of sorts which assures the continued existence of itself. The Lord Himself told the woman that she should bring forth children in great pain—the children are the seed of the woman."

"And the Seed of the woman will break the crown of the serpent," muttered Pellecus. "Interesting."

"And deadly," agreed Lucifer. "The same Seed which yields life to man will yield death to us."

"So we are to war with the children of Eve?" asked Tinius.

"Yes," said Lucifer, "but not just any child of Eve. One day there will be a child with which we must contend—provided we allow such an event to occur. The prophecy clearly speaks of a coming one. But since we cannot ascertain who that one is, we must do our best to exterminate all of them."

"What do you mean, my prince?" asked Pellecus. "We cannot stop the blessing of the Lord. He has willed that A'dam and Eve fill the earth. What are you proposing?"

Lucifer looked at the Council with a malevolent stare.

"Death for death," said Lucifer. "That is what I am proposing. Death to humans. Death to A'dam and to Eve and to all who come after them. Destruction of the human seed. War against mankind. Death to the plans of the Most High!" He looked at the group with cold, savage eyes. "The only way we will stop the prophecy from being fulfilled is to corrupt the Seed before it has a chance to turn on us."

The Council looked at each other in melancholy glances.

"When you say 'death,' my prince," said Pellecus, "you are advocating..."

"Murder," said Lucifer. He began his customary pacing as he spoke. He paused. "I felt the serpent dying, you know. I know what death feels like. A'dam shall return to the dust of the earth. He was not permitted to eat of the Tree of Life. He only ate of the tree which will destroy him. He can die. He will die. As will all humans who follow him. Of course there are only two of them presently..."

Rugio smiled at the thought of tearing A'dam and Eve to pieces. Lucifer looked at the angels, reading many of their faces.

"I'm telling you that if we do not compromise the race," Lucifer pleaded, "A'dam shall breed the Seed of our own destruction! The Lord has left us no choice. The humans must die—to themselves, to each other, and most importantly to the Lord."

"But how can we approach them, much less destroy them?" asked Tinius.

"The same way I approached the serpent," said Lucifer. "Remember, we now have legal possession of this world and all of its resources. The Lord has distanced Himself from it. We now may approach the humans, influence them, even control them if they let us. I once sought to guide their destinies as their steward—now I shall drive them as their master."

"But how?" said Kara. "What will be our strategy?"

"We will set them to war against each other," said Lucifer. "Brother shall fight against brother in hatred. We shall stir up base qualities of jealousy and greed, lust and anger, strife and bitterness. All that God holds in contempt we shall encourage among men. Everything that is profane we shall inspire. This will be the fruit of *our* seed in mankind! We will thoroughly corrupt that which the Most High once held so dear. By the time we are finished He will see no reason to continue this conflict. Why would He desire to preserve a race of humans who have nothing but contempt for Him? What seed of such perversion would hold fear for us? This earth will run red with the blood of men before we are through.

"However, violence will not be our only weapon. We are thinking creatures, are we not? We shall be subtle and cunning in our dealings with man. We shall create great systems of worship—some of you shall become gods of this planet—idolized and adored. You shall have images erected in your honor and placed in great temples—something strangely contemptible to the Most High. We shall divert the attention of man away from the Lord; he will look to the Heavens and see many gods; he will look to creation but miss the Creator; he will look for God within his own corrupted pride. Instead of looking at a star and bowing to its Creator, he will bow to the star itself! What delicious irony to allow creation itself to be worshiped!

"As humans grow and organize themselves—and they will—you shall be placed over families, villages, cities—even whole nations should it come to that. You will be given authority to manipulate those people for the common goal of sowing to their own destruction. If seed is to be the cause of strife then so be it! We shall sow seed—bloody, rebellious, violent seed—in all of mankind!"

He looked at the angels grimly.

"We shall influence their bodies when possible and cause them to fall prey to all manner of disease and sickness. Death opens up a whole new possibility of settling the issue. Sickness of the mind, body and spirit we shall visit upon humans. We shall make their existence burdensome. They will grow weary of life!

"We shall corrupt and destroy the Seed of woman before the Seed of woman destroys us. We have a struggle ahead, brothers. Make no mistake about that! What we have obtained by legal right is meaningless until we are able to secure it. So long as the pretenders in Heaven have authority, we must wage war—brutal, ugly, merciless war. And as you, the commanders of our movement, carry the war to earth, so shall I carry the war to Heaven. I shall ever remind the Lord of the rebellious nature of humans; I shall ever accuse them to His face; until that day that He relents and gives us leave to rule earth—unhindered, unloved, unjudged."

⊹≓————————≒⊹

"One of the most difficult tasks I ever had to perform, Gabriel," said Michael of having expelled A'dam and Eve from Eden. They were seated in Crispin's study at the Academy of the Host. Crispin nodded his head in sympathy. Gabriel smiled a knowing smile. Serus simply looked with compassion at Michael.

"How did they react to you?" asked Serus.

"They were quite afraid," said Michael. "They thought I was the death angel and were sure I was sent to destroy them. I ordered the angels who escorted them out to be resolute but gentle. And not to exchange words with them."

"Did they resist the expulsion?" Crispin wondered.

"Not once they understood what was happening," said Michael. "We simply pointed them out of Eden and walked alongside them. They were both weeping bitterly. And so we forced them out of Eden..."

"And into Lucifer's hands, I suppose," said Serus.

They all looked at him.

"What do you mean by that?" asked Michael.

"He means that since A'dam has surrendered his authority to Lucifer," commented Gabriel, "Lucifer now has legal rule on earth. A'dam is at his mercy."

"Only so far as A'dam allows himself to be led of Lucifer," interjected Crispin. "Choices do work in two directions, you know. Just as A'dam chose to disobey and played into Lucifer's hands, he may also choose to obey God now and at least protect himself in some measure from Lucifer's grip. I mean legally earth is Lucifer's until A'dam takes it back—if that was possible. But A'dam and all humans can still resist. It all goes back to the mind and will of man. We know that. A'dam knows that all too well. And I am certain that Lucifer realizes that too. He will be positioning himself to capture A'dam's mind."

"But why continue the struggle?" said Sangius, who had just joined them. "He has done the damage to God's plan for humans."

"You forget that the Seed of woman holds some very interesting and challenging possibilities for Lucifer's crowd," said Crispin. "Lucifer is finished when the prophecy is fulfilled. He will do all in his power to prevent it!"

"Which leads me to the point of the meeting Gabriel and I just had with the Elders," said Michael.

Michael began explaining the new ministry that angels would be called upon to perform in the struggle ahead. Angels were to be the messengers of the Lord to humans. The Host would not simply be bringing word from God, but critical help in the form of protection, deliverance and encouragement. Most importantly, angels would be involved in holding back the darkness of Lucifer's angels who would seek to undo the Lord's plan for reconciling the fallen humans back to Himself. How that would be accomplished was a mystery, but for now angels were to prepare themselves for war.

"So, the battle for Heaven will be fought out on earth," said Crispin, thinking about Michael's words. "Quite interesting."

"Yes," said Gabriel, "with the will and choices of men and women being the primer. It will be a tremendously difficult task given man's apparent propensity to disobey the Lord!"

"Lucifer certainly has the advantage," agreed Michael. "But we all know that the Lord's plan will ultimately succeed. It must!"

"If it depends on the will of man alone it has failed already," said Crispin.

Lucifer roamed through Eden alone. Although the garden still retained much of its former beauty, the place seemed desolate and was beginning to become overgrown with thorny vines and bushes. The fruit trees had stopped producing and the flowers no longer budded. The animals which once filled Eden with their noises and activity were no longer around. Only an occasional bird flying overhead broke the stillness. Lucifer walked to the center of the garden. He saw the trees, now guarded by two mighty cherubim, their flaming swords moving in every direction. They didn't look at Lucifer. He merely scoffed out loud and turned away. He silently vowed that he would yet establish his throne at this place.

Lucifer thought about the events leading up to this moment. He recalled the planning and jockeying that had gone on in Heaven. He thought of the subtle nature of it all. It was really a good effort. He merely had misjudged the Lord's resolve in the matter. But what now? Legally he was now the authority on the planet. Even though it would not set well with Heaven, it was something with which they would have to come to terms. Why continue fighting a foregone conclusion?

A'dam had fallen. His nature was abased. The image of God inside had been distorted. Lucifer had seen to it that man was corrupted and compromised. From this point on every human born into the world carried with him the stain of that distortion. This was Lucifer's one glimmer of hope. He knew that as long as he could appeal to humans through their fallen nature, he need not worry about the coming One.

"Well, Most Holy One," he said, addressing the Heavens, "it has come to this. Whatever the contest brings, and whoever it involves, it becomes an issue between You and me. I have my angels, You have Yours. I have my mission, You have Yours. I have earth, You have Heaven. I have A'dam, You have…what?

"What do You have, Most High God? A'dam and all who follow are now corrupted. They will no longer fellowship with You, much less worship You. They will be afraid of You and will run from You. I will see to that. Your presence is no longer required nor welcome here on earth. Don't You understand?"

Lucifer looked around Eden.

"Eden. Lovingly designed by a Creator for His most beloved creation. And yet even in this place of near perfection, where there was no want or need, the creatures still turned on their Creator! How can that be? Does that not tell You anything, Most High? It tells me a great deal. It tells me that You are finished with mankind and he is finished with You. And yet You insist that out of these fallen, muddy, rebellious creatures will come One who will crush my head?

"Lord, why would You persist in adding agony to the plight of these pitiful wretches? You leave me little choice but to see mankind destroyed. I would rather let them be slavish brutes populating the earth under my guidance. But You seek somehow to restore them to Yourself? Most High, forgive me, but they are not worth it! Let them go. Create a new world, with new people if that is what You need—but leave earth alone. Leave A'dam alone. Leave me alone. I will see man undone and I vow by all that is unholy to see Your name brought low on earth. The only name on earth which shall be on the lips of men is Morning Star. This I vow. This I promise!"

Kara and Pellecus joined Lucifer in the garden. They had been following A'dam's progress since leaving Eden.

"Well my prince," said Kara, "A'dam is gone. He moved eastward with his wife: soon gone, soon forgotten."

"Gone perhaps," agreed Lucifer, "but he will be remembered. The Lord will not be slack in filling the earth with humans. It is His will. And their destiny—for now."

"His will perhaps," said Pellecus. "But as we have seen, lord, destiny can be altered."

"That is precisely what I have been considering," said Lucifer. "We cannot alter the Lord's will regarding man. But perhaps we can alter man's will regarding the Lord. A'dam desired knowledge so that he might be blessed by the Lord. Instead he was judged by Him. Now that knowledge of good and evil will bless us!"

"It always goes back to knowledge, hmm?" said Kara.

"Correct, Kara," said Lucifer. "We know now that man is a curious creature who can be manipulated; therefore, we have the knowledge to defeat him."

"Knowledge is indeed power, lord," admitted Pellecus. "I have always said so."

"Yes, Pellecus," Lucifer responded. "And as you have pointed out countless times, the reason the Lord has all of the power is because He possesses the greatest knowledge. I shall never have the knowledge that the Most High enjoys. I freely admit this. Therefore, I shall never be more powerful than He."

Lucifer walked to a small brook and looked at his reflection. Rugio and Pellecus stood at a distance behind him. "I don't ask to be more powerful than God. I never did. But can I deny the knowledge that I *do* possess—and therefore its power? What use is knowledge if unapplied? What good is power that is not exercised?"

He sighed, peering deeply into the reflection his eyes made.

"No, I'll never have His knowledge. But, one need not have all of the knowledge. It is only the critical knowledge which proves advantageous."

"Which knowledge, lord?" asked Pellecus rather timidly.

"You weren't listening Pellecus," Lucifer snapped, turning away from the reflection and facing the two angels. "If one possesses knowledge of another's weakness, then one has a definite advantage over that person."

"True, lord," said Pellecus. "We have a definite advantage over A'dam."

"I was not referring to A'dam," said Lucifer.

"Whose weakness are you referring to?" asked Pellecus.

He looked up at the two angels, his bluish aura beginning to glow. "You don't see it, do you? Of course not. No angel sees things as I do. I am the only creature the Lord made with the understanding that can oppose Him. You see, I now understand where the Most High is vulnerable."

He smirked at Pellecus' facial expression. Kara remained impassive.

"You look bemused," Lucifer continued. "Do you recall when I said that some day I would discover where our Lord was vulnerable and that everything would turn on that discovery?"

"I remember," said Kara.

"I'm well aware of your prodding into the Lord's Person," said Pellecus, "digging around His Throne as it were. But I was not aware that you had discovered that which made the Lord...vulnerable did you say?"

"Yes, Pellecus, I said our Lord is vulnerable. All this time I have sought a way to best Him—to trip Him up—to counter any resistance to our plans. I tried to position myself to defeat Him. And I failed."

He looked at Kara and Pellecus dramatically.

"I realize now that He will prove to be His own worst adversary. I won't really have to oppose Him at all. He will defeat Himself!"

He smiled, satisfied.

"And where is the Most High vulnerable?" asked Kara.

"It is so obvious, Kara. So obvious that I never really understood until I saw how He dealt with the humans after their little indiscretion in the garden. I always considered His primary nature to be that of order and law and government. But no! It is not for law and order in the cosmos that He made man. It is for love."

"Love?" asked Kara.

"Yes, Kara," responded Lucifer. "Love is the very nature of the Most High. It is what drives Him. His love for the Kingdom. His love for the Host. His love for His creation. It was for love of man that He made the world. And His love shall be His own undoing in this great struggle."

Lucifer's eyes bored into Pellecus and Kara, the bluish light now streaming around him in waves. The two angels recoiled as the center speck of Lucifer's eyes suddenly became like bluish stars in the night sky. He pointed toward the distant Heavens.

"I prophesy here and now that for love our Lord will one day pay a terrible price. For the sake of love He will be humiliated. Love will see Him hurt, even scarred. And hear me now—this love, that goes beyond reason, will mean the destruction of one Kingdom and the rise forever of another!"

He turned back toward the two angels and whispered harshly, "Victory or abyss!"

"So be it!" both Kara and Pellecus repeated uneasily.

CHRONICLES OF THE HOST
Get the entire series today!

EXILE OF LUCIFER
The unthinkable—a revolt in Heaven—is about to begin!

UNHOLY EMPIRE
Lucifer reigns on Earth, but for how long?

RISING DARKNESS
The search for the prophesied Seed begins!

FINAL CONFRONTATION
The final showdown between Jesus and Satan!

Additional copies of this book and other
book titles from DESTINY IMAGE are
available at your local bookstore.

For a complete list of our titles,
visit us at www.destinyimage.com
Send a request for a catalog to:

Destiny Image ® Publishers, Inc.
P.O. Box 310
Shippensburg, PA 17257-0310

*"Speaking to the Purposes of God for This
Generation and for the Generations to Come"*